hope you enjoy

7/8/01

Act of Contrition

Other books by Janice Holt Giles
published by The University Press of Kentucky

The Believers

The Enduring Hills

40 Acres and No Mule

Hannah Fowler

Hill Man

The Kentuckians

The Land Beyond the Mountains

A Little Beter than Plumb

Miss Willie

The Plum Thicket

Tara's Healing

Act of Contrition

Janice Holt Giles

THE UNIVERSITY PRESS OF KENTUCKY

Copyright © 2001 by The University Press of Kentucky

Scholarly publisher for the Commonwealth,
serving Bellarmine University, Berea College, Centre
College of Kentucky, Eastern Kentucky University,
The Filson Club Historical Society, Georgetown College,
Kentucky Historical Society, Kentucky State University,
Morehead State University, Murray State University,
Northern Kentucky University, Transylvania University,
University of Kentucky, University of Louisville,
and Western Kentucky University.
All rights reserved.

Editorial and Sales Offices: The University Press of Kentucky
663 South Limestone Street, Lexington, Kentucky 40508–4008

01 02 03 04 05   5 4 3 2 1

Library of Congress Cataloging-in-Publication Data
Giles, Janice Holt.
Act of contrition / Janice Holt Giles.
p. cm.
ISBN 0-8131-2172-8 (acid-free paper)
1. Italian Americans–Fiction. 2. Separated people–Fiction.
3. Physicians–Fiction. 4. Catholics–Fiction. 5. Widows–Fiction.
I. Title.
PS3513.I4628 A65 2001
813'.54–dc21   00-012273

This book is printed on acid-free recycled paper
meeting the requirements of the American National Standard
for Permanence of Paper for Printed Library Materials.

Manufactured in the United States of America

Foreword

Wade Hall

Born in Arkansas in 1905, Janice Holt moved to Kentucky in 1939 and during World War II met her husband, Henry Giles, on a Greyhound bus in Bowling Green. After he was discharged from military service in October 1945, he returned to Kentucky and the two were married in Louisville. In 1949, Janice Holt Giles and Henry Giles moved to Giles Ridge in Adair County, Kentucky. It was here in Henry's home community that Janice found her writer's vocation and many of her subjects. In 1946, at the age of forty-one, she had begun her first novel, and three years later it was published as *The Enduring Hills*. Before her death in 1979, she would publish twenty-four books of fiction and nonfiction. Now a new title, *Act of Contrition*, can be added to the list.

The novel chronicles a year in the lives of Regina Browning and Mike Panelli, from the opening of school in the fall through the following summer. During this seasonal year they go from strangers to passionate lovers. Browning had been freed from a loveless marriage when she became a widow at age thirty. She fills her life with library work and her love of music and art. She has no plans to bring another man into her life. One day, however, she goes out into the countryside to draw near a lake and sees an attractive man fishing. Sensing that here is "an artist's delight," she begins to sketch his handsome physique and continues at home to struggle with the lines of his head. One night she dreams of almost drowning on a stormy lake and being rescued by a stranger who says, "You can walk on the water if you try." (Later Panelli will reassure her with the same words as she attempts to cross a narrow foot bridge.) A few days later a sprained ankle brings her face to face with Dr. Mike Panelli, the fisherman and the man with "the troublesome head."

They quickly become aware of their mutual attraction and compatibility. He takes her to his secret camping and fishing spot. After a few weeks she is totally smitten with him. He seems attracted to her but reluctant and erratic in his attentions. Eventually, Regina learns that, three years earlier, Panelli's wife Eva had run away with another man and that he is still married to her. Furthermore, Regina learns that he cannot be divorced from his wife and remain a good Catholic. The relationship seems hopeless until Mike confesses his love to her and promises that nothing will keep them from being man and wife—not his Italian family or his church. Rather naively, Regina and Mike begin to make elaborate plans for their wedding and for the renovation of his family's large home, where they plan to live.

Because of her great love for Mike, Regina decides to accept his church and maybe even take instruction in becoming Catholic. At her first Mass, however, she feels like a stranger and out of place. When she realizes that the religious obstacles to their marriage are implacable, she turns caustic: "It seems foreign, even, to the nature of this land, of America, born as it had been of rebellion to autocracy, than which nothing was more autocratic than the Church. . . . It so stressed the Cross and the Sacrifice, the suffering, the flowing of blood. It so flagellated and doomed the sinner."

In addition, one of Mike's sisters, a nun, and his priest remind her sternly that he is still a married man and in the eyes of the Church will always be a married man. He cannot divorce his wife and marry Regina and remain in good standing with his Church. Mike has been weakened by his passion, they say, and she must make the right decision for him. If you love him, they insist, you must leave him.

A visit to his large Italian family confirms that she can never be a part of his family life, that she will always be "outside the circle." Despite her deep love for him, she begins to question their compatibility. "She wondered if she would ever truly know this man she loved, ever be able to follow him into those strange places of his soul which were so alien to her."

Mike's love for his family and his Church looms ever larger as a barrier between them. At an accident scene with a dying man pinned underneath a wrecked car, she sees Mike the doctor become Mike the priest as he leads the man to "an act of contrition" so that he can die in grace. As their illicit affair continues, it brings conflicting emotions of love, shame, possession, and guilt. Even though Mike promises Regina that he will defy his family and his Church, Regina finally realizes that she must make the decision for him.

Act of Contrition is surely in the grand tradition of love stories about two people, who, despite monumental obstacles, are consumed by their love for each other and will test even the gates of hell to be together. Here is a man who loves a woman so much he will give up family and Church for her, and here is a woman who loves a man so much she will give him up. It is a story of two people who refuse to repent of their love. They will not confess that their love is evil and beg forgiveness for it. They will not confess to a lie and perform an "act of contrition." Like Hawthorne's *Scarlet Letter,* Janice Holt Giles's novel is about lovers who violate the laws of church and society and appeal to a higher law of love. What Hester Prynne says of her adulterous love for the Reverend Arthur Dimmesdale is true for Regina Browning and Mike Panelli: "What we did had a consecration of its own."

Great love stories are generally focused on women, and *Act of Contrition* in no exception. Regina will give all to love. For the first time, she knows the wonder and miracle and danger of love. Her first husband taught her nothing of such love, "its sweeping, wonderful engulfment, and nothing of its perilous encroachment upon the emotions. To be in love was to be terribly vulnerable to the probability of pain and loss and heartbreak. . . ." To be in love means being in torment when Mike is away from her. It means that she can be happy only when she knows he's "not sharing himself with others."

Baring her lovesick soul, she confesses the torments of her passion: "It was terrible, she thought, beautifully terrible to love someone so much. It left one with so few resources." With the strength of a liberated woman, however, she must stand defiantly against creeds, laws, and traditions. She is not at all apologetic for their technical adultery: "She did not, she assured herself, feel the least bit of guilt over the situation. They were mature people, fully grown, intending to be married, and they were responsible only to themselves."

Indeed, although the story is narrated in the third person, the focus is almost always on Regina and the boldness of her rebellion against the boxed-in society of the 1950s. In those days attitudes and actions were not petty or taken casually. It was a time when an illicit affair could lead to dreadful consequences. It was a time when there were rules and a sense of decorum that most people obeyed. There was a social etiquette, a church etiquette and a courtship etiquette that assumed delayed consummation. When someone violated the rules, it meant risking scandal and exclusion. Because of such iconoclastic content and the inevitable controversy the work would have caused, Giles was unable to get her book published at the time she wrote it.

Until he met Regina, Mike had observed the rules. About his unfaithful wife, he says: "How could you distrust your own wife? I knew she wasn't very happy. But she was my wife. We were married. It didn't occur to me she could be unfaithful. I wouldn't have been. No one I knew ever was. Except people . . . but not us, not our kind."

Indeed, it was an old-fashioned time; and theirs is a love that in its expression and fulfillment is, *ipso facto,* a serious violation of social and clerical rules. It was a time before the sexual revolution, before women's liberation, before Vatican II, before air conditioning. It was a time when doctors made house calls, even to remote country shacks, to deliver babies. This story, then, of the love of Regina and Mike, is a story of illicit love, of adultery, and it occurs at a time when respectable people took abstinence and marriage vows seriously. It is a story that will engross but not shock the reader.

Some fifty years later, the world is a vastly different place for lovers. Society is much more tolerant of sexual relations out of wedlock, and religious strictures have been loosened. For Catholics, the Second Vatican Council convened by Pope John XXIII in the 1960s led to a relaxing of prohibitions against Protestant-Catholic marriages and made annulments somewhat easier to obtain. According to Father Eugene Zoeller, professor of theology at Bellarmine University, the pre-Vatican II Code of Canon Law made annulments virtually impossible for practicing Catholics, whether or not both partners were Catholic. If a priest had performed the wedding, the bond was considered inviolable. The bond could be challenged only on canonical grounds, such as a failure to consummate the marriage, the discovery of a blood relationship of husband and wife, or the insufficient consent of either party. Even under such circumstances, it would have been rare for the long, detailed investigation to lead to an annulment.

After Vatican II, says Father Zoeller, marriage is still considered a sacred and permanent bond and an annulment is still difficult to justify by Canon Law. Nevertheless, psychological incompatibility and other circumstances (such as the elopement of one partner with someone else, as occurs in *Act of Contrition*) would make an annulment possible and would thus allow Mike and Regina to have a marriage sanctioned by the Church.

Act of Contrition is set during an old-fashioned time, but it is surprisingly up to date. The love of two people from radically different backgrounds is consonant with today's multi-culturalism and its goal of celebrating while transcending differences. In such a story as this, we can see that once upon a time, say almost fifty years ago, in an uptight society, two people showed the healing, unifying power of love.

Great love stories always involve obstacles to fulfillment, and the barriers vary from time to time. In the case of Mike and Regina, it was the strict Canon Law of a Church that was viewed by many Americans with suspicion and condescension. The beleaguered Church thus had retreated into a fortress of prohibitions disallowing involvement with the enemy. At other times and in other cultures, the obstacles would have been differences in race or class or age or position or politics or wealth. Perhaps in today's permissive, anything-goes society—with only an occasional benign prod from religious authority—it is no longer possible to have an old-fashioned love story. There are few crucibles left in which to test true love.

Act of Contrition is more than a story of liberated love. It is a work of exemplary craftsmanship that displays some of Giles's finest writing. There are exquisitely created scenes of emotional extremes, such as a surprise visit from Mike that turns Regina's dirge of despair into an ode to joy. There are sensuous descriptions of the turning seasons of one calendar year, from fall through the following summer. The emotional and physical attraction between the two lovers is depicted with surcharged sensuality and with artistic restraint. In this novel Janice Holt Giles handles a controversial, even explosive, subject straightforwardly and evenhandedly. The publication of this novel some twenty years after her death reveals new dimensions of her talent and achievement.

Chapter One

∞

The westering sun, slanting through the wide, high windows, laid broad, hot bands across the room. On each window ledge, great bowls of ivy, rooted in water, were thrown into translucent relief, the blue of the glass, the white tangled root-threads reflecting the light prismatically. The oak grain of the long, heavy reading tables was glossed and veined by the burnished light, and the coarse brown leather of the chairs showed every ancient crack. From the street at the foot of the campus came the sounds of increased traffic, homeward bound at the close of the September day. Distance and the thick walls of the library reduced it to a low but steady hum.

Regina gave the cart a push with her foot and placed the last three books on the shelf, automatically aligning the backs with the shelf edge. The task gave her time to reflect how much of a librarian's work was simple housekeeping—tidying, straightening, picking up, replacing. She did not doubt that even in this small college library the work would remain endless and uninspiring.

She pushed the cart into a small closet, divested herself of the smock she had been wearing over her dress as a protection, and returned to the reading room. With an eye trained to notice every detail, she looked about. It was beginning to shape up into something she could recognize and which, competently, she could handle. The last librarian, she remembered, had had the excuse of age, as well as insufficient training, to allow it to become the shambles she had found it; but she had difficulty, even so, in condoning the patience of the administration. To her the library was the heart of a school, its workshop and laboratory, and its efficient functioning was as necessary as a strong faculty, adequate buildings and dormitories. It was just as well, she thought, that she had come on a month early, before the fall term began. She would never have been able to organize it adequately once the students and faculty began to overrun it. She had the satisfaction of knowing she had done an excellent job.

She went into her office, which was a small room to the left of the broad, curving stairs of the entrance hall. Hilton College had built itself around this old mansion which now housed its library. In its beginning it had been the home of the town's wealthiest citizen, who had given it and the surrounding acres for the formation of a college. It had once housed all of the college. But as new buildings were added the old mansion had become, in succession, the administration building, a girls' dormitory, and now the library. It was a gracious and stately old building, but hardly, Regina thought, adequate for a library. However, there was nothing she could do about that.

The office was a pleasant room. There was that to be said for the conversion of a mansion—there were no tiny cubbyholes for the staff, although to use the word staff was to give it undeserved grandeur. Her staff would be untrained students on work grants, and they would remain forever untrained, for they would change each year.

The room had evidently been the library of the home, and its rich paneling, its recessed shelves, its dark flooring and the exquisitely beautiful rosewood desk gave one a sense of continuing grace, for which Regina was grateful. Though she had never put it into words, beauty in grain, texture and pattern, were requisites of her nature.

She played idly with the letter opener on her desk, uncertain whether to go home now, an hour and a half before dinner, or to work a while longer on the records. They badly needed it, goodness knew, but she felt stuffy after the full day indoors.

There was a knock and she spoke, turning her chair toward the door. The red head of her student helper peered around its edge. "Mrs. Browning, I've shifting the biographies in the stacks. Should I start now on the travel?" He looked at his watch, a discreet hint that he would rather not at that late hour, but trying at the same time to look willing if that was what she wanted. He probably has a date, she thought.

"I think not, Herbert," she said, smiling at him. "It's too late. There's only an hour or so before dinner. Tomorrow will do just as well. You've done a fine job today. Why don't you run along now? If you can come at nine in the morning, though, I should appreciate it."

His freckled face broke into a grateful grin. "Yes, ma'am. I'll be here."

He closed the door hastily, as if afraid she might change her mind. The smile lingered on her face. Herbert had been a willing but singularly clumsy helper. Still, she supposed, she should be thankful for any help at all.

Coming to a definite decision, she tidied her desk and took from the shelf in the closet her bag and gloves. It was five-thirty. The records, as well as Herbert's travel section in the stacks, would wait until tomorrow. She glanced at the window, making certain it was closed, and she noted the shadows on the close-cropped lawn. There was time enough, she thought, for a short run into the country. She might be able to catch the last light for a sketch or two. She flexed her slender fingers, feeling the pencil in them already. She hadn't done any sketching for months. She had been much too busy, deciding suddenly to come to this small Midwestern college, supervising the move, choosing a house and getting settled in. She felt a positive need, now, to find a small stream and to catch its lights and shadows on paper.

Her car was parked in the rear of the building and she walked toward it purposefully, her finely bred, disciplined face reflecting both humor and pleasure in her decision. The late sun tarnished the deep, thick brown of her hair with glints of red, and her slim green dress looked as cool as lime sherbet. It was an old dress, but she had the virtue of choosing clothes with a classic simplicity and of superb quality which age only enhanced. She wore them with the casual acceptance of good breeding.

Joining the flow of traffic, she gave her attention to driving. She was an excellent driver, as are most people who can barely remember a time when they did not drive. She was relaxed and casual, because she was certain both of her own reflexes and the tremendous power she governed. She was not without appreciation of that power. That was why she had allowed herself the luxury of the small convertible. She had too much respect for it, however, to abuse it in traffic and too little impatience to use it at the expense of others.

It was good, though, to come to the edge of the town finally, to leave the crawling caravan behind and to nose the car into open country. Feeling freed, she settled herself and pressed her foot down, enjoying as she always did the swift and immediate response. Following the rise and fall of the road, its bends and turns, she yet had an eye for the rich, fertile farmlands lying to either side. The fields stretched, roundly curving, under the heavy light of the sun, picking up a sultry, golden glow from it. In the distance the hills were hazy, as if the heat had pressed there during the day. In a meadow three cows were going toward a barn, udders full, heads nodding, ambling patiently and slowly in single file along a path their feet had made. The sky was softly blue in the east, just beginning to reflect the gold which so flamboyantly gilded the west. It was a time of day she loved, sunset, and the twilight which came on so gently afterward. The wind pulled at her hair, and her face felt beaten by it.

She slowed, remembering a narrow lane opening off the highway, just beyond the lake. It had tempted her more than once before. It bent out of sight, into woods, and she felt certain a stream ran there, feeding the lake. She came to the bridge across the dam of the lake, which provided the town with its water, found the lane opening sharply to the right and eased the car down a steep embankment into it. She thought as she did so how it was a very good thing there had been no rain lately. It was little more than a trail and it probably would be slippery and treacherous under mud.

The lane twisted and wound along and she found herself wondering how she would ever turn if there shouldn't be an open space in the woods. Deciding to let that take care of itself, for it was really too late already since she was in the lane, she kept moving slowly ahead. The road made a sharp bend just before reaching the woods and with relief she saw that they were clear of underbrush and that the floor was fairly level. She left the road and drove into the dim and leafy shade, bringing the car to a stop under a tall elm tree.

Stepping out, she breathed deeply of the still coolness and knew by the quiet calmness which overtook her exactly how hard she had been pushing herself and how much, in the strangeness of new surroundings, she had been missing her own familiar countryside. It surprised her a little, for she had always prided herself on her adaptability. She would have to make these new hills and streams her own.

From the trunk of her car she took out a folding camp stool, her sketching materials, a pair of sensible, rubber-soled shoes, into which she changed. She had too often had to walk over rough country to find the combination of water and light, and she wanted not to go unprepared. She had wondered sometimes why it was she liked best to paint water. Not being analytical, however, she hadn't pursued it very far. "Oh," a friend of hers who also painted had said, "everyone has one thing he likes to do best. Mine is mountains. It's just one of those things."

There was no path through the woods, but it was so dense that there was remarkably little undergrowth and she had no difficulty making her way. She walked over moss and old leaves which deadened any sound and gave spongily under her feet. Occasionally, in a sunny spot, a clump of wild asters grew, blue-lavender blooms looking a little ragged now. On an old fence, bittersweet was yellowing, and beyond the fence which edged the woods, the lake spread calm and deeply blue under the sun. She did not like lakes. Her love of water did not extend to large, still bodies. She liked best the clear, rilling streams one came across unexpectedly. This, too, she had never analyzed, but she knew it was at least partially true because both depths and heights gave her uneasy feelings, and lakes were usually deep. She said, however, that they had no character.

After some ten minutes of walking, she heard the sound of running water ahead, and, quickening her steps in anticipation, she came out on the bank of a clear, fast little creek with shoal water shallow over a beautiful white pebble bottom. The far side of it was touched by sun, and she was delighted with the contrast between the sparkling water there and the deep shadows nearer. It pleased her, also, that her guess about a stream here had been right. Some bushes grew to the edge, and she bent them aside for better vision, set up her stool behind them and opened her pad.

For a few minutes she worked with deep preoccupation, sketching in boldly the outlines of the stream, the trees beyond, the tip of a hill in the background. Then as she began to fill it in, the warmth of the sun on her head and shoulders, piercing an opening in the trees, and the drowsy murmur of the running water began to fill her with a lazy sense of well-being. She dropped the crayon and, leaning against the trunk of the tree at her back, closed her eyes. Almost dozing, her mind slipped into easy channels of remembering.

The strangest thing of all was that she should find herself here at all, for at thirty-three she considered herself quite mature and not given to acting upon impulse. And yet it had been an impulse that had brought her, and one which, without too much consideration, she had followed.

She remembered the weekend Tom and Lucia Rhodes had spent

with her. She and Lucia had been at college together and had kept up their friendship. She had been delighted when the Rhodeses could stop over on their way east. She could remember the lazy conversation by the fire after dinner, in which Tom had mentioned, almost idly, how badly his college needed a librarian.

Until that moment she had been very satisfied with her pleasant life. When Walter died he had left her a small but adequate income. With good management she was quite comfortable and upon occasion could even have a few luxuries. The house, of course, was free of encumbrance, and it had not occurred to her to do anything but follow the pattern of the days established during Walter's lifetime. She served on committees, lunched, played bridge, went into town to the theater, worked at her music and painting.

These last were more than hobbies with her, but she was the first to confess she was far from professional in either. They did, however, give her great enjoyment. They were among the things Walter had had so little patience with. She was aware that he had often thought of her interest largely high-hat, because he understood so little.

"You just put it on," he had told her once, "because you think it sets you apart from the common herd."

She hadn't, but there was no point in telling him so. She refrained, also, from telling him that their marriage had been so disillusioning that without such personal and private interests she could hardly have borne it.

It had been a mistake. She had known it almost from the beginning. But she had a conviction about broken marriages and had tried very hard to make it go. She was beginning to think they had salvaged the best of it when Walter was suddenly and horribly killed in an automobile accident. Not, she admitted honestly, that there would ever have been a starry-eyed excitement between them. It was too late for that—but there had been more peace and less of the frustration of the earliest days.

Again in honesty, she had confessed to herself that although his death had shocked her, for he was too young to die, she had not felt the heart-burdening grief natural in a young widow. There had been instead, once she recognized it for what it was, a sort of relief that the tension and strain of effort were over with, and in the end she had felt a quiet happiness to go about her own way.

That had been three years ago, and nothing had yet occurred to stir her out of the tranquility which had overtaken her.

She had been twenty-six when she married Walter Browning, however, and before that she had had several years of the work for which she had been trained. She wondered, sometimes, if it had not been the quietness of the university library which had made Walter's exuberance so vividly attractive to her. Being a librarian was very like being a schoolteacher. There were few opportunities for a very exciting social life. And Walter had been exciting.

They had met, of all places, in the library itself when he had stopped in on a rainy afternoon for no more purpose than to use the public telephone. A downpour had followed, keeping him, and they had got to talking. "It reminds me," he had said, "of that beastly winter of 1944 when I was in the army—in Belgium. It rained constantly."

She mentioned the rain in Paris, where she had spent a year at the Sorbonne. In the end, having their brief sojourns abroad in common, he had persuaded her to have dinner with him. That was the beginning. He had had so much gaiety, so much vitality, so much zest for living that she had been entranced. The six months of their courtship had been a dizzy whirl of laughter, of dining and dancing, driving, going places. He had had an inexhaustible fund of ideas for having fun. "Let's run up to that old inn on the river for dinner." And the old inn had been dimly lit, uncrowded, with soft, seductive music to dance to. Walter had been strong, handsome in a blond, Viking sort of way, protective, and she had been easily persuaded that she loved him.

There had been no way she could know that life went no deeper than the surface with him. Courtships, she supposed, were always like this—gay, joyous, happy, a sort of coasting along until one took up the more serious things of home, family and settling down. When occasionally she thought, slightly troubled, how little he knew or wanted to know of the things which made up her world, books, music, painting, she put it away from her. We are young, she thought, and there's time for all that. He made it so very fascinating.

Not until they had been married several months did she begin to realize that he both expected and wanted only a playmate, not a wife. He agreed to a home, but it was only a place to start out from. It bored him to spend any time there. And children he would not hear of. "They tie you down," he said.

"Of course. But parents expect to be tied down for a time, don't they?"

"There are enough kids in the world without us adding any," he said. "I don't intend to be a parent, and that's final, Regina."

She was glad, now, that it had been.

Women, she mused thoughtfully, especially well-bred, withdrawn women, can do exceedingly silly things sometimes. Marrying Walter had been her silliest. But that was all over.

Then Tom and Lucia Rhodes had visited and, like a pebble dropped into a still pond, rippling and disturbing the water, reaching in widening circles to the edge, his careless remark had touched her own shore. He was stirring his coffee when she had asked him if he liked his work. "Very much," he said slowly, "if only the library were adequately managed. There's a very decent endowment. But the old witch who has had the library has been a thorn in the flesh. Thank goodness, she's passed on. In English the library means everything."

"She died?"

"A month ago. They are putting out feelers for a new one. I hope they insist upon someone competent this time. Miss Lewes had been there forever, and I suppose they hated to let her go. She had outlived her usefulness, but," he had lifted his shoulders, "Lord knows what the poor old soul would have done. At any rate it has solved itself if only they take care finding a successor."

It was Lucia who had suddenly come up with the idea. It was Lucia, Regina remembered, who had usually come up with the ideas in college. She was a small woman, richly dark, almost voluptuously lovely. Tom, big, awkward, easy, simple in manner and with an uncomplicated mind, was a perfect foil for her. He adored her and Regina had sometimes thought they were the one perfect and happily married couple she knew. Lucia had said suddenly, her eyes crinkling with excitement, "What are we thinking of? The job is perfect for Regina. How could we be so stupid as not to recognize it?"

"For me?"

"For you! Do you want to sit here and vegetate all your life in smugness? Oh, don't tell me you aren't smug. Of course you don't know it. But all your training is going to waste. It's a nice town, Regina . . . really a lovely little town, and the college isn't bad, either. Do say you'll consider it. It would save Tom's life. And think of the fun we'd have together."

"But, Lucia—they may have someone else in mind. It may be settled already. It's been seven years—I'm terribly rusty . . . besides, I have my home here."

"Nonsense. Tell her, Tom."

With amusement at Lucia's enthusiasm, he had spoken. "It might not be a bad idea at that, Regina. Because of their endowment the salary is fairly decent."

She spread her hands. "It isn't that . . . it's just . . . oh, it's ridiculous. My friends are here, my life is here . . ."

"What life?"

Lucia had pierced all the veils with one thrust, and immediately Regina had seen all the committees, the parties, the friendships, the easy, pleasant days for exactly what they were; a trancelike floating along, an escape, a rut, a routine. An uninteresting, uneventful habit. Obstinately, however, she continued to object until Lucia had worn her down and she had promised to think about it. "Tom will pull wires," Lucia had said. "Say you'll come if it's offered . . . please."

"I'll consider it," was all she would venture.

Following their visit, however, the idea had grown on her and her dissatisfaction with her effortless way of living had palled increasingly, so that when the offer came she had virtually decided. She made arrangements to rent the house, packed her most treasured belongings, including her piano, and before she had time to change her mind, headed her car for the Midwest. And here she was, installed, at the helm, the library in excellent shape for the opening of school next week.

Into the dreaminess of her mind, and over the lulling ripple of the water, there came the louder sound of twigs crackling, pebbles slipping and leaves scattering underfoot. A cow, coming down to drink, she thought, lazily opening her eyes. The sound came from across the stream and continued, though discreetly, oddly muffled as if care were being taken. Peering through the screen of bushes before her, which she had only bent, not broken, and which had now risen back to something of their natural erectness, she picked up her crayon. A cow drinking at the edge of the stream would bring her sketch to life. It would be exactly the center of interest it needed. She waited, watching, ready to set to work.

There was no steep bank on the far side of the stream as there was on the side on which she sat. Instead there was a narrow beach, some five or six feet wide, of the same clean, white pebbles that floored the creek, as if it were simply a dry extension of the same. Framing the beach was a thicket of young willow sprouts, thick, dense, intensely green. Waiting as she was, her eyes fixed on the willow thicket, she was yet taken by surprise and somewhat dismayed when, instead of the cow she had been expecting, there broke through the thicket a man. He carried a fishing rod, held high beyond the reach of the willows, and a creel and landing net were slung across one shoulder, dangling at his thigh.

Forgetting momentarily her screen of bushes, she drew back, made an impulsive movement to withdraw. The last thing she wanted was to get involved in chit-chat with a stranger. Seeing her sketching, people invariably wanted to look over her shoulder, ask inane questions, and look at her askance as if she were a little mad to be occupying herself so. It invariably made her self-conscious.

The man went about his own business undisturbed, however, and she realized, belatedly, that she was entirely hidden from his view. He was a tall man and her familiarity with anatomy made her aware that in spite of the awkwardness of hip waders, the burdens of creel and net, he was beautifully proportioned and put together. The shoulders were powerful and slightly rounded. The torso tapered in a perfect wedge to slender waist and thighs, the legs long but solidly supporting.

So narrow was the stream that when he came to its edge and removed the hat on his head, bedecked with dozens of flies hooked into its crown, she could see not only that his hair was dark, but that in spite of the very short haircut, it was tightly and crisply curled and slightly flecked with gray. He knelt to remove a fly from his hat, and she approved of the thriftiness of effort involved in the movement. She recognized the type. He was one of those people born with good bones, with good muscular coordination, with instinctive grace, who never in their lives know a physically awkward moment.

He tied the fly, faced more squarely toward her, without putting his hat back on. He stood directly in the sun now, and she could see the structure of his face and even the texture of his skin. They were an artist's delight. The good formation of the eye bones and cheek bones was emphasized by the hollow planes beneath, and the skin, very dark and stretched tautly over the bones, had the smooth, tight look of mat. It surprised her a little, because it was a quality of youth usually, and he was a man her own age, she judged, or a little older. He must be, she thought absently, in remarkably good condition.

He fed out his line quickly, economically, and she saw his long, mobile mouth quirk once when the fly caught on some obstruction. He had the patience, however, to let it float free instead of jerking at it. Outlined freely against the green willow thicket and the white, pebbled beach, the sun full on his head and face, the water running rapidly around his feet, she suddenly realized that here was her perfect subject. Instead of a cow, fate had given her a fisherman. She forgot herself and the possibility of discovery and set to work hurriedly sketching him in, grateful that she had already done the stream and background, hoping she might catch him before he moved on.

He was a thorough and patient fisherman, however, and she need not have been in haste. He stood for a full ten minutes in the same spot, almost in the same position, shifting only to cast to one side or the other. Once he laid the rod down and she watched him run his hands, absently, over his person, searching for something. "Damn!" she heard him say mildly, and she amused at the ruefulness of his look when he came up from his hip pocket with a pipe whose stem had been snapped. Walter had been a cigarette man, but her father smoked a pipe and forgetfully he had too often sat on his pipe and broken it. She wondered if all pipe smokers were so absentminded.

He never waded far enough into the stream for her to know the color of his eyes, and eventually he wandered slowly and aimlessly on up the creek. She studied the sketch, approving it. She would do it in oils, she thought. The effect of the sun on the head and face would be tremendous. The contrast in the green of the willows, the white of the beach, the shadow of the water would be too muted in watercolors.

Only in passing did she wonder who he was. Probably a farmer from some nearby place, trying for a fish or two for supper. She closed the pad, folded the stool and made her way back to the car.

The sun was almost completely gone now, and the woods were deepening into a darker shade. There were little rustlings of woods creatures all about. Birds twittered softly, fussily, before settling down to sleep. A rabbit ran suddenly out of the fence row, saw her, was startled into stillness, then scuttled before her, bouncing jauntily, his ears peaked, his white scut bobbing. A lizard jerked into motion on a still-warm rock and fled swiftly up its side, poised a moment at the top, flicked its tongue in her direction, then was gone. Bats circled the lake's edge silently, swiftly, blindly.

She walked slowly, feeling a quiet contentment in the hour, in the movements all around her, in the last warmth of the sun, in the slowly purpling sky. She was happier than she had been in years, she realized, happy in a full, unquestioning way. It had been wise to come here, she decided. It was going to be good to be at work again, to have a reason for each day's beginning.

She suddenly realized that she was very hungry, and she thought of the big, old-fashioned kitchen in the house she had taken, searched mentally the refrigerator. There was a steak, there was fresh asparagus and lettuce, there were frozen berries and a tray of ice cream which Nettie had made the day before. She quickened her steps, the sketch now forgotten in the interest of food.

She drove swiftly home and reached it as the first stars came pricking through the night. She went straight through to the kitchen and put the steak to broiling. She set the table with a blue cloth and thin white china, and for the first time in a long time she ate with an appetite which reminded her of girlhood. She really must, she thought, get out in the open more often.

Chapter Two

❧

Term opening, which descended upon her the next week, was as frantic a scramble as she had expected it to be. There were, for one thing, the six students assigned to her, as helpless as infants, to be instructed. Then there were the faculty reserve lists, neatly typed in the beginning but so scrawled over with afterthoughts penciled on the margins, between the lines, top and bottom, as to be almost indecipherable. There were the reserve sections to be set up, the special filing to be attended to. She was amused at a new professor's list for his course in Sixteenth-Century English Literature. *Astrophel and Stella,* indeed! He was due for an awakening, she thought. This was Hilton College, not Columbia.

Finally, there were the students themselves, crowding, packing, haunting the reading rooms until it seemed at times they overflowed the doors and windows. They were always in a rush, clinging querulously and petulantly around her.

"Mrs. Browning, where is Dr. Lister's section?"

"But *why* can't the Collins be taken out? I haven't *time* to do my notes here!"

"The catalog doesn't list this reference book, Mrs. Browning."

And, accusingly, "You've shifted the history. Miss Lewes always kept it in the east end."

Patiently she met each problem as it arose, coped with the students, met with admirable restraint the impatience of the faculty, kept her temper with her inexperienced assistants. This last tried her more than all else. She had never before worked without competent assistance. Occasionally she felt like a mother with a brood of clinging children dragging at her skirts, as she told them over and over and over what to do and how to do it, showed them, led them around so that they might observe. Only their obvious goodwill and clumsily honest efforts saved her from sheer temper more than once.

After several weeks she had hopes of three of them becoming fairly efficient and she assigned one to each shift so that she might know she had someone halfway dependable on duty at all times. For six weeks, however, she spent a full twelve hours each day in the library herself. She didn't dare not.

On a gray afternoon, when the rush had abated a little and some semblance of routine had been established, she felt headachey from the heat of the overcrowded rooms and decided to slip away for an hour or two. Nettie had spoken to her of needing an extra towel rack in the kitchen, at the same time mentioning cautiously that the supply of dish towels seemed low to her, and she herself needed new and heavier gloves for driving. She would run downtown; and then an hour or two in her big chair at home, with some quiet music perhaps, and she would have the lift she needed to see her through the evening's work. Soon, she thought, she might safely take several evenings off each week. She would be glad, for she had missed puttering around at home, and when *had* she seen Lucia and Tom? Not since the president's reception, and that hardly counted. In that milling mob they had barely spoken. She might as well be cloistered, she thought.

She spoke to the girl at the desk. "Jean, I'm going downtown on some errands, and I may go home for an hour or two afterward. Do you think you can manage?"

The girl was one of the alert ones, bright-haired, fresh-faced, smiling and cheerful. "Oh, sure, Mrs. Browning. I'll manage."

Regina patted her arm. "I'm sure you will, too. Give me thirty minutes for the errands and then you can reach me at home if anything comes up. I'll be back in time to relieve you for dinner."

The girl, busy already with the inevitable cart of returned books to sort, nodded, and Regina left her. Until five o'clock when the last class was over, the library would be quiet. She would be back by then.

A keen, cold wind was blowing when she came around the corner of the building to get her car, and she clutched her hat, grabbing at the same time at her coat which blew open and whipped around her. She looked at the sky, thinking its dull gray looked full of snow, or a cold, wintry rain. She slid under the wheel. Well, she reflected, the autumn had held fair an unusually long time. One couldn't expect it to last forever. At least the wind was cold and brisk and fresh. After the stuffy heat of the library, with its musty smell of old books and the acrid dryness of the furnace it was indescribably good to breathe. Backing the car she thought wryly of the lost autumn and its splendor of woods and fields in their fall colors. Philosophically she put it aside. Perhaps the winter would offer something special in the way of snows, frozen streams and frosty drives.

Quickly she made her purchases and was back in her car when she noticed she was much too near the car ahead of her. She frowned, distinctly remembering that she had left plenty of room. She twisted around for a look behind and saw what had happened. There were no parking meters on this side street and someone, drawing up behind her, had nosed her car up to make room. Not in an hour of wrenching and turning could she maneuver out of the tight fit. There was nothing to do but wait until one or the other of the owners returned, and, a little put out at the prospect of her dwindling time being wasted in waiting, she settled herself with a new magazine she had picked up in the drug store.

It was a brief wait, for she was still idly turning through the advertisements at the front of the magazine when voices disturbed her and she looked up. She was startled into an absurd amazement. Two men stood at the curb beside the long, gray car in front, eyeing it. The man nearest her was the fisherman she had sketched. He was no farmer, she saw, unless farmers in this section of the country were much better dressed than she thought. For he wore, and wore well, a beautifully cut tweed suit, which her expert eye told her was not an American tweed. It was much too smoky and heathery and restrained. A pale, creamy pullover, cashmere she was certain, showed under the unbuttoned coat, and above it there was a soft, tan shirt and a narrow brown tie. The tweeds were perfect for him, not bulky as they might have been on a man less well-proportioned, settled and fitted by time to the sloped shoulders and the long legs. He was bareheaded, a pipe in his mouth, and his face was ruddy from the edge of the wind. He wore a look of rueful amusement.

The man with him spoke. "By golly, Mike, you're going to have to do some tall wiggling to get that chariot of yours out of that place. How did you ever get it in?"

15

"I didn't," he said. "There was plenty of room when I parked." The implication was plain. What could you expect of women drivers?

Stung, oddly, into quick resentment and wishing to put herself at rights, she slid over on the seat and rolled down the window. "I'm sorry," she called, "I left you a good two feet, but someone has pushed me up to make room behind."

He raised his eyebrows and took the pipe out of his mouth, smiled at her. "They often do."

"Can I back any at all?"

He walked past her and looked. "About six inches, I'd say. But I've got a foot in front, and it would help, if you'll be good enough."

"Of course."

He watched as she eased the gear into reverse and slowly fed gas. He motioned her with his hand. She watched him intently, her foot ready on the brake. She applied it smoothly when he signaled. "That does it," he said, "many thanks."

With long strides he returned to his own car, said something she could not hear to the other man, slid in and dexterously maneuvered into the open. As he drew free he put out his head, grinned at her, waved, and pulled the big car into the street. Well, she thought, watching him weave into the traffic expertly—I really should have managed that a little better. She assessed her guilty feeling at being thought a fool of a woman driver. Why on earth should it have mattered? He was a complete stranger and it couldn't have been less important. She shrugged it off. She *had* been working too hard to let it get under her skin.

Seeing him again, however, reminded her of the sketch which she had not touched since that day she had drawn it. Perhaps the book store would have some canvas. She got out of the car again. She really should work on it, now that the winter was setting in and her time would be more free.

She began on it that night, and she was pleased with the way it worked up. With no idea what she would do with it when it was finished, she spent all her spare time for two weeks on it. She remembered a thing her teacher had said once about the way an artist works. There are pictures and pictures. There are those that one does on commission, and does as good a job as possible. There are the ones, then, one does because of necessity . . . a pull toward the subject, a feeling of having to do this for no known reason. He had said wryly that they were inevitably the best. This picture was one of those. There was the combination of water and trees, light and shadow, which she loved. The figure of the fisherman was only incidental, to draw the whole together. Anything with life and action would have done as well. It puzzled her, therefore, that she had a little trouble doing him and thought seriously of leaving him out altogether. She spent hours on the head alone and left it at last, still uncertain and dissatisfied.

Lucia called her that night. "Would you like to hear the college orchestra tonight? Tom says they're playing an all Beethoven concert. They're not bad, really."

"I'd love it." She seized upon the invitation. Bad or good, she needed to get out.

"You're certain we won't be taking you away from something?"

"I need to be taken away from it," she laughed. "I've been moping around over a painting that won't come right. What I should do is throw it in the fire."

Lucia's laugh echoed hers. "Don't do that. It's probably better than you think. I remember how low you used to get in school."

"I've not improved, then. This thing is giving me the fidgets. What time?"

"Eight-thirty, or near about. We'll pick you up."

"Fine. What does one wear?"

"My dear," Lucia's laugh rang out joyously, "it couldn't matter less. The auditorium is a little drafty. Just make sure you are warm enough. The administration seems to go on the theory that a chilly audience makes for a warm reception."

They talked on for a moment or two longer and Regina hung up in a mood of happy anticipation. She decided, at length, on a black sheer wool dress, with which she could wear antique gold bracelets and necklace and over which her furs would go comfortably. It should be warm enough, she thought.

Seeing her, Lucia exclaimed, "How lovely! My, but you look expensive and smart."

"Do you like it?"

"I love it. That dress is a masterpiece."

Lucia, whose taste ran to color and fanciful designs, lushness and a little gaudiness, was as overdressed as a Christmas tree beside her, and her own smartness made her feel a little uncomfortable. But Lucia could always carry off her extravagances. She had the coloring for it and the gaiety for it. What was good on Regina would have been drab on her.

The audience was very small, occupying only the center section and not more than two-thirds of that. Shrugging out of her furs, Regina thought how typical it was. The auditorium would have been flowing over the edges if a dance band were playing. Ah, well, she thought, a discriminating few would be better than an undiscriminating mob. It was a shame for the orchestra's sake, though, if they were any good at all. Performers always did better with a good audience. Perhaps they were accustomed to it, however.

She read the program and wondered. They had chosen the *Corialanus* overture, for one thing, and unless the strings were exceptionally good it might be a mistake. The director must have complete confidence in them, for there was also listed one of the Rasoumovsky quartets. The sonatas were more what she had expected to see. She settled back happily as the orchestra entered and began the process of tuning up. What, she wondered, was there about the tuning up which always sent shivers down one's back? Anticipation? Excitement? Pleasure? It always happened to her, at any rate.

The house lights were still up and the hum of several hundred people talking had not yet ceased. She looked idly on, Tom and Lucia for the moment engrossed in conversation with a couple beyond them. She recognized many of the faculty, and would have known their wives anywhere in the world. Wives of college professors wore an almost universal uniform of shabbiness, except Lucia, she thought with amusement. Lucia's plumage was that of the bird of paradise, and among the brown wrens surrounding her, she stood out like a travel poster advertising the Caribbean.

A man two rows down, in the aisle seat, twisted around to speak to the people behind him. With a jar which suspended her pulse and then sent it racing to make up the suspension, she recognized him. Really, she told herself, squirming uncomfortably, forcing herself to look away, you're getting a positive obsession about the man. It occurred to her, then, that it was a good opportunity to observe the head, and she let her eyes come back to him. What have I done wrong, she thought. Where is the trouble? With an excuse she allowed herself to study him covertly. Is it the way he holds it? Is it the bone formation itself? Was it the lighting that day?

He was turned so that his arm lay casually across the back of the seat next to him, in which a woman sat. His wife, she judged, and unaccountably she had an odd, queer, flat feeling. She had worked so long over that head, and with such desperation, it had given her a sense of proprietorship. But of course he was married, and of course it was stupid of her to think any more about that exasperating painting. She would paint him over and put a cow there. With determination she turned to Tom, but at that moment the lights dimmed. She sighed with relief and gave her attention once again to the orchestra.

Boldly the *Corialanus* opened the program, and after the chords of the first fourteen bars the strings took up the restless and agitated qualities of the hero's character. Almost immediately Regina relaxed, impressed. That little white-haired man on the podium was drawing an almost professional performance from the section. It was far better than she could have guessed it would be. She gave herself up to pure enjoyment, then, following the beautiful and moving second theme, the majestic, heroic coda. The audience was breathlessly still for a moment when it was over, then with tremendous energy they tried to fill the half-empty house with applause. The lights came up for the intermission, and the buzz of talk lifted. She leaned across Tom. "Lucia, they are very good. What background has the conductor?"

Tom answered her. "He is a refugee. An Austrian Jew. I don't know what his musical background is, but it includes an excellent training, that's certain."

She nodded. "More than that. Training alone doesn't make a good conductor. And he is very good. Why does he stay here?"

"Because he is grateful, I suppose. The college took him when he badly needed work. Sight unseen, in a way. They made a place for him. It's one of the good things they have done without much credit for it."

Thoughtfully she looked at her program again. The Waldstein sonata was listed next, in her own realm, the piano. She looked forward to it. An usher brushed against her, made his way down the aisle and stopped to whisper in the ear of the man with the frustrating head. He rose immediately, grimaced at the people he had to leave, and taking up his topcoat followed the usher up the aisle. Passing, his eyes rested briefly on her, and she saw them register recognition. He nodded pleasantly, but did not pause. Tom and Lucia were intent upon their programs. She could, she supposed, have asked them who he was, but for some reason which she did not plumb, she let the opportunity pass.

She found the balance of the program disappointing. For one thing she became aware of the chilliness of the hall. Lucia had certainly been right about its draftiness, and Tom had to settle her furs about her before the sonata was over. It was not very well done, she thought critically. She did it better herself. The quartet was better, but it lacked the inspiration of the overture. It sounded thin and distant in the large, unpacked hall. She felt herself becoming restless, which was not usual with her, and wishing the concert would end. Outside, they found a dismal rain falling and without too much compunction she refused Lucia's invitation to have coffee with them before going home. She felt tired and still chilly. It would be better, she thought, to have coffee at home, alone, in front of her own fire, without the necessity for talk. With only minor protests they drove her home and she thanked them, trying to make it whole-hearted, for the evening. "You're to have Thanksgiving dinner with us," Lucia told her, as she got out of the car.

"I am?"

"Yes. I won't have you moping about alone on a holiday. I have a turkey big enough to feed twenty. You'll have to help eat it."

"Is anyone else coming?"

"At the moment I haven't asked anyone," Lucia said, laughing. "But I'll probably end up asking everyone I can think of. Thanksgiving is for a big family and if you haven't one, friends must make up the lack."

Her lightly spoken words reminded Regina of the tragic fact that Lucia could not have children. She rarely mentioned it, seemed to have become entirely accustomed to the idea. But they would have been such wonderful parents—and her instant sympathy had much to do with her immediate acceptance. "I'll be there," she said, "with a tremendous appetite. Don't ask too many others."

Laying aside her furs, she went to the kitchen and made a pot of coffee. Nettie would not approve, but it was impossible to go directly to bed. She brought it back to the sitting room, stirred up the fire, the building of which was Nettie's last chore before leaving. The house was centrally heated, but she liked an open fire.

It had been a stroke of luck to find this small house, furnished with the essentials but with room enough for her piano, a phonograph, books, several good rugs she treasured and a few other possessions which turned it into a home for her. It was a small Georgian house, set in ample grounds, which were fenced with an ivy-grown stone wall. It was sheltered, almost hidden, by trees and shrubs. Lucia had been horrified when she took it, thinking it too isolated for her. An apartment was more her idea of what was suitable and she had thoughtfully listed the more convenient ones. Regina knew her own nature too well, though, and she had had for too long the privacy of her own home. She knew, also, that a piano does not make a welcome neighbor in apartment houses with their thin walls. She would have been cramped and constantly aware of other people surrounding her. So, when she ran across the house, surprised that it could be rented, she had taken it at once. It belonged, the real estate agent had said, to the heirs of an elderly widow, none of whom lived in the town. Under the terms of the will it could not be sold, thus it was for rent, much as the old lady had left it.

Regina had respect for the deceased woman's judgment. The house was furnished with Victorian and Edwardian pieces but not crowded with them. There was space, and the rooms were beautifully proportioned. She was comfortable in it, and she enjoyed coming home to its mellow antiquity and shaded privacy.

She drew a chair up to the hearth, now, and put the *Corialanus* on the record player. Listening, watching the fire, sipping her coffee, she decided she had been carried away undeservedly by the musicians themselves. One could do that easily. Performers sometimes distracted from their performance. She had been prematurely enthusiastic, and her admiration for the little white-haired conductor was probably just as ill-founded. Cutting off the machine she wondered why she was feeling so disappointed. It was a college orchestra, after all, and they had done very well indeed.

She went up to bed, and then lay awake, hearing the rain slash against the windows, hearing the creak of the leafless trees as the wind bent and twisted them. There was a faint reflection of light in the room, from a street lamp a block away, only just enough that when her eyes became accustomed to the dark the outlines and placement of the furniture were discernible, and the streaming panes of the windows were a little less dark than the night. She watched them awhile and then, in spite of her, the problem of the man's head returned. She remembered how he had looked, turned in his seat to talk to the man and woman behind him. His face had been animated, the long, pleasant mouth smiling, the brows occasionally lifted in amusement or question. Perhaps that's it, she thought. Perhaps that's what is needed—more expression. But his face had not been animated when she had sketched it. It had been peacefully quiet, relaxed, placid. And it was that look which went with the fisherman, that calm and happy look of a man doing what he most enjoyed doing.

She remembered, then, that he had spoken no special word of farewell to the woman who had been seated beside him when he left. It had been to the man and woman behind he had made the wry face and some comment. She could not have been his wife, then, or even someone he had brought with him. Her sudden feeling of solace amazed her. It also amused her, and she turned on her side, aware now of the comfortable warmth of her blankets, her snug immolation against the rain and the wintry winds outside.

She recalled that even as a child she had loved this secure feeling of being curled up comfortably when it rained, and she wondered, idly, if it were an instinct universally felt by an uncertain mankind battling the god-permeated elements. The first man must have huddled so in his cave and timidly dared the wind and the rain, the lightning and the storm to invade his kingdom.

He likes music, too, she thought irrelevantly, then smiled drowsily as she remembered the concerts to which she had dragged a protesting Walter. It didn't signify.

She slept and dreamed of a deep, deep lake on which she was rowing—why she did not know. It was only very much against her will. A dark sky threatened and with that forewarning which one knows in dreams she had known she was going to be overturned and that she would be plunged into the horror of those black depths. She waited for the moment in dread and a mounting fear which almost choked her. What she did not know was that when it came and the waters rolled over her, a hand would be outstretched to her and a deep, reassuring voice would say, "You can walk on the water if you try."

With perfect confidence and a surge of joy she had placed her hand in his, knowing without looking to whom the voice and the hand belonged.

Chapter Three

❧

All through November the weather had been unpredictable, varying from warm, sunny days to heavy, cold rains. On the day before the Thanksgiving holidays were to begin, however, it became intensely cold, and a slushy mixture of rain, snow, and sleet began falling in the early afternoon.

From the window in her office Regina could see it was fast freezing and coating the walks, the grass and the bushes with a thick white pelt. She thought of the young people planning to go home for the holidays and wished it could have kept fine. Many of them, now, she supposed, would not be able to go at all. The roads would be treacherous and traffic would be slow. It seemed a pity it had turned off so bad on their first long weekend of the term.

At five when she prepared to leave, she spoke to Jean at the desk. "If you are driving home tomorrow, Jean, you must be careful. If this slush ices over during the night it will be dangerous."

"Oh, we'll be careful. It's only fifty miles and Bill has chains if it's slippery. You be careful yourself, Mrs. Browning."

Regina buttoned her coat. "No fear for me. I'm only going to Dr. and Mrs. Rhodes' for dinner. I can walk if it's bad underfoot. Have a nice holiday."

Jean's smile broadened. "Yes ma'am, we will. It's too bad you can't have the whole time off, too."

"I don't mind. I had nowhere to go in any case."

Knowing that there would be many students staying on through the holidays, she had decided to keep the library open with a skeleton staff, herself and one of the boys.

"Don't you have any family, Mrs. Browning?"

"Oh, yes. But they are too far away for me to go home for such a short time."

Her parents had recently moved to the west coast and were living in southern California. Her father was retired and they had decided to seek a softer climate. She had not yet visited them in their new home but planned, somewhat desultorily, to do so if the summer offered an opportunity. It occurred to her as she slipped on her gloves and settled her scarf about her neck that the urgency of the homing instinct was lost forever once one had been married. She loved her parents, but not for years had their way of life been hers and she never visited them without feeling out of pocket. She did not much regret missing holidays with them. With another admonition to Jean she left.

The next morning she awoke to a dazzling world of ice-crusted surfaces glinting and glistening brilliantly in a bright sun. From the kitchen window as she prepared her breakfast she looked out into the garden. Each vagrant leaf, left hanging by the kindly autumn, had bloomed into an ice flower whose stem was silver wire. A hemlock tree in the walled corner shimmered in plumes of spun glass and the wall itself was furred in a white, woolly coat. The grass was frozen foam and the sun, never more bright, caught a million tiny refractions and turned them into iridescent rainbows. From one window to another she wandered, enchanted, and breakfast proceeded slowly as she carried the first cup of coffee about with her, unable to tear herself away from the scene.

Inevitably she wanted to catch it on paper. The full-paned door of the hall, opening onto a back entry porch, offered the best view and she brought the kitchen stool and propped the pad on her lap, set quickly to work. An idea came to her, then. Why not photograph it, in color, so that she might have a better guide to work by later when the sun had done its damage.

Her camera was always loaded. She flew to the desk at the front of the hall and without dressing, still in her soft crimson wool robe and her slippers, went out onto the porch. Three shallow brick steps, slightly protected by the overhang, led down to the walk. Concentrating on the angle she wanted, and already adjusting the lens opening and shutter speed on the camera, she stepped absently down.

On the ice-sheeted step her foot slid and she wavered, teetering for balance. Seeing she was going to fall, then, she jumped instead and came crashing down, twisting her left ankle under her. She went down in a heap, the camera flying out of her hand into the frozen grass beyond. There was an excruciating pain in the ankle and she sat for a moment, dazed, the ankle doubled under her, her eyes closed, lips bitten, suffering the pain in silence.

It must be broken, she thought. Only a break could hurt so badly. She opened her eyes. What should she do? She shouldn't move, she was certain, but she couldn't stay out in the cold. How *could* she have been so careless? Cautiously she eased her weight up with her braced hands and moved the foot, straightening the leg. Pain like a hot knife ran all the way up her leg to the knee and she grew faint with its intensity. She looked desperately about her. The nearest house was a block away. She could never make herself heard. Nettie would not be coming in, for she had given her the day off. Somehow she must get herself into the house and to the telephone. It made her ill to think of it.

She looked at the foot and ankle again. On the outside of the ankle there was a cut which was bleeding profusely and lesser abrasions had scoured the entire surface. What a fool, stupid thing to do! Twisting about she looked at the steps and gave thanks when she saw that she had left the door ajar. Summoning her courage, then, she set her jaw in a dogged, defiant way which those who knew her best would have recognized, turned herself and began slowly to pull herself, on one knee, the other leg dragging, up the steps. The recurring pain sent waves of nausea into her throat, but she swallowed it down and allowed herself no rest from it. She could faint, she told herself firmly, once she was safely in the house.

She had no idea how long it took her to get inside—it might have been ten minutes, it might have been twenty—but eventually she was back in the hall, the door closed, blessed warmth flowing over her again. She shook as if with an ague and it surprised her when she put up her hand to find that her face was wet from the pain and the effort.

She rested before starting on the long crawl down the hall to the telephone. When she reached it she felt almost lightheaded. She braced herself against the wall and took the phone in her lap. Then she realized she knew no doctor to call. The directory was on the other side of the desk and she shrank from making the effort to reach it. She dialed Lucia's number. Lucia's voice, answering, was cheerfully happy.

"Lucia—this is Regina. I've done the stupidest thing. Slipped on the steps and turned my ankle."

"My dear! I'll come right over." There was a smothering exclamation. "Oh, Regina, Tom has the car. I've sent him on some errands."

"Never mind . . . it doesn't matter. If you'll call a doctor? I don't know one."

"Of course. And I'll start walking."

They lived on the other side of town. Regina interrupted her. "Whatever you do, don't get out on foot. It's much too treacherous. I'm perfectly all right, now that I've got back in the house, but I *do* need a doctor rather badly."

"I'll have one there in five minutes, darling. And Tom and I will run over the minute he gets back. Regina—if there's a chance it's broken don't move about."

"I won't," she promised, laughing humorlessly. She wasn't likely to do much moving with that pain.

"Where are you?"

"At the downstairs phone. It's as far as I could get."

She didn't add that she was sitting on the floor, propped against the wall.

"Well, try not to worry, dear. Perhaps it's just wrenched. Does it hurt very badly?"

"It can be borne."

"I think you're just being brave."

Feeling reluctant to let go of the warm, comforting voice, and the ankle being temporarily easy, Regina said, "I'm sorry to miss your party."

"It probably would have been very drab. Think nothing of it."

"Who was coming? Besides me, I mean."

"Just Mike Panelli—and the Forbes."

"Who is Mike Panelli?" She knew the Forbes. They were faculty.

"He's the doctor I'm going to send you, and I'd better be about it before your ankle is beyond patching up."

"Yes, of course. Don't bother to come, Lucia, if it's inconvenient. You have your dinner to see to."

"Oh, it's hours yet. We'll see you as soon as possible."

When the line went dead she had a forlorn feeling of loneliness, a forsaken, small and purposeless feeling. She had never felt more helpless. She shook it off with an effort and examined her ankle again. It was starting to swell now, but the bleeding had stopped. She felt very disheveled and vaguely she pushed back her hair, noted that the skirt of her robe was streaked with blood and that she had left a trail of it on the floor. She wondered if she could reach the couch in the living room. It was somehow so undignified to be found sitting here on the floor. Measuring the distance, however, she decided against it. Dignity would have to go by the board. It would be much better to be found sitting on the floor in her right senses than to be found in a dead faint halfway across the living room.

Not until she heard the car turn into the drive with a scattering of gravel did she remember the front door was still locked. He would not be able to get in. Oh Lord, she thought, then gritting her teeth she hauled herself up by the desk. Again the pain ran through her and she fought it and the almost engulfing waves of weakness. She couldn't stand much more of this, she thought. Bracing with the desk, the wall, the stair rail, she pulled herself along.

The bell pealed through the house. She reached for the door handle just as the walls began to spin about her, and the light started going. She gave it a tremendous tug, then felt herself falling. She could see no one, but she heard his voice. "Mrs. Browning? I'm Dr. . . . ."

The swiftly descending darkness overtook her and she was sucked into the whirling vortex of spinning walls and floor. But not before she had time to think, ungrammatically, surprised, and somehow deeply comforted, "Why, it's him!"

When consciousness returned she was lying on the sofa and the troublesome head with its dark, crisp hair was bent over her ankle. A hand, warm, big, held her foot and turned the ankle, probing, pressing it. There was the pain again and she stirred in protest, moaned slightly in spite of herself.

He straightened and turned to face her, smiling. Her mind was instantly clear. He had drawn up a hassock so that his face was a little lower than hers. Its structure, she saw on closer look, was definite and forceful, the jaw line quite emphatic and clean. His eyes were gray, the pure gray of a rainy sky, and the irises were cleanly white. She saw, too, that he was a little older, by perhaps two or three years, than she had guessed. There were fine lines about the corners of his eyes, and the gray, which in his hair was only carelessly peppered, was quite distinct at the temples and over his ears. There was also the beginning of a line between his brows. She wondered how many troubling cases had started it there and wanted, oddly, to reassure him. Hers was a simple turned ankle, perhaps a small fracture.

"So you're awake," he said, his voice low and pleasant. "I hoped you'd stay out until I had finished. I hate to hurt you any more. It must have been pretty bad."

She took a good breath. How could she have known exactly how his voice would sound, in a dream or out of it? "I'm sorry to have keeled over just as you came. It was the door . . ."

"Why did you try to open it? You might have called out."

"It was locked."

He dismissed that carelessly. "I'd have broken in. Better a shattered window pane than for you to try to stand on that foot."

"Is it broken?"

"I won't know until it's been X-rayed, but I think not. It seems to be badly sprained, of course, but I'll need an X-ray to make sure."

"Yes, of course."

His bag was on the floor beside him. He bent over it and took out gauze, some tape and scissors, some antiseptic. She noticed that he handled the things of his profession with the same economical grace as when kneeling to tie on a fly. There was no excuse, no effort. She supposed that doctors were trained so, but no amount of training could have given him the ease and purity of movement he possessed. Only an inherently well-articulated and beautifully boned body could have done that. He smiled at her. "I'm going to clean this up a little, and bandage it so we can get you to the hospital. It's going to hurt," he warned her, "but I'll be as easy as I can."

He did hurt her, swabbing the cut, turning the foot, but not as much as she expected. His big hands were amazingly gentle. Once he frowned a little, probed the bone under his fingers and glanced quickly at her. She had time to compose her face. He spoke sharply. "Don't be heroic. I want to know if that hurt."

"I wasn't being heroic," she denied quickly, stung by the guilty knowledge she *had* been being a little heroic. "It didn't hurt any more than the other places you've been poking about."

"Good." He chuckled. "How did it happen?"

She told him, and because she felt rather foolish she went into more detail than she had meant to.

"So you paint. Is it just a hobby?"

"More or less."

"I like a hobby that lets me move around more."

"Like fishing?" It was out before she thought.

"How did you know?"

"Oh, you're the type."

She would never, never let him know she had seen him that day and sketched him. It was too much an intrusion of his privacy for one thing, and for another she felt too self-conscious about it.

He bent his head in the direction of the piano. "I don't recall that Mrs. Webster had that grand piano in her day, either."

"No, it's mine."

"Do you play, too?" His hands were busy with the gauze, now. "I saw you at the concert the other night."

"Yes, I was there."

What a silly remark, she thought. Obviously she was there.

"What did you think of it?"

It was far enough behind her now that she could be honestly objective about it. "I thought it was remarkable for a college orchestra."

"We think so, here in the town. It's a pity there's no more interest."

"It's always an uphill pull for them, I suppose."

"But it's still a shame. They play to half-empty houses constantly. People don't know what they're missing."

She felt a sudden elation, though she couldn't imagine why it should matter that he did like music after all. He didn't consider supporting the college orchestra a duty or something. "I hated to miss the second half," he continued.

"You heard the best. They did better on the *Corialanus* than on the other things." A little shyly, she confessed, "It was my car that was parked too near yours downtown that day."

"Oh, I remembered. How do you think I recognized you?"

He darted a sideways look at her which reminded her a little of a small boy daring an admission whose reception he was uncertain of. Remembering his reaction to women drivers, she wanted to laugh, but restrained it.

"But, of course," he continued, "the whole town has known since August that the new librarian was here."

"There must be more than one strange woman in town," she protested.

"Not that fit the description," he said dryly.

He had finished. He rolled up the remainder of the gauze, gathered up the spool of tape, the scissors, the bottle of antiseptic, and bent to put them back in his bag. From the stooped position, his back turned, he said with detachment, "I was looking forward to seeing you at Lucia's today." He said it a little hurriedly, throwing it upstage.

The feeling of pleasure that swept over her startled her by its intensity and warmth. She started to ask why, then thought better of it. It could only bring on confusion. What answer could a man make to such a question? "Is it going to be impossible for me to go?" she asked instead.

He snapped his bag shut and straightened. "I'm awfully afraid it is, much as I'm tempted to allow it. And I think we'd better get you over to the hospital for that X-ray, now."

Her mind flew to arrangements. "Tom and Lucia are coming when he gets back from some errands. They can take me."

He smiled down at her. She had no way of knowing how appealingly young she looked lying there, her red robe soft and dark against the pale gold of the couch, her hair pulled back in a ribbon, her face drained of color so that her eyes showed deeply blue. "I'll take you. They may be hours yet. I want that X-ray immediately."

"But I must dress!" She caught the soiled skirts of the robe, looked at her bare legs, ran a hand distractedly through her hair.

"Nonsense. You'll need a wrap and that's all. If that ankle is broken you'll have to stay on, and if it isn't, I'll run you home again. Tell me where to look for your coat."

She thought frantically of the disorder of her room. She was usually very neat, but she had been so entranced with the scene outside when she had wakened that she had not picked up the room, or even spread up the bed. She remembered stockings, underwear, possibly even her girdle still thrown carelessly on a chair, and the bed was bound to be terribly rumpled. What an idea of her housekeeping he would get. But there was no help for it. He looked fully capable of picking her up exactly as she was, wrapping her in the afghan on the chair, and carting her off unless she told him. "There's a brown coat hanging to the left in the large closet," she said. It was a heavy, warm coat and full length so that it would almost cover her robe. "If you can't find it, take anything there."

"I'll find it," he assured her, already mounting the stairs. "Oh, which is your room? Mrs. Webster's old bedroom?"

"No," she said, laughing, "I found that one a little overwhelming. Mine is the one at the back, overlooking the garden."

"Sensible choice," he said approvingly. "But Mrs. Webster always loved that old dungeon in front."

He went lightly and quietly up the stairs, his voice drifting back behind him.

He must, she reflected, have known Mrs. Webster very well to know the house so intimately. He had probably been her doctor for years. Not so many years, she thought, remembering his age. He couldn't have been practicing more than six or eight years, ten at the outside. That was time enough, however, for a crotchety old woman to become fond of and see often her doctor.

She heard him close the bedroom door and her face flushed at the thought of what he had seen. He came down the stairs, the coat slung over one arm. He held it up when he reached the hall. "This the one?"

"Yes."

"No trouble at all. Don't try to put it on, though. We'll just sling it around you and button the throat." He slipped an arm behind her and raised her from the pillow, tucked the coat expertly about her. "I liked your room."

"I can imagine—with all that clutter." She felt flustered and awkward. It was always better not to apologize, but the room had been such a mess.

"I didn't notice. I liked the colors. You're fond of red, aren't you?"

It was self-evident in the bedroom, she thought, with its old Sarouk rug, the paisley throw on the bed, the crimson curtains.

He twitched at her robe. "I hope this will clean. It's too pretty to spoil."

She forgot her discomfort. "I don't think," she said, weighing the chances, "I'm going to be able to walk to the car."

He looked at her, astounded. "Who said you were? Or did you think I would allow it? For heaven's sake, woman, that ankle may be broken and you've abused it enough already. I'll carry you, of course."

He set the door ajar. "I'll just open the car and be back in a second."

The cold air struck around her shoulders and she shivered a little, tugging the coat more closely about her. When he returned he picked up a pillow and plumped it in her lap. "That's for your feet. Now, all set?"

With a somehow familiar feeling of confidence she looked up at him. "All set."

He bent and slipped his arms under her knees and her shoulders, lifted her effortlessly and stood for a moment holding her. She did not know what to do with her arms until the only possible thing was obvious to her and she placed them lightly about his neck. "I'll try not to hurt you," he told her.

She barely heard him. She was conscious of only physical things— of the strength and hardness of his shoulders under her hands, the feeling of warmth there, of the scratchiness of his coat against her cheek, of the nearness of his face and his astringent, faintly sweet smell of shaving soap. She found herself strangely breathless and with her heart suddenly beating as rapidly as a girl's. To compose herself she murmured, "I must be rather heavy."

"A ton of bricks would be no heavier," he told her solemnly, then he laughed and shifted her slightly. "Here we go—full speed ahead."

Chapter Four

It turned out that the ankle was not broken, only very badly sprained. And it was Tom and Lucia who drove her home from the hospital instead of Mike Panelli.

She had collected her wits sufficiently by the time she got to the hospital to ask that they be called, and they reached the place just after the X-ray had been taken. Lucia was concerned, in a sympathetic, responsible way. "What *ever* possessed you to stroll outside in the ice and sleet? In nothing but a robe and your slippers, at that! Really, Regina, I think you need a keeper."

She was glowing with the cold, her rich, dark skin warm and faintly luminous. It made Regina feel like a waif. She could imagine how she looked without make-up or lipstick. She was naturally pale, in any case, and she had visions of her face being as white as a winding sheet and her lips turned blue and bloodless.

"Don't scold, Lucia. I feel stupid enough as it is. See if there's a mirror in that cabinet, will you? I must look a fright."

She had been put in an outpatient room. Tom was comfortably occupying the only chair and Lucia had perched herself on the foot of the bed. Tom chuckled at her request. "The eternal feminine."

Unabashed, she laughed. "On her deathbed a woman will wonder how she looks," she admitted. "It's a morale builder, Tom."

"I thought it was vanity."

"What is vanity but self-esteem?"

Lucia was opening and closing drawers. "There's no mirror, dear. Could you do with my little one? The one that's in my bag?"

"If you'll loan me a lipstick, too, I can do with the top of a tin can."

She was squinting into the tiny mirror, applying the lipstick, when Mike Panelli came in, carrying the still wet X-ray. "Well, *you* made a quick trip," he said, by way of greeting to Tom and Lucia.

"We thought she was dying," Lucia said, shuddering. "The very word hospital terrifies me."

"It shouldn't. It should be a very comforting word. Its purpose is healing."

Lucia pointed to the crucifix hanging above the bed. "And extreme unction."

"That, too, when it's necessary." He turned to Regina. "There's no fracture. You're very fortunate."

She had had time to think of all the inconveniences a broken ankle would cause not only herself but the school and to let them weigh rather heavily on her. It would have been such a nuisance, just as things were beginning to go smoothly. She was not at all certain that the student staff could have managed for so long a time, and she had been turning over in her mind the alternatives, of which there seemed very few. "Thank heaven," she said, relieved, "I've been wondering what my youngsters would do without me."

"Oh, I expect they'd have managed."

He might, she thought, have been a little more appreciative of the problems, instead of turning it off as if competent librarians were a dime a dozen. Chillily she agreed.

Without noticing, he continued. "It's a very bad sprain, however, and there are some ligaments pulled here," he showed her on the picture, which felt cold and glutinous in her hand, "and here. And then there's that cut."

"You sound as if you were leading up to something."

"I am. I want you to stay off that ankle until I tell you otherwise. You are *not*," he emphasized, "to try hobbling around on it."

"Did you ever notice," she said to Lucia, grimacing, "how domineering doctors are?"

"Oh, it's their sense of power. They always have you at their mercy."

"Never mind my sense of power," he said, laughing, "just do as I say."

"For how long?"

"I don't know yet. Probably for the best part of a week—maybe longer. We'll see how it gets along."

It didn't sound too bad, after having faced a month or six weeks in a cast. "I may go home, though?"

"Do you have help in the house?"

"Yes, I have Nettie White."

"You'll be all right, then. Nettie will pamper you and take excellent care of you. Otherwise I'd have to say no, for you'd be on that foot in spite of everything."

"*Couldn't* we take her to our place for dinner today, Mike?" Lucia said. "It's Thanksgiving."

He hesitated, looking at Regina. Common kindness would have made him wish to let her be with her friends on the holiday, she reminded herself. His hesitation did not necessarily mean that he himself wished for her to be there. At last he shook his head. "It would be better if she went straight home and to bed, Lucia." He smiled as if trying to ameliorate his sternness.

There was a soft knock on the door, and then, without waiting for permission, one of the floor nurses came in. "Dr. Panelli, there's an emergency."

Regina saw his face become instantly alert. Even his eyes, she thought, narrowed and his mouth steadied into a stricter cut. He became all at once a stranger again, a doctor, impersonal, intent, everything forgotten but the immediate need. She was aware, suddenly, of feeling very tired, the cumulative effect of the strain and the pain, no doubt.

"Yes?" he said to the nurse.

"A man has been shot—a hunting accident. Sister says will you please come to the operating room as soon as possible."

"Give me three minutes. Where?"

"Chest, Doctor."

"Tell Sister to go ahead and prepare him."

"Yes, sir."

He turned, very businesslike and professional, to Regina again, but she felt as if his mind was following the starched immaculateness of the nurse. "I expect you'll have some pain today and tomorrow. Can you take codeine?"

"So far as I know."

"I'll send it along, then."

"Does this emergency mean," Lucia interrupted, "that you won't be with us for dinner?"

"I wish I knew, Lucia. It depends entirely upon how badly the man is hurt. A chest wound is likely to be pretty serious. I'm afraid you'd better not count on me." There was genuine regret in his voice.

Lucia lifted her hands helplessly. "Something will happen to the Forbeses, Tom, I feel it in my bones. We'll end up eating our elegant dinner alone."

The look Mike turned on her was indulgent. "For you two, that would be bad?" A recognition of the loving bond between them was inherent in his words. Then he made a swift movement to the bed, scooped up the X-ray, disarranged the blanket and smoothed it, all in one motion. He smiled at Regina. "I'll be by tomorrow to have a look at you. Be a good girl."

She felt as if he had patted her on the head, as if she were about ten years old. Left helpless by the inanity of the remark, she looked at him, and the self-conscious look on his face told her that he realized and was slightly embarrassed by it himself. It was the sort of thing one said when there was so much more to be said but none of it permissible. Or it was just an adolescent farewell, awkward, obvious, and meaningless? He looked very nice today, she noticed, in a gray suit and blue tie, both of which she approved on him.

He was at the door when he remembered. "Oh. You'll drive Regina home, won't you, Tom? Since I'm tied up?"

The name had evidently slipped out unnoticed, either because he was still confused or because Tom and Lucia had spoken of her so often to him that the name had already become familiar. She wondered why Lucia had never mentioned him to her. But then it was natural, she supposed, for them to speak of a newcomer to an old friend, and it did not necessarily follow that they should remember all their friends to her.

She was wrapped up and taken home, feeling very much like a package of dry goods, and deposited in her own bed. "I'll call Nettie," Lucia said, stacking magazines beside her on the table, "and I'll bring your dinner on a tray as soon as the Forbeses leave."

"You needn't." She was really feeling pretty done in and wishing rather impatiently to be left alone. "Nettie can do for me perfectly well."

"Oh, fiddle-dee-dee. Poached eggs and tea and toast are what Nettie would give you." Lucia carelessly and undiscerningly brushed the suggestion aside. "You're to have turkey and cranberry jelly and I'll sit beside you and see that you eat every bite."

Weakly she gave in. Her ankle was aching again and she only wanted them to go, as good as they were, and leave her to her bed and quiet room. Nettie would be here soon. The codeine would arrive and she could have some hours of relief and sleep before she need be disturbed again.

At last they left, Tom promising to see that arrangements were made at the library, and she turned miserably in her bed, wanting a little to weep, wanting more . . . she didn't know what . . . comforting, she supposed, though she had just turned away the only comforting hands she knew. She felt a little like a child away from home, all familiar things left behind, beset by a sense of loss, loneliness, and dislike for the strange newness all about. Nettie and the sedative arrived simultaneously, however. Nettie was clucking and fussily concerned, and the codeine brought the blessing of sleep.

When she awoke refreshed the next morning, she realized how wise he had been to send her home. It had all been more grueling than she had suspected. She had been asleep when Lucia came with the tray, and either she or Nettie had not allowed her to be awakened. She had slept, wakened at dusk, eaten, then slept again. But the size of her ankle and its continued throbbing told her she would certainly have no difficulty following doctor's orders today. In fact, she had no desire to do anything else.

She supposed he would call during the afternoon. There would be hospital rounds and office calls to take care of. He could not make it much before then. With more concern than she cared to let Nettie see, she watched her tidying the room. Nettie was competent, but she had no imagination. When she dusted a table or chest, the bowls, ashtrays, vases, were apt to be set back in any order. When she moved chairs to vacuum, they were more likely than not to be aligned like sentinels when she finished. Pillows were fluffed and set rigidly and squarely upright.

Not wanting to make an issue of it, Regina asked only for a fire. The house being old, there were fireplaces in the bedrooms as well as in the lower rooms. The room was really lovely, she thought, with its softly jeweled old rug, the crimson curtains, the ancient prayer shawl thrown across the bed. What difference did it make if Lucia's huge pot of white chrysanthemums was set squarely and uncompromisingly in the middle of the table by the window? The flowers were at least fresh and pure, in immaculate contrast to the rich red tones all about them. She loved this room. It expressed, she thought, more of herself than any other room in the house. It was so intimately and personally hers.

Nettie grumbled over the fire. "Don't see why you're always wanting a fire. Just makes a mess to be cleaned up."

"I know," she said apologetically, "but a fire is cheerful, Nettie. I can do with a little cheering today."

"I expect you can, at that. I'll get to it soon as I've done the room."

"Fine."

Determined not to anticipate his call (it would be hours yet, she told herself), she settled herself after lunch with a book. The sun shone through the window and made a bright splash on the rug. The fire crackled noisily and the flames and the smell of the applewood added to a sense of comfort. The book was one she had been looking forward to. She felt very snug and neatly tucked in.

When an hour had gone by she found her attention wandering from the book. It was either unconsciously dull or she was unduly critical. She fidgeted, a thing of which she disapproved in anyone, and scanned the pages, turned them back when she realized she had not made sense of a single paragraph, and finally deciding the pajamas she was wearing had been shrunk in washing and were making her uncomfortable, she rang for Nettie to bring her a fresh pair. Then she changed her mind and asked for a new yellow silk nightgown. "It's too much trouble getting this ankle into pajamas," she said, "and there's a yellow bed jacket to match in the same drawer, Nettie."

Nettie took the discarded pajamas and looked at her admiringly. "You sure look pretty in that. Now, if it was me I'd look like I was coming down with the jaundice. Never could wear yellow."

"Some people can't."

"It's your dark hair, I guess. Mine," she pulled at the graying, mouse-colored locks, "don't take well to any color, but yellow is one that strictly don't do a thing for it."

The telephone rang and she went to answer it. Regina found herself waiting tensely for the message. For heaven's sake, she told herself when she noticed, it's probably Herbert at the library. Something has come up he can't cope with. Nettie stuck her head in the door. "It's Mrs. Rhodes. She says if you don't need her they'll wait till after dinner to come over."

"Tell her that will be quite all right. I'm perfectly comfortable."

She felt inexplicably relieved that Lucia would not be coming during the afternoon.

The time wore on and finding at last that she was not doing justice to the book, nor was she likely to, she put it aside and tried to sleep. She heard every car that passed, however, knew she was waiting for one to turn in the drive. She plumped up her pillows, flounced in the bed and was rewarded with a sharp pang which reminded her she could not afford recklessness. At last she gave it up and compelled herself to lie still, compelled her mind to blankness, drew a velvety dark curtain across her thoughts, which was her last resort when she had an occasional white night. Slowly she felt the tautness of her neck and shoulders relax.

The peal of the doorbell awakened her. The room was shadowy, the light against the window going. She heard his step coming up the stair and she roused herself to pull her pillows behind her and sit up more straightly. She felt drowsy and drugged with sleep. He *would* wait until night to come, she thought crossly.

He came in briskly, purposefully, bringing a tang of cold air with him. "You look comfortable," he said.

"I was asleep," she confessed.

"Good." He glanced at his wrist. "I'm running late. Suppose we take a look at that ankle, now."

He took off his topcoat and laid it on a chair, lifted the blanket and exposed the foot and ankle. It was still considerably swollen. He eyed it with interest, then said abruptly, "Where's your bath? I must wash up."

"There." She motioned. The bedroom was self-contained, having its own bath. She tried to think if she had seen Nettie change the towels. Why must she always be bothering about housekeeping details? "If the towels aren't fresh," she called, "there are some in the cabinet."

"They're fresh."

He came out sniffing at his hands. "Why do women always use scented soap? This smells like verbena."

She thought she detected disapproval and she said, "It *is* verbena," a little acidly. Did he think she would have the disinfectant kind he probably used himself? Keep a bar of it handy especially for doctors, perhaps?

He undid the bandage, probed and pressed here and there, nodded approvingly. "It's coming along all right. The cut is already healing nicely. You must have a nice, clean bloodstream. This swelling will begin to go down by tomorrow, I expect."

She peered. "It looks rather like a basket now."

"It takes time." He busied himself silently with dressing it again, tossed the old dressing in her wastebasket carelessly, and buttoned his cuffs again. "Stay off of it another day or two, however." He picked up his coat. "And don't go knocking it about or the cut will reopen."

Still feeling cross and feeling, besides, an accumulating anger at being so casually dismissed, she said, "How *could* I knock it about in bed?"

He glanced at her. "You don't lie perfectly still in bed, do you? Be careful how you roll it about."

She started to say that the pain itself would make her take care, but obstinately she closed her mouth on the words. She would volunteer nothing more.

He picked up his bag. "If there is any discomfort tonight, don't hesitate to take the codeine. There's no need to suffer."

Well, she thought, that was something. He said nothing, however, about another visit. He glanced again at his wrist, said he must be going, and left.

She was left with a blurred impression of the smell of cold on his clothing, of hurry and preoccupation in his manner, and of general dissatisfaction at having been awakened, roused, and summarily surveyed and dismissed. His arrival and abrupt leaving left her feeling at odds, fully awake, with time hanging heavily over her, something unfinished and shoved aside besieging her. The room seemed cluttered and disordered and the fire needed mending badly. Completely out of sorts, she rang for Nettie. So much, she thought ironically, for vanity. He had barely looked at her, and she regretted the impulse which had made her change to the becoming yellow silk nightdress.

Chapter Five

For two days, then, he did not come.

So determined had she become to put him where he belonged in her thinking—a personable, nice man she happened to have seen fishing, and sketched—the doctor whom Lucia had called for her, but entirely unimportant to her beyond that, that she almost succeeded.

Lucia came and went and she gave herself up to enjoying the hours with her. They were such old friends that little effort was required between them. Lucia could sit with her knitting, and she with a piece of needlepoint she had begun in a reckless moment long ago, and which she thought now would be a good time to finish, in a serene companionship. Lucia had a felicitous and rather catlike flair for domesticity, and when she was with her, Regina caught something of it. She found that she rather liked doing the needlepoint again. She had laid it aside, half done, impatient with its slowness. One could *paint* a picture so much faster. But the needle working in and out of the fabric, the changing of wools and colors rather intrigued her. It was oddly soothing. It had something, she supposed, to do with her enforced inactivity, and much to do with Lucia's presence.

On Sunday Tom carried her downstairs and she was ensconced on the sofa, grateful for the change from her room. However pleasant a room may be, it can become stuffy when one is forced to be in it constantly. Tom and Lucia stayed for dinner and afterward they listened to some records, talked quietly, and the time passed happily. When Tom carried her back to her room she felt sleepily content.

The next day, however, with school resuming, she was restless. Tom had assured her that arrangements had been made with a woman from the city library to come over each afternoon. "Just forget the place," he had advised, adding jokingly, "enjoy your vacation."

It was not a vacation she wanted or needed, though. She missed the business of the reading rooms, the flow of students, the questions, the problems. She felt set aside and frustrated. The needlepoint no longer amused her. She was very weary of her room, and she badly wanted to get up and hobble about—the precise thing she had been warned not to do. Irrationally she blamed Mike Panelli for much of it, believing that if he would just take the time to stop by he *might* find the ankle in better shape that he thought. After all, she reflected, one could coddle an injury beyond all common sense. He couldn't possibly know, without seeing it, that the swelling had gone entirely down, that there was no pain at all, and that she felt a perfect fraud lying here in bed. Furthermore, she had other and better things to be doing.

By the middle of the afternoon she had reached a state of mind, in her fussing and stewing, which made it not difficult to persuade herself it would hurt nothing to try out the ankle. Just here in the room, she told herself, holding onto things. Gingerly she slid out of the bed, eased up on her feet. The ankle felt a little wobbly, but there was no sharp pain. Holding to the bed she crippled along its length, and felt such triumph that it could be done without the ankle giving way that she made a round of the room. That accomplished successfully, she determined to have Nettie help her downstairs. At least she could listen to some music and have her dinner in front of the fire. She put aside any thought of how she would get back upstairs. She would cross that bridge when she came to it.

Nettie was doubtful, but when Regina proved adamant, lent a strong arm to the top of the stairway. It was simple from there. She had only to sit and slide gently from one step to another, Nettie hovering nearby. At the bottom Nettie's arm about her guided her to the couch and she sank gratefully onto it. She felt more weak than she was willing to admit, but when pillows had been piled behind her and her foot slung up on the couch, she was glad she had done it. If necessary, she said defiantly, but to what or whom her defiance was addressed she did not know, she would spend the night here. She was determined to begin using the ankle.

It was twilight when he came. The afterglow of the sun lingered and touched a mirror, the glass of a picture, the satiny sheen of an old table, with a thin, green-gold light. The fire had burned down and glowed softly. As she heard Nettie crossing the hall to answer the door, an ember dropped, and she pushed herself up on the pillows, knowing instinctively who it was.

He stood for a moment in the doorway, looking at her, and her vexation disappeared in a single second in her pleasure at seeing him. "Come in," she called, "I'm not infectious, am I?"

"What are you doing down here? Have you been up on that ankle?"

"Don't be cross," she begged, "I couldn't stand my room another minute."

"It depends on how much damage you've done whether I'm cross or not." He crossed the room and stood on the hearth rug, his back to the fire, looking about. "I was just considering the contrast. I've come from a farm home with linoleum on the floor, a sheet iron stove, and a very tired woman trying desperately to give birth to a child very unwilling to be born. This," he waved his hand, "is almost more than I can take in. Whatever you've done to this house, you've made it charming." He drew up a chair and sank into it.

"It is nice, isn't it?" She felt a warm elation at his approval. "Is the woman very sick?"

"Sick enough." Absently he searched his pockets, came up with his pipe. He shook tobacco into it and tamped it down. As he went to light it he remembered. "I'm sorry. I wasn't thinking. Perhaps you'd rather not have me smoking in here."

"No—go ahead. I rather like it. Will she live? The woman, I mean."

"I hope so. She has a good chance, in any case." He added in a voice that had gone flat. "The baby died."

"Oh. That's a pity."

"It could be said, I suppose, under all the circumstances, that it isn't. But I hate to lose a baby. I don't think I will ever grow used to it."

"I don't suppose one could," she murmured.

"The least they're due," he said thoughtfully, "is their chance at life. I like to give it to them." He moved his shoulders as if to ease them. "Lord, but I'm tired."

"I thought you were."

It occurred to her, then, that since he had come so late she might as well offer him dinner. Nettie always fixed enough for three or four people. "Have you had dinner?" she asked.

"No. I'll stop off at home when I leave here. This is my night for evening office hours. I don't usually take time for more than a sandwich."

"Will someone be expecting you at home?"

The question was more or less academic. No one had said, but she judged that since he had been asked to Lucia's alone, since he had been at the concert alone, he was not married. Something, however, made her ask, something that wanted it settled one way or another.

"My housekeeper will have left sandwiches for me," he said. The pipe was going well, now, and he leaned his head against the chair back, eyes on the fire. "Sallie," he said with amusement, "likes my evening office days. It means she can go home at a decent hour."

Regina laughed with him. "I think Nettie likes my library evenings for the same reason."

He turned his head lazily on the chair cushion. "They're sisters, you know."

"Nettie? And your Sallie? I'm afraid I didn't know. Nettie has never mentioned having a sister."

It struck her as a pleasant coincidence that their housekeepers should be related.

"Oh, yes. They live together. They're both widows. Sallie has told me a good many things about you and your house—passed on by Nettie, of course."

It hadn't occurred to her that Nettie might have discussed her with someone else and she felt a little shock. "What on earth have you been hearing?"

He drew suddenly on the pipe, sending a cloud of smoke out. "Well, for one thing, that your husband is dead."

"Oh. Yes . . . he's been dead nearly three years now."

The memory of Walter was difficult to recall, in this place, in this room. Vaguely she knew how out of pocket his blond bigness would have been sitting in that chair. She was indefinably disturbed, seeing the dark, crisp hair against the pale fabric, seeing the finely drawn profile against the firelight. The silence lengthened until she put the overlaying disturbance out of her mind and recalled her intention. "I was going to offer you dinner. Nettie will be bringing mine soon. There'll be ample, but you've made me uncertain about your time."

He roused, drew himself back into the moment. "You needn't be. I don't have to be at the office until eight." He looked at his watch. "That's nearly three hours yet. It won't put Nettie out?"

44

"I'm sure it won't. She'll be greatly honored, in fact. I don't know what she'll give us though. She seems to be convinced I should stick to an invalid's diet."

"It won't matter. Beef broth and custard in company will be infinitely preferable to ham sandwiches alone. Shall I tell her?"

"Would you mind? I hate making her take unnecessary steps. All this has been as hard on her as on me."

He stuck the pipe in his mouth and stood, shoving his hands in his pockets. It was the tweed suit again today, she noticed, and for some reason was glad. "Then we'll take a look at the ankle," he said. "Has it been giving you much trouble?" He was passing the couch, walking to the door.

"None at all—for two days."

"I expect it's doing all right. I'll not be long."

She heard him whistling as he went down the hall. It had an oddly boyish sound and made her smile. Then there was his voice speaking to Nettie, Nettie's voice replying, some teasing she suspected, and raillery, for she heard Nettie's laugh, then he was back. "You wronged her," he said. "She has lamb chops and baked potatoes, peas and a salad, and she says she'll just pop another chop under the broiler and it will be no trouble at all."

He looked more rested now, even gay. It must be lonely for him, living by himself, she thought, forgetting for the moment that she lived alone herself, coming home to solitary meals, to solitary evenings. When she recalled that that was pretty much what she did she reflected that it was different for a woman, women being fairly domestic under any circumstances. She was glad she had thought to offer him dinner. "You must like lamb chops."

"I do. Properly cooked, of course. Now, let's get the ankle inspected."

He turned on the lamp at the foot of the sofa, snipped the gauze and let it fall, nodded judiciously and approvingly, ran a cool finger over the surface. "When did the swelling begin to go down?"

"The next day—as you said it would."

"I'll bandage it once more, then when you start using it you probably should wear one of those elastic gadgets—to brace it—for a week or two. I'll have one sent out."

Wrapping the new bandage he began whistling softly, almost under his breath. She recognized a tune from *Bittersweet.* "Do you like Noel Coward?"

"Not especially. Why?"

"You were whistling that thing from *Bittersweet*."

"Which thing?"

She couldn't tell if he were teasing or not. She hesitated, wondering why. "'I'll See You Again.'"

His face was hidden as he bent far over to reach around the ankle. "Probably just a whistleable tune." There was something stiff about his shoulders, as if he'd gone a little self-conscious, something even a little awkward. So he *did* know what he was whistling, she thought, in an amused triumph. It made her feel very light-hearted suddenly.

When he had finished and cleaned up the clutter, snapped his bag shut and put it with his coat, he wandered over to the phonograph. "Do you feel like some music?"

"Of course." She was delighted, because she was a little proud of her record collection.

"Anything in particular?"

"Whatever you like."

She started to tell him there was a new Mussorgsky about which she was enthusiastic, but curiosity as to what he would select overcame her and she remained silent.

He ran a finger down the backs of the albums, hesitated thoughtfully, passed over one and then came back to it. Withdrawing the records he still hesitated, weighing them. "This may be a little heavy, but I haven't heard it in quite awhile."

"What is it?"

He smiled at her. "Wait and see."

When the mechanism had been started, instead of returning to the chair by the hearth, he folded himself as easily as a boy would have done onto the rug by the side of the couch and locked his hands about his knees. Because he sat with his back to the lamp, his face was in shadow. Her own was in the full light and it troubled her the way it fell across her eyes. She found that if she turned on her side she could shade them. He noticed, however, when she turned, and was immediately on his feet. "Why didn't you tell me the light was bothering you?"

"I didn't like to disturb you. You looked much too comfortable and settled. There's a small lamp near the phonograph."

"Let's not have any. The fire gives enough light."

He had said it easily though, but there was not quite the ease of posture when he returned to his place on the rug. It was a little too good to be true, and she felt a small tremor of alarm. It had too much the appearance of setting a scene. She would be disappointed if that turned out to be the case, she thought. She somehow didn't expect him to be commonplace. The music demanded her attention then. She smiled when she recognized the Scriabin *Prometheus*. Whatever had made him choose that?

He was the sort of listener who grew rapt as the theme progressed, and it was a noble theme Scriabin had chosen—that of the giving of the fire of heaven to human beings, the conflict of good and evil as the nobler of mankind strove to use it for creative activity and the baser strove equally hard to make an evil use of it. There was no sound in the room save the music as it moved into the majestic conflict, and, caught up by its grandeur and great sweep, Regina forgot everything else and was swept herself into an exultant response.

When the piano, expressing man's joy of life, stood forth clearly against the orchestra, his hand reached out for hers and unthinking and unquestioning she fitted it into the broad palm which enclosed it. It seemed the most natural thing in the world, and it was as if another sense had been added to her own, as if through his hand she made use of a supplementary instrument for hearing and for enjoying.

When it was over there was no awkwardness. He simply released her hand and rose to shut off the phonograph. He didn't ask if she wanted to hear anything else. He seemed to take it for granted she would not. He returned to the chair, however, instead of the rug. "What is that 'mystery' chord of Scriabin's?" he asked.

Still bemused she had to concentrate. "Do you mean the notes?"

"Yes. I can't make it out."

"I think they are C, F-sharp, B-flat, E, A, and D."

"My word!"

She laughed. "Oh, no one but Scriabin ever understood his theory of harmony."

"I can see why. I don't know him too well."

"Did you know that the *Prometheus* was intended to have color lights combined with the music?"

He was immediately interested. "No. How could that be done?"

"He invented a rather elaborate color-keyboard which projected the lights as the notes were played."

"I should think it would be distracting."

"They say it was. Altschuler played it that way once. It didn't come off at all."

"No, it wouldn't. The music has grandeur, though, doesn't it?"

"Well, after all, it's a very grand theme."

He gazed into the fire, pondering. "I've always thought that it isn't the conflict between good and evil which is so troubling. Oh, universally, perhaps. Of course it is—one of the eternal problems. But not so much to the individual. A man knows, in his soul, what is good and what is evil—if he is a decent sort at all. It's the conflict between one good and another good which can be so disturbing."

Trying to follow him but feeling perplexed, she said, "I don't quite know . . . do you mean something such as a conflict between loyalties, perhaps?"

He stirred in his chair, shifted one leg to cross it over the other. "Well, that . . . yes. But I was thinking more of . . . oh, for instance, the good one had been taught all one's life, that's been ingrained so that it is almost an instinct, which one *believes, knows* is good. Suppose it suddenly becomes a barrier in the path of another good thing, one equally as good—which perhaps one longs for even more deeply . . ."

Utterly bewildered, she could only gaze at him. What *was* he talking about? That it was personal and not a bemused abstraction was quite evident, both from his halting speech and from the seriousness of his face. It rather jolted her. "Can't they be reconciled?"

"No." Then, as if sensing her confusion, he made an abrupt movement, as if brushing aside the question. "Oh, never mind. I talk a lot of silly rot sometimes. I'd much better stick to Aeschylus' conception. Or do you think it was Aeschylus' *Prometheus* Scriabin had in mind?"

"Well, he'd certainly read it somewhere, and that seems the most logical—for a Russian."

"I've always thought so."

The fire sputtered and as if it were a signal his eyes met hers, held them for a long, searching look, taking in, she felt, every feature of her face, until it became embarrassing to her and she turned her own eyes away. It was disconcerting to be stared at so, and she wondered if her hair was tumbled or her lipstick faded. If so, his face had not reflected any notice of it. Not until she began to be self-conscious did the stillness become awkward, and to ease the moment over she said, "We'd better have some light."

"Must we?" he said, but obligingly he turned on the standard lamp beside his chair. "It was so restful, without."

"Nettie will be bringing dinner in a few minutes."

"I suppose so. Hadn't I better put a log on this fire? It's beginning to look pretty discouraged."

Without waiting for an answer he chose one and dropped it in place. Then, with an air of triumph and something of a flourish, Nettie came wheeling in their dinner. Watching her, Regina smiled. How universal it is, she thought, this feminine pleasure in serving a meal to a man. No amount of trouble is too much, and the reward is the instinct itself. Women, eating alone, are apt to become careless of food and Nettie, serving her, had never troubled to put ruffles on the chops, or to top the salad with slivers of almonds. The man so honored was properly appreciative. "That looks wonderful, Nettie."

Archly Nettie laughed. "Go on with your flattery, Mike Panelli. I know how Sallie feeds you. Where shall I put the doctor's tray, Mrs. Browning?"

"There's that folding table in the hall closet, Nettie."

The matter was taken out of her hands. "Nonsense. I'll have it in my lap right here." He pulled his chair around to face her. "I like to see my dinner companion."

Nettie settled the tray on his knees, then put another pillow behind Regina's back, and laid the other tray beside her on the coffee table. She withdrew rather reluctantly. "There's plenty of coffee in the pot here."

"Thank you, Nettie. I think we have everything now." She smiled to ease her dismissal.

Seeing the tray jiggle a little as he cut into the meat, Regina said, "I didn't think men liked to eat off trays."

"Whatever gave you that idea? They're perfectly manageable if you know the hang of it."

"Walter didn't."

It was out before she thought and she was instantly conscious of a jarring intrusion. Now he would ask if Walter was her husband, and there would be more talk of him, explanations, questions, answers. The last thing she wanted was to talk about Walter now, his likes and dislikes, or to listen to meaningless sympathies. But the comment was left unremarked. If he felt the ripple of discomfort which spread over her he gave no sign of it. He simply nodded, his face expressing nothing but a hungry man's interest in his dinner. With relief she heard him say, "Some men don't, I suppose. But I've had to snatch too many meals where I could find them. My chop is perfect, incidently, how about yours?"

She was finding it exceptionally good. "I think Nettie outdid herself for you. By the way, I meant to ask. How is your emergency? The man who was shot in the hunting accident?"

"Coming along famously. It was the most interesting thing..." and he was off, talking shop furiously, as if she understood each detail, explaining the type of wound it was, the problems involved, the minor frustrations.

His eyes changed when he talked of his work, she saw. They became lit, the pupils widening as his enthusiasm mounted until there was only a rim of darkening gray showing. He used his hands a lot, illustrating, and his entire body seemed more vividly and energetically alive. She lost the thread of what he was saying, watching him. "But I'm boring you. Why didn't you shut me up? I get started on something like that and don't even realize what I'm doing."

"I wasn't bored," she denied quickly. "I found it fascinating."

His face changed, became impassive and a little set with withdrawal. "Most women don't."

"But I did." She wondered who had repulsed him when he had been taken out of himself with some bit of surgery or some troublesome case. How cruel it was of her. His mother? A woman he had loved? She felt a deep resentment for him.

He looked at her suspiciously, saw her smiling, and smiled in return. "There's such a fine excitement in operating, you know. Especially in an emergency like that. You never know what you may run into. It's like pitting yourself against a tough adversary, one that may be more skilled than you. When you bring it off successfully, there's no other feeling quite like it. It's a little like getting very satisfactorily drunk. As heady as that."

"I can imagine."

"No, I'm sorry . . . you can't. It takes another surgeon to know."

His denial was not rude. It was a simple statement of fact, and she knew he was right. She had made a merely polite, perfunctory remark.

Both gave their attention to food, until presently she said, "You know, I don't believe Lucia ever said—did you get over to her place for dinner after all?"

"No. The man was on the table over two hours. They were finished by then. I was too tired, in any event." He looked up and grinned ruefully. "I am a trial to hostesses."

"Well, you can't help it," she said cheerfully. She didn't add that with so presentable a bachelor any hostess that did succeed in bagging him must have a feeling of triumph akin to his own description.

"If you really mean that, you'd be a blessing as a doctor's wife." He said it with detachment, pouring himself more coffee, motioning to her cup in question at the same time.

She nodded to the coffee. "It would seem to me that the importance of a man's work should be understood." It sounded a little stuffy as she said it, but she honestly meant it.

"It would seem so. It often isn't." Once again there was the expressionless look on his face.

Nettie created a distraction then, arriving to clear their plates and bringing the dessert. Seeing it Regina laughed. "You're going to have the invalid's custard at any rate."

Defensively Nettie spoke up. "There wasn't time to make anything else, Mrs. Browning."

"Of course not," Regina soothed. "Dr. Panelli had said . . ."

"I had said," he took it away from her smoothly, "that I hoped you'd have some of your famous custard, Nettie. You may not know it," he continued, raising his brows at her, "but Nettie is known far and wide for this custard of hers. It is even said," he leaned forward conspiratorially, "that she guards the recipe so carefully that not even Sallie knows it."

It was successful and Nettie broke into a laugh. "If Sallie knew the recipe she couldn't use it. That girl will always have a heavy hand with custards."

When she had gone Regina's mouth quirked. "You're quite a diplomat, aren't you?"

"Did you want Nettie on a high horse?"

"Of course not. I was only approving your tact. I think there's some fairly good brandy in that cabinet. This custard seems to call for it."

When they had finished, all but the last of the coffee, the last half glass of brandy, he lit his pipe. "You don't smoke at all?"

"No. For some reason I never have."

"It's just as well. It's a dirty, expensive habit." He looked at her over the match. "I'm rather glad you don't."

She laughed. "That sounds as if you're a little old-fashioned."

"Not particularly. It doesn't become some women, though."

"And I'm one of them?"

"Well . . ." he surveyed her humorously, "yes."

"Suppose I'd said I did."

She felt rather excited, dueling with him thus.

"If you'd handled a cigarette naturally, I'd have approved."

"If I ever take to it," she said emphatically, "I'll practice until I have it down pat before allowing you to see me."

It all sounded, she thought, as if they were beginning a long and friendly relationship, one in which he had the right to speak his mind, one in which she valued his opinion. It was borrowing from the future, and a most unlikely future at that. She changed the subject, told him a story dating back to her college days and the girls' defiance of the rules about smoking in their rooms. He found it appropriately funny and laughed.

The clock in the hall struck the half hour. He glanced at his watch quickly, looked toward the windows, which had become quite dark. "Good Lord, how late it's gotten to be. It doesn't seem more than . . . I've got to run, I'm afraid."

She was reluctant to see him go. "Was that seven-thirty?"

"It was. Miss Hopkins will be cross if I'm late."

"Miss Hopkins?"

"My office nurse."

"She must be an old bear, then."

"Oh, no. She's very nice, really."

Regina felt something less than enthusiastic about her.

He was pulling on his topcoat, settling it about his shoulders. "She's very presentable, too," he added, "if you like redheads. Personally, I've always found them a little peppery."

A feeling of well-being warmed her. She could be generous now. "Oh, I've known some quite beautiful red heads—and not too tempery, either."

He shrugged. "Miss Hopkins is a very competent nurse. I'd be lost without her. So would I be without my telephone."

Which seemed to dispose of Miss Hopkins quite adequately and, as far as she was concerned, more than satisfactorily.

"My ankle," she said, "may I begin to use it now?"

He smiled down at her. "You already have, haven't you?"

"That doesn't count."

"It would have if you'd damaged it. Yes, I think so. Around the house. Don't attempt anything more until the end of the week."

"Then I can go back to work next week?"

"Probably. We'll see. It's much better to be certain than to risk it too soon." He picked up his bag, glanced again at his wrist, hesitated, then leaned over and lightly kissed the top of her head. "You were an angel to give me dinner."

Feeling considerably less than angelic and at a total loss for anything to say, she watched him go. She had barely felt the brush of his mouth on her hair, but she put up her hand as if it had left a mark. Whatever had possessed him to do that? It had been done so lightly and casually that it probably meant no more than if he had taken her hand for a moment, to say goodnight and thank you. Just a gesture, she thought, but a nice, sweet one. She lay a long time awake that night, remembering it.

Chapter Six

❦

At the end of the week he telephoned. Pleasantly but almost perfunctorily he asked about her ankle and gave his formal permission for her to go back to work. She thought he seemed preoccupied and he made no effort to extend the conversation, warning her merely to be careful with it, then letting her go. When the connection was broken and she had hung up, she had a feeling of, well, that's that.

It grew as the weeks wore on toward Christmas and she did not see him, though she berated herself about it. Why in the world should she see him? But it did seem odd that she never caught a glimpse of him, downtown, driving on the streets, or anywhere. Only when she assayed that fact did she realize that she had been looking for him wherever she went, which must stop, she told herself emphatically.

The cold, which lingered a full week after Thanksgiving, broke, and December was marked by a resumption of springlike weather, balmy, almost warm. Regina welcomed the mildness and took to making short drives into the country each afternoon. She was becoming more familiar with the surrounding hills and valleys and coming to like their abrupt shifts and changes, the sudden small streams to be found wandering through any of the valleys, the old bridges over them, the white farmhouses and long rows of fences.

She was with Lucia frequently and together they planned the holidays. She was to spend Christmas Eve with them, for the tree, and they were to come to her house for Christmas dinner. Quite domestically she planned the dinner a full two weeks ahead. She wanted it to be very special, and she shopped about for some luxury foods, which, to her regret, she could not find in the local stores. If the weather stayed fine, she thought, she could run up to the city. It was barely a two hour drive; and she might do some gift shopping there, too. She wanted a certain mauve shade in a knit stole for her mother, and she might run across a piece of Italian brass for Lucia.

She set a date the week before Christmas and called Lucia to see if she wanted to go, too. "I wish I could," Lucia's voice came, in a heavy, croaky wail over the wire, "but I've got an abominable cold. Wouldn't you know I'd pick one up just now, when I'm the very busiest?"

She really did sound hoarse and very nearly voiceless. "Have you seen a doctor?" Regina felt anxious about her.

"Oh, I called Mike and he sent over some pills. I'm taking them. I wouldn't dare ask him to stop by for nothing more serious than a cold. He said he was snowed under. It seems there's a real epidemic of this virus stuff."

She did not realize how warmly the relief she felt colored her voice suddenly. "Well, *do* be careful, Lucia."

"My dear," Lucia protested, laughingly, "I don't have pneumonia."

She forced herself to more constraint. "You might easily have. Is there anything I can do for you in the city?"

"No, I think not." Then changing her mind, she said, "Oh, yes. There's a leather shop on Third Street, just across from the hotel. Do you think you would have time to stop in there and pick up a wallet I had them make for Tom? There was a card from them saying it was ready and asking if I wanted it mailed. I haven't got around to answering it yet. It would save trouble if you can pick it up."

"Of course I can. Anything else?"

"No, nothing. Have a good time."

She was in a holiday mood when she left home the next morning. She dressed carefully in a tawny suit made of such fine wool that it was nearly weightless, chose soft brown pumps, gloves and hat, and tied a brilliant tangerine scarf about her neck, aware that it did nice things for her hair and her cream-pale skin. "I may be late," she told Nettie, "so don't wait for me. I'll probably eat in town before starting back."

She was getting an early start and the morning was beautiful. The air was brisk and cool, but the sun, through the window on her arm, was prophetically warm. She was wise, she thought, to choose so light a suit. She doubted she would need the topcoat she had slung into the car at the last moment. However, one never knew. These fine mornings could turn cold with hardly a moment's notice.

She enjoyed the run into the city, the road free at that early hour of heavy traffic so that she could give attention to the passing hills, farms and small towns through which the highway ran. They all had very much the same look. The highway formed the main street for a couple of blocks, on which were crowded close together at either end, and for several blocks to either side. She wondered what drew people to such towns, what kept them there, what their interests were, how they occupied themselves. Most of them, she guessed, had been born in the vicinity. It was home and there was never a thought of leaving. She had had such a feeling about her hometown, she remembered, as a girl. It had seemed the center and hub of the world, and it was not until a break was made when she went away to college that the feeling had left her.

She reached the city just after the shops were open, handed her car over to a garage attendant, and as she rode up to the street level on the escalator reflected that she had timed it exactly right. She would get her shopping done before the stores became crowded. She would have a good lunch, see a show perhaps, then have something light with tea before starting home.

The day moved along as she had planned, except that the time got away from her rather more rapidly than she wished. That was because she spent such a long time hunting for the brass for Lucia. It was rewarding, however, for she finally found it. She checked her parcels, had her lunch, saw the movie that interested her, and was going in the tearoom door when she recollected that she had not yet picked up Tom's wallet for Lucia. Better do it now, she thought—the shop might be closed later.

As she waited for the package she looked at ladies' wallets, thinking she needed a new one herself and they might have something interesting here. She became so engrossed that she was unaware of anyone else in the shop until a voice spoke, quite literally, in her ear. "Are you Christmas shopping for someone, or are you just looking?"

She was so startled that she jumped. "Mike! You scared me. You should give some kind of warning when you approach a person."

"What kind of warning? A bell about my neck? Or should I tug at your skirt and say, 'please, ma'am, may I speak to you?'"

She laughed, feeling ridiculously pleased to see him. "I was just thinking I might choose a new wallet."

"Hadn't you better wait and see what's under the tree? Someone might anticipate you."

He looked as pleased as she felt, and his voice was carefree and bantering. He also looked remarkably brushed, combed down, and pressed. She had never seen him in a dark suit before and it made him look quite distinguished. "It isn't likely," she said, "no one knows I need it. I had to stop here on an errand for Lucia and I was actually only passing time. What are you doing in town?"

"I had to bring a patient up to the hospital. It seemed a good chance to get all my shopping done in one whack. I don't mind shopping if I only knew what to *give* people." He said it plaintively. "Are these ladies' wallets really good?"

"Very good, some of them. It happens that I like a thin, black, grained leather. This, for instance," she pointed, "is a beautiful thing. It can be initialed on the plate. It's just a little more than I care to pay, however. Otherwise it would be perfect."

"But it would appeal to most women?" He peered with interest.

"Oh, definitely, I should think."

She did not intend to sound brusque. There must be dozens of women with whom he was friendly enough to exchange Christmas gifts. She had a sudden mischievous impulse to steer him toward some impossibly ostentatious thing, which she quelled sternly. It was really none of her business.

"I trust your judgement, but I like that one better," he said, pointing to a tan pigskin. "Miss Hopkins has been grumbling about her billfold coming apart at the seams and I thought it might be an appropriate gift for her. What do you think?"

Full of remorse she turned back to the counter. "Do you recall at all the kind she's been using? Women do get into a habit about such things, you know."

"Good heavens," he exploded, "how should I know? I've never noticed the kind of wallet she uses."

Meekly she replied. "I just thought you might have. It would have been helpful. But you couldn't go far wrong on the one you like."

The clerk brought her own package at that moment. "Will you tell Mrs. Rhodes that if the wallet isn't satisfactory in every way we'd appreciate her letting us know. It was a very special order and we want her to be entirely happy about it."

"I'm sure she'll be pleased with it, but I'll tell her."

Mike asked to see the tan pigskin, looked it over, said he'd take it, then as they waited for it to be wrapped, he said, "What are you doing next?"

"Nothing. I've finished. I was going to have tea, then start home."

"Look. Let me give you dinner, then I'll drive you home. Oh, I suppose you are here with someone."

"No, I'm alone—but I have my own car."

"Well, I'll trail you home then, to see that you're properly guarded."

He waited, with an eagerness that was quite apparent, for her reply. There were several reasons why she shouldn't—she was a little tired, it would throw her later than she liked getting home, she had to work tomorrow, but she found herself saying, "All right, then. But we can't linger long."

"No longer than you say."

They had started to the door when he turned about. "Just a minute. I meant to order a belt for my brother. I know exactly the kind, so it won't take long."

She waited, without impatience, at the door, watching the people passing, wondering a little where he would take her for dinner, hoping it would be some quiet place. Vaguely she heard him talking to the clerk, but sooner than she had expected he was steering her out onto the sidewalk. He did not ask her where she wanted to go. Instead, with something of authority he turned her down the street. "There's a place a couple of blocks down that has good food, and the music isn't obnoxious, either."

"It sounds nice."

"I hope it isn't crowded."

"Well, it's a little early yet for dinner."

He adjusted his steps to hers, linked her arm through his and looked down at her happily. "This is wonderful luck—to run into you. I had no idea . . . That's a marvelous outfit you're wearing. I haven't seen you in brown before."

"You've never seen me in anything but a bathrobe, have you?" she said, laughing.

"Oh, no," he corrected her. "You had on a black dress the night of the concert."

"Well, really," she said, surprised, "I had no idea you were so observant."

"I can do better than that," he boasted. "You wore gray the day your car got pushed up too close to mine."

Speechless, she stared at him. He met her look boldly, chuckled, squeezed her arm gently. He was the most erratic man, she thought. He remembered every time he had seen her, even remembered what she had worn, but he could go for weeks without seeming to know she was alive. What could one make of a man like that? Any other man she'd ever known who was interested enough to notice details would have given some indication of it by at least a mild pursuit. But he was a very busy man, she recalled. "Lucia tells me there's an epidemic of colds and flu, and that you've been swamped by it."

He nodded. "I've been working fourteen to eighteen hours a day for three weeks. It's to be expected, though, with this mild, unpredictable weather. It always happens."

"You must be feeling pretty worn out."

"I was. I had to chuck it or die on my feet. I had this old man to get into the hospital here—to see Johnson, the heart man—so I called Barton and asked him to take over. I must have been psychic." He grinned down at her.

A sudden suspicion took hold of her, a very pleasant suspicion. "You're sure you didn't talk to Lucia . . . you did!"

"I've been watching that leather shop for hours," he confessed. "I had begun to think I'd missed you, though I swear I haven't left the window of that hotel across the street for a minute since noon."

"Oh, Mike." She noticed it this time, but she couldn't go on calling him Dr. Panelli forever.

"Now, don't say you mind. I did have the old man to bring up."

"But you wasted such a lot of your time. Why didn't you call me?"

"I only learned you were coming when I called Lucia this morning about her cold. I tried to reach you then. I thought we might drive up together. You'd already left."

"What a fraud you are—pretending it was all pure accident."

"It was fun surprising you. Here's the place."

He piloted her through a doorway. It was a nice place, rather narrow in front but opening into more space toward the back, somewhat Victorian looking with old mirrors and chandeliers, and a small, cleared space for dancing. Not more than a dozen people were there yet, and he motioned to a table for two against the wall not too near the orchestra, which was only just coming in. It was not a luxurious place and, she judged, not too popular, but it had an air of good taste and quiet respectability. She guessed that the food would be excellent.

Catching their reflection in one of the long mirrors as they walked toward the table, she could not help noting what a handsome pair they made—he, very tall, bearing himself with his effortless ease, assured, almost carelessly distinctive—she, reaching even in heels only to his chin, slender but not thin, smartly dressed and with the same well-bred assurance of manner. She approved the quiet understatement in dress of that mirrored pair and saw the approval reflected in the waiter's eyes as he seated her. It added to her already deeply felt pleasure.

Picking up the menu, he said, "They do Italian foods especially well here, if you care for it. Being Italian," he grinned, "I love it. But, first—what do you want to drink?"

When she asked for a martini he grimaced but gave the order and added, "I think I'll have a Scotch and soda."

Her discomfort must have showed. It was very difficult for her to forget the too many Scotch and sodas she had seen Walter drink, the hundreds of times she had protested, unavailingly, and the sluggish, inevitably amorous aftermath. "What's the matter?" he asked quickly, his eyes noticing and anxious on her face.

"Nothing," she denied, just as quickly.

"Yes, there is. You aren't a temperance enthusiast, are you?"

"No. Really, there's nothing wrong."

"But you didn't approve of Scotch and soda. Why?"

Seeing that she had given herself away too completely, and thinking it more courteous to explain, she haltingly began. "My husband . . ."

"Was your husband an alcoholic?"

"Oh, no—nothing like that. He simply drank too much sometimes." She laughed apologetically.

"And he liked Scotch and soda." It was not a question, it was a statement.

She nodded, unhappy that her face had given her away.

He beckoned the waiter. "Change that Scotch and soda to another martini, please."

"Mike, really. You mustn't do that. Not every man who likes Scotch and soda drinks..."

"I am not every man," he said firmly, "and I wouldn't for the world remind you of something unpleasant. Besides, it was just an idea. I don't really care one way or the other."

She felt her face flushing and thought what a fool she'd been, but she gave him a grateful look all the same. He smiled at her, leaning his arms on the table. "Was it very bad, living with him?"

"Sometimes," she admitted, honestly. "But not always. Not impossible, at any rate."

"He didn't deserve you."

"How can you know? You have no idea what kind of a person I am. Or what kind he was."

"I know more than you think." He reached over the table and took her hand, looked down at it, smoothed it with his thumb. "I haven't been entirely honest with you. I've known Lucia and Tom a good many years, you know. I've heard what Lucia thought of him."

"Lucia didn't know him very well."

"What she knew of him she didn't approve. She used to grow quite eloquent over him."

He looked up and met her eyes. She felt a prick of moisture. Lucia had always been so passionately loyal and so passionately disapproving of the marriage. "Was that before he was killed?"

"Long before he was killed. Long before my..." he bent quickly and touched her hand with his lips, gave it back to her across the table, his face suddenly a curiously puzzling picture of distress, self-reproach and humility.

What have I said, she thought, dismayed. What did I do? Wholly to ease him she looked about the room and remarked casually, "We were lucky to be so early. The crowd is beginning to gather."

"Yes." He quickly picked up the direction of her comment. "Christmas shoppers, I expect—oh, here are our drinks."

They ordered then and talked quietly of other things. He asked her if she liked the town, the college, her work at the library. She told him she did, mentioned her training for such work, told him how she had happened to come here, though she guessed he knew. He told her something of his school days, where he had interned. "Have you always lived in Hilton?" she asked.

"Yes. All my life. My father was a doctor there before me."

They spoke of their childhoods, of their families. She learned that he came from a large family. "Six of us kids," he told her, "the noisiest bunch of brats ever raised. How my mother put up with us, I'll never know." He smiled, remembering.

"Is your mother still living?"

"Oh, yes. She lives here in the city with my oldest sister. You'd like her. She's small—dumpy, still black-haired. Like all Italian women she's given to extremes—as happy as a lark one day, so miserable she could cut her throat the next. We aren't a very restrained people."

"She sounds wonderful. Were you the youngest?"

"Of the boys. I have a sister younger. I'm the only one who stayed in the home town."

She told him that she was an only child. "I suspect," she added, "that explains why there is such a bond between Lucia and me."

"Probably. But friendships can sometimes be as close, or even closer, than family ties."

He told her that he was coming here to spend Christmas with his mother if he could arrange it. Sometime before she had learned that he lived in a huge, old-fashioned frame house near Lucia and Tom, much too big and too much trouble for a man living alone. It was odd, she thought, that he had never married. She was on the verge of mentioning it, feeling they had reached a point where almost anything could be said, when their food came and there was the usual distraction of plates being set, glasses being refilled, questions asked and answered. She had forgotten by the time they were alone again.

The music had been a soft and continuous background to their conversation, and as more people had filtered in, a few couples were venturing onto the dance floor. When they had finished, and as they waited for dessert, she turned to watch and listen more attentively. It was decidedly danceable music, reminding her of her girlhood when Tommy Dorsey had played the college dances and a very thin young man by the name of Frank Sinatra had charmed everyone with his special style of singing.

She smiled, remembering that the tune was even Dorsey's own . . . *Sentimental Journey*. Memories crowded into her mind—the beautiful party dresses, boyfriends crushing their own flowers on the girls' shoulders, the girls' way of slipping off their shoes and dancing in stocking feet, the no-breaks which always belonged to one's own special boyfriend, the sad, sad ecstacy of youth. Then his hand was being held out to her and she was being led away from the table.

She had known he would be a wonderful dancer. It was inevitable, given his grace. After a dozen steps, they drew apart to smile delightedly at each other, and then she allowed herself to be drawn close again. In a moment she felt his head lower so that his cheek rested against hers, and she closed her eyes and let her own head touch his shoulder. It had never occurred to her before, she thought dreamily, feeling the smooth warmth of his face against hers, feeling the movement of their steps in the closeness of their bodies, how much the acceptable embrace of the dance could assuage a deeply felt but denied yearning.

Horrified at the thought, she stiffened and immediately his head lifted and he looked down at her questioningly. "A twinge in the ankle?"

She shook her head. "Nothing."

He tightened his arms again and she relaxed. How far afield one's uncontrolled thoughts could go. She had always liked to dance. This was no different than any other time.

They danced three more times until, regretfully noticing the time, she said she thought she must go. He agreed. "I have to get back myself. I'll *have* to make some hospital rounds."

"So late? It will be nine before you're there."

"I know. It's only to take a look at a couple of doubtful cases and prescribe night medications. I wish you didn't have your car."

"I wish I didn't either." She was not in the mood to deny it.

They found themselves lingering in spite of the necessity, and she felt that she must take the lead in breaking away. "We *must* be going."

"I know—I'm coming this minute." He scooped the check off the tray.

Outside the night air was chilly and she shivered, wishing she hadn't left her topcoat in the car. It was clear, and above the canyon of the street a new moon hung, looking as white, as thin, as brittle as frost. He drove her to the garage and waited, then followed her out of town.

She was conscious of him behind her all during the long drive home. He drove with dim lights, considerately, but each time she looked into the mirror he was there. The lighted farmhouses flashed by. Telephone poles and fences unrolled swiftly in the glare of her headlights. The moon raced with the car, forever over her left shoulder. Glimpse the moon over your left shoulder, make a wish and it will come true. Her grandmother used to tell her that.

She flung her hat off onto the seat beside her, loosened her scarf, feeling marvelously young, feeling again like the girl who used to go home at three o'clock in the morning after dancing all night, feeling as if champagne were bubbling in her throat. She glanced at the moon again and laughed. Who needs to wish on the moon?

Chapter Seven

❧

It was a white Christmas after all.

With a swift suddenness of mood the snow came after two days of dark, smoky rain. It began falling in great, wet patches the middle of the morning on Christmas Eve, so thick that, standing at the window, Regina could not see across the garden. There was no wind, and the snow fell in such a calm silence it was almost eerie. The ground is too wet, she thought regretfully—it will simply melt away.

She watched it for awhile, then turned back to the decorating which her dinner party tomorrow was an excuse for doing. She had found holly and other greens at the flower shop. Feeling only a languid interest in it, for some reason, she nevertheless went about it according to plan—the pine boughs on the mantel, with the brass candle holders and the long tapers at either end. The holly for the table—its red berries would be good against the white cloth. A flaming poinsettia in the window. It was a commonplace at Christmas, of course, but she hadn't been able to resist its scarlet beauty.

The house smelled good from Nettie's efforts in the kitchen, heavy with spices from the baking of sundry things without which, according to Nettie, no Christmas would be complete. Regina could hear her singing loudly and entirely off key as she went about her work—something that called for innumerable repetitions of the word "Rejoice, rejoice." She wondered a little what Nettie could have to rejoice about. She knew by now that she was a widow, that her two sons had been killed in the war, that she lived with her sister, Sallie, in a tiny house in the edge of town, and that she was an ardent church member. It was simply the season of rejoicing, she decided, and Nettie was reacting to it normally.

She wasn't, she knew. Unable to identify her continuing sense of gloom she had a solitary lunch, found herself wishing that she had allowed herself the extravagance, after all, of flying to the coast and spending the holidays with her parents. It was a time to be at home, she thought, forgetting entirely that there was nothing of home for her at her parents'.

As she finished the meal the telephone rang. "I'll get it," she called to Nettie. As she crossed the hall she glanced out the door. To her surprise she saw that the garden was already quilted with white and that the shrubs and boughs were quite heavily laden. She saw, also, that the snow was continuing to fall very thickly.

"Would you like," his voice came to her, deep, almost boyishly eager, "to take a long walk in this stuff? It's almost too good to be true."

As if borne up on wings, her spirits lifted. "I'd love to."

"I'll pick you up inside of thirty minutes. Do you have boots?"

"Yes."

"You'll need them."

"I thought you were going to your mother's?"

"Not until tomorrow. I'll see you, then."

"I'll be ready."

Nettie thought she had lost her mind. "Walking? In this snow? Mrs. Browning, you'll catch your death."

She felt mischievously inclined. "Dr. Panelli prescribed it."

Nettie was not to be won over. "Well, he's crazy, too. What time will you be back?"

"I have no idea." She whirled on her toes, feeling her hair swing wildly about her head. "You remember that I'm having dinner at the Rhodeses', don't you? You needn't stay when you've finished the baking."

"Humph," was all the reply she got.

She chose a red, hooded coat, which was light but warm, and hearing him on the drive flew out to meet him before he had time to get out of the car. He leaned across and opened the door for her. "You look like Little Red Riding Hood."

"I doubt if she ever felt as adventurous as I do. However did you happen to think of this?"

She settled herself with a childish wiggle of pleasure and pulled the car door shut. Absorbed in backing through the gate he didn't answer for a moment, and she felt the bump of chains on the tires. He might follow impulses, she thought, but he takes care all the same. When he had negotiated the gate he answered her question, indirectly. "Don't you like to walk in the snow?"

"It's been years since I have, except when necessary."

"Time you made up for it, then."

She didn't ask where he was taking her, but when he turned out onto the road which led by the lake she had a presentiment and felt unexpectedly pleased with his choice. It must be one of his favorite spots, she thought. He couldn't know, of course, that it had become one of hers, too. She had visited it often since discovering it.

He was silent, giving all his attention to driving. The snow was really very thick and it was impossible to see well enough for actually safe driving. She felt no qualms, however, watching him intent on the road, seeing his hands so sure on the wheel. He handled the car with the ease and economy of an excellent driver. She thought of the lack of awkwardness in any of his movements and knew she could have guessed that anything he did he would do well. Under his breath he was whistling softly. It was the same tune. It might be just a whistleable tune, as he had said, but it had certainly stuck in his memory.

He did not turn into the narrow lane just beyond the lake. Instead, he drew off onto the shoulder of the road. "Here's where we start walking." He pocketed the ignition key and slid out of the car, going around to open her door. She waited, allowing him the courtesy. She also pretended ignorance of his intended direction and waited until he had looked up. Taking her arm, he piloted her into the lane. "This way."

They clung together, holding crossed hands, as skaters do, leaning on each other, stumbling occasionally, laughing, recovering, feeling the wetness on their faces and breathing in the stinging, moist air. Mike's bare head was quickly frosted, and Regina felt her lashes grow tangled with the snow. She blinked it away and licked at her cold lips.

There was only a light covering on the ground as yet, but it was enough to make their footing insecure. Except for an infrequent "Watch it," or "There's a rut, here," they walked along without conversation. The lane was outlined for them by the wires of the fence and the snow-topped posts on either side. It was a soft, white, silent world, a drifting curtain drawn all about them. They could see nothing but each other and the fence a few feet ahead. It was a wilderness of snow, and they were entirely alone in it—-as alone, she felt, as the first man and woman in the cold, primordial dawn, invaders of a strange isolation. She shivered compulsively.

"Cold?" His voice was concerned and she got the impression that he very much did not want her to be cold yet. It would have spoiled things for him.

"No. I was thinking—what if we got lost?"

"We won't. I know this road. We can't miss it, in any event, because of the fence."

She came very near saying, what of the woods, but caught it back in time.

When they came to the woods he plunged into them and they stood for a moment, looking back. Already their tracks were lost in the thick smother. "I never saw it snow harder," she said, for want of anything else to say.

They were sheltered, now, from the worst of the fall, and the quiet, which had been so intense in the lane, was here disturbed by the gentle hissing of the snow against the last-hanging leaves and the bare tree limbs.

"There's a stream a little farther on," he said presently, "where I fish sometimes. There's a foot-log to a little island."

They turned to go. She had missed the foot-log. It must be upstream from where she had seen him.

They came to the stream and the narrow path which bordered it. He went ahead to show the way and to hold back the overhanging branches for her. The stream was a rushing, white-foamed torrent now, not at all the gently flowing water she remembered. The rains had swollen it and turned it into a roaring, tumbling force which had narrowed the beach on the island considerably.

She began to dread the foot-log. Surely he would not be mad enough to cross such a slippery bridge on a day like this. Heights made her dizzy, just as depths made her afraid, and with that water roaring and tumbling under a log she didn't think she could possibly make herself do it. It would be foolhardy to try it.

She was a little reassured, however, when they came to it, to find that it had a length of cable stretched across between posts for a support, and it was a much larger log than she had thought it might be. It had been a tremendous tree, for its girth was at least four feet and the walkway had been hewn flat. Just the same, she thought, taking a deep breath as she allowed him to pull her up on it, it was going to extend her courage to attempt it. He went ahead.

She found herself clutching the cable with both hands, inching along, afraid of the moment when she would be over the water. She wanted to call out to him to wait for her, but she wouldn't. Without even making use of the cable he was already halfway across. When she came to the edge of the water, something in her balked and she could not move another foot. Helplessly she looked down at the swirling flood, feeling pulled toward it, which was always her reaction to heights. Just as she was thinking, miserably, that she would have to call him to her rescue, he turned and saw her clinging so desperately to the cable. Instantly he came back. "What is it? Are you frightened?"

With him beside her, her courage returned. "A little. Heights always bother me." She laughed, embarrassed. "I always feel as if I'm being pulled over."

"A lot of people feel that," he said, reassuringly. "Would you rather not go on?"

She wanted badly not to go on, but she also wanted badly not to disappoint him. "I think, perhaps, if you'd hold onto me..."

"Of course." He slipped around behind her, put one arm about her and braced her firmly. "Don't look at the water. The walk is wide. Pretend you're walking on the sidewalk in front of your house."

That was all very well, she thought, but she *wasn't* walking on the sidewalk in front of her house. Still, since she had made up her mind to it, it might serve. Nerving herself she went ahead, wishing she might shut her eyes entirely, wishing she could also shut out the noise of the swollen stream. Men liked the most unforeseen things, she thought, and required you to like them also. What could there be on this island worth making that dangerous crossing for?

Without mishap she gained the other side and was relieved to feel her feet on the ground again. "There," he said, "it wasn't so bad, was it?"

"No," she agreed, knowing he expected it of her. It had been as bad as could be, only possible because he was holding onto her.

Walking along the curving beach she tried to put the thought of the return trip out of her mind and enjoy what evidently he thought was something very special. He pointed out to her the growth on the island, the good fishing places in the water, the white pebbly beach, the way the island widened, and when they came to the tip, he pointed her to a grove of small, scrubby pines.

They grew very close together, but were open a little on the south side, toward the water. He led the way and she followed him, stopping under the low-hanging branches. It was like a small room under them, closed about on three sides, a sheltered spring bubbling up in the center. She saw a crude fireplace of stones and the blackened ashes of old fires. The sandy floor was firmly packed and strewn with brown needles. There was an old camp box to one side, spread with a tarpaulin. She looked at him questioningly.

He nodded. "Yes. I've camped here many times. No one else knows of this place—or at least I've never seen anyone about. It's a sort of special favorite of mine."

He said this last a little shyly and he looked a bit embarrassed, as a small boy does when revealing something so sacred that it makes him afraid. She guessed that he was halfway wishing he hadn't brought her. She might not like it. She and the place both would be spoiled for him then. She was aware how much she was being tested. "It's a lovely place," she told him, tenderly understanding, fully meaning it. "I can see how it would be special for you."

"Do you?" He turned to her eagerly. "A doctor lives such a mad life . . . so public and demanding. There's so little time to build up any reserves."

"I've often wondered how they do it."

He dragged the camp box up to what amounted to a doorway in the grove. "Let's sit here awhile."

It was narrow and they were both forced to sit, a little uncomfortably, on the edges. Uncomplainingly, however, she sat, glad to listen, glad even to be uncomfortable, for his sake. He put an arm about her. "I'll keep you from falling off."

But there was very little to listen to for awhile. He had shown her something extremely private, something which he admitted held deep meaning for him. She had liked it, known what it meant, and there didn't seem much more to be said. In snatches, with long silences between, he told her how it was in the spring and summer—green, cool, quiet. "I often spend the night here."

She was even happier, now, that she had not disturbed him that day last fall, intruded on his privacy. It would have been more than an intrusion. It would have been a desecration.

"Do you fish at all?" he was asking her.

"Not much."

"I think you'd like it."

She wondered why he thought she would like it. It had always seemed to her the most boring way in the world of spending time. She had been on a few fishing trips in her life and had found that invariably she wished she had stayed at home. Of course she had not tried fishing. She had seen to it that she had a supply of books. Even so, however, she had been hot, uncomfortable, miserable. Walter hadn't enjoyed it either, save for the boats, but he had insisted once or twice that they go, when there was to be a congenial crowd. The men had played poker and fished, the women had swam and lain about in the sun. She was always very happy to get home again.

She had missed the thread of his conversation. Giving him her attention again she judged that he had been telling her they would come here next summer, if she liked. He would teach her to fish.

"Just so I don't have to put worms on hooks," she said.

He threw his head back and shouted happily. "Listen to her! Worms! You really don't know anything about fishing, do you?"

"Well, I fished with worms when I was a little girl, and I could never make myself put one on the hook. My father always had to do it for me."

He looked at her tenderly. "I wish I could have known you. I'll bet you were a nice child. What were you like?"

"Fat—freckled—stubborn."

"I don't believe it."

"But I was. I was a vile child."

"Someone lied to you."

She thought how often her mother had told her she was a problem. She hadn't thought in years of those days when she had been made to feel such a nuisance. Not to this day did she quite know how, except that her own will and her mother's had too frequently clashed. There had been some carryover into her adult life, she knew, however, for occasionally Walter had stormed at her for being obstinate. But what was one to do? Given convictions, one had to stand by them. He had never seemed to understand that, any more than her mother had. She shook off what was threatening to become morbidity. "Did you fish here when you were a little boy?"

"Of course. I discovered this place when I wasn't more than eight or nine years old. I ran away once and camped here for two days. My father had whipped me, for what I've forgotten, but I thought it very unjust of him. It probably wasn't, but I was so unhappy I ran off, meaning to become a tramp or hobo or hermit or something."

It was a more special place even than she had guessed. "Did they come to find you?"

"Nothing so romantic as that. I got hungry and went home."

"What happened?"

"I got another whipping for scaring my mother half to death. That's justice for you." He laughed happily and she knew there had been no scars. He must have had a remarkably healthy childhood, emotionally as well as physically. But he couldn't have helped it in that large, laughing, Italian family.

"I suppose all little boys love an island," she said, reflectively. "The Long John Silver influence, no doubt."

"It was more Huckleberry Finn with me, I think. Though of course there's a lot to be said for a treasure and pirates and fifteen men on a dead man's chest. I used to pretend this was the Mississippi. Once I tried to launch a raft from that riffle there." He pointed, laughing.

"It wasn't successful?"

"No. It wouldn't budge—hung up on the rocks. When I dragged it down into deeper water, it overturned with me. I gave it up as a bad job finally. What did you read when you were little?"

"Oh, the usual things."

Trying to remember, she moved, lost her balance, and only his tightened grip on her saved her from slipping off the chest. "Careful," he warned, "there isn't room . . ."

His other arm went round her, too, and feeling suddenly that a crisis of some sort was impending, feeling unready for it, feeling unreasoningly that this was neither the time nor the place, she stood quickly. "Hadn't we better be going? It seems to be growing awfully dark." She peered out into the open.

She must have misjudged him, she thought, for he accepted the suggestion readily, even cheerfully. "I suppose we had. You haven't been cold, have you?"

"Oh, no. I'm perfectly comfortable. But I'm having dinner with Lucia and Tom tonight, and they said come early."

He put the chest back where he had got it, slipped a casual arm through hers and pushed the pine boughs back for her. "They're wonderful people, aren't they?"

"Among the best," she agreed.

"What always strikes me about them is their closeness . . . their happiness together."

"Yes, they've always been like that."

"Sometimes when Lucia looks at him, one gets the feeling that she has shut out everything else in the world and sees only him."

"I think perhaps she does."

"I hope he knows how lucky he is."

She looked at him, quickly, catching a note of bitterness. His face had gone set and closed. "He does, I'm sure."

"It happens so rarely. It's what every man wants, of course."

"Is it?"

She had never noticed that it was what Walter wanted particularly. What he had wanted was for her to be ready to go, anywhere, anytime he suggested it. She had had the feeling that if she had tried to make him the center of her world it would have smothered him and he would have resented it. He had wanted to be left free and alone.

"But, naturally."

There was a lengthy silence, then he burst out with more emotion than the moment called for. "If women only knew how much it means to a man . . . if they only knew how easily they can kill the best in him . . .how dreadfully he can be hurt . . ."

Someone had badly hurt him. She knew it now. It accounted for too many things about him. Someone he had loved had let him down and he had never quite recovered from it. It was no use pointing out to him that men let women down, too; that people did dreadful things to each other, and that it was questionable whether it was more on one side than the other. Right now he was reliving his pain, and whatever blame had been his, she was on his side. The woman must have been a monster to hurt him. Regina's only thought was to comfort him. "One woman doesn't make a world, my dear." Perhaps she was treading where angels would have been afraid, but it was the only thing she could think of.

He looked down at her, studied her face to see if she were teasing, saw it was earnestly sympathetic, and smiled. "No—and thank heaven for that."

"There are a good many Lucias in the world, I should think."

He bent his head to one side and pushed up an arm to avoid a limb, grinned at her. "I doubt it. But another Lucia isn't exactly needed. Only . . ." Forgetting the limb, he let it swing and it caught them from behind, showering snow down on them. He got the worst of it, being bareheaded, and, half blinded, he stopped. "Damn! I've got it all in my eyes."

Quickly she searched her pockets for a handkerchief or tissue, came up with one. "Stand still."

He stood, his eyes closed, as she mopped his face. Intent only upon what she was doing, she was entirely unselfconscious until she felt his breath on her face, sensed the effort he was making to control it, heard it labor a little in his throat as he forced it to steadiness. She saw the pulse in his temple beating rapidly and knew that his heart was pounding. Her own began to accelerate dangerously and she allowed herself no more. Stepping back she tossed the tissue aside. "There. I think you'll do." She would not meet the long look of his darkened eyes, but made herself walk on. "I'm afraid we must hurry."

Taking his cue from her, he said, casually, "That was a stupid thing to do. It might have caught one of us a pretty bad blow. I wasn't thinking, I'm afraid."

"Well, there was no harm done."

At the foot-log he asked her, "Are you going to be nervous again?"

"Not as much as coming over. I'll just go ahead, shall I?"

Though she knew he was close behind her, he did not help her this time. Having crossed it once, however, she had fresh courage for it, and she negotiated it without difficulty. He congratulated her when they reached the other side. "That was very well done. You would soon be tripping over it as if you'd been doing it all your life."

"It does grow easier, doesn't it?"

The snow was falling less heavily when they reached the lane, though underfoot it was much deeper. It reached to their ankles now, and walking through it was tiring. "If we'd stayed much longer," he said lightly, "I'd need a shovel to get us out."

"I thought of that," she said.

Out of the corner of his eye he looked at her. "Did you? I thought you were only thinking of a graceful way to be rid of me."

His effrontery caught her unprepared and left her speechless. Really, it was pretty bad taste in him. She removed her arm from his and trudged on, unable to think of anything to say. He walked beside her for a moment, then took her arm again. "Don't be angry."

He said it so softly, with such little-boy pleading, that her heart melted and she felt a sting of moisture in her eyes. He was completely unpredictable and, perhaps, she confessed honestly, all the more lovable for it. "I'm not angry."

"I'm sorry. I shouldn't have said that."

"No, you shouldn't. It wasn't kind and it wasn't true."

He thought a moment. "It wasn't kind, I'll grant. But I think it was true."

She stopped dead still. "Mike! Really!"

He faced her now, angry himself. He clutched her arms, his big hands pressing painfully. She saw that his face had gone white about his mouth. "Don't lie. Just don't lie. Say anything you want—it can be as harsh as you please. Say you wanted to be rid of me, but don't ever lie to me!"

She felt the tears very near the surface, and more than that she felt confused again. "Why would I want to be rid of you? You're unreasonable, Mike."

"You thought I meant to make love to you—it was unpleasant to you."

"You make it very difficult. I don't know that I thought anything, actually. I felt we had said all there was to be said, for the moment, that it wasn't the time . . . that things were becoming awkward . . ." she faltered.

"Go on."

"And it certainly was time to go, Mike. I had no thought of lying to you. I don't, you know, though you may not believe it. If someone has lied to you and you've been hurt by it, I'm very sorry. But you'll please remember it wasn't I."

He searched her face, then let her go. "I'm the one to be sorry."

"I think you are." She rubbed her arms. His hands had gripped much harder than he knew.

"Did I hurt you?" It was a quick, anxious question.

"No."

He bit his lip, drew in his breath. "Well, I seem to have made a thorough botch of things."

"Please—let's just forget the whole thing."

"I'll be glad to." He laughed, shakily. "If you're sure I'm forgiven."

"If you go on about it, I'll be wondering."

"I'll shut up this very minute. Here's the car, in any case. Let me brush you off. It's a good thing you had that hood on. It saved you getting snow down your neck."

Now he's chattering, she thought, trying to set us both at ease. He acts about fifteen. But she met him halfway and they drove home making unimportant conversation about everything under the sun except what had passed between them.

He wouldn't come in. "You've probably got to hurry. I hope I haven't made you late."

"There's plenty of time. What time do you leave in the morning?"

Standing on the porch with the snow behind him, the light from the hall glinting on his head, she felt she could have forgiven him much more than she had.

"Long before you're awake. They'll be keeping the tree for me."

Absently, thinking of the road, the snow, the early start for him, she said, "You'll be careful, won't you?" Immediately she regretted it. It sounded so wifely.

His mouth twitched and she thought, suspiciously, he was trying not to laugh. "I'll be very careful," he promised.

"Well—thanks for a lovely afternoon, Mike. And have a fine Christmas."

"You were good to come. I hope I didn't spoil it for you. There's no use wishing you a merry Christmas. You'll have it with Tom and Lucia."

"I think so."

"I'll see you when I get back, then." He turned to go, without saying when that would be, then swung around suddenly. "Oh, here—I meant to give you this." He shoved a small package in her hand and was gone before she could recover from her surprise.

Inside, she weighed it in her hand, feeling distrustful of it. She had sent him a card, of course, but it hadn't occurred to her to give him anything, and she wasn't sure she approved of his giving her a gift. She wondered why he had.

Collecting herself, she took off her coat, hung it in the hall closet, and went into the living room. Nettie had left a fire, as usual. She stood for a moment with her back to it, appreciating its cheerful warmth, the small package still in her head. Thinking of his sudden presentation, she wondered if he had meant to give it to her earlier, in the pine grove perhaps, and it had been driven from his mind. All that fuss, whatever it had been about, would drive any intention astray, she thought.

Reaching a decision, she tore the wrapping off. It was just as well to see what he had been about. Carefully done up in tissue was a small, elegant white box which bore the name of the leather firm in the city. He wouldn't dare, she thought. But he had. Within was the slim, grained, black wallet she had confessed to liking so well but which she had also confessed was too expensive for her. It was even initialed, exquisitely. For a moment she was angry. It was graceless of him, she thought, and it took entirely too much for granted. He had neither the right nor any business doing it. What did he take her for? Did he suppose that she would welcome a gift from him that she had felt she could not afford? Had he even thought, perhaps, that she was hinting? It was like a slap in the face. She would return it at once.

She fingered the fine leather, inspecting the beautiful workmanship. It was really a lovely thing. As she opened it, a folded note fell out. He had written, in a bold, flowing hand which somehow she had known he would possess, "I told you it might be under your tree."

In spite of herself she smiled and her anger slowly receded. She supposed he had bought it when he turned back and pretended to be buying a belt for his brother. Remembering the scene in the leather shop, remembering his elation the entire evening, she decided the gift had been bought and was offered in a gesture of innocent pleasure and good will, as a wish to see her have a thing she had expressed admiration of—nothing more. She had better, she reflected, receive it as honestly. He was a complex individual, almost beyond understanding. This afternoon had shown her that. Whatever had prompted him, though, she felt certain now it had not occurred to him she would take it amiss. Suddenly she had no wish to spoil his gesture for him.

She tossed the wrappings in the fire, but, uncritical of her motive, she saved the note, putting it safely away in her desk.

Chapter Eight

꧄

Trying to write him the next morning, and finding it more difficult than she had expected, she eyed the note paper distrustfully and bit the end of her pen. There surely was some happy medium between a girlish gushing and an old-maidish stiffness.

Half a dozen abortive attempts lay crushed and abandoned in the waste basket and it looked as if this fresh sheet was not going to provide any more inspiration than all the others. Absently, her mind refusing to function, she looked out the window. A pair of juncos, feathers roughed against the cold, picked hopefully in the snow. Seizing the opportunity for further postponement, she went for some bread crumbs and scattered them on the sill.

The trouble, she reflected, watching the birds descend on the crumbs, was that their last encounter had thrown her off. She could not come to terms with it. It had been, at least for a few moments, so intensely personal. She weighed her own feelings and, unable to make anything of them save further confusion, shrugged them off with exasperation. At the moment the entire problem resolved itself into writing a simple note of thanks. Surely she was capable of that.

She seated herself at the desk again and pulled the paper toward her, began scratching hastily. In well-bred, courteous terms she thanked him for the wallet, padded her surprise and pleasure a little, and signed herself cordially his. It was surely the most trite thank-you note ever written, she thought. It said nothing she intended or felt. It would have to do, however.

She would have him to dinner, she determined as she sealed and stamped the note, and she could add a more personal touch to her gratitude then. Toward the end of the week would probably be best. She would ask him when he called next. He hadn't said when he would be back, but she supposed he only meant to spend the day. With winter illnesses at their peak he could hardly spare more time than that.

The snow began to melt and the streets took on a drab look, the mixture of slush, dirt, and oil that the passing of hundreds of cars make of softening and moistening snow. Even the garden began to lose its enchantment and became a dripping morass of bedraggled shrubs and bushes and water-soaked grass. That was the worst of snow, she thought. It never went away with any grace. There was always this time of ugliness and discomfort.

She didn't expect him to call on Monday, though there was just enough chance he might to keep her wondering. On Tuesday, however, each time the phone rang she answered it expecting to hear his voice. The cleaner called about a skirt—was the stain chocolate or any other liquid with oil? It made a difference. Lucia called, still full of Christmas happiness. Listening to her, her voice running lightly on and on about this and that trivial thing, Regina thought she had never before noticed how tiresome Lucia could be at times. Guiltily she thought the Christmas festivities must have tired her more than she had thought—Lucia was not a person one had to make allowances for. She answered more warmly and with resolution attended to the balance of the conversation.

Nettie's sister called, and shame-faced Regina found herself listening intently for some clue in Nettie's end of the conversation, a word that might indicate he was at home again. Indignant with herself she went upstairs where she could hear nothing. What had come over her? Never in her life had she eavesdropped before. It went against all of her principles. She set herself the most unpleasant chore she could think of—straightening her dresser drawers—as a sort of penance and as an assurance she was *not* waiting for his call.

A dress shop downtown rang up, then, to say that a dress she had liked had been received in her size. She couldn't have cared less, but she promised to stop in and try it. She slept most of the afternoon and wakened feeling drugged and unrefreshed. The lonely evening which followed added nothing but a continuing sense of forlornness, the constant drip from the eaves and the wet hissing of tires through the slush in the street contributing to a rapidly mounting feeling of neglect.

When he had not called by noon on Wednesday she took herself in hand. There was no point sitting by the phone like a high school girl. Really, why should it matter whether he called or not? She resolutely beat down the suspicion that if he never called again much of her interest in her present life would be considerably dimmed. Angry at herself and angrier at him, she dressed and got the car out. She would go down and look at the dress. If he called now, it would serve him right if Nettie had to take the message. He was in town . . . he was bound to be. Unless—and her heart lurched—he'd met with an accident on the road. But she would have heard of it. It would have been in the papers . . . It would have been on the news over the radio. No, there was no possible excuse for him—save the excuse that it wasn't important to him, and in that event she had better begin making it just as unimportant to herself.

She took the dress, though she liked it less than she had thought. She needed another dress, though, to see her through the tag end of winter. Somehow, one's clothes always began to look a little tired around the turn of the year, and yet there was still a lot of the winter left. Undazzled by the beige crepe, but feeling she had been wise and practical, she left the shop, walked down the street, thinking idly that she might stop at the bakery and see if they had a cheesecake.

The traffic signal went red just as she reached the curb and among a handful of other pedestrians she waited for it to turn. She was aware of a line of cars drawn up, and something, not as definite as certainty, merely a glimpse of his car from the corner of her eye, arrested her. She turned quickly, ready to wave and to speak, feeling inexpressibly lighthearted. The wave of shock which swept over her when she saw the woman beside him startled her both by its unexpectedness and its force.

The woman, quite near since she was on the curb side of the car, was attractive, about his age or a little younger. It was impossible to tell. Her head was bare and the wind-ruffled hair was as dark as his own. A gay, green scarf floated at her neck, and she was laughing. They were both laughing, Regina saw, and she had never seen him look so gay or so happy. The woman was small, for he was looking down at her as he spoke, and the mixture of tender regard and comfortable companionship was reflected in his face. It stabbed through Regina like a sword, leaving her almost ill. A fierce and completely unreasoning feeling of jealousy, envy, and anger surged over her. It was humiliating and shaming.

She fought it down with difficulty. The signal changed and she continued to watch, standing rooted, as the line of cars began to move. As Mike's car edged forward she saw the woman reach up and lay her hand against his cheek in a gesture which was both intimate and affectionate, a gesture which spoke of a right and of long familiarity. There was just time to hear his laugh ring out before the car gathered speed and crossed the intersection.

Numbly she remembered where she was and walked on, unaware of people crowding against her, forgetting even where she had meant to go. Her only thought was to find her car and get home as quickly as possible. It was as if her shame at the strength of her feeling showed on her and she must take it to some private place.

Driving home, reason began to assert itself. He did not belong to her. He had every right to take out whom he pleased. He had given her no reason to believe he did not have any number of women friends intimate enough to drive beside him carelessly, touch him at their pleasure. As attractive as he was, as eligible, there were certain to be. No amount of reasoning, however, could assuage her sense of shock and betrayal. It had, in fact, nothing to do with it, and it simply left her on a flat plateau of disenchantment. It was his pleasure with someone else which hurt so.

Well, she told herself finally, as she drove between the gate-posts of her own drive, that should teach you not to go mooning around reading things into a man's actions. It had been only a casual interest with him, and he was the last person, she thought bitterly, remembering her concern for him, she should waste any sympathy on.

The flat, thin sun of late afternoon filled the house with a shadowy light. She looked about with a feeling of strangeness as if she had returned from a long absence and was seeing the place for the first time. She felt oddly out of pocket and at a loss, sensing before she found Nettie's note that the house was empty. The note was propped against a milk bottle on the kitchen table. It said she didn't feel well and was going home. Supper was ready to put in the oven. She would telephone the next morning if she couldn't come. It was a kind of last straw, a final desertion.

Regina stood, tapping the note with her fingers, thinking of alternatives. She could call Lucia—but she doubted if she would be welcome so soon after the long weekend of Christmas when they had been so much together. It was always a question, in any case, whether Lucia and Tom wanted anyone else very often. She thought a little desperately of going out for dinner but rejected the idea immediately. The noise and clatter of a public dining room would drive her distracted. To her dismay she felt tears of self pity rising and she dashed them away angrily. She would do the normal, sensible thing . . . fix her own supper and eat it alone, as she had done evenings without end already. It was absurd to allow this feeling to get the upper hand of her.

She looked to see what Nettie had left her. There was a casserole of doubtful nature, probably yesterday's roast and potatoes, a green salad lacking only its dressing, and a pudding which looked a little sunken, as if Nettie had been in haste to be off and hadn't given it proper attention. Disconsolately she put a kettle of water on for coffee, set the casserole in the oven to heat, then wandered into the living room. Aimlessly she came to a stop beside her desk with some vague idea of collecting the cards from various gifts and writing the courtesy notes they required. She might as well, she thought, get them done tonight; it would be as good a way as any to spend the time.

She opened the desk and found them where she had neatly pigeon-holed them. As she withdrew them, the note which he had written to accompany the wallet fell out, fluttering on light wings to the green blotter pad and lying there, accusing. She had been going to ask him to dinner so she could thank him more properly, she remembered. Gulping miserably she picked up the note and dropped it in the fire, watching as its edges curled, browned and smoked. Then, unaccountably feeling as if she were destroying something precious, she snatched at it, but it burst into flames and she dropped it onto the hearth. It was quickly consumed, and only a small pile of white ash was left. Melodramatically she thought that was about all that was left to her.

The kettle, which was the kind that whistled when it was hot (it was Nettie's joy and her annoyance), sent its high-pitched sound through the house and she went to the kitchen, ladled coffee in the pot and poured the water over. She peered into the oven and poked at the casserole. It would need another fifteen minutes at least.

She decided to eat before the fire in the living room and got down a tray. The doorbell rang. The cleaner, she thought, with her skirt. Before answering, she took the time to get her bag from the hall closet. It rang again, imperiously, two short, sharp rings. All right, she muttered under her breath, I'm coming.

Impatiently she flung the door wide, and then leaned heavily against it for support. He was still pressing the bell, like a child with a new toy, and its insistent peal rang through her head. "Mike! Stop that."

"I was afraid you weren't home."

He looked eager, pleased with himself, happy and relaxed. There was a touch of color in his cheeks as if he had been driving in the wind, and the gray suit, with its accompanying gray shirt and dark tie, made his eyes look unbelievably deep and dark, bright with a kind of starriness she had not seen before. She steadied against the gust of emotion she had felt on seeing him . . . noted dryly a tiny print of red near his mouth, and her anger returned stormily. How dare he come straight from kissing another woman to her! The shrewdness she felt turned her voice stiff and cool. "If I weren't, it would hardly do any good to ring the bell off the door, would it?"

He chose to ignore it. "Aren't you going to ask me in?"

"I don't know. I'm just fixing my supper."

"Good." He pressed past her. "I'm famished. There's enough for me, isn't there?" He ran his hand over his hair. "Lord, it's wonderful out today."

He should know, she thought cynically. He's probably been for a long drive with whoever she was . . . to one of his favorite spots, doubtless. It must be an old trick of his, showing them to women, playing on their sympathies. Curtly she said, closing the door, "You'll have to take left-overs. Nettie had to go home."

"It doesn't matter. Anything, so long as it's food. I'll help, shall I?" He was already making his way to the kitchen.

Crossly she said, "I don't like to be helped. It throws me off. You'd better wait by the fire."

"Oh, I won't get in your way. Just tell me what to do." He sniffed the air appreciatively. "It smells good, whatever it is."

As if he had done it a thousand times, as if her kitchen was entirely familiar to him, he opened the oven door, peered in. "Meat pie, I'd think. With lots of onions." He drew in the air, exaggeratedly.

She found it unbearable. What gave him the idea he could take his welcome so for granted? It was really going to be a good deal of trouble. There wasn't enough salad for one thing, and she'd been going to do with warmed-over rolls. Well, he'd just have to do with them, too. Silently she went about putting things together. He drew up a stool and leaned his elbows on the table and watched her. It gave her the fidgets and more to ease herself than anything else she handed him the lettuce. "You might chop some more of this in that bowl."

He set about it, without moving, pulling the bowl toward him on the table. A little absently he said, keeping his hands busy, "Have you seen that old mill on the Deer Run Road?"

"No."

"It's a little far out—twenty miles, perhaps. But it's worth seeing. One of the last of the old water mills in the state."

"Is that where you've been today?"

In spite of herself her voice shook slightly. Was he going to confide in her? Tell her . . . oh, all sorts of things which he ought to know would be impossible to hear.

"Yes. I must take you sometime. You'll probably want to paint it."

She slid the casserole out of the oven, hiding her flushed face. "I doubt it. It's very likely too quaint. I don't go for those obviously picturesque things."

"Oh, but it isn't. Not at all. It's still running—it's a working mill. You can even buy cornmeal there. There's an old man . . . he's quite a character. And the mill is built of stone." He stopped his work, interested in describing it to her. "A part of it is covered with moss, it's so old. And the sun this afternoon, on that moss . . . I wish you could have seen it."

She pointed at the lettuce. "I can imagine. Do finish what you're doing, Mike."

He looked at her, then, puzzled. "You're a little out of sorts, aren't you?"

"I'm tired," she said, shortly.

"What have you been doing? Oh, I haven't asked about your Christmas. Was it a good one?"

"Yes," she admitted, grudgingly. "The wallet was lovely, Mike, but you shouldn't have done it."

"Why not? You wanted it. I wanted you to have it."

Suddenly she wanted to be cruel, give him a little of the pain she was feeling, hurt him even in a childish way. "It didn't occur to you that it might be a little ostentatious?"

His eyes narrowed and his face reflected his bewilderment. "What is ostentatious about a wallet?"

Already she regretted the impulse, felt guilty, but stubbornly she went on, the burden of her guilt making her foolhardy. "Well, a book or flowers might have been in better taste."

She saw his mouth set in a firm line. "What you're really trying to say, isn't it, is that I'm just a Dago peasant with no taste at all."

She was shocked into realism. No amount of anger or resentment should have made her give way to such execrably bad taste herself. It was completely inexcusable, because she knew, actually, how innocent had been his intention. She had no right to take her bad temper out in exhibitionism. She smiled, tentatively, trying to recover the moment from its threatened direction. "I don't mean that at all, and you know it. You have excellent taste. It rather surprised me, though, and I suppose, not being accustomed to receiving such gifts, my ideas run to more commonplace things."

"That isn't what you said. You said it was ostentatious."

He wasn't going to let her off easily, after all. Miserably she dumped the rolls in a basket, covered them with a napkin. "I didn't mean it. I told you I was tired, Mike. I'm sorry if I sounded cross."

"You not only sounded cross, you *were* cross. What have I done? *Was* the wallet in bad taste? Your note didn't sound as if it were."

She shook her head, afraid to speak lest she burst into tears. Her hands trembled as she took down another tray, and it clattered as she set it on the table.

"What *did* you mean, then? What has come over you? You've been angry about something ever since I came. I mean to know what it is."

He was impossible. She would have allowed herself to be drawn and quartered before admitting she had seen him with someone else this afternoon, before letting him know it lay behind her unreasonableness. But he was quite capable of continuing to make a scene until she somehow satisfied him. She seized on the first thing that entered her head. "Oh, Mike, you're a doctor. For heaven's sake, you *must* know there are times when a woman doesn't feel too well and says and does silly things."

He looked at her searchingly, sighed with relief, laughed shakily. "For God's sake, why didn't you say so? I thought you were angry with me for something I'd done . . . and I was completely in the dark. I couldn't think . . . here, let me have those trays. Where do you want them? In the living room? Oh, Lord . . . I may be a doctor, but I don't think I'll ever understand women!"

She could have shaken him. How could he pretend it mattered to him whether she was angry or not? But his relief was so obvious . . . it was she who couldn't make him out. She watched him carry the trays expertly through the hall, and with something of resignation she took up the coffee pot and followed him. Maybe it was the other woman who meant nothing to him. Perhaps it was that that was entirely casual. It must be. There had been no mistaking his anxiety when he thought her angry with him, and the remembrance of his face, bewildered, hurt, salved her own hurt pride.

He had cleared the low table before the sofa and set the trays on it. "I've yours there," he pointed. "I somehow always think of you on that sofa." He drew up the hassock.

She poured their coffee. It occurred to her that she was making out a very good case for herself of being one of those delicate ladies who need constant pampering. But there was no help for it now. The only protest possible was in the nature of a joke. "I am becoming Elizabeth Browning, then?"

"Oh, no. You're hale and hearty enough. It's just that—well, you were on the sofa with your ankle that time, and when I had dinner with you the other night . . ."

"The lady of the sofa," she murmured, taking her place on it.

He laughed and shook out his napkin. "Also the lady of the library, the concert, the foot-log, and the snow. About that old mill. Teresa and I drove out there . . . Oh, I haven't told you, have I? My youngest sister was at my mother's for Christmas and she came home with me for a couple of days. She lives in Chicago. I haven't seen her for almost two years. We spent all our time exploring all the old places."

Of course. It *would* be that simple. So simple that it would never have occurred to her. Her relief made her suddenly weak and she set her coffee cup down carefully, its weight becoming much too heavy all at once. She noticed that in spite of her care it chattered nervously in the saucer. Why hadn't he said so at once? It would have saved her so much misery. But, then, why should he? He didn't know she had seen them—didn't know, thank goodness, how absurd her reaction had been. She exonerated him gladly, joyously, feeling, suddenly, as if every cloud in the sky had been rolled away. "It must have been fun."

"It was. She's a nice person . . . all gaiety and sparkle—always my favorite, I'm afraid. If she could have stayed a little longer I'd have brought her by. But she only had two days and there were a thousand things she wanted to do."

"I expect so. Has she gone, then?"

Nettie's casserole was unbelievably good, the warmed-up rolls were almost like new, the coffee was superb. She was ravenously hungry.

"This afternoon. I'd just taken her to the train when I came."

She felt an impulse to tell him she had seen him, but she checked it. She didn't trust herself to talk about it yet. Besides, it was much too much of a confession to make. It gave her away too completely. "Tell me about your day at your mother's."

"Oh, it's always the same. Completely crazy. Anna . . . my oldest sister, has a houseful of kids—just like our own family. They're all over the place yelling and running and romping. Everyone was shouting at everyone else, trying to be heard over the kids' noise. Tissue paper knee deep—the biggest dinner you ever saw—Mama laughing at everything part of the time and crying over Papa the rest of it."

Tenderly she thought of him in the middle of such a family, happy himself, laughing with them, running wild with the children, affectionate with his mother. She envied him the big, loving family with their emotions so near the surface, noisy, bound to each other so warmly. An Italian family had lived near them once, when she was a child. She remembered their noise and their laughter, their wild, shouting quarrels, their passionate and unreasoning affection for each other. Her mother had disapproved of them, thought them unrestrained and not quite genteel. Of course they weren't—by her mother's standards—but she remembered how exciting it had been to visit the Giacomos and what good things they had to eat and how much fun they had had together. The Panellis would be just such another family, she guessed.

"Mama scolded me," he was saying, "for not getting there Christmas Eve to go to church with them. She likes us all to go to the midnight service together. I think she suspected I'd skipped it altogether."

She was a moment taking this in. Then she remembered—the Giacomos had been Catholic, too. But Mike . . . it somehow would not have occurred to her. Feeling a little odd, she asked, "And did you?"

"Oh, no. I went to the cathedral here."

"We watched it on television. It was very impressive."

He buttered a section of roll, giving it serious attention. "I thought of asking you to go with me."

"Why didn't you?"

"You would have gone?"

"Of course. Why not?"

"I thought it might bore you."

He bit into the roll, glancing at her, and she wondered if he felt as defensive as he looked. "Why in the world should it? It was a beautiful service."

"Well," he said, reflectively, "of course, to a Catholic it's more than that."

She felt apologetic without quite knowing why. "I'm sure it is. What I meant is . . ."

"I expect it appeals to you aesthetically. It would—to an artist."

"To a musician, too. What was that flute-like effect? It sounded almost like birds."

"The boys' choir, I think. Their voices are very high. Father Vincent is very proud of them. They're his own boys from St. Raphael's, and he was so pleased to have them sing at the cathedral."

It occurred to her, then, that this was a conversation for which she was not all prepared, either by any previous experience of him, for a part of its strangeness lay in a more sophisticated conception of him, or by her own temperament. She had the uneasy feeling of treading on uncertain ground with nothing to guide her and each step threatening to bog down. Thinking they would soon descend to trivialities, she noticed with relief that he had finished his plate. She remembered the pudding. "I'm afraid Nettie has made a most uninspired pudding of some sort for dessert—rice or bread by the looks of it. And it also looks as if she had left something out, but it might taste better than it looks."

"I couldn't eat another bite." He produced his pipe. "Is there any more of that brandy? Don't get up. You keep it over here, don't you?"

He was really beginning to know her house very well, she reflected, watching him find the decanter and glasses. He moved about it familiarly, as if from old habit. And that, she recalled, flushing a little, extended even to the upstairs. She allowed him to pour the glasses and return the decanter to the cabinet. He stood, then, on the hearth rug, his glass in his hand. There was a long silence, which threatened to become awkward, until he said, presently, "Teresa and I were reading together last night . . . Do you know Henry Adams?"

"The *Mont-Saint-Michel and Chartres*?" She guessed accurately. "Yes, of course. I've always thought it a pretty good summation of his philosophy."

"It's the awfullest tripe, of course—but some of it is rather beautifully done."

"Tripe?" She raised her eyebrows. It struck her as an amusing thought and she had a moment's enjoyment of its audacity.

"He's such a pessimist."

"Well, yes. I don't think he ever denied it. It was part of his temperament as well as his experience."

"Of course you have to remember," he swirled the brandy about in the glass, lifted it and inhaled, "that to him the universe was unintelligible."

She took time to reflect that at that point she and Henry Adams saw very nearly alike and time also to consider that if he were a good Catholic the point itself would be unintelligible to Mike. Aloud, she mused, "It always seemed to me a little wistful of him to hold that the twelfth century was the best."

"Oh, no," Mike took her up quickly. "I think he had something there. It was a very simple age . . . the age of the priest and the soldier, when faith was strong and men were unified by their faith. Life was vastly less complicated. It was never so true again."

It was not an argument he would appreciate, but she felt compelled to say it. "For simplicity, why not the Greeks?"

"For simplicity, yes, perhaps—but they were not unified by faith."

"Not even their faith in freedom . . . in the individual?"

"That was a passion, not a faith." He set his glass down and pulled up a chair. "I've always wondered a little what would have happened if the Church had been taken to Greece instead of Rome."

"It would have been far less dogmatic and legalistic," she said, quickly.

"And less effective, probably. It's the influence of Roman organization which has given it its authority through the centuries."

She considered that, admitted its validity, adding, "At the same time, it's questionable how good it's been."

Immediately she saw that she had shocked him a little, probed a little too deep, gone a little too far. To ease the moment, she got up. "I have the *Mont-Saint-Michel* here somewhere." She searched the shelves. "Some day I must get these books organized a little better. For a librarian I neglect my own books shamefully. Here it is." She brought the book to the sofa where, knocking out his pipe, he joined her. "I'm interested in what you were reading. Can you find it?"

He took the book. "In the ninth chapter, I think. Yes—here."

She bent closer to look and felt his breath on her cheek, smelled the mixture of tobacco smoke and brandy and thought, absurdly, that it could even be tasted if one's lips . . . She drew hastily away. "Oh, that about the windows of Chartres and the presence of the Virgin. Yes, it's good. Read it to me."

Without any self-consciousness he began. "'You, or any other lost soul, could if you cared to look and listen, feel a sense beyond the human ready to reveal a sense divine that would make that world once more intelligible, and would bring the Virgin to life again, in all the depths of feeling which she shows here—in lines, vaults, chapels, colors, legends, chants—more eloquent than the prayer-book, and more beautiful than the autumn sunlight; and anyone willing to try could feel it like the child, reading new thought without end into the art he has studied a hundred times . . .'"

He gave the lines an intense beauty, his voice altering as he read to an almost priest-like reverence, offering the beauty to her as if it were a chalice. Why, she thought, bewildering, except that it was so new a role for him. Then she placed it. It was not only so new a role for him, it was so new a role altogether. In her world, no one believed—seriously, that is. In her world they were all Henry Adamses.

"Then of course he had to spoil it." He thumbed through the pages, found another passage. "'Mary concentrated in herself the whole rebellion of man against fate; the whole protest against divine law; the whole contempt for human law as its outcome.' And so forth—to here. 'She knew that the universe was as unintelligible to her, on any theory of morals, as it was to her worshipers, and she felt, like them, no sure conviction that it was any more intelligible to the Creator of it.'" He closed the book, stroked its back thoughtfully. "Mary, the Mother of God . . . knowing the universe was unintelligible. How presumptuous of him!"

She took the book from him and laid it on the table. "Well, it was one man's point of view."

"That of a man who thought all life tragic."

"He had a good bit of reason to, don't you think?"

"You mean his wife's suicide?"

He had his pipe out again. She watched the long, spatulate fingers tamping down the tobacco, remembered with a shivery feeling their touch on her ankle. "For one thing. It must have been shattering."

He struck a match, drew on the pipe, stood abruptly to throw the match in the fire, remained standing, staring into the flames. "Not so shattering, I'd think, as to be disillusioned in her."

She could have bitten her tongue for her carelessness. Whatever had made her bring that up, to remind him of his own hurt. It was difficult to remember, though. His reticence about it made it even more difficult. If one knew, she thought, it would be easier to avoid. It might also explain his continuing bitterness about it.

He turned about suddenly. "Well, that's quite enough of Henry Adams, I should think. Do you know, I've never heard you play. Do you have to be in the mood or something? Would this be a good time for it?"

She rose immediately. "It would be an excellent time. Is there something special you'd like?"

"Nothing . . . anything."

He settled himself more comfortably in his chair. Passing him she had a childish desire to run her fingers through the dark, gray-peppered hair.

At the piano, she wondered a moment, feeling rather uncertain of his mood, not wanting to carry over or sink him further into unhappy memories. She decided to be a little virtuoso and launched into Ravel's *Jeux d'eau,* which was intricate and vivid and realistic enough, she thought, to put all morbid reflections from his mind.

For an hour, which was a deeply happy one for her, she played for him. At the last, feeling that whatever dark incantations had beset him must certainly be dispelled, and moved, perhaps by the square of moonlight across the rug at her feet, by the paleness of her hands in its white light, she found herself drifting into the slow, sweet clarity of a Chopin nocturne. She sensed, rather than heard him, come across the room to stand behind her, and then his hands rested lightly on her shoulders. He leaned down and she felt his face against her hair. "I'm going now," he whispered. "Don't stop. I want to leave with the sound of it in my ears."

Her fingers moved automatically over the keys. His lips brushed her cheek, the faintest wisp of a kiss, his hands tightened on her shoulders for a moment. "Thank you—so much." And he was gone. Her shoulders, where his hands had been, felt as bare as if the dress had been ripped from them.

Obediently she continued to play . . . to the echo of his swift steps in the hall, to the echo of the closing door, to the echo of his car turning the gravel in the drive . . . to the echo of her own thudding heartbeats. To the end she played the nocturne, and when at length she lifted her hands from the keys and let them fall in her lap, she wondered at the wetness on her face. She touched her lips with her tongue and found them salty. The unbidden tears had found her asking and bereft mouth.

Chapter Nine

∾҉∾

Both January and February were dismal months. The short, dark days followed each other with the dreary monotony of rain until the earth was like a water-soaked sponge, refusing to absorb any more, lying sogged and filled, all its pores and brachials flooded and swollen. Day after day the skies were overcast, until it seemed as if the sun had sought another system and had turned its back upon a planet so discouragingly thankless.

Regina lived in boots and waterproof until she began to feel as if she had taken to the sea and wondered why the ground under her feet didn't heave like the deck of a ship. Such a country! She thought longingly of the sun-drenched beaches her mother wrote about and planned with considerable zeal a visit as soon as the spring term was over.

It did not help any that Mike chose to be erratically inconsistent during the entire time. After the warmth of Christmas it had seemed logical to suppose that they had arrived at some conclusive stage in their relationship, though just where, she had to confess, she had very little idea. But at least, it seemed to her, they had established some sort of *rapport*. They had touched something deeper and more meaningful than the thin plate of the surface, and she could not be, she thought in an effort to be honest, mistaken in feeling it had been true for him as well as for herself. Where it should have led, she would not allow herself to wonder, feeling very sensible in disciplining such thoughts. It would have been quite satisfactory, she told herself, to settle into a comfortable, dependable friendship. That was really all, she added, trying to be convincing, she expected.

If Mike felt any of what she felt, he took an odd, queer way of showing it. He never developed the assurance of habit with her, nor any of its old-shoe ease and comfort. Instead, she never knew from one day to the next what to expect of him. Sometimes he would call her for several days in a row, talking at length over the telephone almost as if he were present, going on interminably about such widely disparate things as a new record he had bought, a miserable run up to the city, a squeak which had developed in his car, much of it so trivial that it was almost womanish in its chattiness. She, waiting to hear some suggestion that they have dinner together, go to a concert, even drive in the rain—anything that would mean being together—would realize finally and disappointingly that he simply wanted to talk to her . . . that some need not pressing enough to make him stop by had driven him to the telephone and an hour of wandering, disjointed conversation. She always hung up feeling still hanging herself, uncertain of what he wanted. Almost invariably she dismissed it eventually with an excuse for him. He was being worked very hard—he was too tired—his hours were extremely difficult and wearying. Naturally when he got home, finally, and could relax in comfort, he couldn't be expected to dress and go out again. It did not always work perfectly, for she was aware she was making excuses for him, but in the main it served her need. It left untouched, however, her awareness that he had never asked her to go anywhere with him in public. A walk in the snow, dinner in the city was all—neither of which could be called appearing together. When they were together it was always in her home.

Sometimes he would stop by, usually late in the evening, usually, also, when she least expected him, when he had not called for four or five days. If she had other plans, which occasionally she did have—evening hours at the library, dinner at Lucia's, or some faculty obligation—he accepted it cheerfully, stayed a brief fifteen minutes and went on. Again, if she was free, he was as likely as not to spend the entire evening, frequently withdrawn into a mood which asked, wordlessly, for the sympathy of her music or her quiet talk. At such times it was almost as if he were driven to her as to some refuge.

It was all very unsettling. Just as she became used to his telephone calls and began to expect them he left her to a long silence of her own company and thoughts. When he had come by three Wednesday evenings in a row, and tentatively she left the fourth one free for him, he failed either to call or to come. It was all the more bewildering because not once had he ever asked more of her than occasionally to take her hand, to put an affectionate and quickly removed arm about her, and once to brush her cheek in the dusk when she stood by his car to say goodnight. He had immediately stiffened into self-consciousness and backed the car too hastily down the drive, spinning his tires and almost hitting a post.

It was as if some private war had made a battleground of him, and she was sometimes his fortress and sometimes his chief opponent. It was partly that feeling which made her, when more than once she determined to put a stop to the whole thing once and for all, relent each time and made her feel she could not fail him too. There were times when she wondered if he were not, slowly, in his own perilous way, trying to learn to trust once more.

Furthermore, by some involute kind of reasoning, which was somehow comforting to her, she also arrived at the conclusion that it would be giving the entire affair more importance than it deserved to do anything but accept it on his terms. By appearing to be casual and busy, not at all dependent on him, she could simulate an approximation of such a state.

It became a point of honor with her never to suggest anything to him. In the give and take of a more relaxed relationship she would have thought nothing of calling him to come over for dinner with her, to go for a drive, to come listen to a new album. Under the circumstances, however, she refused what would have been more natural for her and left the initiative to him.

Once, on an evening when he had been unusually distant, it occurred to her that he might be a little uncomfortable with her because he was a Catholic and she was not. She knew so little about it, but surely he knew better than to suppose it made any difference to her. She gave it little credence but it was a possibility, so rather too brightly she said, "Would it be allowed for me to go to church with you one morning?"

"Would it be allowed?" Startled, he gazed at her.

"I mean—is there any rule against it?"

"Certainly not. Why would there be? Do you want to go?"

"I do—rather."

The windows were dark with rivers of rain, the gleam of the lamps reflected against them. A strong wind was blowing and the window frames rattled like old bones. It was a night when a fire, companionship and hot food should have made the indoors cheerful and comfortable. Instead, he had arrived, just as she was having coffee, wet, cold, doleful, and his mood had transferred to her at once.

Provoked, she had taken his coat, felt his cold hands as she took it from him, and fussed at him crossly. "What *are* you doing out on a night like this? Surely you finished your calls long ago."

He had looked at her with somber eyes, blinking a little in the unaccustomed light. "I was just finishing up. I saw your light. You weren't going out, were you?"

His eyes, dulled by weariness, by chill, by something she could not even remotely guess, rested on her hopefully. Still cross, but melting under his obvious need, she said, "No. *I* have more sense."

"You aren't a doctor, either."

He stood before the fire, spreading his hands to its warmth. He looked so much like a big, bedraggled dog that she found herself wanting, only to reassure and comfort him. He never wore a hat and his hair was plastered down with the rain. His face looked locked in some kind of inner despair, something so hopeless as to wipe it free of all expression and life. It was as immobile as untouched stone. He's lost a patient, she thought, knowing how he hated it—probably a child.

Steam began to rise from his clothing and she saw that the lower half of his trousers was soaked. His shoes were wet, too, and muddy as if he had been in the country. "Are your feet wet, Mike?"

He looked down at them as if aware for the first time that he had feet, and a shiver ran over him. "I hadn't noticed. They are, I think—a little."

"And you've probably not eaten yet."

He looked at her guiltily. She could have shaken him. He knew, better than anyone else, what care he should take. He preached it often enough to others, goodness knows. In a rush of motherliness she made him sit down, knelt before him to take off his wet shoes. He seemed not to realize at first what she was doing, so slack were his responses, then suddenly he pushed her away roughly. "Don't *do* that!"

"I only meant . . . " She stood, turned away from him, invaded by a rush of anger, her voice going sharp. "Well, at least take them off yourself. Really, Mike, you're positively childish."

"Regina!"

She wheeled swiftly, catching him unaware, before he had time to compose his face. She could not bear the look of questioning anxiety. She wanted to catch his head close and tell him not to mind . . . she didn't mean it. She smiled and saw the relief waver across his mouth.

"You really are provoking, Mike. Running about in the weather, getting yourself soaked and chilled . . . not taking the least care. Slip your shoes off, now, and set them by the fire to dry. How would a bowl of hot soup do?"

"It would be perfect," he said gratefully, stooping to loosen the laces in his shoes. He leaned back, sighing. "It's perfect just being here."

With the soup she brought a mug of steaming toddy. "This may be old-fashioned, but I can't help believing it's also a good remedy. Drink every drop of it."

"I intend to. It smells wonderful."

The soup and hot drink thawed him visibly. He brightened, though with some effort still, and when he had finished challenged her to a game of chess. As she set the board up, he said, a little diffidently, "I wasn't entirely truthful just now. I did have a late call to make—but I'd been walking for about an hour."

Horrified she looked at him. "In this rain? Why, this is *Wuthering Heights* weather. Are you mad?"

He muttered something which she only half heard—something that sounded suspiciously like he'd been feeling like *Wuthering Heights* inside, which she thought best to ignore. In spite of her sympathy she felt a little weary of his moods. It was difficult sometimes to remember how he had been conditioned, by the background of his emotional heritage as well as by some hurtful experience in his past, to moodiness and a kind of unrestraint which was foreign to her. After all, he *was* an adult, presumably a well balanced and mature one.

They played one game quietly, intently, and it was as they finished and he drew on his shoes preparing to go that she had the impulse to ask him to let her go to church with him. "If you're serious," he said, knotting his laces but looking up at her, "we can go Sunday."

"Whenever you say."

She couldn't tell whether he really wanted her or not. His face showed nothing but a well-bred impassivity. She wondered. "Mike?"

He was putting on his coat. He turned. "Yes?"

"If you'd rather I didn't—it was just an idea."

He crossed the room rapidly, lightly, took both her hands. "My dear—of course I wouldn't rather. It's only . . . it may bore you."

"I promise it won't."

He needed a haircut badly and she wanted suddenly to free her hands, push back the rough, curling edges around his ears. Funny, she thought irrelevantly, she'd never noticed before how well-formed and really beautiful his ears were.

He gave her hands a reassuring, quick squeeze and dropped them. "Then let's make it the nine o'clock service. That's Father Vincent's."

She followed him to the door and they talked a moment, inconsequently, of the rain letting up, of hoping it would be fair for a few days, of how long it would yet be before spring came . . . of nothing in particular, and particularly of nothing that even remotely touched upon the personal.

As she dressed on Sunday morning she wondered what on earth had possessed her. She felt an awful fool and she could hear Tom and Lucia shouting derisively now. "But, darling," Lucia would say, her voice drawling the words out slowly, "all that Latin mummery. However did you stand it?" Well, she had let herself in for it and there was nothing to do but go through with it now.

She felt even sillier walking in beside him, standing aside in the vestibule as he dipped a finger into the font, crossed himself, then took her elbow and steered her down the aisle. She had stage fright all at once, and she glanced about nervously. The place was far from full, then she remembered there had been a mass at six that morning and there would be another at twelve. It was a convenient arrangement, she thought—one that Protestants might well profit by.

Mike indicated a pew and she slid in, looked up to see him completing his genuflection, made room for him on the seat beside her, and was left feeling oddly embarrassed when, instead of sitting, he went immediately to his knees on the prayer rail. She felt caught out in some gauche act and wondered if she had transgressed some courtesy by not kneeling herself. She told herself not to be silly. She was a visitor, not a member of the congregation.

Covertly she watched Mike's face. It might have been the face of a stranger, it was so quietly remote. The wings of his black brows were serenely drawn, the flash over his cheek bones looked smoothed and firm, the full line of his mouth moved sweetly as he prayed, visibly but inaudibly. With a pang she realized he had gone into some private place, some sanctuary which only his God could enter with him—and perhaps Mary, the Mother of God. Neither this place nor this time had anything to do with her. She was only an onlooker, forbidden by the unapproachable Virgin to enter.

Finished, he lifted himself from his knees and wordlessly handed her his own Missal, taking for himself one of those provided by the church. He had marked the *Ordinary of the Mass* for her with the book's own thin gold cord. It was a beautiful thing, his Missal. The leather was fine-grained and supple and the leaves were thin and gold-edged. Loving books as she did, she found it a pleasure to handle. She caught herself nearly whispering it to him. As if she were not there, he was already engrossed.

He had not taken her downtown to the cathedral. Rather he had chosen this plain little wooden chapel on the outskirts. She felt a little disappointed. The cathedral had an interesting history and she had been told it was unusually beautiful. What she had seen of it in the televised service Christmas Eve had borne out what she had heard, and almost the only thing she had looked forward to about this morning was its beauty and the music of its choirs. But perhaps this was Father Vincent's church, and she had gathered already that Mike was very fond of him.

It was a bare, almost austere little church. Outside of the altar, which was the simplest she had ever seen, the Stations of the Cross between the windows were the only ornamentation. The pews were puritanically hard, uncushioned and uncomfortably straight-backed. The floor was uncarpeted, painted a bleak, sensible gray. A rubber-tiled strip went down the aisle, uncompromisingly useful. There were no choirs, and when Father Vincent entered from one side, he was unserved except by two young altar boys.

The priest was a middle-aged man, short, thick-set, almost blocky in build, with beetling black brows and dark, swarthy skin. There was no mistaking that he was, like Mike, of Italian origins. The chasuble hung awkwardly on him and she knew immediately that he was the kind of man who would always look rumpled. In common clothing he was the type whose coat would always be riding up on him, wrinkling about his neck and shoulders, and his trousers would never hold a crease. Looking at the strong line of his jaw, at the massive bulk of his shoulders, she felt instinctively that he was a man who could not be moved; a man whom one could count on to be just but upon whose mercy one had better not depend. Justice, she thought, in a man of God could be a terrible thing, a pain-inflicting thing, a pitiless denial of humanity in an affirmation of divinity. Uncomfortably, she felt that this man, pitted against any adversary, would be a powerful enemy.

The mass began. *Introibo ad altars Dei: Ad Deum qui lastificat juventutem meam.* She followed the words of the Latin text easily, but she could have followed them in any event. Father Vincent's *sub voce* was not very *sub voce*. She guessed that ordinarily his voice would have a boom and a ring to it which would carry great distances.

There was a business around the altar she had not expected. The altar boys genuflected, changed sides, waited on their knees, hands folded angelically. Father Vincent moved from one end of the altar to the other. Each movement was prescribed, had its own meaning. It was all, she reflected, so old. It had come such a long way down the centuries that its beginnings were almost lost in the shadows of time, except to those priests whose business it was to roll back time in the presence of their unquestioning people. Who among these faithful kneeling knew how carefully, how shrewdly, how wisely this very service had been ordained by the church fathers all those centuries ago, and why? How this movement had been weighed and included . . . how that phrase had been balanced and strengthened, each a significant, binding thing upon the faithful. It was the mass, the Church speaking with authority through its servant, the priest, himself bound and unfree. It was the Church taking the faithful step by step into the presence of God.

The Kyrie Eleison began. *Lord, have mercy . . . Christ have mercy . . .* The murmur of the Latin phrases, said so swiftly, so monotonously, was like a rush of small wings beating the air. The painted, plaster smiles of the Virgin and the Saints looked benevolently down, unmoved either by the words that rose and fell frugally and wave-like about them, or by the up-lifted, beseeching faces turned toward them. Lifting her eyes from the Missal, Regina looked at Mike. His lips moved, soundlessly, his eyes were fixed upon the altar and the tall, slender Mary which dominated it. Our Lady of Remedies...what remedy was it his own doctor's training could not provide? *Pax*...my peace, the Virgin smiled down...my peace I give unto you. What peace had she known toward which all mortals strove?

The Canon of the Mass had started. Father Vincent moved toward the final consecration. "To dispose our days in thy peace . . . preserve us from eternal damnation." What would it be like to believe . . . to believe utterly in eternal damnation? How did one do it? *Hoc est enim Corpus Meum.* A silvery bell rang, and Father Vincent lifted the host high in his hands. This is My Body. *Mea Culpe.* She saw Mike's hand, closed into a loose fist, strike his breast three times gently. *Hic est enim Calix Sanguinis.* This is the Chalice of My Blood. The Very Body and Blood of God, not the idea. The second bell rang, sweetly, with petition and prayer, with warning and reproach, with deadly condemnation. *Mea Culpe.*

She found her heart beating up into her throat as the communicants filed up to the rail and Father Vincent turned, the Body of God in his hands. Mike remained on his knees a moment longer and she read from the Missal the prayer he was praying: "Let not the partaking of Thy body, O Lord, Jesus Christ, which I, though unworthy, presume to receive, turn to my judgment and condemnation." *Domine, non sum dignus . . . Domine, non sum dignus,* Lord, I am not worthy . . .

She watched him make his way forward, watched him kneel at the end of the long row of old women, young women, girls, children, men, his hands chastely held beneath the white cloth of the railing—watched the priest move down the row, murmuring. It seemed almost casual to him, a little hurried, even, as if he'd suddenly looked at his watch and remembered another engagement. Quickly his hand dipped, too, and proffered. But he was only the intermediary. The act was between the penitent and his God.

When he came to Mike, for some reason not in the least clear to her, she closed her eyes against the sight of God being laid on his tongue. She felt a frightening revulsion for all of it, for both the offering and the reception. It was a terrible thing, this theory of transubstantiation, and it was this toward which the entire mass had been directed. This was the moment of grace . . . this was the taking of God into one's own body, which sanctified it; upon one's worthiness to accept, to take, depended one's eternal salvation. To be denied was to die. *Corpus Domine . . .* preserve thy soul unto life everlasting.

As Mike rose and came back to her, she thought his face looked like that of a child—peaceful and somehow innocent. She remembered what a friend of her school days had said once. "I could die without regret, at the moment of taking Communion." The girl had been sixteen, and Regina had been shocked, seeing she meant it quite literally. She felt immeasurably distant from the man who sat down beside her, and in her confusion she dropped the Missal. She had been holding it spread open, but in falling the pages closed and it lay upon the floor open only at the fly leaf. She stooped to recover it and there was nothing to keep her from reading the inscription: "For my love, with all of mine . . . Eva."

Dully she picked it up and left it closed in her lap. So she had been a Catholic, too. It was, she thought, exactly what she might have expected. His hurt and his God were somehow all mixed up together.

It was over. The congregation shuffled out. Following Mike up the aisle she wondered what she had expected to gain by coming here with him. What had been her motive? Dimly she remembered the grave idea that it might make him more comfortable with her, that by a show of interest she might . . . but what did it matter? He needed nothing from her. It had been only her egotism which had read any need into his actions. No one who believed all this could ever need anything from anyone. It was all here, all one could ever need, asked and answered belatedly. No one can ever really understand another nor guarantee another's peace of mind.

She felt as weary as if she had borne a load a long way. Her shoulders ached and she thought, incongruously, that if she came to mass here very often she would soon take to bringing a cushion with her.

Chapter Ten

She was working in the garden, comfortable in faded old jeans and a disreputably worn woollen shirt cast off long ago by Walter. When the day had turned up so fine, she had felt irresistibly drawn outside. It was an old garden, planted much too thickly. Once kept neatly in bounds, it had now run wild, with the shrubs and roses grown to tree size, spreading and overhanging the lawn. The brick walks had all but disappeared in the mat of grass that had overtaken them, and the high stone walls were heavily covered with moss and ivy. It was a wilderness, but it was one of the things she most loved about the place. The neglected garden made an almost impenetrable screen for the house and gave it the privacy she so desired.

There were a few fine beds of bulbs, and these she attacked vigorously, raking out the winter mulch of leaves and dead grass and weeds. The sun was warm on her stooped shoulders, and overhead the sky was a deep, cloud-free blue that looked like polished porcelain. There wavered a soft south breeze, sweetly fresh and smelling a little of green things already. Half a dozen robins walked about almost at her feet, unalarmed by her movements, picking at the twigs and leaves left by her rake.

She felt very earthy and primitive, raking and piling, stooping occasionally to pull loose a dried weed, enjoying the tug on her muscles, the baking warmth on her shoulders, the soft air on her face. She felt strong and healthy and good. She would put, she decided, a table and chairs on the terrace and spend all her leisure hours out here this summer. It was so shaded that it should never be too hot. She could even have supper here if she liked, and ideas for summer meals with tall, cool drinks, crisp salads, tangy sandwiches, took form in her mind. He would like a big chair, she thought, with a high back so that he could rest his head and stretch his long legs comfortably. Into her daydreaming Nettie's voice came, making a shrill interruption. "Mrs. Browning! Telephone."

Nettie had a way, when she called her, of lengthening the last syllable of her name, drawing it out until it hung almost visible in the air. It amused Regina, reminding her of her mother's way of calling "Re-geeeee-na" when she was a child.

The smell of leaf mold on her hands came strongly up to her as she lifted the phone. His voice had a happy, larky sound. "It's like summer outside. It's unbelievable for March. Let's go fishing!"

"Now?" She asked it incredulously.

"Right now—this minute. Have you smelled the air?"

"That's just what I've been doing for the last two hours. I've been raking leaves and digging in the iris bed. Mike, I'm not dressed."

"You must be. You aren't the sort of woman to go about unclad."

She caught something of his mood and giggled. "I suppose blue jeans would go fishing all right, wouldn't they?"

"Perfectly. I'll pick you up in fifteen minutes. You can powder your nose in that time, if you think you must honor the occasion."

The lunch was her own idea. It would free Nettie, and it would give them a longer time in the open. She ran about the kitchen happily, collecting ham, cheese, lettuce, whatever Nettie, suddenly industrious at the promise of getting off early, suggested. Nettie brought a hamper and lined it with a white cloth. "I'll just put a thermos of hot coffee in the bottom, Mrs. Browning. The doctor will want it. He loves his coffee."

"That will be fine, Nettie."

She wrapped the sandwiches in oiled paper, humming contentedly. The island, she caught herself thinking, will be a good place for a picnic, and she smiled at the thought. She had no doubt where he would want to go. They would build a fire, almost certainly, and they would sit under the pines and eat their sandwiches and drink coffee from these paper cups . . . "Nettie—the cups! I almost forgot them!"

"I've put them in. They're under the napkins. This will be good for the doctor, Mrs. Browning. Maybe I shouldn't say so, but I've been glad to see him so friendly with you."

"Why, Nettie?"

She felt a curious desire to hear what Nettie thought of it.

"He needs to forget that other one, Mrs. Browning. The Lord knows it's taken him long enough. Three years, it's been and him never so much as taking a look at another woman. You'd think he'd have got his divorce and put her out of his mind by now."

The sound of her heart was suddenly like the roaring of surf in her ears, and the feeling that swept over her was that of being smothered in its foam. Why hadn't she guessed? Through the roaring in her ears and the choking in her throat she thought, distractedly, that she ought to tell Nettie to hush . . . but it was already too late.

"I don't know why he should have grieved over her so long. She wasn't any good at all." Nettie was folding a square of cloth, laying it fussily over the sandwiches, readying the hamper for closing. "Everybody but him knew she was carrying on with that man. Everyone in town knew she was going up to the city every week of the world to see him. It didn't surprise a living soul when she ran off with him for good. Nobody but him, that is. He was like somebody struck dead for weeks. And never a word from her all this time as far as anybody knows. Him still living in the house like he expected her to come back any time." Nettie sniffed. "Good riddance was what I said. From the start he was too good for her. She was just plain trash."

Was she beautiful, her heart cried, and she lifted her hand to her mouth to keep back the words. Her name was Eva, and she gave him a Missal and all her love. But she took it back again and gave it to someone else, and she left him crippled and alone. The pain came then—an incredibly stabbing, humiliating pain, and she did not know whether it was for him, hurt so publicly, or for herself, knifed so suddenly by her own commitment and the image of a wife—of the intimacy, the shared moments, the touch, the flesh, the spoken and unspoken words, the dark hours. She made an abrupt gesture of refusal . . . my darling! And it frightened her, the strength of it, the demanding force of it. Swift on its heels came anger. He might have told her!

She compelled herself to stand perfectly still—compelled her breathing to become quieter and more normal—compelled her pulse to slow. She knew him too well by now, she told herself, to think for one moment that he had tried to deceive her. There were hundreds of ways she might have known. What was common knowledge and town talk could hardly have escaped her. Of course he had thought she had known. Of course he had thought Lucia, if no one else, had long ago told her. She had only her own hesitancy ever to speak of him to blame for not knowing. She could have asked Lucia at any time. It was not the kind of thing he would speak of himself. Until . . . she had come to the heart of the matter . . . until he trusted her enough, or—but she would not say even to herself—until he loved her enough. It was unbearable that he might not ever.

She drew in her breath. "I think we have everything now, Nettie. Thank you so much for helping. Do you suppose we have enough sandwiches?" She tried, with effort, to make her voice sound light and casual.

"I doubt you'll eat half what you've fixed, Mrs. Browning. All that ham . . ."

"Well a man usually has a pretty good appetite after fishing."

"I wouldn't worry about it. There's plenty. I'll just go on, then. And I'll do the rest of the ironing in the morning, if that's all right."

"There's no hurry."

She was left alone, finally, and she wondered, looking about bewilderedly, what it was she had meant to do next. The kitchen was like the room of a stranger, its equipment confusingly unfamiliar. She found that she had automatically tidied up the disorder of fixing the lunch as Nettie had talked. She had no memory of having done it at all. She wondered if in her distraction she had put the knives and waxed paper in the refrigerator and the butter and mayonnaise in the cupboard drawer. But the instinct that had ordered her had been faultless and everything was in its place.

Whatever it was she had meant to do next, there was no time. His car was turning in the drive.

They were eating and she sat on the goods box with its tarpaulin cover, watching the small fire. He was on the ground at her feet, his legs crossed, blissfully at peace. A little bitterly she watched the side of his face. She wished she could approximate only a third of his ease and happiness. It had done no good after all to bring all those hefty ham sandwiches designed so lovingly for a healthy male appetite. "It's Friday," he said, quirking a rueful eyebrow at her.

"Oh, I forgot." It was the final disenchantment.

"No reason why you should remember. I'm the Catholic—not you. The cheese will be fine. *You* have the ham."

For some reason she could not define she baited him. "Couldn't you cheat just a little? I'd not tell."

He bit cheerfully into a cheese sandwich. "It's not that way at all. Not like one of those things that it's all right to do if you aren't found out. It's much more difficult." He had settled himself comfortably, with his back against a pine tree. "I've often thought the Church puts too much responsibility on the individual."

Bent over the hamper she said, "I'd think it the other way round. It leaves so little to the individual."

"Oh, no. You're all wrong."

"All those rules."

She unwrapped a ham sandwich, thinking it would doubtless taste as dry as it looked.

"Yes, when you're a Catholic, you have all the answers. It should be very simple and easy. The truth is, it couldn't be harder. It's left up to you, you see. No one knows but yourself. You don't have to obey the rules. You can cheat. You don't have to go to Confession. No one will know the difference. You *could* even take Communion in mortal sin. Only God would know it—and that's what makes it so terrible. He trusts you so." He smiled at her a little self-consciously, as if asking her pardon, then continued, hesitantly, "Men are so weak and He is so at their mercy."

It was all quite beyond her. She wanted to be sympathetic, but she did not know how. She had not gone again to church with him, nor had he asked her. There had been no discussion of it at all. She wondered, briefly, if he was trying, a little bit, to prepare her for what a convert must know. But she dismissed it as soon as it entered her mind. She was borrowing from a very uncertain future if she crossed that bridge before she came to it.

The entire afternoon had been difficult for her. She had determined not to let what she had learned make any difference, but it had been hard, especially in the face of his high good humor.

They had come, as she had expected, to the island, and he had praised her negotiation of the foot-log. He had taken out a rod for her, put it together, tied on a lure, and had laughed at her awkward attempts to cast. She had made the necessity for concentration an excuse for silence, and he had apparently accepted it. He had watched her a while, then he had wandered off on his own, going not too far away, but far enough that conversation was not necessary.

There had been one moment of naturalness, when she had caught a small fish. In spite of all she was feeling she had grown excited, and there had been laughter and teasing between them. It had not entirely subsided when they decided it was time to build the fire and eat, but she felt now as if it had never occurred, and there was only this hard core of restraint within her. She descended to a banality. "I think Nettie put in some hard-boiled eggs. Do you like them?"

"I love them. Do you remember when you were little, at Easter time how you could eat all that filled your basket at one sitting? I used to gorge myself on them."

She nodded, not caring in the least. "They used to choke me."

Meticulously she offered him more sandwiches, potato chips, more eggs, olives, and she nibbled at the food herself. At last he shook his head. "I couldn't eat another bite. It was a wonderful idea . . . the lunch. I hadn't thought of it."

"I expect you'd rather have cooked over the fire." She began to put things back into the hamper.

"Well, there is a point there. There's nothing quite like boiled coffee and fried potatoes in the open."

He got up to put another piece of wood on the fire. The sun was getting low and a chill was creeping off the now shaded water. She felt it around her shoulders and shivered a little. She threw the waste bits of wrappings and egg shells in the fire, folded the square of cloth, which after all they had not used, and closed the hamper. Her housekeeping done, she was left at a loss.

He sat down again, nearer this time, so that his shoulder leaned against the end of the box. She started to ask him if he shouldn't have something under him, then closed her mouth firmly. He was not a boy. He was a full-grown man and if he wanted to sit on the ground and risk getting a chill it was entirely his own affair.

The inevitable pipe came out and she watched his fingers, now familiar with every move they would make. His pipe and her, she thought, with a little venom, were about equally comforting. Or no, she had it wrong—the pipe was even more comforting. Finished, he struck a match and puffed, then sighed and moved, and the movement brought his shoulder against her leg, his hair perilously near her hand. Irritated she wanted to move, but some slackness of will kept her from it.

There was a long silence, broken only by the hissing of the fire on the damp log he had laid on. The red of the flames was reflected onto the white rocky beach beyond, turning the small, bleached pebbles rosy, like the inside of a shell. The sky looked as if fire had touched it, too. Beneath, and between its banks, the stream was cobalt and umber, a little smoky already from the loss of the sun. We should be going, Regina thought. The sun will be down soon. It will be turning cold.

He moved, and her leg where he had touched it felt the separation as a hand from which the glove has been removed. "We should be going, I suppose."

"I was just thinking it."

He sighed, stirred restlessly. "It should have been a perfect afternoon."

He had noticed, then. Careful, she told herself, and then disobeyed her own warning. "Should have? Hasn't it been?"

He tilted his head back to look up at her, resting it against her knee. "Something has been troubling you."

He said it simply, not asking to know, only stating a fact, a little sadly, a little regretfully. It placed all the blame on her, and she reacted with resentment immediately. She kept stubbornly silent, willing neither to deny or to admit, feeling only a graceless urge to torment him.

Still looking up at her, his head still tilted back and her knee very conscious of its pressure, he said, "I'm sorry. I hate for anything to bother you—ever."

The weak tears rose to her eyes and she no longer tried to resist the impulse to cruelty. "Then you should have told me before now that you were married."

He jerked around abruptly, almost upsetting her from the box in his swiftness. He put out an arm to guard her and left it there, carelessly, across her knees. "Do you mean you didn't know?"

"How could I have? You've certainly never mentioned it, and I don't discuss my friends with other people."

Her voice held a note of righteous indignation which she would have found absurd in someone else, and which she would have dismissed lightly as play-acting. She did, of course, discuss her friends with other people upon occasion. Everyone did. But the comedy of her statement wholly escaped her.

"But, my dear . . . well, everyone in town knows it. I should have thought Lucia . . . Oh, damn! Why didn't you . . .?" He was completely helpless, of course, and she took a perverse pleasure in his stumbling efforts. "You haven't been thinking all this time that I had tried to deceive you? You surely would know . . ."

"What else am I to think?"

"But, good Lord, Regina. It couldn't be hidden. You'd be bound. . . . Who told you?"

"Nettie." She said it grudgingly.

"When?"

"Just today. As we fixed the lunch, in fact."

He whistled softly in exasperation, then tried to smile, but it didn't come off very well. "I *am* sorry . . . but I don't quite see how I could have . . . well, look. You just don't go about unburdening yourself to everybody. It's just one of those things."

"Everybody?" Her anger mounted.

"Well, of course, you're not everybody . . . in fact, you're very special. But still . . ."

"Still," she interrupted, her voice coming with a rush, "I don't ordinarily go about with a married man."

"I'm sure you don't. I mean, I know you wouldn't . . ."

"But of course I have, since you didn't choose to tell me."

She was beginning to feel better, some of her spleen having now been spilled over. She even wondered, a little humorously, if there was in every woman something of the shrew, something which brought on a quarrel, a scene, even enjoyed it a little. You got so bottled up otherwise. It was such a relief to fling words about like stones.

He was very quiet, and she looked at him apprehensively. Either the firelight was playing tricks with his face, or it had gone pale. "I don't think you mean that . . . not entirely," he said, slowly. "You're angry, of course, and I can't blame you. But I think you know, even if you won't admit it, that I had no idea of deceiving you. And all that bosh about your not going out with married men . . . You know, if you know anything at all about it, that I don't fall in that class any more. It's been too long, for one thing. A man isn't married whose wife has been gone three years."

She felt contrite all at once and she relented entirely. Impulsively she pulled his head against her knee again, and laid her hand on his hair. It was as crisp as she had known it would be. The cut, curling ends felt crinkly against her palm. Under the caress she could feel some of the stiffness go out of him. "I don't really know very much," she admitted. "Only that you were married and that she left you."

"With another man," he said softly. "It doesn't matter any more, you know."

"Doesn't it?" She thought she knew better.

He turned a little, found her hand and held it. "Do you really want to know about it?"

"If you'd like to tell me. Otherwise, no."

"You'll have to know sometime. It may as well be now. I think I've always known I'd have to tell you, even though I did think you'd heard the bare facts from Lucia or someone else."

"Don't, if you'd rather not."

"No. Now that it's come up, I'd rather get it over with. I meant it, though. It doesn't matter, now."

"Why not?"

He lifted his head to look at her. "How could it? Since I've known you?"

She could have wept, or struck him, or snatched his head close and let her hands have their way with his face and mouth. Were men always so dense? Did they think a woman always knew? Instead, she laughed, shakily. "I'm glad I've been good therapy."

"You've been more than that." He kissed her palm and took a long, indrawn breath. "Well . . . there isn't much to tell. We were married only two years, just a little over. I don't think she was ever faithful—not even at first. There are women like that, I suppose—congenitally incapable of faithfulness. She liked excitement, going places, fun, dancing, running up to the city for the theater. Being a doctor's wife, being tied down by the hours I had to keep, the unforeseen emergencies—never knowing whether I'd be free, planning an evening then having it turn into nothing at the last minute. It all got on her nerves."

"Didn't she know you were a doctor when she married you?"

"Oh, yes. But one never really knows how those things are going to be until they're actually experienced. I suppose she thought I could arrange things better if I'd wanted to. She said so, more than once, in any case. She never had much patience. I didn't mind her going without me. I never suspected . . ."

"Had you known her long?"

He shook his head. "No. I met her at a party—she was visiting a friend here. She was from the city. It was all sort of whirlwind, I'm afraid. Neither of us took time to think."

"She was a Catholic, though, wasn't she?"

"Oh, yes. How did you know?"

Feeling a little ashamed she told him. "I saw her name in your Missal."

"Oh, that. Yes. She gave it to me before we were married. I was using an old one that had most of the binding lost. Mama gave it to me when I made my first Communion. Eve made fun of it and one day gave me the new one."

And you, my darling, have treasured it ever since. A deep sadness overtook her. She wished now that she had never brought it all into the open.

He went on, as if having started it, the pathetic end of the story was inevitable. "I don't know how she met the man, or how long she had been seeing him. It didn't seem important to find out, when she left."

His voice had gone dull and flat and he was talking in short, jerky sentences, as if he might be having trouble with his breath. "A friend of mine told me, afterward, that everyone in town knew it—had wondered when I'd find out. But there are things you don't suspect. How could you distrust your own wife? I knew she wasn't very happy. But she was my wife. We were married. It didn't occur to me she could be unfaithful. I wouldn't have been. No one I knew ever was. Except people . . . but not us, not our kind."

She stroked his hair, thinking how, in spite of its crispness, it was soft, like a boy's almost, or a child's. The dull voice went on. "Then I came home one day and the traditional note was there, propped on the hall table. Just like the movies. That was all."

She was silent a moment and then she asked, as gently as possible, "You didn't try to find her?"

"No. What was the use?"

He flung himself about suddenly, buried his head in her lap, and she found herself wishing, incongruously, that she had on something besides blue jeans . . . something soft and silky, something more comforting to his face. She put her arm about his big shoulder.

"It was the lying that was the worst. All the reasons she gave for going up to the city, week after week. There were hundreds of them . . . perfectly logical to me. And they were all lies. It makes you wonder if the truth is in anyone. You can't help it."

She remembered the bruising grip on her arms, the sudden lash of his voice—don't lie to me . . . don't ever lie to me! Never, she vowed silently, never, Mike, I promise. Not even about the smallest things. You shall never have anything but the truth from me.

She waited, keeping her arm about his shoulder, the other hand pushing the hair back from his temple, tenderly. She would have, she thought, if she could, taken all his pain into herself so willingly—rid him of it entirely. It struck her that nature's supreme cruelty must surely be the necessity for each human being to live so locked within himself, in such terrible solitude, so unable either to feel or to bear for another, or even much to express himself. There were no words, now. She could only make of herself a reservoir of comfort, a basin for his hurt to pour out in.

At last he moved, lifted himself away from her, pushed at his hair himself. "Well, that's the story—all of it. I don't know why I didn't tell you sooner."

All of it! There was so much more. What did she look like? Was she beautiful? Did you love her very much? What was she like in those closest moments—tender, loving, kind? Did you expect her to return, and would you have taken her back if she had? Is that why you have waited three years in that big house alone? There were a hundred things she could have asked, but would not. And she knew she would never ask. She would never know.

On what note the moment might have ended she did not know. Mike had pulled her to her feet and was looking at her, searching her face intently. With her heart beating in her chest, she waited. Then there was a thrashing of the bushes and a scrambling on the pebbles, and a farmer in overalls crashed into sight. Mike dropped her arms, looking annoyed, and turned to face the man. Equally annoyed and feeling some-what embarrassed, knowing almost certainly the man must think he had stumbled across a pair of lovers, she bent hastily over the hamper and closed its top, taking time to latch it securely.

The man peered at them. "Oh, it's Dr. Panelli, isn't it?"

"Yes. Are we trespassing? We've been fishing the stream and having a picnic on the island."

The man scratched a stubble of beard. "Well, I don't reckon the island belongs to anybody, Doctor. My land comes down to the bank of the creek, but I guess an island is public domain. It wouldn't matter, any-how. You've not seen anything of a brindle cow and young calf, have you?"

Mike shook his head. "Not a thing. Have they strayed?"

"Since yesterday. I thought she might have crossed over down at the riffle and was browsing around over here. Thought I'd take a look, anyhow."

He seemed in a hurry to move on, shifted from one foot to the other, broke off a twig of willow and peeled it, put it in his mouth. Casu-ally he spoke of the weather, of the difficulty of starting to plow with so much rain, of the state of the stream and its likelihood of offering good fishing later on.

Thinking that this could go on indefinitely and Mike needed rescuing, Regina slung the hamper over her arm. "Mike, we'd better be going. It's growing late."

"Yes, of course."

His response was immediate. He picked up the rods, broke them down and stowed them in their canvas cases, still exchanging trivialities with the farmer, who made no move to leave. At length, the solitary small fish having been given his freedom, he said, "Well, I hope you find your cow. But I don't believe she's on the island."

The farmer spat to one side. "Likely she's not. She'll turn up I guess. Well, better fishing next time, Doctor."

Regina thought she detected a dry note of skepticism in the remark, as if the fishing rod had been merely stage props for a more clandestine business.

"Yes. Thank you."

Mike took her arm and steered her around the end of the pines.

Feeling the flatness of anticlimax they stumbled silently back to the car. Stealing a glance at Mike's face she saw that it maintained a show of poise very like that of a small boy who has brought off an awkward moment as best he could—not entirely sure, but very nearly. It occurred to her that one of life's small ironies is its injudicious staging of great moments. Nothing could have been more ridiculous than the kind of interruption the overalled figure looking for a brindle cow had brought. Calculated, it could not have been more irrevocably destructive of a mood and a moment.

Chapter Eleven

❧

Easter was late that year, falling in mid-April.

The jonquils, tulips, and hyacinths in the garden had come and gone, but the lilacs were blooming and the first tight little fists on the peonies were opening. The great willow tree in the corner was a waterfall of soft, trailing green, and the maples by the drive were rusty with buds. The iris, which had been only timid little tips when Regina had raked them a month before, were foot-long spears now, bladed and strong. And the robins which had picked worms at her feet were nesting in the crotch of an apple tree near the back door. Late Easter—late spring, but both had finally arrived.

She went to the Pascal service with Mike on Easter Eve.

It had come about casually. She had been to the dentist's that day and, passing a drug store, remembered he had told her to begin using a stronger brush. She might as well stop in now and get it, she thought.

Mike was sitting on a stool at the fountain. Spying her in the mirror, he wheeled and called over to her. "Hi! Come have a drink with me."

She crossed over to him. "Thanks just the same, but I won't be able to drink anything cold for a month."

"Why not? Are you suddenly allergic to cold drinks?"

"The dentist just got through cleaning my teeth."

"Br-r-r," he shuddered. "It's what I've been putting off. How about a lukewarm coffee?"

She considered, then nodded. "That might do."

He gave the order to the boy, specifying emphatically that the coffee be warm, not hot, then taking her arm he picked up his glass and led her to a booth. Seated in semi-privacy, the padded booth coming up about to their shoulders, the noise from the juke box respectably muted, they talked awhile. She never knew quite how they got around to Easter, but they did, and then he was telling her about the Pascal service. "It's new—first change that's been made in the ritual in nearly four hundred years. It's a candle-lighting service. Father Vincent has been in a dither about it for days. It has to be sung and it's been so long since he sang a service that he's got stage fright."

"When is it?"

"Tonight—at eleven. Would you like to go? It should be rather pretty. I warn you, though, it will be long, for mass starts at midnight. Two hours may be too much for you."

She felt a little lukewarm about it, but looking up and catching his eyes just then she thought they looked eager, so she agreed to go. There was no reason for admitting to herself that she wanted to be with him enough to bear two solid hours of church in the middle of the night.

When they reached the little chapel that night the congregation was gathered in small groups at the door, holding slender tapers and waiting for the lighting of the Holy Fire. There was some evidence of lack of rehearsal. Soon after they arrived the server and Father Vincent came out, and the server was rather awkward getting the fire going. The faces of the people wore questioning looks, as if they were not certain what was expected of them.

Mike got tapers for both of them, and she accepted hers, suddenly determining to take a more active part this time. The service began in the open with the lighting of the fire. Father Vincent looked a little harried and more unkempt than ever and he shooed the small altar boys about with muttered undertones. When he and the server had completed the ritual of the lighting and gone inside, the people formed in a long file and slowly followed, solemnly lighting their tapers from the flame of the seminarians' candles at either side of the door.

Recognizing that there was always something awesome and beautiful about a candlelit procession, Regina was yet moved by it. The thin torches were so frail; the face above each one, lit in the circle of immediate reflection from below, was so quietly and yet so passionately reverent; the sway of movement was so hypnotic. She followed, her eyes bent on her own candle flame, her mind going back down the centuries to the catacombs, to the guarded torches of the martyrs, to the dark and feebly lit aisles and tunnels underground; going even farther back to the ancients, who had believed that all life came from the womb of the earth and returned to it at death. This was both the flame of life and the lighting of the soul to its first and last home. Almost she came under the spell of its mourning incantations.

Inside, the candles provided the only light, and the bare, ugly chapel was softened and made nearly beautiful by the dimness. The pews were grayed out of their harshness. The white walls were pale frames reflecting a thousand tiny, flickering shadows. The vaulted roof was lost in darkness, and the grotesqueness of the Stations of the Cross, with their blood and their agony, was almost hidden. The altar was plain and unrelieved by any splendor, and the faces of Mary and the Saints were swathed in veiling. Imitating Mike she sat, opened the booklet he had handed her. She risked a whisper. "Why are the statues veiled?"

"They always are—in mourning until the resurrection. They'll be unveiled at the last."

It was a tedious service, with much kneeling for long periods of time, and the hard, uncushioned prayer rail became an instrument of torture to her before it was over. She wished, too late, she had remained an onlooker, but Mike's smile of gratitude when she first knelt beside him had been so warm and happy that she could not now bring herself to deny him. Stubbornly she went through with it, trying to keep her mind on the service, suffering the ache of her knees, the stiffening of her back an the weariness of her leg muscles.

The chant of the two seminarians, apparently all this small new chapel warranted by way of ecclesiastical gesture, held her for awhile, but it soon became repetitious and monotonous. The smokeless flames of the candles burned steadily, lit the faces of the penitent and, slowly, almost mesmerized by the drone of Father Vincent's voice, the monotonous polyphonic responses of the seminarians, it all began to seem to her a weird and votive enchantment, utterly alien to her very nature.

It seemed foreign, even, to the nature of this land, of America, born as it had been of rebellion to autocracy, then which nothing was more autocratic than the Church. Her mind wandering along, it seemed right to her that the Church should have had its birth in those hot lands of the Mediterranean—should have come from a sultry and passionate people.

There was still something of the ancient blood rites in its offerings and its atonements and its passion. There was still something of exultation and ecstacy in its emphasis on suffering. Pascal—the Sacrifice of the Lamb—it was such a blood-washed religion. It so stressed the Cross and the Sacrifice, the suffering, the flowing of blood. It so flagellated and doomed the sinner.

Glancing at Mike she saw that he was not following the service. Instead he was fingering his rosary—each bead a prayer, she remembered. The thought of the prayer sticks of the western Indians—the feathers a prayer to the clouds, the arrows a prayer to the forests, the shells a prayer to the sea—all born of fear and hope that they could be merciful and remove the menace—the hope of every man, down through the ages, since the first man who had dreamed of immortality had willed it and had then created his vision of it. It was all a part of the same thing, fear and incantation, faith and vision, spirit and dream and hope. It was such a pitiful, such a splendid, hope—such a victorious hope. It assuaged such terror, comforted such pain, lit such darkness. It was so toweringly triumphant on such a thin base—merely the web of a dream, spun by the spirit of man.

She was numb by the time the mass began. Her emotions, toward which every word had been directed, toward which all the words of every mass were always directed instead of to the intellect, had been dulled by the reiteration and the steady tom-tom effect of the rhythmic rise and fall of the tonal voices. How sonorous it was and how little they said. One idea, one thought and phrase, repeated and repeated and repeated until somnolence ensued. She thought it would never end, and she felt stupefied when at length it did.

She did not see him for two weeks afterward, except once, on the street. He was walking with Father Vincent. It was the priest who, striding along bulkily beside the taller, slimmer man, was talking, with rapid, strong gestures emphasizing whatever he was saying. Mike's head was bent, listening, and his face was grave with attention. They passed within a yard of where she stood in the entrance of a shop, but Mike did not see her, he was so engrossed. She caught a part of what the priest was saying. She had been right about his voice. It was deep and strong and resonant. As they passed she heard only a phrase: ". . . no alternative, Mike." And she saw him slice with his hand as if cutting off something. She thought Mike's face looked troubled, and she put it down to a problem of some patient. He was so conscientious about them. He would have carried the full burden of any one of them, wherever it led him. It had doubtless led him to the priest just now.

Growing weary, at length, of his long silence and beginning to feel neglected, she seized eagerly upon the opportunity for some social life when Lucia telephoned and asked her to dinner. "I'm long overdue the courtesy to Tom's new assistant," she said, "but I've been lazy. Spring fever, I suppose."

At the beginning of the spring term Tom had been given some much needed help in his department. Regina had met the man in the library and had spoken with him several times. She was not much drawn to him. His name was Charles Garrett. He was young yet, as teachers go, thirty or thereabouts, slender, with fair hair and skin and very light blue eyes. She had thought him a little anemic, but she had become so bored with the sameness of life lately, with its dull immediate level and its lack of promise for the future, that she found herself thinking he might be more interesting than she supposed. "Of course I'll come," she said.

Lucia was an inspired cook, and the meal was excellent, the table beautiful with Lucia's flair for interesting combinations of flowers, linen, silver and china. There was never anything commonplace about one of her dinner parties. And, listening to Tom slowly drawling the witty, satirical talk he was famous for, listening to Lucia's sparkling rejoinders, to Charles' less than brilliant but entirely adequate contributions, she thought how in her absorption with Mike she had been missing exactly this sort of thing, which really was second nature to her. These were the people she was most at home with, the kind that had always made up her circle. This was the talk—of books, of academic life, of campus and classroom and lectures and students, which she knew best and enjoyed most. Exhilarated, she felt as if she were sipping wine after a long thirst. It had been foolish of her, she decided, to allow herself to be so monopolized by Mike.

When they gathered in the library after dinner there was a spirited discussion of a new translation of *Madame Bovary,* of a phrase which they all knew in the French and which she and Lucia held out had been badly mangled. Tom settled it by saying, authoritatively, "There is no way that phrase can be translated without taking liberty. It's simply the difference in the languages. There isn't any English word which even approximates the French there."

Charles, interestingly, took up the same problem with Greek. "You have, finally," he said, "to read it in the original or miss the best of it. It loses too much in translation."

They went, then, into a discussion of the spareness and leanness of Greek poetry, and Regina illustrated it by some taut chords on the piano, a little dissonant against the more lush tones of the accepted harmonics. "That's the way I always hear it."

From there it was simply one more move into music and willingly she played for half an hour. Then Lucia, remembering, said, "Charles records bird songs and he's brought his tape recorder. I almost forgot."

With no reluctance he played his newest recording and Regina, watching his absorption, the bent head tilted to hear, listening to the plaintive, sweet notes of the bird calls, had a moment of astonishing insight, seeing for one brief second Mike's amused face when he learned of this. "You mean he goes out and tracks down birds and records them?" With a perceptiveness grown out of her slowly developing understanding of him, she knew that to Mike birds would be simply a part of nature, part of the woods and streams, to be accepted and enjoyed without making much to-do over them. Belatedly she realized it was the more loving and more honest way, and that she preferred it too. It rather ruined the recording for her.

Just the same when the evening was over she offered the man a lift home. He had explained that his Volkswagen was momentarily in the shop. "That's the dickens of these foreign cars. Repairs are so difficult."

At his door, he stood beside the car a few minutes, making small, unimportant talk, then he asked her, surprisingly, if she would like to run up to the city for an evening. "We could do a play if you like—or perhaps there'll be a concert. Have dinner. Whatever you'd rather."

It was precisely the sort of thing she had waited so long to hear Mike propose, and which he never had. With something approaching a feeling of triumph she agreed. "I think it would be lovely."

"Fine. I should have my car again by the end of the week. Shall we say Friday night? What time would we have to leave here?"

"It's a two hour run. Probably five. Is that too early for you?"

"No. My last class is at three. Thanks so much for the lift. I'll be looking forward to Friday."

Driving away she had a moment of regret. He really bordered upon the insipid and she would probably be bored the entire evening. A spark of malice made her lift her chin in the old, dogged manner, however. She would not sit at home and wait for Mike Panelli any longer. She had her own self-esteem to bolster occasionally. It had suffered sadly the past two weeks and it was high time she took it in hand. Even if she were bored with the company, she consoled herself, a play or a concert would do wonders for her.

The evening when it came was beautifully fair, mild and warm, with a sunset, into which they drove, so boldly colorful as to defy description. The air was almost luminous with brilliance, and the rolling fields to either side of the road were like green plush, so soft, so rich, so deep-piled. Charles drove expertly and smoothly, with a casual competence which permitted conversation.

She had taken care with her appearance and knew that she had never looked better. The dress was the soft, pale beige she had bought at Christmas time, so simply made that its elegance lay in its understatement. With it she wore the antique gold bracelets and ear drops of which she was so fond, and she topped it with a brief, black jacket. The dark, reddish brown of her hair carried it off well, she knew, and she knew also that her hair gleamed and shone from the last minute washing she had given it.

"I hope you haven't seen this thing I've got tickets for," Charles said, "in New York. This is the road company, of course, and it would be quite a let-down for you if you've seen the original cast."

She knew from the city papers what was playing that week and she shook her head. "I haven't got up to New York this entire season, so it will be new to me. I'm looking forward to it."

He was a good host, though not a particularly inspired one, and the evening was a success—enough of one, at any rate, she told herself later in bed, that it had been worthwhile. She had promised Charles they would go again sometime. She felt unusually tired, but she laid that to the unaccustomed drive and the late hour.

She was a long time going to sleep, her mind at first reliving the play, then drifting to Mike, wondering what he had been doing for so long a time, why he had neither telephoned nor come by. At the last, drowsy, in that confused moment of being half awake and half asleep, her mind stripped of all conscious pretenses, left honest and defenseless, she knew it would have been twice the fun with him. She giggled, remembering the cramped, rough-riding small car. The vapid mannerisms of Charles were a poor substitute for the healthy, masculine normalities of Mike Panelli.

Chapter Twelve

❦

She was doing the dishes after a late supper when he came the next night. He gave the doorbell an impatient trill, then walked on in without waiting, whistling to let her know who it was, and calling, "Where are you?"

Unashamedly pleased and not caring if it showed in her voice, she shouted back, "In the kitchen. Come on back."

He sauntered lazily in, stopped in the doorway and leaned against it. "You're looking very housewifely."

"I'm being very housewifely. A revival is starting at Nettie's church tonight and she left early. *You're* looking very outdoorsy. Been fishing?"

He had on old jeans, a thin, worn jacket over a faded pullover. His face, she thought, was already beginning to darken from his afternoons in the sun. She felt a pang that he had evidently been going alone—that he had not suggested again that she go with him.

He strolled across and picked up the dishtowel, began wiping the dishes with a lack of concern which bespoke a habit that the interruption of three years had not broken. He must often have dried dishes for Eva, she reflected, then put the thought, unpleasant to her, away.

"I went to the old mill today," he explained. "I must take you sometime."

A fleeting annoyance crossed her mind. It was always sometime with him—never now, unless on impulse it occurred to him. But, then, she reminded herself, he could rarely make plans. "Did you have any luck?"

"Three beauties. Oh, that reminds me. They're in the car. I brought them to you."

He went for them and she looked when he showed them, as proudly as a small boy, and found the proper note of admiration. "Put them in the freezing compartment," she directed. "Nettie will probably have them for lunch tomorrow."

She had got ahead of him with the dishes and he wiped industriously for a moment. "The garden's looking nice," he said, indicating with his head the window from which it could be seen.

"I've been working in it quite a lot. It's really very nicely planted, but it's been badly neglected."

They were really at a loss for conversation, she thought, when they had to descend to a discussion of her garden. They would soon, no doubt, be discussing the weather. Glancing at him she saw that his face looked somehow lit and happy, a little smug, even, as if he knew something importantly nice. Maybe it was catching the fish, she thought. Success in any effort was always gratifying. There was also an undercurrent in his voice. It was always deep, pleasant to the ear, but it had a note of vibrancy now which underlay the trivialities he was speaking. Something pleased him very much, she decided, and while she wondered about it, she reflected that he would tell her when he was ready. In silence she washed and rinsed and placed into the rack the diminishing stack of dishes.

"I came by last night," he said, at last, carefully wiping a platter, "but the house was dark. I thought you might like to go with me today."

"I wish I'd known," she said, honestly sorry. "I went up to the city with Charles Garrett."

The circular motion of his hand stopped for a moment, then resumed, more slowly. "Who," he said, his voice very careful, "is Charles Garrett?"

"Tom's new assistant. Haven't you heard? They gave him one at the beginning of spring term."

"I see. I suppose he's young."

"Oh, very. Barely thirty, I'd say." She reached for a pot in which something had been scorched, leaned over beyond him for the scouring powder. "Lucia had him to dinner the first part of the week and we arranged this thing about going up to see a play . . ."

He had seized her arm, at the same time laying aside the now thoroughly dried platter and the enveloping dish towel. "I don't care when you arranged it. I don't like it."

She was so surprised that she did not quite take it in, stood blinking at him. Then, furious, she tried to disengage her arm. "I don't think it matters whether you like it or not."

"Don't you?"

He was looking steadily at her, his brows drawn together in a scowl, his mouth thin and angry, his face beginning to flush. She tried again to free her arm, but instead of letting her go he grabbed her other arm and held her, his strong hands gripping the flesh, digging in, hurting. She was completely helpless. "Mike, let me go!"

"I won't. Going off up to the city the minute my back was turned! And it doesn't matter. How do you think it makes me feel?" He shook her rather roughly. His teeth were clenched and his voice came through them, bitten off short and smothered.

"I don't care how it makes you feel! I don't think it's any of your affair. What I do is entirely my own business and none of yours. And if your back was turned it was your own doing."

As she spoke she became more angry. She quit trying to get loose and stood within his grasp, drawing herself up as proudly as possible. He was so tall that he towered over her, and looking up at him, so near, was already making her neck ache. To her horror, she also felt very near tears.

"Well, by God, I'll *make* it my business! I won't have you . . . out . . . with other . . . men!" He punctuated the words with shakes, as if she had been a child. She felt her head doddling ignominiously.

She lost all control then and heard her voice shrieking at him like a fishwife. "What right have you got to tell me who I'm to go out with? You can't make it your business! I'll go out when I please, with whom I please, do you hear? What do you think I am? I sit here for days on end, waiting for you to call or to come . . . all at your own pleasure. You never even think of me! You go your own way until it suits you to remember me! Then you walk in here and make a scene because I've been out . . . just once I've been out when it pleased you to come by! Let me go! You're hurting me, Mike. Let me go!"

She struggled, twisting and wiggling, turning about, kicking at his shins, even trying to get her head down to bite. She was suddenly as elemental as the first woman in that ancient cave, all reason fled, only raw fury and weeping anger directing her. As they swayed, struggling, the kitchen stool was overturned, and blindly Mike kicked it out of the way. Slowly he backed her against the cupboard, and the loose dish towel, caught in her twisting movements, carried the platter he had been drying crashing to the floor. Its wreckage about their feet, they stood, both of them short of breath, both of them red-faced, both of them disheveled. "Be still," he hissed at her. "You can't get loose, don't you know that? You'll only hurt yourself worse. I don't intend to let you go. Be *still*, I said."

She quieted, looked up at him, her hair hanging forward, her eyes stinging. "Mike, are you out of your mind?"

He loosened his hold a little. "I think I am . . . a little. I never expected to feel like this . . . with you. Listen . . ."

Sullenly she said, "You act as if I were your wife."

"That's exactly what I intend you to be. I came to ask you tonight. I never meant . . ." His arms closed around her, pulled her near. Her face buried in his jacket she felt his lips on her hair, on her temple, and then his hand turned her head and they closed on her mouth.

At first she struggled, then the strong, hard pressure of his mouth, holding her own so irrevocably, had its way and she relaxed, slowly returning the kiss. Dreamily her mind accepted the fact as her mouth accepted his lips. She had, she thought, known it would be exactly like this. She had known, as if by foresight, that all the bones of her body would feel just this way—as loosely jointed as if unhinged—that her knees would go so weak as barely to support her, and that at that small spot on the back of her neck there would be a hotness of sheer, quivering nerves. She had known that the long, firm mouth would be hard against her own, and that it would, given time, go as soft as a child's, as full and sweet. She gave herself up completely to the unreasoning joy which surged over her, put her now uninhibited arms about his neck, held his head close and felt with unbelievable tenderness the crisp, crinkly short hair under her palms again.

When he loosened her finally she was short of breath, there was an unbearable ache in her shoulders and her ribs felt as if they had been crushed. A little dazed and rather self-conscious she let him hold her away and look at her. He was not laughing. He was looking at her hungrily, as if he could not get enough of her. "I love you," he said, "I love you so much."

"Darling!" She snatched his head close again. "I love you, too."

He sighed, bending his head against her shoulder. "I think I'd have gone out of my mind if you didn't. Have I hurt you, really? Let's look."

She protested but he insisted on rolling back her sleeves. The prints of his fingers were red against the pale skin. He looked at them with shocked eyes. "Regina! I ought to be horsewhipped."

Although she knew that by tomorrow they would turn the purplish blue that all bruises turned on her, she tried to console him. "It doesn't matter, darling. It really doesn't. You just have no idea how strong you are." She laughed a little. "Whatever got into you, Mike?"

He pulled her into his arms again, nested his chin in her hair. "I don't know. I just saw red for a minute or two. I was so mad I felt like beating you." He laughed uneasily. "I didn't know I could get that angry. But it was all so different than I'd foreseen. I came here . . . do we have to stand here in the kitchen?

"Of course not."

In the living room he stared at the empty fireplace. She had a feeling that it disconcerted him. "There's always been a fire. Do you think it's too warm tonight?"

Guessing that he had visualized the scene, had wanted to tell her and ask her before the fire, where they had so often sat and talked, she was quick to respond. "It's not too warm at all. I just hadn't got around to it. You do it. Everything's there, ready."

When the fire was going he pulled her down beside him on the hearth rug and she knew that this, too, had been part of the setting in his mind. She felt so perfectly at peace, so calmly, beautifully happy, that she had no desire to do anything but what he wanted. He stretched out on the floor, pillowing his head in her lap. He closed his eyes and she thought he might be dozing when he was still for such a long time. But he opened them at length and looked up at her. "Can you forgive me?"

She bent to kiss him, quickly. "I already have. I told you, dear . . . it doesn't matter."

"It does. It was brutal of me. I think I hardly knew what I was doing. You can't imagine how it felt."

She grimaced. "I can do better than that. I can tell you exactly how it felt."

He rolled over, propped his chin on his elbows. "I don't mean that. I mean the sick feeling . . . the fear . . . the sudden horrible . . . I mean, it was as if I'd lost you entirely, and I hadn't even told you yet. It drove me wild."

"Don't think about it any more, Mike. I'm sorry I went. It never occurred to me you'd . . ."

He took her hand, bent her fingers. "Well, you couldn't know, after all. I should have thought of that, too. But it's been such hell . . . it was as if you'd known all along. I didn't see how you could help it. I thought it was plain . . ."

Bewildered, she waited for him to go on. Nothing was plain to her except that he'd said he loved her . . . that he intended her to be his wife. Instead of continuing, however, he buried his face in her lap and took a long, shuddering breath. She felt like all the witches in the world for having tormented him. It made no difference that she hadn't known. She should have understood him better. If the love, which she now admitted she had felt since the first time she went to church with him, since she had followed him out the church door feeling her own defeat in the immeasurable distance he had gone from her—if that love wasn't true enough to understand him in any extremity, it had already failed her. She bent and touched his neck with her lips and he turned, reached up and pulled her across his chest, held her tightly and began kissing her with a hunger that seemed insatiable.

When he let her go they were both trembling, and she arranged her disordered hair with shaky hands. He watched her, smiling. "You did say you loved me, didn't you? I think I remember that."

From under her bent arm she smiled back at him. "I did say it. I do."

He reached for her hand. "I have to be touching you. I feel empty if I'm not. Don't move away from me."

"I didn't, darling. I only wanted to . . ."

"Oh, let your hair go. You look beautiful with it all rumpled and blown about. I love your hair. It's the most wonderful color. I love everything about you. Your littleness—and the way you walk, as if your legs were longer than your body—and your hands. Do you know," he sat up suddenly, "they're amazingly strong. You very nearly got loose from me in there."

"It's playing the piano, I expect. All that practicing."

"After awhile, will you play for me? Not now, of course . . ."

She murmured that she would, and in the midst of her assent, he stopped her mouth greedily. "Nothing, nothing at all matters, now. It couldn't. Lord, I didn't know I could be so happy."

"I'm glad."

She tilted her head to ease the crick in her neck. She would have been so much more comfortable on the sofa, but not for worlds would she have moved. If this slightly dramatic scene on the hearth rug before an open fire was what he had dreamed, she would suffer all sorts of cricks and discomforts.

He stared into the fire. "Was this fellow—this Charles Garrett—did you like him?"

"Don't be an idiot, Mike. I barely know him."

"Yes, but you'd know if you liked him, wouldn't you?"

She laughed, humoring him. "Well, then, I didn't—particularly. He's dull and tiresome and vain and affected. And, he's a little effeminate." She told him about the bird songs and rejoiced at his whooping laughter. "I only went with him because I'd got tired of sitting around waiting for you." She could afford honesty now.

"Have I made a convenience of you, darling?"

"Well, you have—rather. But of course I allowed it."

"I haven't meant to. It was just . . . I thought you understood."

"I did—really. I know how busy you are."

"It wasn't that so much . . ."

A little shyly she said, "I didn't mean to act like . . ." but the name wouldn't come.

He assured her quickly. "You haven't. Believe me. I just went off the deep end. You never *did* go out with someone else before."

"I won't again."

"Well, I should hope not! You're properly engaged, now, and don't go forgetting it."

She looked at him fondly. "Forget it? How could I? It means as much to me as it does to you."

"I doubt it. It couldn't."

He said it simply, but it was freighted with meaning. His face was suddenly sober, serious, and his eyes dropped.

A log on the fire crackled unexpectedly, sending a shower of sparks onto the hearth. He had forgotten to set the screen in front and they both jumped, brushing at their clothing. He got up to put the screen in place and remained standing, his hands shoved deep in his pockets, his lower lip caught in. "I saw Bruce Clark this morning."

Seeing his mood had shifted she thought it a good time to move to the sofa. "Bruce Clark?"

"An attorney. He's to get the divorce proceedings started immediately. He thinks it may take around three months."

Her heart started pounding. "That's not very long, is it?"

"It's too long."

He came to sit beside her, pulled her over and held her draped across his chest, his arms enveloping her closely and smothering once more. "Will you marry me as soon as that?'

She tried to arrange her thoughts, tried to sit up to make it easier, but he refused to let her move. Limply and helplessly she lay, thinking how possessive he had suddenly become, how arrogantly male and superior. It amused her and at the same time made her feel tenderly small and protected. "It depends, Mike. Will you be expecting me to leave the library?"

"I'd rather you would. It's a full time job, being a wife."

"I know." She hadn't meant to say that. To cover it she hurried on. "I'd rather, too. But there's the school, darling. I'd hate to leave them in the lurch."

"You aren't thinking very clearly. This is almost the first of May. Spring term ends in June, doesn't it? It will be well over before I'm—free."

He doesn't like that word, divorce, she thought. Well, it was an ugly word. He couldn't be blamed for that. Unfortunately, however, it was a necessity. "I wasn't thinking only of the term, dear. I should stay until there is a replacement. Do you want us to set a definite date?"

"I want us to be married on the very day, the very first day it's possible. Before anything can happen—" His voice broke off shortly.

"But, darling, what can possibly happen?"

"Nothing. I suppose I'm just eager. I just don't want to wait any longer. It seems such a long time already."

He kissed her, gently at first, and quietly, then with the bruising lack of restraint which was beginning to make her mouth feel crushed. He had not shaved since morning, either, and she was aware that the slight roughness of his face had made her own feel almost raw. She thought they must stop this for awhile. It was beginning to become exhausting. She insisted on his releasing her, pleading aching shoulders and her cricked neck.

Full of apology, he did so, straightening his tie and pullover when she stood clear of him. She eased her twisted skirt and, thinking now was as good a time as any to play for him, she went to the piano. It was only when she had sat down, lifted her hands, that she realized there was no music that could possibly be played now. Anything would have been too much, and in its excess would have been anticlimactic. She laughed ruefully, turning away from the keyboard. He smiled at her. "I think so, too. It isn't the night, is it?"

"I'm afraid not."

She went to stand by the fire. He watched her. The last of the light had gone now, and she switched on a lamp behind the sofa. He promptly reached up and switched it off. "We don't need that. The fire is enough."

With his arms lifted, his head turned slightly, she knew all at once what had been wrong all the time with the head in her sketch of him. The pose was similar, for in the painting he had his arm uplifted, ready to cast. It was that lift of the chin which had escaped her. "Mike," she said quickly, "Wait a moment—don't move. Stay just like that."

"What in the world . . .?"

"Please don't move."

She hurried to the hall closet and brought back the painting and a sketching pencil, stood off from him and quickly drew in what she needed. "Now—you can relax."

"I felt a perfect fool. Let me see that!"

Unabashed, now, she gave it to him.

"When did you do this?"

"Last fall. You were fishing."

"At the island—I can see that. But where were you? Why didn't you tell me?"

"Across the creek—in those bushes. It was the first time I ever saw you. I'm afraid I was rather selfish about it. I didn't want to be bothered with having to talk to you." She said it teasingly, with some triumph.

"Oh, you didn't? How do you know I would have bothered to talk to you? It's good, Regina—really good. All that light and shadow on the water. And you've done me very respectably, too."

"It was the head I had so much trouble with. That's why it isn't finished. When you reached up to turn off the light it came to me."

"Funny. I had no idea there was anyone within miles of me. There never is there. Can you remember the date at all?"

"September, I think. I'm not sure."

He studied the picture awhile longer, then laid it down and drew her close again. "The way I feel now it seems I should have it just by some sort of vibration. You sort of set it up in me, you know." He grinned mischievously. "What are you going to do with the painting, now that you've got the original?"

"Oh, I've always had the original, didn't you know? An instructor I had once told the class that anything one painted became one's own, indestructibly—became a living part of one."

He turned a face lit by some inner light toward her and it surprised her to see that his eyes had misted over. Softly he said, "I like that. I like it very much—knowing I've been a part of you all this time. It's a very . . . a very lovely thought, isn't it?"

She felt shy confessing. "It's been true, though I haven't known it, I suppose. I never got you out of my mind after I sketched you."

In the way of all women in love she wanted to know when he had first known. "Oh, men are more stupid, I expect," he said. "All I knew for a long time was that I was more restless than usual—that I only felt really good when I was with you. I didn't analyze it—just put it down to overwork."

"Yes, but *when* did you finally know?"

He thought about it. "In the snowstorm on the island, I think. It seemed so natural to be there with you."

"That island is a very special place now, isn't it?"

It pleased her that it should be so. What it had meant to him all his life was now enlarged, included her and their love.

She had been standing before the fire and he had been sitting on the sofa. Even as they talked she had a restless feeling, not understanding why. Not until he stood, abruptly, and pulled her into his arms again did she realize that it had been because already she missed them about her, felt cold without them. His lips lingered on hers. "You haven't said yet whether we'll be married in August."

"But I did . . ."

"No. We only dispensed with the school term. Do you want to wait longer for some silly female reason? Oh, God, don't say you do!"

The outburst made her laugh. At her age and having been married before, it was a little silly to think that she would need time. "Of course not, darling. The very day the divorce is granted, if you want."

He cut the last word short with his mouth. She was next aware of an inner quivering in herself, and of his breath coming roughly against her mouth, very short, as if he barely had it under control. Then she felt her own trembling extended to him. This, she thought distinctly, will never do. She moved to free herself, but he held her tightly, refusing to let her go. "Mike."

He lifted his head, gulped in air, but he did not let her go. "Oh, Lord . . . three months . . ."

"It won't seem long."

"It will seem forever. Don't say it won't. It seems forever right now." He held her away, stared down at her. "Is there any good reason why we have to wait that long?"

Her first thought was that she had not heard right. Then, a little numbly, her mind not taking it in fully, she knew she had. "Well, the divorce . . . you said . . ."

"I don't mean that. You know what I mean. It will never be quite like this again. We shall never be so perfectly ready. It needs tonight to make it whole . . . make it complete immediately."

"Mike, I don't think you . . ."

"Yes, I do know. I want to be wholly committed, entirely, irrevocably . . . now. I can't explain it . . . but, please. We're going to be married."

"That's just it . . . in three months..."

"Let's be married now . . . tonight. Then it's final..."

She felt as if her breath would choke her and she pulled loose to give herself time. She walked away from him toward the window, aimlessly arranged the curtain. She had not expected this. But, yes . . . she should have known. He followed her, finally, wheeled her around, compelled her to look at him. "Have I made you angry?"

She shook her head, unable to speak, feeling she would cry if she did. She didn't know why she hesitated. It wasn't as if she were a girl, or they were both children. They were old enough, mature enough. They were responsible to no one but themselves. It seemed cruel, it seemed even prudish of her, under his urgency, and under her own if she was honest. She weighed her scruples and found they were less moral than simply uncertain. If she knew why . . .

She argued with herself, feeling his eyes upon her, waiting. She could, she thought, have felt less torn if he had compelled her—but she would never have forgiven him that. It was like him to leave it to her, to accept whatever she decided, and she knew he would.

At length he took her gently into his arms. "Darling, you look as if I had betrayed you. Don't . . . forget it. It will be just the same. I didn't mean it, really. When we're married will be soon enough."

As if she needed just that gently denial she reached her decision. "No—it wouldn't be the same. You're right, of course. It would be three months of punishment, and at our age and under the circumstances, unnecessary."

The tenseness went out of his face and he laid his cheek against hers. "You won't be sorry, I promise."

She caressed his face, kissing his eyes, his brows, his roughened cheek and finally his mouth. "No. I won't be sorry."

They went up together, arms about each other's waists, reluctant to lose touch even for a moment. "How perfect that you have a house," he said, when they came to her door.

She felt a little light-headed and giddy. "Isn't it? Imagine if I were in an apartment."

"Then we'd just have to use mine."

She felt a small electric shock. His house? She wondered, as he held the door open for her and she felt for the light beside the bed, if he expected her to live there when they were married. She wondered, finding the switch and turning it on, if she could. She put it out of her mind. They would cross that bridge when they came to it.

She looked quickly about the familiar room. He was standing just inside the door, doing the same, although his hands were already busy with his tie. "I've always liked this room. It's not all fussy and prim," he said.

Each object in the room reflected her own taste, she thought for the hundredth time. It was the real setting for herself, with its soft jeweled tones, the red of the curtains, the faded velvet of the rug, the ancient prayer shawl on the bed. Her eyes flew to it, drawn as if by a magnet. "If I'd known," she murmured, for something to say, "we could have had a fire."

"We shouldn't need it."

He seemed entirely at ease, almost at home. He crossed over to the dressing table and sat down to remove his shoes. She remained rooted where she was, filled suddenly with an awkward shyness and apprehension. It was so much more difficult than she had expected it to be. What did one do?

Her mind sought the only comparison she knew. It had been a hotel room with Walter—a sumptuous, elegant, bleak, impersonal hotel room. They had registered late at night, had gone up together, then after kissing her Walter had done the obvious and trite thing. He had meaningfully left her alone until she was ready. When he had returned she was safely undressed and in bed. Nothing of that night prepared her for this moment. She stood, uncertain and wavering.

He looked up at her questioningly. "What is it?"

Feeling a small shiver run down her back, she took her courage in her hands. "Darling, would you mind leaving me alone for a little while?" With a rush she confessed it all. "I think I mind undressing before you."

He looked surprised, then his face turned impish, bedeviling. "Why should you? Have you forgotten that I'm a doctor?"

With sudden spirit she retorted, "It isn't the doctor I'm shy of."

Smiling at her as if she had been a child, a child just a little dense and uncomprehending, he crossed the room. "You're pretty silly, aren't you?" He clicked off the light. "It's easily remedied."

She had time to notice that the moon laid a great, white square across the rug and made a silver lake of the mirror before he drew her into his arms. In the comforting dark she could laugh at herself, and allow his hands to help her with her buttons and hooks, allow them finally to lead her, without protest, to the bed.

Chapter Thirteen

❦

"Don't let me go to sleep," he begged, "I must leave by midnight."

She was comfortable and warm and snug, her head on his shoulder, his big length curled around her. Drowsy, she could not bear to think of his leaving. "Why? That's only a couple of hours."

The bed shook with his laughter. "There's nothing I'd like more than never to move again, but don't you think it would look better if my car were seen or heard leaving at midnight than at dawn? I'm afraid your reputation would never recover."

"I hadn't thought of that. Where did you leave it?"

"In the drive, naturally. I had no idea . . ."

She couldn't resist teasing him. "Oh, yes, you did. You came fully intending to spend the night."

"I'll swear I didn't! It just came about . . ."

He felt her body shake and gave her a little spank. "I ought to compromise you good and proper for making fun."

"I wouldn't worry about it if I were you," she said, between giggles, "I think you have—very successfully."

He pulled her over toward him. "Don't keep your back to me. It's a lovely back, but I like your front, too."

"Mike . . ."

When they could talk again, he said, "Just the same—in a small town there's always gossip. I imagine there's been enough of it already."

"About us?" She was genuinely surprised.

"About us. You are a very attractive young widow, my love, and you have a whole house entirely to yourself. There are people who would say it's for no good reason. Especially when I come and go rather freely."

"They wouldn't!"

"They would, and probably have. But we'll put a stop to it. We're going to be seen together from now on, openly and publicly. And I'll start the rumor that I'm getting a divorce and that we're to be married as soon as possible, if you like. How is it done? Would Lucia do it for us?"

"Well, she would—but I don't think it would be very good taste until..."

"Oh, I see. One can't very well be married and engaged at the same time, can he?"

"Hardly. Perhaps I'd better go out with Charles a few more times."

"That won't be necessary," he said, with great dignity, which dissolved into a scuffle and a pretended smothering of her with her pillow. He gave it up and subsided breathlessly. "Oh, Lord, I feel wonderful. Do you feel like that too? As if you'd just been born, all fresh and new, with a whole lifetime ahead of you for happiness?" He stretched out long in the bed, kicking the sheet aside, complaining as his foot touched the rail, "this bed is too short for me."

"I'm not surprised. It wasn't meant for a man."

There was a brief silence, then he said, softly, "You mean it never—it wasn't yours before?"

As glad as she had ever been of anything in her life she assured him, "No. It's mine—bought when I came here."

He seized her. "How wonderful! Just yours—and mine." After a time he said, gently, "I suppose you loved him very much."

"No. I never loved him at all, really. I was infatuated, I suppose. It wore very thin in time—almost at once. You're truly the first, darling."

She knew it was what he wanted to hear, and while she willingly would have lied, she was glad it wasn't necessary.

"I'm glad. I've been horribly jealous of him."

"You needn't be. I'll tell you an awful thing, if you won't be shocked."

"I won't be."

"I was sorry he was killed, of course. Anyone would have been. It's a terrible thing to have to die, and he died horribly. But I didn't mind the way I should have if you . . . Oh, dear God, Mike, don't ever let anything happen to you!"

She dug her head into his chest and clutched him.

"I won't. I promise I won't." He stroked her hair and comforted her. "I'll live so long you'll have to help me out of a wheelchair. I'll live forever. I'll be an old, thin stick of a man tottering around with a young, beautiful wife."

Recovered, she retrieved her pillow and settled herself again. "It'll be the other way around. You'll be a fine old man with a wrinkled old crone to take care of."

They descended to the foolish, silly banalities of love, murmuring the fond endearments, the small words that were in themselves so meaningless but with love become so precious.

The time sped by as if borne on wings. They lay and watched the square of moonlight move across the room until it was only a narrow finger of light, touching first the foot of the bed and then laying itself across their faces. He dozed, finally, and she watched him, not sleepy at all. He was so fine, so wonderful, so good, she thought. With light fingers she traced the wing of his brows, the strong line of his jaw, the column of his throat. His nose wrinkled as she disturbed him a little and she left off, content to look at him, to taste all the wonder, all her happiness.

She thought how it had been with Walter—so greedy, so quickly satisfied, so uncaring of her, wounded and exhausted. How he had then turned on his side away from her and was so soon asleep, leaving her to all the strangeness and the aching and the crying loneliness. She shuddered, remembering. Nothing could have been gentler than Mike's kindness and care, his control and concern. It was so perfect it had made it seem easy and simple, though she knew it had required all his discipline. She was grateful to him.

She dreamed the time away. Should they be married here—in the living room, perhaps? Or at Lucia's? Lucia would be in heaven arranging a wedding, and she would make it so lovely for them. That might be best. In the way of all women since Eve first worried about her fig leaves, she began to plan clothes. A heavy, raw silk dress, she thought, to be married in—very plain, in ivory or palest beige—a small, flowered hat with only a tip of a veil—blue shoes, perhaps. Would they be going away? A navy linen suit for that. Her luggage was nice, she recalled. It would go anywhere decently. Then she giggled. He would very probably not be able to take a minute off.

He stirred, gathered her into his arms and sighed, still asleep. Then something brought him awake with a start. He peered at his watch. "Can you tell the time? I can't see this damned thing."

"I'd better turn on the light. It's growing late, I'm sure."

She switched on the lamp, giving thanks for the heavy screening of shrubbery and trees, and they both blinked, blinded for a moment by the glare. "Oh, Lord, it's twenty to one. You should have waked me."

"I dozed myself, darling. There's no great harm, is there?"

"I suppose not." He stretched his arms and yawned comfortably. "I hate to go."

"I hate for you to go. In three months you won't need to."

He dropped his arms about her and closed his eyes again. "Do you think we could get by with it if I stayed until daylight?"

She kissed him lightly. "Since you've brought it up, I don't think we should try."

He heaved himself up and swung his legs off the bed. "Probably not. My telephone has very likely been ringing off the wall the way it is."

The bed already felt wide and empty to her. It was going to be lonely without him. "Was anything important coming up?"

He walked across the room to the bath. "No. If there had been, I shouldn't be here."

"Not even for me?" She knew it sounded coy the moment she had said it.

"Not even for you, sweet. A doctor can't run out on his job."

He had a fine body—long in the torso, equally long in the legs—almost perfectly proportioned. He was entirely unembarrassed before her. Some day, she thought, watching him disappear into the bathroom, she would make him pose for her in the nude. She tried to compose herself comfortably in the space he had left, solacing herself with the warmth his body had created. It was a poor substitute, she found. She missed him curled around her. She heard the water running, then when he came back, saw that he had washed and looked much less sleepy. He began to dress briskly. She watched him without comment.

He came over to her, then, sat down on the bed beside her and kissed her. "I'll call you sometime today. I'm going to be pretty busy—there's an operation this morning—but I should be able to get to it before night.

"Will you come tonight?"

He held her away and looked at her, surprised. "Of course. You didn't think I wouldn't, did you?"

"You might have been busy," she murmured.

"I'll tell you ahead of time if I'm going to be—if I can, of course. Goodbye, darling. It was perfect. It's going to be a long day."

He snatched two or three quick kisses and mournfully she realized that he might as well be gone already. His mind had shifted and the kisses were almost perfunctory. It was a thing she must get used to.

She heard his steps on the stairs, careless, heedless of noise, heard him whistling softly. Then she heard the door close. He took care with that, she thought, for she had barely heard it. But the sound of his car starting up was not to be subdued. She wondered if old Mrs. Logan up the street would be awake at this hour. It was unlikely—and what did it matter? It wasn't too horribly late.

She curled round in the nest of the sheet and blanket and found that she was sleepy after all. With his pillow drawn under her cheek, a faint smell of his hair still lingering on it, she closed her eyes. Drowsily she wondered if he would want her to take instructions from Father Vincent. Vaguely she knew that it wasn't absolutely necessary. Catholics did marry Protestants without it, but it would probably make him very happy if she did. In sleepy good humor she thought she would ask him, in any case.

It was not until she had been at work some time that morning that she recalled this was her evening on duty. Herbert had had it last night. Irritably she thought how it would throw everything off, and she considered asking Herbert to take her stint. That would make three evenings in a row for him, however, and it really wasn't fair. Reluctantly she decided against it. There was nothing for it but to call Mike. Better wait until after lunch, she thought, when he would be in his office.

It was a bright day with the sun glaring through the high, uncurtained windows. As the day wore on she was conscious of feeling tired and of her eyes feeling as if they were rimmed with grit. She was glad it was not a terribly busy time. She thought she would not have been able to cope with a throng of young people and a group of fussy professors. There was only the usual run of students reading, and some office work to be done.

Around three she tried to reach Mike. His office nurse told her, in cool accents, that he was busy. Could he call her back when he was free? He could, she said, and gave the library number without giving her name. She busied herself with some cataloguing which had piled up.

It was nearly four-thirty before he called, his voice pleasant, courteous, and professional. Remembering its vividness the night before, she smiled. He did not know, of course, whose call he was returning. He had only an emergency number. She liked his professional voice. It was quiet and cheerful without being self-conscious, ready to be interested, even sympathetic, but until the need, rather detached. "Mike? I'm sorry. I won't keep you a minute. But this is my night on the desk. I didn't remember until this morning."

He muttered a smothered damn. "I had it arranged so that we could go out to dinner."

She wondered if Miss Hopkins had hung up yet. It was possible she was still on the line, so she made herself reply lightly. "That *is* too bad. We'll do it another time, shall we?"

"You sound pretty remote, and not very interested. What's up?"

"Well, I thought . . . are you alone?"

"Of course. I never make a call in the presence of a patient."

"What about Miss Hopkins?"

"Oh. I see. She's gone. Now, what about this thing tonight?"

"It's just what I said, dear. I have to work at the desk until nine. That isn't too late, is it?"

"By about three hours. But it'll have to do, I suppose. You can't rearrange things?"

"I shouldn't." Again she was tempted, but she decided to stay firm. "It's really not fair. Herbert worked last night. I don't leave the girls here alone at night."

"No. You couldn't. Well, then—shall I pick you up?"

She considered. "No. Come straight to the house. I'll leave the door unlatched."

His laugh was warm. "Are you preparing to set the stage?"

"Would it help any?"

"Not a bit. You don't need stage setting. I'll be along, then, around nine-thirty. O.K.?"

"Fine."

The rest of the day went better, just from having talked with him.

Nevertheless, and in spite of his teasing, she did set the stage a little. She hurried home, on the dot of nine, glad the evening was chilly. She had a quick bath and put on her most becoming dress gown. Then she laid a fire in the bedroom, fixed trays of small sandwiches and cookies and took them up, along with the electric coffeepot. She arranged them carefully in front of the fire and had just time to settle herself, hair brushed and lipstick fresh, with a book, before he arrived. She was conscious of the fact that she looked unhurried and unruffled, which belied her accelerated heartbeat as she heard him coming up the stairs, and at the last moment she couldn't hold the pose and got up quickly to meet him at the door. He enveloped her in a smothering hug and immediately disarranged both her hair and the fresh lipstick, a good deal of which came off on his face. Drawing away and seeing the oddly clown-like effect, she burst out laughing.

"What's so funny?" he asked.

"You should see your face."

She drew him over before the mirror and he peered, then laughed himself. He picked up a tissue and started wiping at the smears. "Why don't they invent a lipstick that won't come off?"

"They have. But it makes my lips dry. I can't use it."

"Well, always see that I'm clean when I leave, then. Imagine the effect if I had to make an emergency call and walked in with a face like that!"

"It would be rather disconcerting, wouldn't it?"

"It would be scandalous." He drew her into his arms again. "Lord, how long the day has been. Did you sleep at all last night—after I'd left?"

"Like a baby," she confessed. "I didn't think I would, though. And you?"

"I was too keyed up. I lay awake until all hours."

"And with an operation the first thing this morning! Mike, we must do better than that. You might do something wrong." She was horrified at the thought.

He rumpled her hair and grinned at her, wryly. "I couldn't stand many such nights, it's true. But I was wide awake during the morning, so it was all right. It was a little rough this afternoon, though." They were standing on the hearth and he gazed into the fire reflectively. "I'm glad you thought of the fire. I suppose we'll settle down eventually, but last night I could only lie there and wonder if it was all true—if you'd change your mind before we could be married, or if . . . oh, all sorts of things."

"How morbid of you. It's true—and I won't change my mind, darling."

He swung her off her feet suddenly, kissed her quickly and carried her to the bed, dumped her unceremoniously onto it and sprawled lazily beside her. "See that you don't." Comfortably he pillowed his head on her shoulder and she felt the rough tickle of his hair on her neck. "Ummh, you smell good."

"It's that scented soap you don't like," she murmured, "remember?"

"I like it fine on you. Do you mind the antiseptic smell I can't seem to get rid of?"

Eva hadn't liked it, she thought. He wouldn't have thought of it otherwise. "No. I like it. Besides, there's your tobacco—and whatever it is you use on your hair. I wouldn't mind it, in any case."

He played absently with the belt of her robe, then drew it tight about her and as suddenly loosed it entirely, shifted himself to lean over her, looming very large. He was heavy, and something, his belt buckle or a button, caught edgewise, cut into her. She winced and, immediately noticing, he said, "What is it? Am I hurting you?"

"Well darling—" she smiled, unbuttoning his coat, "I think it was that button."

He sat up, laughing. "I can take care of that in ten seconds."

He draped his coat over the back of a chair and she wondered if all men, disrobing, went through the same procedure. Walter had so often begun in just that way. Coat over the back of a chair, trousers folded, on the seat, shoes set under it. It must be a masculine pattern. She turned the spread back and heaped the pillows.

When he slipped in beside her, he said, "Have you told anyone about us yet?"

"No." She made room for him. "There's only Lucia, really. I'll tell her—sometime. And my parents, of course, when I write next."

"Will they approve?"

"Why not?"

It surprised her that he should ask. She tried to see his face, but it was hidden against her shoulder.

"Oh, a divorced man, and all that."

"In this day and age, that's a problem?"

"It is—sort of. Don't you think?"

"Not under the circumstances." She felt a sudden uneasiness. "Not unless we make it one." She squirmed her shoulder away and turned to look at him. "Mike, are you feeling guilty about getting the divorce?"

"Positively not." His reply was reassuringly firm. "I wouldn't mind three divorces if it meant you in the end."

"Then what is it? Why is it a problem?"

"It isn't." He pulled her close to him, kissed her lengthily and effectively. "I suppose I was just wishing, futilely, of course, that . . . well, that I'd met you first. I feel a little—spotted."

"But, darling, I've been married too."

"It isn't the same."

"Why isn't it?"

"Walter is dead."

And Eva, of course, was still living—some place, somewhere. Not knowing exactly what he *did* mean, she said impatiently, "It's exactly the same. Divorce makes a marriage just as dead."

He was remarkably sensitive to her mood. "Of course it does. And since I can't undo it by wishing it away, I'm very glad it's possible to undo it legally. I only wish it didn't take so long."

It occurred to her that he might have done it long before, but she didn't say so. There had been no point, actually, or not much of one, and she really did understand how only the necessity might prod him. She felt remorseful for having been sharp with him and she turned to him, generously. He gathered her to him and whispered, "Turn out the light."

There was further talk but it had nothing to do with divorces or problems. It was, rather, whispered in the dark and took the form of the inspired language of love in all of its varying nuances.

The windows were gray with dawn and the birds were twittering noisily when they awoke, horrified. "My God," Mike said, leaping from the bed to draw the curtains, as if that would help the situation, "How could we be so careless?"

From the bed, fully awake and immeasurably refreshed by the hours of sound sleep, Regina could not bring herself to be too alarmed. "We were both so tired, darling."

They had got up around eleven, puttered around a bit, eaten, and Mike had smoked a pipe. They had not meant at all to go back to bed but it had developed very naturally. "What time is it, actually?"

He glanced at his watch. "Four-thirty. Tired or not, we must *not* do this again. Thank heaven I walked over. I suppose there is a back way— out the garden?"

She felt a quick distaste for the idea. It was to be expected, she told herself, trying to reason about it, that they must be careful, but she had no liking for slipping about. She did not, she assured herself, feel the least bit of guilt over the situation. They were mature people, fully grown, intending to be married, and they were responsible only to themselves. Anything needing secrecy, however, carried with it the taint of guilt. Hidden things always did. She put it aside. It could not be helped. It was part of the price and she refused to allow it to become weighty. "There *is* a back gate. It comes out in that little park behind the house."

"Good. I'll take that way. Fancy, if I had to start the car at this hour!"

The room was gloomy with the curtains drawn, and disordered from their snack. She eyed it with distaste. It also smelled noticeably of Mike's pipe. She got up and pulled her robe about her. "There's no need having the curtains drawn, dear. The windows only look over the garden and the trees make a screen."

She pulled them back and flung up a window, wrinkling her nose. "I hope that tobacco smell goes away before Nettie comes."

"I shouldn't have smoked. Why did you let me?"

"Oh, I can always say I've taken up cigarettes. Perhaps I'd better."

They laughed. He tightened his belt about him. "It might be a good idea to leave a package around if we're going to be so thoughtless."

"It *is* difficult to think of everything, isn't it?"

Absently she stacked their trays, noticing that they had dropped crumbs on the rug. Nettie would think nothing of his having had a tray with her in the living room, but crumbs in the bedroom would baffle her. She had better run the sweeper. How deviously one must plan, she thought.

He had finished dressing, with an economy of movement that amazed her until she remembered that he was probably accustomed to dressing quickly upon call. It had only taken him five minutes. Knotting his tie before the mirror, he looked around at her. "It's going to be very late before I can get away tonight. There's a staff meeting and it'll probably last till all hours."

Feeling more than a little disenchanted, what with the grubby room and the shabbiness of the entire situation, she determined to handle things more efficiently. "Mike—look. We can't possibly be together *every* night for three months. Why don't we skip tonight?" Seeing him frown, she went on hurriedly. "I'll tell you. This is Saturday. I'll go to church with you tomorrow, and then let's be very bold and spend the afternoon with Tom and Lucia and tell them the news, shall we?"

He gazed at the knot of his tie, spoke rather distractedly. "I'll probably drop in at the hospital chapel in the morning. You aren't growing tired of me, are you?"

"You know I'm not. But you also know, darling, that I'm right. Let's at least *try* to be sensible."

Satisfied with his tie, finally, he turned and swept up his jacket. "Of course you're right. But I'll miss you tonight. Funny, isn't it, how easily one adjusts—it's so natural, being with you."

She took his face between her hands and gently kissed him. "I know. I feel that way, too. But we mustn't overdo it. You'd grow tired of me."

"You slander me—or else you doubt me." He kissed her once more, then put her aside. "I've *got* to go. What is this about tomorrow?"

"You weren't listening."

"Yes, I was. Something about Tom and Lucia." He slapped his pockets and looked about. "Have I got everything?"

"Unless you've forgotten part of your underwear—or your socks," she teased.

"No, I'm complete. I have a better idea, darling. Let's not be cooped up tomorrow with Tom and Lucia. If it's fine, let's run up to the old mill. We can eat there. The people run a—well, a sort of motel."

She looked at him suspiciously and laughingly he raised his hand. "I swear I wasn't going to suggest a thing. It wouldn't do, anyhow—too close to home. Besides, I can't be gone overnight."

She couldn't forbear saying, "You *have* been, I should say."

"And I mustn't again."

When he had gone she remembered, feeling oddly neglected, that he had not kissed her goodbye, and then she laughed at herself. There had certainly been kisses enough.

She picked up the room, took the trays to the kitchen, washed the dishes and put them away. Returning to her room it jolted her to see, almost at once, forgotten and in plain sight, his pipe on the bedside table. Provoked, she put it in the drawer. How often, she wondered, would they so easily allow such things to occur? It took considerable doing, she was beginning to realize, to become adept in secrecy. It comforted her, though, in her discomfort over the necessity, to remember that it certainly proved what novices they were at it—if that counted for anything.

Chapter Fourteen

❦

It wasn't so easy, not seeing him that night, however.

Until Nettie left it wasn't too bad. There was someone to talk to, and someone in the house with her. After dinner she worked awhile in the garden, Nettie's rejoicing voice lifted over the dishes following her about companionably. But when she had gone and dusk had come and the sleepy birds were fussing softly, the house seemed very large and lonely.

She wrote to her parents, which seemed to occupy quite a bit of time, but when she looked at the clock had taken only forty-five minutes, and that left her at quarter of eight with practically the entire evening yet ahead of her. She tried to read but could not keep her mind on the book. Tried her needlepoint again and found it tedious and dull. Wandered to the window and peered out, looked at the clock innumerable times, feeling certain it had stopped.

When, for what seemed the hundredth time, she had aimlessly walked from the sitting room to the dining room to the kitchen and back, she stopped by the telephone in the hall. She had only to lift the receiver, dial a number, and this evening of self-imposed loneliness would end. She was tempted to the point of sitting down and looking up the hospital number. Then she put the directory away. Nonsense, she told herself. This was her first test, her trial run at being a doctor's wife. There would be many such evenings and she had better start getting used to them.

It didn't work very well, for there was no appealing the fact that she was not yet a doctor's wife. When she was, he would be stopping at home during the day, she would know where he was, he would be sharing with her the information about his calls and meetings and all his routine. When she was left alone it would be a normal thing and he would be coming home to her eventually. As it was, she was alone by her own wish and there was nothing to look forward to until tomorrow.

Leaving the hall she went back into the living room, made herself pick up the book again. Its pages were meaningless, and across them she began to see in her mind's eye the staff meeting—in some conference room at the hospital, with cups of coffee and pipes and cigarettes going. She could see Mike there, in his element, laughing and joking with the other doctors, enjoying himself, taking up with them all the problems so unfamiliar to her, herself entirely forgotten, put completely out of his mind. It made her feel very forlorn.

At last, around nine o'clock, seeing she could not lift herself out of the misery of her mood by rationalizing about it, she dressed and went to see a second-rate movie. She was bored throughout, but it had the virtue of making the time pass, and it kept her from yielding ignominiously to the temptation of calling him.

The night was muggy and warm and she did not sleep well. She dozed and waked, dozed and waked, and finally could not even doze any longer. Her room felt close, though all the windows were open. It was not until she heard a rumble of thunder that she realized how still the air had become, in forewarning of a storm. She flicked on the light to see what time it was and was aghast to find that it was only a little after midnight. She felt as if she had been tossing and turning for hours. Eyeing the rumpled bed she thought it looked as if she had been, also.

Impatiently she got up, smoothed the sheets, laid the blanket off entirely, got back in bed, turned off the light, and then gave herself up hopelessly to the misery of missing him. She clutched the other pillow and wished that it was occupied. Never, she vowed, would she refuse him again. It was her own doing, this business of being here alone. She had only herself to blame. He would have come. He wanted to come. He had taken it for granted he would come. And then, inconsistently, she began to wonder if he *had* really wanted to come. Irritably she remembered he hadn't protested much. He had accepted her suggestion rather easily, hadn't he? Why hadn't he swept away her objections and insisted? It must have suited him very well not to come. Her present helplessness made her abjectly unhappy. In exasperation she turned on the light again and picked up a book. She looked at its title miserably—*War and Peace*—and felt an immense dislike for it. She wondered how many thousands of people had stuck, as she had, halfway through the huge tome, and on how many thousands of bedside tables it rested in the determination to read at least twenty pages nightly until it had been waded through.

There was a cautious whistle from the garden. Unbelieving, and with a suddenly light and hopeful heart, she flew to the window. He was standing in a patch of moonlight, looking, she thought, a little wildly, for all the world like Romeo himself. She had a mad and giggly impulse to quote Juliet's speech at him. Instead she called down, in a carefully low voice, "I'll let you in in a moment."

She was so happy she was quivering. She couldn't find a robe. She couldn't find her slippers. Her hair was all tangled and uncombed. It didn't matter. She snatched up the first thing she laid her hands on, found too late it was her oldest and shabbiest dressing gown, a faded and ancient cotton that was almost disreputable and, barefooted, ran down the stairs to the back door. He was leaning, nonchalantly, as if they had forever, as if he came whistling to her garden every night of his life, against a post.

Her rush carried her into his arms and she held to him as if she would never let him go, murmuring small reproaches, touching his face and kissing him, lightly and quickly, a dozen times. "I thought you'd never come."

"Look who's talking! I wasn't supposed to come, remember?"

"If you hadn't, I'd have died."

She couldn't see him too clearly, but she thought he raised his eyebrows at her. She shut his mouth with her own before he could protest. "Well," he said, finally, lifting his head, "for such a welcome, I'd be willing to be told not to come *every* night."

"Don't tease. I've been miserable."

His shoulders were so big, so strong, so dear, under her hands.

"Have you, darling?" His voice was tender.

He swung her off her feet and walked with her to the glider-hammock on the terrace. Without releasing her, he sat, cradling her as comfortably as if she had been a child. She felt like a child who had had punishment lifted from it, the threat of banishment removed. "Will you be cold?" he asked.

She tucked her feet under her. "No. But aren't you coming up?"

"I daren't. I only came by to say goodnight."

"But, Mike . . ."

He kissed her. "Darling, we'd be certain to go to sleep again. It's too late."

"Why didn't you come sooner?"

"The staff meeting is only just over."

"Did you really come by just to say goodnight?"

She felt the movement of his head. "I didn't expect you to be up, actually. I just drove by—just to have a look, think of you, asleep. Your light went on just as I got here."

"I couldn't sleep. I'd just decided to read awhile. What would you have done if the house had been dark?"

"Gone home." He said it so matter-of-factly.

"Without waking me? Without seeing me?"

He laughed at the shocked disbelief in her voice. "Next time, sweet, you'd better say what you mean."

She pulled his head down. "Next time, don't pay any attention to me."

He only stayed an hour, and it was a quiet time, full of silences which were comfortable with love, full of soft exchanges of murmured talk. They watched the flickering play of lightening, low on the horizon, against the banking darkness; watched the moon ride in and out of the massed, fleeing clouds; pointed out the few courageous stars to each other, smelled the penetrating sweetness of the first new blooms of honeysuckle on the wall, felt the dew rise damply on the new-cut grass. It was all infinitely peaceful and happy.

Then the first few drops of rain began to fall, and they ran, hand in hand to the porch. For the first time he noticed her bare feet. "What are you doing running about without shoes? Suppose you'd cut your foot. Aren't you ever going to learn to take care of yourself? Wasn't it on these steps you hurt your ankle?"

She admitted it was but could not resist adding, "In the very slippers you're scolding me now for not having on."

"Well, there's no ice tonight, and there might be sharp stones or even broken glass."

"But there's a doctor handy," she teased.

"One who does *not* want his lady's foot bruised." His arms went about her and rocked her gently to and fro. "Ah, Regina, do you know how much I love you?"

"Tell me."

"More than anything in the world—more than anyone in the world—more than my life—," his voice deepened, softened until it was barely a whisper, ". . . more than my soul."

"Darling!"

They held to each other a moment longer, and then he had to go. She watched him leave in the rain, his coat turned up against it, and wished tenderly he had never to go.

When she was again in her room, in bed, she thought about it, the entire evening, and she soberly and frankly faced the full extent of her committal. She had learned, once and for all, in misery and aching loneliness, that nothing could ever be the same for her again. She was hopelessly and helplessly involved with him, and all her happiness, present and future, depended on him. At a whim, a word, or a touch, by his presence or his absence, she could be lifted to the heights or sunk to the depths. She was no longer a free person, independent and certain of herself, in command of her own life. What she felt, what she did, what she became, was all in his hands.

It was a shiveringly fearful feeling. She had not counted on it, she realized. She had not known how demanding her own love would be of her. She had no experience of such love. She could have prevented all this. It had been in her power to prevent it. She had had only to say no two nights ago (was it really only two nights? Already it seemed half a lifetime.) He would have accepted it, and the reins would have been in her own hands. But she had not chosen to do so, and now it was too late. All her resources were gone. Her abandonment was final. The power was entirely his.

With swift decision she put it away from her. Something essentially and passively feminine in her was even glad it was so. She thought of the Chinese symbols for light and dark—the Yin and Yang—the feminine and the dark receptacle, the receiver—the masculine, the giver, the bringer of light. It was the way of nature, she reflected, and trustfully she was content to have it so.

The mill was as beautiful as he had said. Built of stone, it was gray with time, leaning a little toward the narrow, cliff-held stream. Vines covered one end entirely and the dark hills behind it made it a somber picture. The old wooden wheel turned creakingly, as if its bones were tired and its flesh water-worn.

Like teenagers they clambered over the rocky hillsides, looking for wild flowers which they did not pick, taking amazingly adolescent pictures of each other. One of Mike, with a water hyacinth behind his ear, she knew she would forever treasure.

Late in the afternoon they climbed by a hard and rocky path to the top of a cliff and stood in the sweeping wind, Regina's skirt blowing about her and, hand in hand, looked down on the green-pastured valley below. The air was sparkling, like wind-roughed water in the sunlight. The flash of a metal roof on the hill beyond was diamond-clean and the trees which fringed the rim of the hill were picked out in stark counterpoint. The mill was small and quiet on the white-watered stream in its narrow race. The cabins, built of logs, which the mill owner rented to week ending visitors, were hidden in a grove of trees. The sky was gold and sapphire, with long coral streamers reaching up to the zenith. The wind in the pines was like a lute, making sighing music, and the voice of a lark rose up to them, soaring high from the pastures below. A dog barked somewhere near the mill, the sound coming to them brokenly, bent and barred by the wind. From a cove across the valley a cowbell tinkled faintly. This moment, Regina thought in an ecstacy of happiness, this very moment is as much of heaven as a mortal can ask, and she turned to lift her face to Mike, as if asking him to set his own seal upon it.

They ate by candlelight in the mill dining room. It was low-ceilinged, with old, smoked beams overhead. The huge stone fireplace, not needed now, was banked with red geraniums in white pots, and the ancient walls which enclosed the great room were a fresh and still slightly odorous white themselves. The tables were covered with red-checked cloths. There were only a few people dining. "We're lucky," Mike said. "Later in the season the place gets rather crowded."

"I can imagine. It must be a paradise for city dwellers when the weather turns hot. I love it, Mike. I'm so glad we came. I want to come again and paint it."

Affectionately he smiled at her. "We'll come some week day when there'll be no one but us. You can paint while I fish."

They ate trout, caught from the mill stream, with fresh, tender asparagus drowned in new butter, and tiny, crisply tangy radishes. For a sweet they had great, fat red strawberries, so sweet and juicy they dripped on the way to the mouth. Still feeling the sense of height from the climb, Regina thought it was food for immortals, too.

Toward the end of the meal there was the stir of an entering party.

With her back to the door she could not see, and she had no curiosity to see in any case, but looking up she saw that Mike's face had altered from the relaxed, happy quietness it had worn all day. She caught a glimpse of acute dismay, and then a settling to impassivity which was almost stoical in its discipline. Even his eyes had gone dark and remote. She felt a little frightened. "What is it, darling?"

He made an abrupt motion of pushing his plate aside, drew out his pipe. "Nothing. Why?"

"You look different . . . so . . . Mike, you haven't eaten half your berries."

His smile was strained. "I ate too much of the fish, I expect. You have them, if you like."

"Oh, no—there're plenty, but . . ." She gave it up, realizing belatedly she should have said nothing at all.

He was restless as she ate the rest of her berries, glancing about the room, drumming on the table with his fingers of one hand, fidgeting in his chair. He wanted to leave, she thought, and she sipped the last of her coffee. "Do you want to go, dear?"

"Whenever you're ready." He denied his restlessness, the shift of mood. "There's no hurry." There was no mistaking his relief, however, when he saw that she had finished.

"I think I'll just find the ladies' room, then," she said, making an effort to be casual and normal, "and repair the damages. I've probably eaten all my lipstick off."

She was pushing back her chair, he was standing to help her, when she was aware of someone approaching them. She turned, hearing Mike draw in his breath, a sinking feeling swept over her. It was only the priest, she saw. She did not know who she had expected, or rather she did not put into words her sudden great fear. Her knees felt weak with her relief.

The priest's black cloth was upon them and she subsided into her chair. He held out his hand to Mike and his voice rang, as she had known it would. "Mike . . . I haven't seen you in some time, boy. You've been busy, I expect."

"I have, Father, quite busy. Father Vincent, this is Mrs. Browning, the librarian at the college."

"Yes." His hand was big and warm, dry in the palm, broad and capacious. It swallowed her own. "I've heard many good things about your work, Mrs. Browning. Mike, don't let me keep you. Sit down."

Mike's eyes sought hers, and there was, puzzlingly, defeat and sorrow in them. They held for a moment then returned to the priest. "You'll have some coffee with us, Father?"

"No. I haven't eaten yet. But I'll sit with you for awhile." He drew out a chair and placed himself to Regina's left. "Do you like Hilton, Mrs. Browning?"

"Very much, Father. I enjoy the work at the college, too."

He nodded. "Pleasant work nearly always makes a place pleasant to live. I could tell you, though," he laughed heartily, "about some parishes of mine, when I was driven to call upon the Lord to know what I had done to deserve such punishment."

He launched into an amusing story of his first parish, a tiny, new chapel in the country, which had a leaky basement that regularly flooded during the rainy season. "I had to pump that basement for eight hours at a stretch," he concluded, "in order to have a fire in the furnace on Sunday mornings." He sighed. "I seemed fated in those days to be a tender of septic tanks and cranky furnaces."

He told a story well, Regina thought, and his rich, heavy voice underscored each point as he made it. She would have enjoyed it except for Mike's bleak, unhappy face across the table. Whatever is the matter with him, she thought, acutely conscious of his uneasiness. She laughed rather more than she might have, to make up for his total lack of response.

To carry the situation, and as a shield for him, she told something of her own problems in the old, made-over residence which housed the library and its dilapidated, cranky furnace. Father Vincent could listen as well as talk, and he seemed attentive, unaware of Mike's distress, and properly appreciative of her anecdote.

When she had finished, however, he turned to Mike, and she saw that it had all been but a prelude. "I heard," he said, soberly, now, "that you have made a decision, Mike."

Mike's chin came up and she recognized the gesture from her own way of meeting a challenge. "Yes, Father."

The priest rose, laid his hand on Mike's shoulder, and his voice softened unbelievably, was as gently as a child's. He loves him, Regina thought. He loves him very much. "God keep you, Mike."

Mike's voice was so low as almost not to be heard. "Thank you, Father."

The warm, dry hand was extended to her. "And Mrs. Browning, I hope you will continue to be very happy."

The eyes that looked down at her were far from warm, though.

They were dark and appraising, a little cold, and more than a little re-moved. She felt as if they held a warning, which she could not fathom, but she thrust up her own chin as she met them. There could be no mistaking it. He knew of their engagement and he did not approve. In-deed, he disapproved enough to dislike her. Because she was not a Catho-lic, perhaps? Did he think she would take Mike away from the Church? Deliberately she made her voice cool, echoing Mike's words, "Thank you, Father." But she added, "I think I shall."

The eyes flickered, either from the candlelight or from the chal-lenge picked up. His broad, swarthy face showed no expression. Bowing slightly, he turned away.

She watched the massive shoulders, the bulky, short torso, make their way back to his table, and she knew, without knowing why, that he was her enemy. She had known it, she reflected, the first time she had ever seen him—in church, that time. There had been a presentiment, and she remembered that she had thought, even then, how powerful an enemy he would be, how implacable.

She made her face cheerful and calm before she turned back to Mike. Whatever underlay the priest's disapproval, she was no mean an-tagonist herself. She would meet him with as much guile as he could dispense. He had his Church—but she had her love. "Shall we go, dear?"

Chapter Fifteen

❧

As if to compound the note of anticlimax on which the day had ended, the next morning was darkly overcast with a cold, west wind blowing. Regina looked at the weather and brooded.

The sting of the encounter with the priest still burned inside her. Perhaps, she thought, she should ask to see him and talk with him. Perhaps if he knew she had no wish nor desire to estrange Mike from him or his Church, he would look with more favor on their love. If Mike were only not so reticent about what he expected of her—but there was time. They would discuss it one day, when he was ready.

She dismissed it thus and turned her mind to more practical matters. She had had her winter things cleaned and had put them away in mothproofed bags for the summer. With an aversion to opening them and getting out a heavy coat, she decided to make do with a lightweight suit, unwilling to believe winter had returned.

Nettie warned her. "This is dogwood winter, Mrs. Browning. It'll be cold for two or three days. You'd better dress for it."

"Oh, nonsense, Nettie. Why, it was like summer yesterday."

"That was yesterday. We always get a cold spell like this early in May, and in my opinion we'll have a heavy frost tonight. Two years out of three it comes and nips the peach trees and the early gardens. You can take my word for it."

"I don't believe it. The sun will be shining and it will be hot again by noon."

"You'll see." Nettie nodded gloomily.

She was right. Unbelievably, the thermometer dropped forty degrees during the day, and when Regina put her car up that evening she had to run, shiveringly, through a sleety blast from the garage to the back door.

Standing, absorbing the good heat of the house, she looked out the door at the garden. All the young green things looked so unguarded and defenseless. They looked so cold, so drenched by the rain. It was as if they had been betrayed. The ancient lilac bush was weighted down and even the tall spikes of the irises were bent, as if punished beyond bearing. The peony bushes looked as if their great, heavy heads would break. She remembered the bed of lilies-of-the-valley against the north wall. They were just opening. On impulse she gathered up an armload of old newspapers and went out to cover them. It would probably do no good, but they were too tiny to be left alone and unprotected.

"Don't feel too bad about the flowers, Mrs. Browning," Nettie told her, "the rain will keep the frost away."

"It's such a cold rain, though, Nettie."

"Not as bad as frost would be. They'll come to no harm from the rain."

Glad she did not have to go out again, she went up to get out extra blankets and, accepting the inevitable, to find heavier clothing for herself for tomorrow. Her arms were full when the telephone rang and she called down to Nettie to answer. It was Mike, she knew, and after dropping her load on the bed she started down. Instead, Nettie met her. "It was the doctor, ma'am. He was in a hurry and he said not to bother you. He's coming for supper. He says he's sent Sallie home with the flu."

"Oh? I'm sorry. Is she very ill?"

"He didn't say. She had the sniffles when she went to work this morning and I told her then she ought to stay home. But she *would* go. He said she had a temperature."

"Well, perhaps a day or two in bed will take care of that. It often does, you know. What do we have planned for dinner?"

"Nothing a man would like—but there's steaks in the freezer. Don't worry. We'll give him a good meal."

It occurred to Regina that this would be as good a time as any to tell Nettie. She searched for a tactful way of putting it and could come up with nothing but the blunt truth. "The doctor and I are going to be married, Nettie."

The leathery creases of the plain Scotch face stretched and softened. "Are you now? I'm mighty glad to hear it." She bobbed her head knowingly. "I've been thinking you might. He and Sallie both have spoken of it. If you don't mind me saying so, Mrs. Browning, it'll be a good thing for both of you. Him living by himself in that big house, and you living by yourself in this one. It's not good for you. Have you set the date yet?"

"Not definitely. Sometime this summer, probably."

Nettie laughed. "Well, don't put it off too long. He's a fine man, the doctor. He's got a heart of gold. The whole town loves him."

And some, Regina thought, remembering Father Vincent, love him enough to be possessive.

With a happy lifting of heart, probably, she thought, from having finally told someone, she went into the dining room. A little amused at herself, for after all no one would have been more horrified or condemning than Nettie had she been privy to the entire affair, she surveyed the room and decided that since this was the first time she had ever offered him a meal at table, she would make something of a ceremony of it. It was a nice room, she reflected, with good paneling and good proportions. She wished a little wistfully that the place could be bought and they might make their home here. It was such a gracious, charming house, and the grounds were so lovely.

She looked at the gleaming mahogany surface of the table, at the drooping mass of lilacs in its center, and got out cobwebby lace squares for place mats. Using her thinnest china and finest silver she set places, then rearranging the flowers she left them for a centerpiece. The whole room was scented by the heavy sweetness of the lilacs. There was something rather sensual about them, she thought—the close form they took, their abandoned weight, their almost overpowering odor. Even their graceful droop was loving. Stepping back to see, she decided it all looked very nice.

She ran upstairs to bathe and change. Deciding to live up to the table she chose a soft blue crepe which clung to her figure. It was an old dress and it had always been a favorite of hers. It settled about her now with the comfort of all familiar things. She brushed her hair until it shone, noting its fly-away fineness and deep-swept waves. Her hair was one of her nicest assets, she thought—but the blue dress was very good with her pale skin. She looked at herself in the long mirror between the windows, feeling more than a little satisfied with the results. She remembered that Walter used to say she had a damned seductive figure, deeper bosomed than her clothing indicated, firmer hipped and longer legged. She was suddenly fiercely glad of it. She wanted to be beautiful for Mike—wanted, even, to be seductive.

She heard Nettie letting him in downstairs and she waited a moment, wondering if his voice would always send these small, electric shocks over her skin, raising the tiny bumps of flesh, making the fine down on her arms feel singly and individually alive, bringing a burning feeling to her neck and throat, making her bones go soft. Lazily she lifted her arms, as if feeling them already about his neck, savoring the feeling in anticipation, then laughing at herself she went down the stairs.

Nettie was taking his coat, putting it away in the closet. Regina saw that he had on the old tweed suit she liked so well. There was a spattering of rain on his hair, which glistened in the light as if sprayed with silver. There was red high on his cheeks from the cold. He put up both hands to run the palms back from his temples. Then, seeing her poised on the stairs, his face changed. The tiredness smoothed out, the brows relaxed, the wide, firm mouth shaped into a smile and the whole face was lit, almost incandescently, with love. A warm rush of love for him engulfed her and she went to him. Boldly, she kissed him. He flicked a cautious glance at Nettie and she laughed. "She knows."

"Good." His arms went around her then and when Nettie emerged from the coat closet he was holding her tightly. Over her he laughed, "I'm a very lucky man, Nettie."

"I would say you are, Doctor," Nettie said, joining his laughter, "I'd say you both are, for that matter. Seems to me you're just made for each other. I'd like to wish you happiness, sir."

"Thank you, Nettie."

"Now, I'll be getting back to the kitchen. I expect you're not too much in love to eat a good dinner." Her starched skirts bustled down the hall.

Regina watched her go. "I'm sure she thinks I've got the best of the bargain," she said, laughingly. "You stand very high with Nettie."

They went in to the fire and he stretched out on the sofa, making himself at home easily. "Well, she's known me since I was a boy." He held out an arm. "Come sit here with me. Lord, but you're lovely in that blue dress. It exactly suits you. Is it new?"

Settled in the curve of his body, his arm about her, she shook her head. "As old as the hills." Then she laughed. "Where did that saying come from? It doesn't apply, but we use it constantly."

He nuzzled his face against her thigh. "No idea. Nothing could be as old as the hills, could it? You smell good, too. You always do. What have you been doing today?"

"Trying to keep warm, mostly—and the usual thing at the library. The youngsters are beginning to worry about finals and term papers. They're doing a terrific amount of reading."

"It's always the same, isn't it? I used to get in a blue panic as the end of term neared. I never believed I'd pass another final." He tried unsuccessfully to hide a yawn, smiled at her apologetically. "I'm pretty tired, I'm afraid."

She felt deeply tender and leaned down to kiss him. "Has it been anything special?"

"No. Nothing unusual. It's the weather, mostly, I expect. It'll bring on a round of spring colds and flu. I had to send Sallie home at noon."

"Nettie told me. How will you manage?"

"Eat out. The house can go until she's back."

"When we're married," she promised, "that sort of problem will end for you."

He pulled her down against him. "When we're married . . . isn't that wonderful, doesn't it sound fine? When we're married you'll be at home every night when I come in. I won't have to go out in weather like this to see you."

"No."

His laugh rang out.

"What is it?"

"I was just thinking—I'll never want to make a night call again."

"Take a partner to do the night calls for you."

"I wish I could afford it. It's beastly enough having to leave you now. It will be intolerable when there's the whole night."

"Oh, you'll grow so used to me you won't mind at all."

He held her away to look at her. "I'll never grow used to you. I'll never have enough of you. You're already like the blood in my veins—as necessary for me to live."

"Darling . . ."

When he let her go her hair was rumpled and her lips felt familiarly bruised. He had no idea, she thought, how punishingly hard at such moments his mouth could be. It was as if he wanted to absorb her into himself, and by sheer pressure made the effort.

"By the way," he said, squirming around more comfortably, "you probably should come by the place one day before long and take a look at it. You'll very likely want it done over completely, and the furniture may not suit at all."

He expected them to live there, then. She felt a dull, weightiness in her stomach. It was really too much, she thought. He couldn't possibly expect her to want to live there, in a home which had been Eva's, furnished by her, alive with the presence of her choices and the memories of her domination. She knew it by sight only. It was a big white frame house, of no particular style or period, with its gincracky porches dating it around the early nineteen hundreds. It looked like a comfortable old family home. That thought made her ask, hopefully, "Was it your family home, darling? Or did you buy it after . . .," she stumbled, but feeling she must get over these blocks in her thinking—they were going to live a lifetime together and it wouldn't do to keep on avoiding them—she continued, "after you and Eva were married?" The name had come hard, but it was a triumph that it had come at all. There *was* a difference, she thought. Walter was dead. Eva was still living.

"It was the family home. It's much too big, of course, and terribly old-fashioned. Eva never liked it. She never did anything to it, not even to rearrange the furniture." He laughed. "She said it was impossible and there wasn't any use trying. She kept wanting to build." His eyes had a wistful look in them, however. "I've always been fond of it. I grew up in it, and that made the difference, of course. Would you rather live somewhere else?"

He had noticed her difficulty a moment ago, she thought, and with her sky suddenly bright and clear again she caught his head to her. "Of course not. I'll love it, too. I'm sure I shall. If you were a little boy there, I wouldn't dream of living anywhere else."

"You always understand, don't you?" he said, against her throat. "That's the one completely perfect thing about you. You always know what I want and how I feel."

"I mean to. I hope always to. Tell me about the house. Why doesn't your mother live there with you?"

"She did—until I was married. She decided to live with Anna, then. The place is mine," he said. "It's my share of what Papa left. It was what I wanted."

"Then it's what I want, too. You won't mind if I change it about? Paint and decorate a little?"

"Change it as much as you like, darling. There's only a little of the old furniture I'd want to keep, if you'd like to get rid of most of it. Papa's desk and . . ." he hesitated, looking at her awkwardly, then evidently changing his mind about what he had meant to say, finishing lamely, "and a few personal things."

She refused to be ruffled or curious. "We'll see. It may all be usable. If it is, fine. I won't turn you upside down, dear."

"Turn me any way you please, I shan't mind."

Talking about the house brought her mind around to the wedding. "I've been thinking," she said, "that it would probably make Lucia very happy for us to be married in her home . . ."

Nettie's appearance in the doorway, announcing dinner, interrupted her, but not before she noted an anxious look on his face. Well, she thought, never mind. We'll talk it over another time.

When he had seated her and taken his own place, she looked up from unfolding her napkin to see him just finishing crossing himself. She guessed that he had murmured a private blessing and that he did this regularly when at home. She started to tell him he might make his prayer aloud but decided it was, after all, his affair.

They looked at each other across the table, their eyes saying the same thing to each other—that this was the first time of many for them to sit thus together. He smiled at her wryly. "It's an awfully big table, isn't it?"

"Too big. We'll not have one of our own this large."

He cocked an eye at her and grinned widely. "I expect we'd better."

"Why? This is almost a banquet table."

"So was ours at home. Give us time and we'll fill it up."

It embarrassed her to find her face heating. She remembered, among the hodgepodge of assorted notions she had about Catholics, that they did not believe in birth control. That, at least, was common knowledge. If one read the newspapers at all one knew that. She managed a laugh. "There isn't time for too many, darling. We aren't youngsters ourselves, you know."

"Time enough for half a dozen," he said, contentedly and to her horror. Did he really mean it? Really want that many? She left the idea hanging in catastrophic mid-air. A little desperately she said, "That many?"

More seriously he said, "Don't you like children?"

"Of course, Mike. But half a dozen . . ." She spread her hands, helplessly.

"Oh, that's just a good round figure. You do want them, don't you?"

159

She felt a melting tenderness at his smile and could not have denied him a dozen as a good, round figure if he had asked.

Nettie served the soup, and she waited until she had gone before answering. It gave her time to think that there were so many things about him unfamiliar to her, things out of his background, so different from hers, things out of his faith, which could not have been more unknown to her if he had been a Hindu or Buddhist. She had never had the slightest curiosity about Catholicism—she had never even known well another Catholic, not since school days at any rate. There were going to be so many things to learn, so many things to become accustomed to, and once again she wondered if he would want her to become a Catholic, too. She thought with a little longing of the stodginess of her Methodist upbringing.

Feeling his eyes on her she knew he was really waiting for her to answer. "Dear, I hope we have as many children as we can afford and I have the courage to take care of."

He took a spoonful of soup. "I'm glad. We hadn't spoken of it, and I wouldn't have insisted, naturally. But a big family is such a lot of fun."

He began to talk about his childhood, then, about the whole other time, when her ankle had been hurt and the hospital nurse had come for him—his doctor's look. "I've got to go." He was already looking about for his coat.

She hurried to the hall. He wouldn't have noticed, of course, where Nettie had put it. "What is it?"

"There's been an accident on the highway north of town."

"But don't the ambulances take care of accidents?"

"Normally. We only have two. One has taken a patient to the city, and the other is on another emergency call."

She helped him on with the coat. "Was that Miss Hopkins?"

"No, it was the hospital. You don't mind, do you? I've explained that I can be reached here occasionally, when I'm needed." His eyes crinkled. "Until a discreet hour, of course."

"Of course," she murmured. They would never have a moment free of the threat of a call now, she thought, and then horrified at her selfishness she said, more generously, "Naturally, darling. I'm glad you thought of it." On impulse, reluctant to let him go, she begged, "Let me go with you—please."

"On a night like this? It's miserable out."

"I'll dress warmly, and I won't get in your way, I promise. If you get tied up I'll get myself home."

"Oh, you can have the car, once we get to the hospital." He thought about it briefly. "Come along, then. But hurry. It may be pretty messy, though, I warn you."

"I may be able to help," she threw over her shoulder, already mounting the stairs. Rather proudly she added, "I did some Red Cross work during the war."

The road was very slippery and in order to be careful of their own safety he had to drive more slowly than he wished. She saw that his impatience was eating away at him. "How far out is it?" she asked.

"At the old stone bridge. It's a death trap. I've been saying so for years."

She had no idea where the old stone bridge was and she refrained from any further conversation. He needed to give his entire attention to handling the car on the treacherous road.

The highway north led to another and smaller town some fifteen miles distant. It was hilly and full of curves. As they wound along, the rain-slick pavement a shining, twisting, black snake ahead of them, it began to seem an interminable distance to her. Just as she began to think it must certainly be nearer the other town than theirs and it therefore would have been more sensible of whoever called to telephone there, they rounded a long, climbing turn and found the crowd gathered, the blink of lights, she knew they had arrived.

The state police were there, and the usual group of curious people. The car, which had quite evidently hit the stone bridge, crumpled and then rolled, was perched precariously on the very rim of a steep embankment. It made her shudder to see it. It looked as if the touch of a hand would send it tumbling on down. Mike was out of the car in a second. She followed more slowly, hearing him ask, "How many are there?"

The crowd made way for him and the police closed about him. "Just the driver, Doctor," one of them said.

"You haven't moved him?"

"We couldn't. He's pinned down. We've even been afraid to try to move the car."

Regina struggled through the crowd. A policeman barred her way. "Keep back, miss."

"I'm with Dr. Panelli," she said.

"Oh, beg pardon."

She knew that he thought she was a nurse, but it did not matter. If she could help Mike in any way she wanted to be near enough he could call on her. He was stooping, trying to find a way to the man pinned down so brutally. The car rested on its side and only the legs of the man protruded from under it. It must be crushing his chest, she thought, and wondered if he could possibly be alive. Mike went to the front of the car and bent down. "Can you hear me?"

Because she was only one step behind him, she also heard the man's reply, sobbed out in great gusts of bubbling breath. "Are you a priest?"

She saw Mike stiffen, then heard him suck in his breath. At almost the same time he wheeled to dig his heels down the embankment to get nearer. She was terrified for him. The whole, delicate balance could give way any moment and come crashing down on him. She put out her hand and clutched his coat. "Mike, please . . ."

Roughly he tore loose. "Get a flashlight from that policeman. Hold it here for me."

The policeman heard him and came to hold the light himself.

The rain was a drizzly mist now, and she noticed that it made the glow from the flashlight hazy and dim. He won't be able to see she thought. Somewhat peremptorily he told the policeman where he wanted the light. In an agony of fear, then, she stood helplessly and watched him fling himself down on the soggy ground, begin to inch his head and shoulders under the car. If he so much as touched it, it might be sent hurtling down on him. It was so foolish of him, she thought wildly. Surely the most sensible thing was to get the car lifted and get the man to the hospital as fast as possible. What could he do for him in that tight space under it? Give him a shot to ease the pain, she supposed. There was nothing else he *could* do until the car was lifted. She found herself staring tensely as he wriggled under, and saying over and over again, "Please, please, please," in some kind of incoherent prayer.

There was a murmured, indistinct conversation, questions from Mike and answers from the man, then the man's voice, clearer, asked again, "Are you a priest?"

There was a long silence, long enough she thought that Mike should be through and inching back out again, then she heard his voice, clear and firm, but somehow gentle and reassuring, not denying, not confirming, only urging. "Make a good act of contrition, now. Say it after me."

She heard a long, choked sigh and felt the effort of the crushed chest to draw breath as the man tried to speak. Out of what anguish he was trying! She felt as if her own breath hung in her throat, as if by holding it, she could help. Mike's voice was tender and loving and kind. "Try hard. Try once more."

And the essential words began to come. As in a trance, fixed by pity for the man, by fear for Mike, by horror of the fragilely balanced car, and by a strange sorrowing feeling of loss as the doctor in Mike was replaced by the priest, the obligation of his faith inevitably upon him, she listened to the slow-spaced words, the agonizingly uttered words, which somehow, by some sanctification of dogma and ritual, would enable the man to die in peace.

For he was dying, of course, and Mike knew it. There was nothing more to be done for the body—there was only now the state of the soul to consider. To murmur this act of contrition, whatever transgressions stained one's soul, to die in grace, was the final necessity. Not as a doctor, but as a good Catholic, Mike administered it comfortingly. At the risk of his own life, as reckless of it and as lovingly as if he were truly a priest, he administered it.

The haze of mist on her cheeks was cold, and she wondered if she would ever truly know this man she loved, ever be able to follow him into those strange places of his soul which were so alien to her. They wound terrifyingly far from her and they left her only the solution of humility and promise.

"I . . . I can't . . ." The anguished voice faltered.

Mike's voice was firm. "Yes, you can. Try."

It was cruel of him. Shudderingly she flung up her hands to hide her face.

"Most heartily . . . sorry . . . for having . . . offended Thee."

What kind of a God was it that demanded this ghastly effort for His glory? Surely a penitent heart must be enough. Must the words be said, even with the last, dying breath?

It was over.

Mike was standing beside her once more, drawing her hands down from her face. He was almost unrecognizably muddy and wet, covered all over with the heavy, sticky clay. Even his face was ploughed with the slime. It dripped from his hair and was mixed with his brows. But he was safe. The priestly office was finished. She swayed toward him, weakly crying, and he put an arm about her. "He is dead, now," he said, in a voice as dead as the man. "We can go."

Chapter Sixteen

❧

Two days later he called, growling hoarsely, barely able to talk at all his voice was so near gone. "Either Sallie's germs were terribly contagious, or all that muck and water on the highway the other night have laid me low," he explained. "I've got a fabulous temperature and an assortment of aches and pains that have confounded the combined medical knowledge of the entire staff."

It was just what she expected, she told herself. He had been wet through, on that soggy ground fully fifteen minutes, and there had been that long drive home. He had shivered almost uncontrollably the entire way, she remembered, and she remembered, too, that recovering from her fright she had been anxious and had scolded, that he had answered her brusquely and told her not to nag. "Just how much temperature do you have, Mike?" she asked.

"I don't really know," he said, trying to laugh. "My eyes are so blurry I can't read the damned thermometer. It looked as if it went right on out the top, but it couldn't have. It doesn't really matter. It's to be expected, actually."

"Well, you sound horrible. Is it mostly in your throat?"

"It's not mostly anywhere—it's all over, in my head and in my chest and I could swear it's in my back and legs, too. Oh, it's a honey. I'm going to have to stay in for a few days."

He sneezed prodigiously, nearly breaking her eardrums, and she saw him in her mind's eye, drooped over the telephone, hot and achy, with a head that felt swollen and tight and a throat as raspy as a file. Poor dear. "Has Sallie come back yet? Is she there?"

There was a silence, then he said, "Damn! I haven't a handkerchief. Wait a moment, will you?" She waited, hearing various knocking noises which she identified as drawers being opened and closed. He was in his bedroom, at any rate. She heard him clear his throat before he picked up the phone again. "Darling? No, she isn't here yet. She'll be here in the morning, though. She's doing fine—now that she's passed all her bugs on to me."

She disregarded everything but the fact that he was alone. "Mike, have you been there all day, with no one to see to you?"

"Oh, I haven't been here all day. I only gave up tonight." His voice cracked at the end and she heard him gulp to get it back.

To some extent the weather had moderated, but there was still a sharp chill in the air. She was horrified that he had gone about all day, probably with fever. It made her sound more cross than she intended, when she scolded him. "You would go right through the roof if a patient of yours behaved the way you've done. Why *don't* you take better care, dear?"

Patiently he explained. "There were things I had to do. Please don't worry about it. I've asked Barton to see to them for a few days."

"I should think so. Mike, I'm coming over. I can at least make you comfortable for the night."

"You'll do no such thing! I'm highly contagious. You'd just come down with this bug yourself. I'm all right, really. I'm going straight to bed and stay there until this fever breaks, and Barton will look in in the morning."

"Promise?"

"I promise. I'm just sorry not to see you tonight."

"Well, that's your own fault. I'd risk the germs."

"I know, but I won't have it. What will you do tonight—since I'm not coming?" He sounded rather wistful.

"Read, probably. Get to bed early." She answered at random. The evening having been left hanging loosely so suddenly, she hadn't thought.

His effort at laughter was painfully harsh and croaking. She winced, knowing how it tore his throat. "You can probably do with a good night's sleep. You've been very good to let me come so often."

Good? It was unbearable to think of an evening without him. He surely knew that. "I'll miss you," she said softly.

"And I'll miss you."

"How long do you think it will be?'

"I wish I knew. Three or four days at least, judging by the viru-lence. I'd tell a patient that, in any case."

The habit of him was so strong that the idea of three or four days without seeing him stretched like an eternity to her. But her anxiety for him tempered it. "However long it is, Mike, don't get out too soon. Don't be impatient."

"I'll try not to be."

He was taken with a coughing spasm which really alarmed her then. She waited until he had it under control. "Darling, don't keep talking. It's irritating your throat. Get to bed, now, and don't try to call again until you're better. I'll call Sallie tomorrow. I'll want to know."

"I expect you're right." He sounded tired. "Goodnight, then—and I love you."

Even over the telephone he could make it sound like a miracle.

She expected the evening to drag out interminably, remembering her restlessness before. Instead she rather enjoyed puttering about. She went upstairs, got comfortably into the old cotton dressing gown and set for herself a series of small chores she had been putting off—sewing the crystal buttons on a blouse back from the cleaners, lengthening a skirt, rinsing out stockings and gloves, mending a burn in a sweater. The last made her smile, recalling how it had occurred. A matchhead, when Mike was lighting his pipe, had flown off wildly, lodged, burning, against her sweater. There had been a flurried moment, his hands hurrying, beating, trying to recover it. Then, when it was safely out, the slowing, the linger-ing, the melting sweetness. There were beginning to be so many tender memories.

She wondered why she should feel so at peace this evening, when the other time had been so intolerable. There was even a comfortable, housewifely content tonight as she puttered about, lazily. At length it dawned on her, making her feel rather ashamed, that it was because this time he was safely at home, in bed, ill. Before he had been at large, spend-ing the hours with other people. The knowledge that if he was not here, he was at least not sharing himself with others, had been subconsciously acting as a sedative on her. Could she really be narrow and small-minded? So easily inclined to jealousy? She must be more careful of that emotion, she thought, soberly. It could be a corroding, rusting thing—it could even be destructive of everything good and fine between them.

It was especially surprising to her to recognize it in herself because she had never felt it before. With Walter she had been happy to have an occasional evening to herself, and when they were married it had often been a relief to her to have him go out alone. She reflected that marriage with Walter had offered her very little in the way of experience with love. It had taught her nothing of its sweeping, wonderful engulfment, and nothing of its perilous encroachments upon the emotions. To be in love was to be terribly vulnerable to the probability of pain and loss and heartbreak, and its best reward was its joy of necessary giving.

She thought of Tom and Lucia, of how there was almost no barrier between them, of either thought or emotion, and guiltily she realized she had been neglecting them woefully. They would never need her, for they needed no one else, but they *were* old friends and they deserved better of her. She determined she would see Lucia during this time Mike was laid up.

She awoke the next morning remarkably refreshed from a long, unbroken eight hours of sleep. Ruefully she admitted that Mike had been right. It was what she had needed. She hoped his night hadn't been too miserable, and she called, as early as she dared, to have word of him. "He's still asleep, Mrs. Browning," Sallie told her. "He must have been worn clear out."

She felt a pang of conscience. If she had needed rest, how much more he must have needed it. His work was so much more demanding, too. Probably that was more responsible than Sallie's germs or the exposure as a contributing factor to his taking cold. Sustained weariness, she recalled, was often at the bottom of such things. "When he wakes," she told the woman, "tell him I called, and do make him stay quiet, Sallie." She would have liked to say more, but decided against it.

"I'll do my best."

She had the morning free, since she had desk duty that night, so, remembering her intention to see Lucia, she got out her car and drove over around ten. It was going to be a fine day, she thought, glad the wintery spell was over and the sun was warmer. The sharpness was rapidly going from the air and it had the lift and lightness that comes only in spring. In a day or two it would be really warm again.

The town was one of old homes and spacious gardens and she enjoyed the short drive along the tree-shaded streets. There were many locust trees, and the heavy, sweet odor from the blooms was almost cloying. With some amusement she thought how little she had known, when she came, that this place would be her permanent home. It was a pleasant place to live, though, large enough for all the conveniences of a city, small enough for the friendliness and ease which go with short distances and the more or less intimate knowledge of one's neighbors. She felt content to think of it as home.

Her mind turned, practically, to her own affairs. She had better, she thought, sell the home that had been hers and Walter's. It would be a problem to keep it leased and it would soon run down and become expensive. As soon as she had seen Mike's house she would know better what of her own furniture she wanted to keep. It would entail a trip, she supposed—a conference with her attorney about selling, then there would be the necessity of selecting the furniture and seeing to its moving. But there was no hurry about it. Sometime during the summer, say July, would do very well. It would be wise, she decided, to have Mike's house done over, all the painting and remodeling, if that proved necessary, out of the way before having anything shipped. It was exciting to think about—and she had always enjoyed doing a house. It was so flexible and plastic in one's hands. She had no doubt she could make a charming home of Mike's place. Given space, which it had, and enough money, one always could.

She found Lucia supervising spring housecleaning, the place entirely topsy turvy, Lucia looking very efficient in white drill coveralls, the smoke from her cigarette curling above her rumpled head, standing in the middle of it giving orders. "Oh, Regina. Come in, if there's room. We've moved everything out and are doing windows and floors today."

She felt a little thrown off to find Lucia so active, when she had been thinking of a long, quiet talk with her, but she put it aside and offered to help.

"Oh, no. Once they're started we can leave them. We'll go upstairs where there's less confusion." She interrupted to shout at a colored boy. "When you've finished the windows in here, Zeke, start on the ones in the dining room."

"Yessum."

"Now, come along, my dear." She linked her arm through Regina's. "Let's have some coffee, shall we? I've just made a fresh pot."

Taking their coffee to the upstairs sitting room, they settled comfortably in the deep, shabby old chairs Lucia used in this informal room. She lit a cigarette, ran her hand through her hair. "My Lord! Every spring we go through this upheaval. I've told Tom it would be simpler just to pitch a tent some place."

"You'd die," Regina said, laughing. "You love all this—you know you do. If it weren't necessary, you'd create the necessity. I remember how you turned out our room at school."

Lucia stretched, cat-like, curling her arms above her head. "I know it. I've got to move things around every so often. Tom is being very patient this time." She dropped her arms. "It's been ages since we saw you. We were talking about it just the other night. What have you been doing with yourself?"

It might as well be now, she thought. A little demurely she dropped the bomb. "Getting myself engaged."

"What!" Lucia sat bolt upright, amazement making her face look blank. "You're teasing."

"No. It's true."

"But you haven't said a word . . . you haven't been . . . Who is it?"

"Mike Panelli."

Lucia sank back against the cushions. "Of course. I should have known." She laughed. "For one horrible moment I thought it might be Charles Garrett. But you've got better sense than that."

"I hope so."

"But, tell me . . . when did it happen? You've been so quiet about it. I didn't even know you'd been seeing him. Oh, your ankle—that started it, didn't it?"

"I expect so. But I'd seen him several times before without knowing who he was." She was conscious of her deep pleasure in talking about him, telling someone, finally, who would understand all she felt. "I had even sketched him—there was something about him . . ."

Lucia bobbed her head. "I know. He's very attractive. Regina, I'm so glad, so very happy for you. It's precisely what I wanted for you—not Mike particularly—but someone. I told Tom . . ."

"I know exactly what you told Tom," she interrupted, "I think I knew it even when you were urging me to come here. I can almost hear you telling him—'What Regina needs is to get married again. If we can bring her to Hilton, we can see to it ourselves.'"

"No such thing," Lucia said, with spirit, "what I said was only that I wished you could find some nice man and get married again. And you have, very slyly, too, I might add."

"Not really. It's been so gradual I hardly realized it myself. Just a few times together—then, bang!"

"That's perfect. Bang! That's the way it should happen. That was the way it was with me." She sipped her coffee, then frowned slightly. "Isn't he still tied up with that witch he was married to? I don't recall his having been divorced."

"He's getting it now."

"Well, it's high time. I've wondered so often why he waited . . ." she broke off, stared absently out the window. "Do you mind at all that he's a Catholic?"

"No. Why should I?"

"You shouldn't, of course. I just wondered. Sometimes it does bother. But then one has to be broad-minded about these things. I've often said that if Tom had been Mohammedan I'd have married him just the same. I don't know much about it—one has such vague ideas—but don't Catholics get annulments instead of divorces? I seem to have heard . . ."

Regina thought of the vague things she had heard, also, about which she had no actual knowledge. "They do have annulments, don't they? But I suppose they have divorces, too, under certain circumstances. Mike wouldn't be getting one otherwise. He's a very good Catholic, Lucia."

"Is he?" Lucia's eyes were speculative. "Does he expect you to become one too?"

"I don't know. He hasn't made an issue of it. He really hasn't said anything at all about that part of it. But if it's important to him, I suppose I will."

"I don't think you'd like it."

It was too near her own discomfort and she moved restlessly under it. "Probably not. But I would rather, if it made him the least bit unhappy for me not to."

Lucia shrugged. "Perhaps Mike would leave his church, if it became an issue."

About that she was now certain. "No—he wouldn't. I told you. He's a very devout person. It surprised me, terribly, but he is. His whole family is. He has a sister who is a nun. And they're Italian, you know. If he were more like us . . . from a plain American background—but his grandfather came here from Italy only fifty years ago. His father was born there. They're like a family that lived next door to us when I was a child—the family and the Church—that's their life. He's been trained to it since he was born."

"Well, then," Lucia raised her brows, "it's pretty much up to you, isn't it? But there are people who marry Catholics and don't go into the

Church, aren't there? So long as you're willing to be married by a priest and promise to rear the children in the Church. Seems to me I've heard something of that sort."

"Oh, I don't know, Lucia. I'm woefully ignorant about all of it. I've been waiting for Mike to say something, but he hasn't. He probably will, when he thinks of it, or when the time gets nearer."

"When are you planning to be married?"

"August, probably. That's about as soon as it will be possible. The divorce will take three months, and it's only just started. Mike wants it immediately when that's final."

"Are you going to your parents' for it?"

"No. I was wondering . . ."

Lucia took the words out of her mouth. "Then we'll have it here. Don't say a word—it'll be fun. Tom can give the bride away . . . oh, that room must be painted. It's far too shabby for a wedding."

"Oh, Lucia—who will notice? There'll only be Mike's people and you and Tom. Don't start dithering about it, please."

"Who's dithering? A wedding is a wedding, my dear. You'll be glad to remember a magnificent one, in your old age." She made a wide gesture with her arms. "We'll have a whole wall of flowers, with the altar in the middle . . . what are you going to wear?"

She gave it up and fell to planning with as much enthusiasm and excitement as Lucia. It added to her pleasure that after marriage she would always be living near this one good friend, whose knowledge of her went so far back, and whose love and concern had weathered the storms of that first, inauspicious linking of herself and Walter. It was just part of the goodness about it all.

They had only got through the wedding and halfway through re-decorating Mike's house when it was time for her to go. There was a small, giggly contretemps when she could not find her car keys, and Lucia teased her about being absent-minded, going with her when they had been located to the car. "Tell me anything at all I can do, dear," she said, leaning over the door to plant a quick, affectionate kiss. "And I wouldn't worry about this religion thing. It will work out all right."

"You're very encouraging. I think it will, too—really. Mike's very capable, and he won't be impossible about it."

She drove away still glowing, and feeling very young, very girlish, and very bride-like.

Chapter Seventeen

❦

"Mike, there are any number of really good pieces here. We can use most of them nicely. Some of it, of course . . ."

"Some of it," he said, laughing, "is pure junk. Throw it out if you like. Give it away—burn it. I am only sentimental about that bedroom furniture. It came from the old country with my grandfather."

She had seen his face when he showed her that bedroom, which had been his parents', and she had known it was this he had hesitated to speak of that other time. The room had every look of having been closed up a long time, a musty smell pervading the air, and the large pieces being covered with dust covers. Feeling uncertain, not knowing whether his hesitation had been because it had been his and Eva's room, or whether Eva had not liked the heavy dark pieces and he was afraid she might not either, she had looked first at his face, when he had thrown off the covers, to give her some clue. It had revealed only a hovering anxiety and quickly she had determined it was more important to set him at ease. "They're beautiful old pieces, darling. Really beautiful. How fortunate that you still have them."

The look of happiness which rubbed out the anxiety was her reward. "Are they really good? I don't know—I've always loved them."

She looked more closely. The bed was immense, deeply carved, and blackened with age, but she thought it was rosewood. A chest, also enormous, and a tall armoire, a desk and two heavy, much used chairs, were all of the same wood. "They need refinishing—the varnish has cracked—but they'll be very special pieces when that's done. I'm certain of it. If we do the walls very light—white, or a pale ivory, they'll be show-pieces. I have a rug—oh, you've seen it. That one in my bedroom. It will go beautifully in here."

She looked about. The room needed the large pieces. It was a tre-mendously large room, with windows on one side going from the floor to the ceiling. It had been kept fairly simple, however, except for the gilt and red paper on the walls. It would be easy to replace that. The wood-work was good and would take paint nicely. In her mind's eye it began to shape up. But he was talking.

"That's fine, then. Do you mind if it's our room? I've always wanted it. Of course it was Mama's until she left. Then Eva didn't care for it." Rather shyly he glanced at her, smiling a little awkwardly. "I'm sure glad she didn't, now."

"So am I." She could be entirely honest about it, now that he had said it. "Are you getting tired, darling? This is just your second day out of bed, after all."

"No. I'm doing fine. But you've seen most of it, now. There's just my room and the attic."

"They can wait. Why don't we go downstairs again and I'll have Sallie make us some tea and you can lie on the sofa."

"It might be a good idea at that. My legs are pretty wobbly still."

What had begun as a heavy cold had turned out to be a virus infec-tion which had kept him in bed the best part of the week. Worried and unhappy about him, she had obediently kept away until Sallie told her he was getting up one day. Then she had overridden his protests and come to see for herself how he was getting along. It had shocked her to see him thinner and looking very wan and drained of energy. "It's the damned drugs," he had told her. "They're worse than the disease. I know now why so many of my patients don't like to take them. They hit the infection hard, but they do something to you if taken a long time to get over. I feel like an empty sack."

She had come the next day, bearing good, nourishing things to eat. Not, she told him, that Sallie had neglected him, but Sallie's invention stopped with the basic things and he had grown tired of them. Today, then, he had been dressed, feeling much better, and had suggested they make a tour of the house.

She was almost overwhelmed at its size. There were fourteen rooms, some of them small. Even the two bathrooms were immense, and the parlor, as Mike called it, was almost barn-like in its vastness. There were small inconveniences, as in all old houses—not enough closets, too many dark doors and windows, an ancient furnace with ugly, space-taking radiators scattered about, and the kitchen was hopelessly labor-wasting in its arrangement and size. None of the problems were insurmountable, however. The floors were good, the rooms were not too badly arranged, and by shifting doors and windows about, painting, doing the kitchen over entirely, it would become comfortable and rather lovely. The grounds were roomy and while the plantings had been done hit or miss, they had the virtue of age to cover the mistakes. None of it was impossible and she felt very happy about it. She even felt eager to begin work on it and thought it none too soon.

She brought the tea tray into the library, which apparently Mike used most of the downstairs rooms. It was a very masculine room, all books and leather, even the couch on which he lay being covered in dark, well-worn leather. He was used to this room, she thought, handing him his cup, and she would leave it alone almost entirely. He needed at least this one retreat untouched. "When could we begin on it, dear? It will take several months, I'm afraid."

"Well, then, we'd better get started. Shall I see some people about it?"

"If you will. Then I'll spend all the time I can spare supervising. Mike, it's going to be such fun!"

He stirred his tea, laughing at her, his eyes warm and affectionate on her. "I'm glad you think so. It's not my idea of fun, I'm afraid. You look like a little girl with her first doll house. Do most women like such things?"

"Of course. It's the most feminine of instincts—making a home. I'll love every minute of it. I expect it's going to be pretty expensive, though."

They had never discussed finances, either, it occurred to her. She guessed that it would be no problem. He was a successful doctor, and she had her own small income—but nothing had been said about money at all.

"How expensive?"

She tried to think and arrived at a rough figure. "Around five thousand, I'd say—to make it really liveable and comfortable." She added hastily, "Of course, you've been living here all your life and I imagine it seems all right to you the way it is."

"No. I've lived here, it's true, but I haven't had to keep it. I know it's difficult, because even Mama used to complain. Five thousand can be managed."

He was eating hungrily, she saw, and was glad of it. He couldn't afford the loss of much weight. He ran a little to slenderness anyhow. She gave him another muffin. "If it pushes you, darling, I have a little of my own."

He smiled at her, generously. "Keep it for your own needs. Maybe I should say that I have around fifteen thousand a year. Does that seem too little to you?"

"Heavens, Mike! Do you think I'm accustomed to luxury? That seems a princely amount to me. I'm a *very* good manager, in any case."

She had finished her tea and she had laid the napkin and cup back on the tray, got up and wandered about the room. "Your father bought a lot of books, didn't he? Or are these yours?"

"Some of them. Most of them were his. They're largely medical things. You have to keep up, you know. These muffins are wonderful. Did you make them?"

She nodded.

"You're a very good cook, too, aren't you?"

"I like to cook. It's as creative to me as painting. You like this room, don't you, Mike?"

He was filling his pipe. Over it, he looked at her humorously. "I have a lot of memories connected with it. This is where Papa lived, when he was at home. This is where I was called to account, more times than I like to remember. This is where punishment was meted out, too seldom for my own good, I suspect. Papa hated to punish, but Mama wouldn't, so it fell to him. I've stood before that desk many times and wiggled until he finished a lecture. I feel rather close to him, working in here."

"We'll leave it just as it is then, darling. And we'll leave your bedroom until last, so you can have a place to sleep in all the clutter. When we have to turn you out, our room will be finished and you can move in there."

"Our room . . ." He drew on his pipe slowly, then he laid it down. "I love that plural possessive. It has such a nice, married sound. Come here. You haven't been near me all afternoon. I'm not infectious now."

"Mike, I have! I kissed you when I came . . ."

"That doesn't count. You know what I mean. Come here."

Obediently she went to him on the sofa. She knew by the piercing tenderness she felt when he kissed her how much she had been missing him. It was terrible, she thought, beautifully terrible to love someone so much. It left one with so few resources. He lifted his head and said, softly, against her ear, "Let's go up to our room."

"Now?"

"Now." He stood and drew her to her feet, swaying her toward him a little. "It's been a terribly long time."

"I know, but . . ." She said the first thing that came into her mind to give herself time. "There's Sallie."

"I'll arrange that. There are errands."

"Mike, I don't think . . . it's really . . ."

"Please," he said, urgency in his voice. "Let's make it *our* room truly. I want to—very much."

He was usually so thoughtful of her. The picture was all wrong, somehow, and she was very reluctant. Yet, seeing him so urgent, she knew that whatever his reasons they were more than physical. He had some dream about that room—he had confessed to a special feeling for it. Her decision to make it their room had confirmed her place in it to him. But oughtn't it to wait? Was this truly the fortunate hour? Her reason for reluctance was so vague as to be only a disturbing thing, not really valid against his great wish. She only knew, uneasily, that she would rather not. Searching his face she saw that he was waiting almost tensely and she had not the heart to deny him. "The bed, darling, it isn't . . ."

Brusquely he motioned to the stairs. "There are things in the chest in the hall. You go on up. Can you manage?"

"Of course."

She still felt very unhappy about it, something indefinable holding her back, and her unhappiness disturbed her more than the reasons for it. If it was just the house—his house, she thought, climbing the stairs slowly, she had better come to terms with it immediately. She was going to live here a long time.

They were lying, lazy, sleepy, and almost drugged with content, talking only a little, now and then. The sun was shining almost hotly through the tall windows. "Why did they make those windows so tall?" she asked, "they aren't, in the rest of the house."

He turned his head and looked idly at the windows, nuzzling her hair with his chin. "There's a little balcony out there. They open."

"How nice." She raised on an elbow to look.

He pulled her back down. "You're disturbing my pillow."

She laughed at him and let him rest his head against her shoulder again. "Your siege with that virus has made you terribly lazy, darling."

"Has it? I think I've always liked your shoulder, haven't I?"

Gaining courage from his drowsiness and his relaxed and peaceful mood, she asked, "Mike, why did you want this—today—here?"

"Oh, just an idea."

She refused to be put off. "No, but why? There was some good reason."

"Not really. It has been a week, you know."

"That wasn't it. There was something else, and you may as well tell me. I'll keep nagging until you do."

"Can't you guess?" He tilted his head to look at her.

"It had something to do with it being your parents' room, but beyond that . . ."

He took her hand and bent the fingers one at a time. It was a thing he often did when he was searching for words. She waited until he looked at her again, helplessly. "You'll think it's awfully silly."

"I won't. I promise."

"Well, then—it's just—there was simply the feeling that Mama and Papa ought to know . . . and approve. I knew I'd know instantly if . . . I'm making a hash of it. It can't be properly said. It was just a feeling I had, and it had to be settled at the moment."

"I know it did," she said, wryly.

"You didn't mind, really, did you? You see . . . all their children were conceived in this bed, and . . ."

She looked at him in amazement. "Mike, you're not suggesting . . ."

"Oh, shut up! Of course not. I told you. It was just a feeling that they'd somehow like it . . ."

Gently she said, "I think what you're trying to say is that, like a little boy, which you were when you used to come into this room often, you needed their permission."

He drew in his breath. "I knew you'd understand."

"Darling, couldn't you have said so—downstairs?"

"I didn't quite know how." He looked at her ruefully. "It sounded so asinine."

"It doesn't. But you really are an amazing person. You're such a mixture of sentiment and common sense. And you're so astonishingly young in so many ways." She couldn't help adding, teasingly, "Do you think they approve?"

"I'm certain of it."

"My guess," she said, daringly, "is that they wouldn't. They'd probably think we made very free with their room."

"Oh, that. I wasn't thinking of that. I meant us—in the larger term. Us, being married."

She was puzzled beyond all understanding, now. He really made no sense at all. "You sound as if this had been a test of some sort. I'm beginning to wonder if I passed it."

The face he turned to her was so unhappy that it shocked her. She snatched his head to her. "Darling, what is it? What did I say? I didn't mean anything . . . I was just talking."

"You," he said, his face muffled against her throat, "would always pass it. It's I who fail."

She was never more bewildered in her life. What could he be talking about? She comforted him in the only way she knew, holding him, stroking his hair, kissing him softly. "I think you'd better give over such morbid ideas. You can never fail at anything, my darling. You're the most wonderful, the best, the very best, the one I love most in all the world . . . how can you fail?"

He only shook his head, refusing any more words.

The silence which followed was so long and so deep that when the doorbell shrilled suddenly, it pierced it as shatteringly as if it had been glass. Frozen, they stared at each other. A fire alarm could not have been more shocking. The bell splintered the stillness again. "Damn!" Mike muttered, scrambling for his clothing, "Who can that be?"

Tiredly, Regina closed her eyes. She knew, now, what had been wrong. It was this that had given her such uneasiness, this that had been subtly wrong with the picture. It was inevitable that they should be disturbed here, and that there would be this sudden, shocking, shaming guiltiness.

"For two cents," Mike said, "I'd let them ring. Except the door may be open and they might be capable of walking right on in. You stay here, darling."

She turned over and dug her head in the pillow, finding herself incapable of replying. She knew when he left the room because she heard the door close gently. But she did not lift her head from the pillow for a long, long time. It was not in her to feel less guilty than she did. It suddenly seemed so sordid, so grimy. It was on a level with all lewd and hidden things, and it did no good to say they were different. They were different only in their intention, not at all in the act. There, they were no different than the commonest street loafer, picking up the commonest streetwalker. In the essentials, it was alike, and in the eyes of nature at least, with the same purpose. It made no difference, actually, that they meant to be married as soon as possible. With decency they should have waited. To lie here, closeted away, in a horror of being discovered—she thought of all the vile four-letter words that described it and shuddered away from them. There was neither grace nor beauty left, and barely the shreds of love. She had felt so innocent—but then, all lovers felt innocent, she supposed. It was the glaring light of discovery, or this shattering fear of it, that brought the shame and guilt.

So she continued her flagellation, lashing at her bare flesh, feeling the whips on her tender conscience, feeling revulsion for herself, and what was more terrible, feeling it for Mike. If he hadn't insisted—but some measure of honesty required that she take her share of the blame. She had been willing—from the start she had been willing. Her face felt hot and she wished she could leave at once. She did not even want to see Mike right now—could not, she thought, in an agony of embarrassment.

When she had worn herself out with her self-imposed hair shirt, she roused and dressed, being as quiet as possible. She wanted her bag, with its small pocket comb for her hair, and her lipstick. From experience she knew that her hair would be tousled and her mouth ravaged. In spite of herself, she smiled. Mike did such a thorough job of kissing her. Some small feeling of tenderness for him returned, and with it a little of her self-esteem. What *did* it matter? It changed nothing between them. It was the merest accident, and he was evidently handling it beautifully. She had been hearing the murmur of voices from below for some time. She had allowed herself an excess of emotion, she thought, and an unnecessary excess at that. Just the same, she told herself, hunting vaguely around for her bag, never again here. He could plead all he wanted. There would be no opportunity for this sort of thing again.

Realizing she was only half-searching for the bag, her mind almost entirely preoccupied with her thoughts, she stopped still to think. Had she brought it upstairs at all? Her heart lurched as she had a sudden picture of it, lying quite conspicuously on the desk in the library. To her astonishment it struck her as so completely the last straw that it was funny, and she giggled uncontrollably. She clapped her hand over her mouth, knowing she was at the stage where hysterical laughter could overtake her, too devastatingly to be stopped.

She sat down in one of the deep chairs to wait. It surely couldn't be much longer. If it were a patient Mike would send him along in a moment. If it were a friend of his, he would certainly do the same as soon as he decently could. Sitting there, idly looking about the room, she began to plan its reordering. Ivory walls, she thought, and woodwork—and the old pieces restored, dark and shiny against them. Her beautiful old rug on the floor, and red curtains, of course—a rich, crimson spread for the bed. She tiptoed to the windows. She wanted to see the balcony. She was halfway across the room when Mike called. "Regina? Can you come down? Father Vincent is here."

She stood as if she had been speared in her tracks. What could have got into him? Didn't he know she would look exactly as if she had been in bed? He could order his face and hair and clothing in a moment. Hers would be a dead giveaway. She was suddenly furious with him, until she remembered the bag. Of course—he had had to do something about that.

She answered. "Just a moment, darling."

She looked wildly about. If she could just find a comb. She ran her hands through her hair, conscious that she was probably only making it worse. The bathroom! She flew down the hall and sighed with relief when she saw his comb. In the mirror she saw that her worst fears were true. There wasn't a vestige of lipstick left. And of course there would be none here, unless . . . but she would not use any she might find here! She decided to wash her face—then she had a brilliant idea. If she went down slightly rumpled, with dust on her hands, perhaps even on her face, there was the perfectly good excuse that she had been going over the house prior to redecorating it—had even been browsing in the attic, maybe. There had been enough dust on that chest in the bedroom, she remembered, to do it. Feeling conspiratorial and rather elated, she smeared it around, did an excellent job of a spot on her nose and one high on her cheek, made her hands unsightly with it.

On impulse, then, she picked up an ornate figurine from the chest, and with it in her hands, went slowly downstairs, her heart thudding painfully hard in her chest. She tried to assume a puzzled look as she went into the library. "Whatever is this, Mike? It isn't bisque. I don't recognize it at all. Oh, Father Vincent." She wondered if she overdid the surprise. "I'm sorry. I didn't know you were here. Mike's voice was rather indistinct. I only heard him say come down."

She did not allow herself to glance at Mike. She didn't dare. If he was surprised at her act, however, he didn't give her away. He waited until she and the priest had shaken hands and seated themselves, then he took the figurine from her, turned it up and looked at the base. "I'm not sure what it is. It's one of Mama's pieces, I suppose. Where did you find it?"

"On the chest in that room at the end of the hall. We're going over the house, Father." She might as well, she thought, be hung for a sheep as a lamb, so she added, "We're planning to be married this summer and the house must be redone before then."

"I see." His face was as smoothly placid, as bland and unrevealing as a child's. He glanced about the room. "I suppose it's going to be a rather large order."

"Not too large. Mike's parents had many nice pieces. I've been trying to choose from them. But I'm forgetting. Did Mike give you tea?" The role of hostess came easy to her. There was, after all, no reason for him to suppose there was anything more than what appeared on the surface. She felt a small lurch of triumph at being in command of the situation, at being so acceptably, so rightly, the lady of this house, and he the guest.

"No, but I'm afraid I haven't time. I only stopped to see how he was doing. You seem to be taking very good care of him. He looks very nearly well again."

The remark stung her. It meant so little, or so much. Very well, she thought, her chin going up—if that's the way you want it. Who had a better right to take care of him? They were not hiding . . . her thought faltered—well, they were not hiding their intention to marry. "I think," she said, deliberately, "he had picked up a little since I began feeding him." Let him make what he would of that.

Mike made his contribution, smilingly. There was none of his reluctance to meet the eyes of the priest this time, she saw happily. Instead he looked contented, a little amused, and his eyes on her were reassuring and affirming. He was standing beside her all the way. "Sallie's cooking lacks something in the way of creativeness," he said. "Regina has an inspired way with food."

"That's good." The priest rose. "I must be going, Mike. I'm delighted to see you looking so well. We'll be seeing you out again soon, I suppose."

Mike stood, to escort him to the door. "Next week, I hope. Barton seems to be managing well, so I shan't be in too much of a hurry."

"You're probably wise. These things take longer than one realizes. Mrs. Browning . . ."

With the poise that was so natural to her she took his hand. "When we are married, Father Vincent, I hope you will come often. Mike is very fond of you."

A little sadly the priest looked at her. "And I of him. He is a very rare person, Mrs. Browning. You have . . . he means a great deal to me, and he has been of inestimable help in the parish."

"I'm sure he has."

For the first time, Mike looked uncomfortable, but it passed as he led the priest down the hall.

When he returned they looked at each other, then collapsed onto the sofa, helpless with laughter. "Whew!" he gasped, when he could, and wiping his eyes, "that was too close for comfort."

"It certainly was! Never again, Mike—don't you dare ever suggest it here."

He raised a hand. "I'll swear it. Darling, you should have been an actress. However did you think of all that dust?"

"Oh, just a womanly thing. I was in such a terrible predicament— my hair, no lipstick. He saw my bag, didn't he?"

"He couldn't have helped it. There it was—larger than life. There was only one thing to do. Get you down here. I knew I could count on your coming up with something."

"I could have killed you at first. Then I remembered. I'd been look- ing for the bag. Otherwise I mightn't have."

Their laughter was a healing thing, and she blessed it later, when she was at home again, remembering the torrent of emotions when she had lain there alone. It had got them over the worst possible time, and it had been like balm on all the bruising soreness. A man might be able to take such things in his stride—but not a woman, she thought. Not this woman, in any event. She would be very glad when it would all be over and they could be safely, legally, and publicly together. It would take a long time, she reflected, for the memory of that searing shame to be erased from her mind.

Chapter Eighteen

❧

May turned into June with an abandoned flowering of roses all over the town. Regina thought she had never seen so many. Every garden, including her own, was suddenly aflame with their profusion and color. The town called itself, through the Chamber of Commerce, the City of Roses, and with good reason, she thought.

There was also the first heat of the summer, and a flurry of activity centering around commencement. Seniors went about with a haunted look on their faces. Hopefully they had committed themselves to invitations, to class rings, to the rental of caps and gowns, but now at the last moment, with finals and term papers rearing their ugly heads over them, they felt harried, doubtful and fearful. They made desperate efforts to make up, by long hours in the library and in their rooms, the effortless hours they had spent loitering in the Casbah, their name for the dingy little corner restaurant they had appropriated for their own use. Feeling pity for them, for it was always so, Regina did what she could to help them.

With failure and all its catastrophic results a grinning specter over their shoulders, they begged for extra hours in the reading rooms, for extra time with the reference books, for extra privileges in the stacks. It would have been cruel to remind them there had been the entire term. She had done the same thing herself, as had almost every other college student since time began, and she knew the sudden, grim awakening which had come to them, felt sympathetic, and granted as many privileges as she could. She spent long hours with them, tracking down the most remote references, borrowing volumes which she did not have from the university, calling upon her vague knowledge of languages to help interpret ambiguous passages. She began to feel as if she were trying to graduate herself.

She neglected Mike a little during those weeks, and when he protested, finally told him, "It will soon be over, darling. Think of it as an epidemic of flu—it's quite similar. Your time wouldn't be your own in that case. And if I'm a good librarian, mine is not my own now."

"But you haven't been free an evening this week. And look at you now. Your face is almost as white as your pillow. You're wearing yourself out, and I don't like it."

"It's mostly the heat, dear."

She knew she must look tired, her face drained by the heat and the long hours. He had come late, catching her by surprise. She hadn't had time for a bath, she hadn't repaired her face, and her hair felt limp and ragged and, she was certain, must look the way it felt. When he had arrived, whistling and full of energy, fresh from a tub, she had looked at him helplessly, more than a little provoked with him for not giving her warning, and not at all in the mood for him. She had gone up with him, however, without protest. She *had* been using him rather badly, and he looked so happily anticipatory. All the same, she thought, a residue of irritation remaining, he was taking a lot for granted—coming and going as he pleased. It was what one got for being so readily available.

There had been a small feeling of triumph in being so busy herself that he must be kept waiting these past weeks. She hadn't voiced it, even to herself, but there had been a small satisfaction in putting him off, reversing the situation. It had been a sort of legitimate paying him off for all the times she had waited. He would know better how she had felt so often now. It did something for her self-esteem, which had never quite recovered from the shattering afternoon when Father Vincent had surprised them. However vaguely, it restored a measure of her independence.

He raised himself on an elbow to look at her. "How did you get home tonight? Walk? I noticed your car isn't in the garage."

She wished he wouldn't hover so—it was too hot. They had turned the lamp back on to keep from falling asleep, since it was so late, and the room, usually cool enough, seemed stiflingly close to her. The heat from his body only increased her discomfort. "Charles brought me." It was so unimportant to her that she barely thought of what she had said.

Immediately, however, she felt him stiffen. "Charles? Isn't that the fellow you went to the city with?"

Rasped by the heat, by her knowledge that she looked tired and drained, by weariness, and most of all by the sudden chill in his voice, she became stubborn and refused to ameliorate the bald fact. He could take it or leave it. He had no right to question her. "Yes."

"Well!" He flounced away from her, making the springs shake.

Her head was beginning to ache and the movement jarred it. "Don't *do* that, Mike," she flared out at him, more sharply than she intended—but he could just behave like an adult, instead of like an adolescent. She wasn't going to have every move she made questioned, she wasn't going to suffer any teenage spasm of jealousy. She quite forgot her own agony of jealousy when she had seen him with Teresa. The shoe was altogether on the other foot now.

"Sorry—but you took me by surprise. I thought you weren't going to see him any more. I suppose he's around the library quite a lot, though—and brings you home when he likes."

She could have laughed at the forced dignity with which he spoke if she hadn't been so provoked with him. "Don't be silly." It was really ridiculous of him and she would not explain. Not content with that, however, she added, "But if he did bring me home every night, it would be nothing for you to get in a dither about." Even in her exasperation she caught the false note in that and wondered what possessed her to say it.

"Who's in a dither?"

"You are. You're behaving exactly as if you were eighteen, instead of thirty-five."

"I am not. But after all, we *are* going to be married—or have you changed your mind about that, too? The way you've been putting me off these past weeks I'm beginning to wonder."

"You know why I've had to put you off." She was growing rather weary of all this play-acting. "I've explained it."

"And with Charles very handy all the time. Oh, yes, you've explained it." Like a wounded Adonis he lay as far as possible from her in the limited width of the bed, very careful not to touch her at all.

"Well," she said, resignedly, "he *does* teach at the college and it *is* necessary for him to use the library."

"And I'll bet he uses it more than he needs to, too!"

"You're being ridiculous."

"Well, doesn't he?"

"How should I know what his requirements are, Mike? How much he needs to use the library?"

She knew that one simple word of explanation would end the whole childish situation, but some obstinacy in her refused to say it. Something long hidden, an irritation with her own helplessness in their relationship, an exasperation with being the feminine and passive recipient, a sense of guilt over the necessity for secrecy, and an irrational desire to blame him for the necessity, had overtaken her and was urging her to cruelty. She did not recognize it as such—she thought he was being preposterously immature and she did not intend to humor him.

"Why couldn't you have called me? The telephone is very convenient, you know."

"And *you* know I never call you. I never have, except when you were ill. Not even when I've been the most uneasy about you, or you've kept me waiting the longest."

There was a considerable amount of heat in the remark and he was quick to catch it. "Oh, so now it's I who have kept you waiting."

"Many times. I can't recall the times I've sat here waiting to know whether you were coming or not. I *never* know until the last moment. Do you think I like it?"

"You knew I was a doctor."

His voice was entirely cold and with dismay she realized he must have gone through this a hundred times before. But she could not bring herself to abandon the tack she had taken. She was too angry herself now. "I think you take full advantage of it, too."

He stared at her, and she was aghast at the steeliness of is eyes. "What do you mean by that?"

She had no good idea what she had meant, but she returned his look, aware that her heart had begun thumping wildly. She had gone much too far, further than she had intended, but she knew no way to back down. "You certainly have the opportunity to be out with someone else. I'd hardly know it if you were."

"Do you really think that?"

She shrugged impatiently. "How do I know what you do when you aren't with me."

"I said do you *really* think that? If you do..." he seized her wrists. "Do you?"

She was invaded by an unreasoning and boiling anger at the grip of his hands. If he was going to grab at her every time he got angry . . . she twisted with instinctive resistance, and getting an arm free struck out at him, hitting him hard across the face. It stopped them both, as frozen as marble, and he hung over her, his face slowly blanching until the red marks of her fingers were like welts against its whiteness. "I think I had better go," he said, slowly.

Still possessed by the blind force of anger she made no move to prevent him. "Perhaps you had."

Dazed, breathing hard, feeling very like a fishwife, it was only when he was out of the bed, dressing swiftly, that full realization of what she had done reached her. The quick fear that shot through her was sickening in its impact. She had never meant . . . she was only trying . . . she couldn't bear him to go. What had come over her? What she had done was inexcusable. She had baited and tormented him beyond all bounds. She had been more childish than he, simply to satisfy her female vanity. It would serve her right if he walked out of her life forever, and the merest thought of it sent her heart down with such a sinking as to make her physically ill. "Mike," she called to him, softly.

He was putting on his shoes, bent over, and he looked up at her without answering. His face was still white and she could have wept over the red marks her hand had made. It was also still very stern, and the eyes he turned on her were as remote as if she had not even been there. She had gone too far—he would never forgive her. She held out her arm, appealingly, "Please . . . Mike."

With a rush that brought him stumbling to his knees beside her he was in her arms. "Darling, darling . . . it was so beastly of me . . . so cruel. I didn't mean it . . . truly I didn't. It was only . . ."

His breath came in gusts against her throat. "It doesn't matter. Say you love me. Just say you love me."

"You know I love you. It must have been the heat, darling . . . and I'm so tired. It's so simply explained, really. My car is in the shop. He only gave me a lift this once. And he's hardly ever in the library. I hardly ever see him. He's the least important thing in the world . . . you surely know that."

"I know . . . I do know, believe me. I don't know what got into me, either. Not seeing you for so long, perhaps. Feeling like a child whose mother had gone away. But it doesn't matter."

She made room for him on the bed, felt how cold his hands had become. "Mike, you're cold! In all this heat."

He shivered a little, "I felt like death." Quieter, he kissed her. "Oh, Regina, Regina, never quarrel with me again. I am too far committed . . . I couldn't live without you . . . you've replaced. . . ."

She soothed and reassured him. "You won't have to. I couldn't live without you, either. We're both too committed." She laughed shakily. "What *was* all this about, anyway? Such a tempest in a teapot."

He kissed her again, more lingeringly, and with a kind of radiant tenderness she turned to him. The restoration of peace and happiness made them both exhilarated beyond sense and they were alternately silly and tenderly loving. She had the feeling of having climbed out of a swampy bog, of having rid herself of earthiness, of standing, finally, on a cool, windswept peak, everything commonplace and mundane left far below.

As if inspired by the same winged feeling, he stayed until the inexorable hands of the clock told them that dawn would soon be coming, and even then, though he was contrite, he was reluctant to go. He got as far as the door a dozen times only to come back to kiss her once more, to hold her, touch her again, as if fearing to let her go. "Two more months," he said, "just two more months and this will all be over."

"I know. It will be wonderful, won't it?"

"It will be more than wonderful. Regina . . ." he paused, repeated her name reflectively, "Regina . . . do you know what your name means?"

"Of course. Queen, I think."

He was sitting once more on the side of the bed. "Queen. Queen of heaven." He continued softly. "*Salve Regina, Mater misericordise, vita, dulcedo . . . Ad te clamamus, exules filii Evae.*" Lost in reverie, he gazed at the pool of light on the floor, and said, at length, out of that reverie, slowly and very softly, "A man could pray to the woman he loves."

She knew instantly what he meant, was made uneasy by it, but she kissed him lightly and said, "Mike—you really *must* go. It's very late, or early, or something."

"I know," he gathered himself together. "I'm going this minute. Tonight?"

She hesitated. She would be tired beyond all endurance tonight, after no sleep at all, or at best only three or four hours, but she was uncertain of him now. He saw the hesitation and was quickly contrite. "I'm brutal, aren't I? I'll not come at all—I promise. Get to bed early, and sleep the clock round. Doctor's orders."

"I need to," she confessed. "But I'll miss you."

Cheerfully he said, "We have a lifetime ahead of us. Sunday, then."

"All right. Sunday." On sudden thought, she added, "Shall we go to church?"

He was noncommittal. "If you like."

She hadn't been to church with him since Easter and she had rather a wish to go again. It might, she thought, more or less as an afterthought, bring him to say what he expected her to do about things.

When he had finally gone she lay sleepless for a long time, troubled and thinking. He was so mysteriously bewildering at times. That affair of his parents' room—this reference to her name and the *Salve Regina*. There was no making him out, but it was almost as if he had made a substitute of her for something very important to him—equated her, in some way, with his religion. It made her uncomfortable. No mortal was ever made for that high throne. She could not be Mary, Mother of God, to him, nor should she be called upon to be. Mary's smile was divine, and for the altar. Hers, as he had the most valid reasons for knowing, was quite human and very earthily for him. He could not say his Hail Marys to her, for she was limited by the very humanity of her love.

One had only, she thought, to hear mass said a few times for it to become familiar. There really wasn't much mystery to it, upon analysis. As she listened to the *Kyrie* and then to the *Agnus Dei* she was struck once again by the lulling repetition, and it occurred to her that it was very cleverly designed for exactly that lulling, trance-like effect. Every movement was prescribed, every word indicated. The familiar was so safe, one needn't think, one need only murmur the words that must surely be the outward sign of the inner security. To touch the beads, to say over the words that had come down, unchanged, through the centuries—it must give one a feeling of timelessness and a sense of an eternal home. If one followed the rules, one was never in danger.

Father Vincent had turned and the communicants were going up to the railing. She glanced at Mike, who remained motionless, his eyes fixed on the altar. Perhaps he was waiting. There were always some who did, until the first line had finished. But as they left the altar and others took their place, he remained seated beside her. She had no idea when or under what circumstances one took Communion. Perhaps it wasn't necessary every time. He always had before, though.

When they had been dismissed, however, and were in the car driving home, she felt curious about it. She mentioned it. "You didn't take Communion today."

"No."

He had been very quiet all morning, his face wearing the deliberately impassive look which she had come to know was his mask when he was troubled. She doubted that he knew how much it gave him away. His face was ordinarily so mobile, his eyes so expressive, that the assumption of that set, impassive look always told her of some inner disturbance. She imagined it was second nature to him, that he had trained himself to it to keep from frightening patients when he had to give them bad news. She knew him now in all his moods, so well that she knew, also, how often it occurred when it was a personal and emotional thing with him. He hadn't a poker face. He had recourse only to this unnatural inexpressiveness. Her question had set the lines about his mouth now.

"Don't you have to?"

His foot was restless on the accelerator and the car jerked ahead. "I hadn't been to Confession."

"Oh." She knew it would be better not to pursue it any further, but she was beginning to resent his reticences, and she decided it might as well be discussed now. "How often must you go? Before Communion every time?"

He shook his head impatiently. "Not necessarily. Once a year is mandatory—but as often as you feel the need—as often as you have . . ."

"How often do you usually go?"

He looked at her, his exasperation showing. "Once a week." They were meeting a line of traffic and he maneuvered the car through it. Then, a little absently, he added, "It's very difficult not to sin—longer than that."

"Sin?"

He smiled at her, awkwardly. "What do you think Confession is for? You know—you forget and break a fast day . . . you forget and swear . . . you forget and are guilty of envy...there are a thousand things."

As well as if he had marked it in black and white she knew now why he had not been to Confession, and why he, therefore, could not take Communion. "You forget," she said slowly, "and make love before you are married, don't you?"

The eyes he turned on her were stricken. "Darling, it doesn't matter."

"You haven't been to Confession, and you haven't taken Communion since . . . since we began. Isn't that it?"

Miserably, he nodded. The car, swerving dangerously, recalled him to his driving. "But if I don't mind, it shouldn't bother you."

"I think you *do* mind."

"*No*. I had all that out before . . . I went over all of it . . ."

She was silent, trying to sort out what she had to say. That it must be said, there was no doubt, but how to say it best. "Mike," she began slowly, "what would Father Vincent tell you if you did go to Confession . . . about us, I mean."

"It doesn't matter what he would say." He was becoming obstinate.

"No, but I want the truth now. What would he say?"

"I expect you know—but I tell you, it doesn't matter."

"He would tell you it was wrong, wouldn't he—and he would tell you to give it up. This being together before we are married—he would tell you to give that up, I'm certain."

He did not answer and the stillness grew between them into a palpable thing, as heavy and as solid as the heat that pressed down on them and made the car an oven. They turned into the driveway of her home, but neither of them made any move to leave the car. They sat, instead, as if something held them there. She looked at the heat waves shimmering up from the grass, felt her head beginning to ache from the tightness behind her eyes, knew that somehow this wall must be broken down and removed. "Mike, I can't have your sin on my conscience."

"It isn't on your conscience," he said, his voice flat and dull.

"But it's on yours, and I am the cause of it. We'll have to stop. I would never have started it if I'd known."

"Does that mean you won't marry me?"

"Of course not! It only means . . ."

Swiftly he turned to her. "Then what is all the bother about? Will you trust me—please. I *tell* you it doesn't matter. I knew what I was doing. I made my choices. Stopping what we are doing will make no difference—not in the long run. Nothing would be altered in the end. Please, Regina . . . believe me. Deliberately and of my own free will I made the decision. I know what I am doing. I have no regrets, truly I haven't."

It was very hot in the car and sweat was forming in fine beads on his forehead. She gazed into his eyes, saw them clouded with misery and knew she could not press him further. With unexpected clarity of vision she realized her own motives were not entirely pure. She wanted her own mind set at ease, she reflected. It occurred to her that he had every right to think for himself and that it was a little superior and condescending of her to try to decide for him. It was something which, after all, was private and personal with him. She took her handkerchief and wiped the moisture on his face away. "I do trust you, darling. I don't want you unhappy is all. I don't want to be the cause of any unhappiness for you."

"Then forget this—just leave it to me, will you? I am not unhappy. My Lord, I'm happier with you than I've ever been in my life. *You* could never cause me any unhappiness."

The emphasis did not escape her, and a little sadly she thought, No, but through me there is some conflict which *does* make you unhappy, my darling. If she only knew more about it, knew what lay at the root of it. It was at that moment she determined to see Father Vincent herself. Not at all for the purpose of confession—*she* owed him no confession, but if Mike was not going to discuss with her the steps she must take—and she realized, now, that she had long ago decided to take them—she must find out for herself. She said nothing, however. There was something called instruction, she recalled. When she was fully committed to it, embarked upon it, she would tell him. Perhaps this closed door would be unlocked then.

She opened the car door. "Are you coming in?"

"I can't right now. There are some calls to make. Shall we go out for dinner tonight?"

"Unless you'd rather eat at home."

"We've done that so often." Suddenly animated he said, "Let's splurge. Let's drive up to the city. We can go back to that Italian place and dance again."

Warmly, feeling some threatening danger almost, but not quite, removed, and wishing now to keep it at a distance, she agreed. "That will be fun."

He kissed her quickly, patted her cheek affectionately. "I love you, you know."

Watching him drive away she reflected, thoughtfully, that that itself might very well be the trouble.

Chapter Nineteen

❧

She parked the car in front of the ugly little chapel and looked at it distrustfully. It sat, small, its white paint raw and already peeling, in a sandy plot, its drabness unrelieved by any shade of trees or any softening of shrubs. The ground around it was red and hard-baked. The heat of the sun reflected from it as if it had been concrete. There was a belfry and a cross above it, but they added nothing of beauty. It borrowed nothing from its surroundings, had only itself to offer, stark and plain and dreary, as the House of God. It was as if it said, within my walls God dwells and that is sufficient, that is acceptable, nothing more is necessary.

She opened the car door slowly, reluctantly, wishing she had never got herself into this. It was too late, though, now. She stiffened her back and went up the walk to the parish home, as ugly in its square, boxed way as the church. Father Vincent lived there and he had told her to come to his study.

A housekeeper answered her ring, a gaunt, gray woman of indeterminate age, as bleak and forbidding as the house. "I'm Mrs. Browning," Regina told her. "I have an appointment at three with Father Vincent."

"He told me," the woman said, grudgingly, her face remaining suspicious and unwelcoming. Regina wondered what she had interrupted. Some chore of the woman's, no doubt, which she resented. "He's busy right now. You can wait in here."

She led her to a small room on the right of the entrance hall, pushed the door open into an oven of heat, and motioned her to enter. "Will he be long?" Regina asked, as the woman turned to go.

"I wouldn't be knowing. He didn't say. You can wait as long as you like, though. You won't be disturbed."

She pushed her hair back wearily and Regina noticed that the large shoes she wore were slit in a dozen places. Her feet hurt, probably. Constant pain would account for much discourtesy and she was willing to overlook it. It didn't really matter.

The room was small and shabby and there was neither a fan nor shades at the windows to relieve the glare and heat. She seated herself on an uncomfortable straight chair—there were no others—and studied the room trying to get some clue to the man's personality. It offered none. It was deliberately impersonal—merely a study—and it was almost bare of furniture. There was a plain graceless oak desk beside the windows, which were not only shadeless but curtainless. There was a very worn old Axminster rug on the floor, so frayed that the bare boards showed through in places. There were three straight chairs, plain kitchen chairs, unvarnished, unpainted, and they were mercilessly lined up in a row against the bleak white wall. There were shelves of books behind the desk, but they told her nothing. One glance showed her that they were all theological studies. There was a telephone on the desk, and a hook-neck lamp, and nothing more. The desk itself was so uncluttered as to look unused. A crucifix hung in the space between the windows, just over the desk. It was so placid, she saw, that every time anyone working at the desk lifted his eyes, they met the crucifix. It was a constant reminder, a constant plea, a constant rebuke, and it may have been a constant solace.

She remembered that Mike had told her St. Raphael's was a new parish, only three or four years old, divided off by order of the bishop from the cathedral parish downtown. It had grown unwieldy in time and it was decided to start this suburban parish. She recalled, also, that he had said it was having hard going. It was very poor, new parishes always were, and Father Vincent was working terribly hard to bring it up. That accounted, she thought, for the poverty of the study. If it did not, then the austerity here was a clue, of sorts, to the man she had come to see. There was no precise way of knowing, however, whether this room was a hair shirt or not.

The heat was so oppressive that she felt herself beginning to perspire and knew that the fresh linen dress would soon be wilted. Her hair felt damp already and was clinging to her forehead. Wryly she thought that the goodly Father had a foretaste of hell in this small box-like room. She wondered if he were deliberately leaving her all this time alone as a kind of psychological punishment. She refused to allow it to trouble her and set herself to endure the heat, the hard chair, and the waiting with dignity and serenity. She would not let him win the first round by finding her, when he returned, restless and frustrated.

Outside a group of boys were playing ball and she watched them, deliberately removing from her mind any further thought of why she had come, or what might be the results. When she had called the priest and asked for an appointment he had sounded pleasant enough, had offered her a choice of times, and had even made a small joke about the heat with her over the telephone. She would have to go on that slender evidence that he would meet her at least halfway.

He came into the room wiping his brow. His dark suit, the white collar very wilted, must be awfully hot, she thought. She noticed also that it was so dingy it was turning brown at the seams and cuffs. He was broad, bulky, and corpulent enough that heat must bother him considerably. She left the opening of the conversation to him, only watching him carefully. He seated himself behind the desk, ordered the telephone and lamp slightly, which told her that he was not entirely at ease himself. One did not fidget with things when one was perfectly comfortable. "I'm sorry to keep you waiting, Mrs. Browning. There were things . . ." he flourished his hands defensively. They were massive hands, hairy on the backs, thick-fingered. She wondered if the palms were dry today.

"Of course. I've been entirely comfortable. Are you certain you have the time now?" Hearing herself, she wondered if her voice always sounded this way, cool and with a certain amount of detachment. It came to her ears as from a stranger.

"Oh, yes. It was the organ. The man who looks it over regularly has come today. I had to see him started, but I'm free now. There are a hundred things, in a small, new parish." He sighed, and she saw that he looked a little tired. Then he collected himself and smiled at her. "This parish is another of those I told you about at the mill."

"I'm sure it must be." It was time, she thought, to get down to the subject. "I've come, Father Vincent, to talk with you about beginning instruction. I want to become a Catholic—if it's possible." There was an edge of virtue in her voice.

She noticed with satisfaction that he was startled. He didn't expect that, she thought. He looked at her a moment, then swung his chair around toward the windows. In the harsh light she saw what a strong face he had, the brow very high, with a heavy thatch of black hair above it, the jaw line reminiscent of another Italian's, who had led his people so disastrously. The swarthy skin was thick looking and a little pock marked. He had evidently had a very bad case of acne as a young man. He swung back around and his black eyes rested on her piercingly. He had so much power in his hands. "Yes," he said, at last, "I see. It depends, Mrs. Browning. Your husband is dead, is he not?"

"Yes."

"Well, there is no problem there." Then he attacked swiftly. "Why do you want to become a Catholic, Mrs. Browning?"

There was no use ducking it. Her chin came up and she made her hands, which had instinctively clutched at her bag and gloves, remain quiet. "Because Mike is one and I think he will be happier when we are married if I am in the Church, too."

"I see."

He looked away from her, out the window again, watched the boys at their ball game, and she thought his face had become inexpressibly sad all at once. For what seemed a very long time he stared out the window, then he turned to her again, lifted a big hand and pleated his lower lip with it. "I'm sorry—very sorry, indeed, but I have to tell you— it won't be possible."

Her heart felt as if a huge hand was squeezing it tightly. There was not only pressure, there was pain, and a colder perspiration broke out on her forehead. "But, why? If I am willing."

"All your willingness makes no difference. The difficulty is, Mrs. Browning, that you and Mike cannot be married in the Church."

It came so suddenly that she was entirely unprepared for it. She could only look at him blankly. She had known he did not approve. She had known he would condemn their intimacy before marriage. She had expected him to be grueling about her preparation. But she had never once thought he would deny them the right to be married. She swallowed a time or two before she could speak, wishing she could have a glass of a water. Slowly she recovered her poise. "I'm afraid I don't understand."

"You are not familiar with Catholic doctrine, are you?"

She shook her head. "I know very little about it."

"Mike is a married man, Mrs. Browning. He cannot have two wives."

"But he is getting a divorce. It will be final in August."

"With a Catholic, there is no divorce. 'Whom God hath joined together, let no man put asunder.' Catholicism does not recognize divorce."

It was so harsh a blow that she felt as if she winced under it visibly. "Should he have got an annulment, then?"

"An annulment wasn't possible, either. His wife is a Catholic, too. They were married in this church. I married them myself. Nothing but death can undo that marriage."

"But Catholics do get annulments. I've heard of it...."

"Of course. When one or the other is not a baptized church member. In that case God has not joined the two. It has been merely a legal ceremony. In Mike's case it is altogether different."

"You mean he can never marry again?" It did not seem possible that any doctrine could be so dogmatic under the circumstances.

"He *is* married, Mrs. Browning. There is no way a man may have two wives."

"But she left him. She ran away with this other man. He hasn't heard from her for three years. How can you call that a marriage?"

"Eva has sinned grievously. But as far as Mike is concerned, the facts remain the same. The marriage cannot be undone. There is no alternative."

She remembered the phrase and the sudden picture came to her of him and Mike walking down the street together, talking together, she overhearing from the store entrance that unappealable sentence . . . there is no alternative. She saw again his hand, slicing the air, as if cutting something off. It was she who must be cut off, then.

"Did Mike talk to you about it?" she asked.

"Many times. He knows."

"Before he decided to get the divorce?"

"Before he decided to get the divorce. I gave him the only counsel I could."

"And what counsel was that?" She knew, but she was compelled to hear him say it.

"I told him he could only give you up. I urged him to, before he was too far committed."

It explained so many things, she thought wearily. It explained the long, outstretched times between seeing her; it explained the coming and going, the snatches of happiness, the other times of dark moods. She recalled how she had thought it was as if he had become a battlefield, and she thought she could not have chosen a more apt term. It was what he had been. A little proudly she remembered what his decision had been, and in her pride in him she took pride in herself, in her own worth. "I cannot believe," she said, "that God is without mercy Himself. Surely He must love His creatures more than that. He couldn't want them condemned to unhappiness."

The priest spread his hands. "There is a greater happiness."

"How can there be?"

He smiled. "Their love of God."

She stared at him. "Mike is human. He wants a human love. He wants to belong to someone, to have a home, to have children."

He leaned forward suddenly. "I have been afraid of exactly this, Mrs. Browning. I know Mike, you see. I know what he wants and misses. I am not inhuman. I can see that, and it grieves me that it cannot be different for him. Believe me, if it were left entirely up to me I think I should pray God just this once to lift his judgment."

"His judgment? Or the Church's interpretation of it?"

"The Holy Word says . . ."

"I *know* what the Holy Word says. I also know it says many other things which may be variously interpreted. Not your church nor any other puts into practice everything it says. All of you pick and choose, according to your own needs and understanding. This one thing your church has picked . . . and I think it did it very shrewdly. It was a very certain way of holding Catholic families together and in the Church."

"Perhaps. But for whatever reason it was selected to become a Catholic rule, it *was* selected, it *is* a rule, and the rule is inviolate. I am absolutely helpless before it."

"You are cruel. Your Church is cruel. Your God is cruel, to deny Mike this happiness."

"In denying him this happiness, God offers him another, greater, fuller, richer happiness—doing His will."

"I don't believe it *is* His will."

"But Mike believes it."

"No! How do you know he does?"

"Because he was born as a child of God. He was brought up to seek God first."

"He no longer does."

"He will again, in time."

Abruptly she realized how bitter the taste of his words was in her mouth, as if they had entered her and she had bitten down upon them, sour and puckering. She licked her lips with her dry tongue. "How can God have made it possible for us to love, have given us the passion, the intent, the promise, and then deny us, take it away from us, hurt us with the very emotions he made into us?"

He looked at her sadly. "I do not know. I only know the will of God through His Words."

"You talk so glibly of the will of God. It is so easy for you. You know nothing of what Mike feels, or of what I feel. You don't know what you are doing when you say it can't be. You have no idea of the waste and the futility and the sin, the *sin* it would be!"

"I do not know, I confess. There is still nothing more I can say. If you want to become a Catholic under those circumstances, knowing the marriage is impossible . . ."

She cut him off rudely and coldly. "My only reason was for Mike's sake. I couldn't be less interested now. I'm afraid I'm only wasting your time." She gathered her gloves and bag together, made as if to rise. "What happens if Mike and I are married anyhow?"

"Mike will be excommunicated."

"What does that mean?"

"It means that he will never take Communion again—so long as he lives with you. It means that he becomes an exile from a country inherited and believed by him. It means that each Sunday morning he will sit and watch the truly penitent, the confessed and shriven, come forward to receive the Host, and that he may never again be among them. It means that he will live with you in adultery, for we cannot recognize the marriage, and therefore he will live in mortal sin. It means that he cannot even die in grace unless he denies you and repents. It means the end of living for such as Mike Panelli, Mrs. Browning."

The words were like small stones pelting her, inexorable, bruising, hard. She felt as if nothing could shield her from them, not even a lifted arm or hand. They fell, remorsefully, telling her the irrevocable truth—that through her Mike would be condemned. Only her pride sustained her. She would not bow her head before them. "I cannot believe that what Mike and I feel is wrong, Father. I cannot believe God would look upon it so. I think *He* would have more pity than you."

The priest's face altered, twisting with emotion. "I can only interpret the Church's rule."

She rose. It had been foolish of her to come. There had been only this shame in it for her. Her body, when she stood, felt light and weight-less, as if she had been ill for a long time. Her head was dizzy, and for fear that she would fall she held to the back of the chair. The priest stood, too. "If you really love Mike, Mrs. Browning, there is only one thing for you to do. Go away. Go back where you came from. Take your-self out of his life."

She lifted her eyes and gazed at him wonderingly. How could he suggest such a thing so calmly—decide for them so inevitably? "I think Mike must have something to say about that. It isn't my decision to make alone."

"It will have to be your decision. Mike is too weak to decide now. He has committed himself too deeply. He cannot, of his own will, give you up now."

And what about me, she cried silently. I am committed too deeply, too—I am committed by all the hours with him, about which you know nothing—the close, beautiful, lovely, warm hours. I am committed by my knowledge of his body, and by his knowledge of mine. There is no way you, a poor, chaste, virgin man can know how deeply we both are committed. Strangely, she wondered if he had ever known temptation. But he would have had the strength to turn his back upon it. He would have had his priesthood as his refuge. Mike would have . . . what? *Pax* . . . she remembered, from the mass. Was peace more important than love? He had laid so heavy a burden upon her. Even her mind stumbled under it and she cried out, "How could Mike ever love God again if He de-manded such a sacrifice? How could one believe in a God who asked one to deny the human love between those He had created?"

"The Church says . . ."

"I don't care *what* the Church says. It says nothing valid for me . . . and in time it may say nothing valid for Mike!"

He shook his head. "There you are wrong. Mike will never forget. He will live out his life with you, empty and increasingly conscious of his irreparable loss."

Her head came up. "I will not let him. If he must have God to be happy, there are other churches."

"For you, yes. There is always the rule of invincible ignorance. That is not open to Mike. There is only one Church for him."

She could have beat him with her hands. She felt a hatred for him and his arguments that boiled over and made her want to scream at him. He *could* not be so right. He did not know Mike in the way she knew him. He saw only the Church and Mike's training under it. For love, a man could remake his life. For her, Mike would remake his. But tears rose to blind her, and she would have begged if she had known how. Instead she could only grope for the door. She felt the priest beside her and he put his hand, gently, on her arm. "Mrs. Browning, I am very, very sorry. I wish you had come to me sooner."

She shook the hand off, angrily. "It would have done no good. Nothing you could ever have said would make me believe you are right—or your Church. You are cruel, and if Mike is made to suffer, it will be through your cruelty. He is a good Catholic and I would have tried to be one. You, too, will lose something."

"Don't think I don't grieve for that. We always grieve at such a loss. Mike is a wonderful help, and I am sure you would have been, too. But there is no other answer I can give you."

She left him without another word, wanting only to get away, get home into the coolness of the old, shaded house, be alone and try, in some way she could not now perceive, to lick the wounds he had inflicted and mend them. She felt as if she would never be the same again and with all her heart she wished she had never come to this place today. She should have trusted Mike.

When he came that night she told him, quietly and with as little bitterness as possible, what she had done and what had transpired. He listened without comment until she had finished, then he took her in his arms. "I wish you hadn't gone to him, darling. I could have told you . . ."

"Why didn't you? Mike, I went there, ready to become a convert, wanting to become one, for your sake and for the sake of our marriage. He slammed every door in my face . . . in our face."

He drew her to the sofa and held her, consolingly. "I suppose I thought you knew. To a Catholic everything is so plain . . . so well-known. It seems inconceivable to us that others don't know, too."

"But I didn't know. How could I have? I have never known anything about Catholicism. I had no idea our being married would make you have to leave the Church."

He stroked her hair and kissed her gently. "It was what I was trying to tell you the other morning . . . that it made no difference in the end."

She wept quietly. "I can't bear it. It's the most inhuman thing I ever heard of. I can't believe it. Isn't there someone higher up you can go to? Couldn't you even go the Pope?"

"It would do no good. He explained it to you, dear. It's because Eva and I were both in the Church, you see."

"He said you talked to him about it."

"Oh, yes. I knew, really, what he would say. But one has to hear for himself."

"Is that why you used to stay away sometimes for so long? Was it hard to make up your mind?"

He tightened his arm about her. "Not when I really knew, darling. In the beginning . . . well, it was forbidden, you know. I knew I had to live out my life alone . . . if I stayed in the Church, that is, so I've never allowed myself to think of it. I've never even been tempted before. Then you came . . ."

"I came along and became a problem for you."

She felt as if they two were alone, stranded on some strange, barren rock, flood waters raging about them. Their only hope lay in each other, in clinging fast to their rock together. But what was their rock? Love?

"You came along," he said, so sweetly and reasonably that her breath caught in her throat, "and you were your own beautiful, lovely self, with whom I fell in love—whom I love more than anything in the world— whom I love more than the Church, and for whom I regret nothing."

She lay against him, his arms strongly about her, his heart beating evenly beneath her head. How could he be so calm, when she felt so storm-tossed? But then, she recalled, he had already had weeks to get used to the idea—months, even. He had, in fact, considered it at length, made his own decision long ago. Since that was true, hadn't the burden already slipped from her shoulders? She lifted her head. She knew the question was footless even as she asked it—there was only one answer, but she was compelled by the memory of the priest's voice. "Will you ever regret it?"

"Never."

His answer was so prompt that she knew, at least for the present, he believed it himself. He smoothed her hair back. "You are so hot, Regina. You've worked yourself into such a state over this that you're almost feverish. Look, why don't we run out to the island, fish a little, cool off."

Twilight had darkened the room and outside the sun had entirely gone. The light that was left, however, had that pale, luminous glow which lasts for an hour or so past sunset at that time of year. The birds were still twittering in the garden, as if they knew there was plenty of time before they need tuck their heads under their wings. She had a feeling of time suspended, caught in its rhythm for a moment, stopped and held back for them. Almost bemused she said, "It's very nearly dark."

"There's time."

He smiled, and it was so gentle, so tenderly loving that it almost broke her heart. Surely even God could not help loving Mike enough that He could not withhold His infinite mercy from him. It would work out. It must. Even a very mortal human would have that much compassion.

The island lay like a white and gleaming jewel in the late light, the pines pointed and darkly green, the willows more pale but thick and shrubby along the beach. The stream was low and clear, and the riffle was very noisy. Its babble over the rocks was somehow soothing and comforting.

They fished until they could no longer see their lures on the water, then, with a glance of complete understanding, of complete accord and wanting, they turned to the pine grove.

There was an abandon in their love that there had never been before, a kind of desperate rapture and wildness which took them winging beyond all time, past, present, or future, which blotted out everything but themselves, seeking and murmuring and touching. There was ecstacy, a kind of trembling delirium, mixed with a deep hopelessness and clinging. They sought some manifestation, some expression between themselves beyond any they had ever made, of hope. They said, "I love you" a thousand times and sought new ways to say it, feeling the futility, the insufficiency of the old phrase. "Why isn't a new one invented?" Mike questioned in a whisper against her ear. "There are so few ways...I love you, I adore you, I worship you..."

She picked it up, and continued the chant. "I cherish you, I treasure you, I love you . . ."

"You're repeating already."

"It's so easily said . . . and it has to mean so much."

In the dark of the pines, she felt as if she had never been so transported, never knew such mystery and such enchantment, never felt so complete a loss of herself in him. She could, she told herself fiercely, have died happily at that moment, lain buried with him forever under the dark pines.

The one thing she had not told him, Father Vincent's counsel to her, was even blotted from her mind.

Chapter Twenty

❧

"It seems impossible, doesn't it?" They were standing in the doorway of the kitchen watching the workmen fitting the last screws in the last knobs of the new cabinets. This room was then finished except for her own touches. "It seems impossible they could have done so much in one month—even with six men working I wouldn't have believed it could be done." She wiped her paint-smeared hands down her blue jeans. "Do you like this yellow, Mike? With the blue tile it's a little gaudy, but it's a north room and it's rather dark . . ."

"If you'd painted it red, I wouldn't have minded. I have no eye for color, but it looks fine to me. Very gay. What are those things you're doing on the doors of the cupboard?"

She laughed. "I don't really know. A sort of formalized Swedish design, I hope. It makes the room a little busy, perhaps, but it's so large." She pushed her hair back, tilted her head to consider the cupboards.

"They're nice." They turned back into the dining room. "What amazes me," he continued, "is the way you've achieved an effect of light and space all over the house. I don't see how you did it."

"Taking out windows, moving doors, using lighter paint . . . there are dozens of ways. It does look nice, though, doesn't it?"

"It looks wonderful. You're going to be awfully tired, though, by the time it's all finished."

"No," she shook her head. "I love doing it. I'm even going to make the curtains myself."

"All of them? For the entire house?"

"All of them. But not," she said, laughingly, "until after we are married. The main thing now is to get the painting done and the floors finished. Then when the furniture from the other place comes, it can all be put in place and we'll have something halfway comfortable to come home to."

They had decided, after all, to have a short wedding trip.

Mike looked at her reflectively. "I don't think you're going to be able to go. You're looking thin to me, and I'm sure you're losing weight over this." He made an effort to span her waist with his hands. They lacked only a little of meeting around her. "I couldn't have done this a month ago."

She looked down in surprise. "I hadn't noticed."

"Well, I have. I wish you'd take it a little easier. I don't want you overtired and too thin. You'll be getting nervous and edgy."

"I won't. I promise. I expect it's the heat more than anything else. Heat has always bothered me, and it's been a very hot summer. I'll be rested and fresh for the wedding, you'll see. Mike." She drew him into the library, the only undisturbed room on the lower floor. "We've been so busy with the house we haven't discussed the wedding. Lucia wants us to be married at her house. What do you think?"

He made the business of finding his pipe and filling it a lengthy one. She thought how much awkwardness the act of filling a pipe, or even of lighting a cigarette, could cover. She had noticed it in everyone who smoked. Given a situation which requires thought, they always had the device at hand for providing time. "If you like," he said, finally, scratching a match and puffing.

"You don't much like the idea yourself, though, do you?" she asked, sitting on the leather couch, suddenly aware that she *was* a little tired.

He sat beside her, leaning comfortably back on the worn, cracked old leather cushions. "There's just one thing . . ."

"Yes."

Without turning his head he sent a guarded look her way. "I'd rather not be married by a minister, if you don't mind."

"Why? Oh—because Father Vincent can't marry us."

She realized she hadn't given the matter any serious thought at all. She had assumed that, since Father Vincent couldn't marry them, some

Protestant minister unobjectionable to both of them would be found. "Do you have someone in mind?"

"I thought perhaps Judge Walton . . . he's a very good friend of mine." He leaned forward and took her hands. "Do you mind very much?"

"Not at all, if I know what's back of this. But I think you should tell me why you object to a minister."

He fidgeted with his pipe, then blurted out bluntly, "I can never get back in the Church if we are married by a minister. There's a chance, a very slim one . . . for instance, if Eva should die . . . or there might be some other thing come up later that would make an opening . . . I'd just feel better if we didn't entirely close the door—but I will," he added quickly, seeing her face, "if that's the only way you'll be happy about it."

There had been nothing more said between them since the day she had gone to see the priest. It had seemed to be a buried issue and it shocked her to find this continuing feeling in him. A little flatly, because of an undercurrent of resentment and some uneasiness, she said, "You want a legal ceremony and that's all, is that it?"

Looking at him she saw that his face had gone darker and she knew he was flushing, either from shame or from embarrassment, she did not know which. It didn't matter. They were about equal in emotional discomfort. At least, she thought, he wasn't happy about what he was asking of her.

Adultery, Father Vincent had called it. It was a very ugly word, and she recoiled with a wince from it. What Mike was asking her to do was simply to make it legal—and that meant that deep within him he accepted Father Vincent's interpretation. She tried to be just. He would, of course, having been reared under the rule. A man cannot have two wives. But he would go to law and rid himself of one, and he would go to lay again and take unto himself another. Neither action, however, changed the essential status, which would apply to her as well as to him in the eyes of his Church. In the eyes of hers, for what it was worth, and it was worth nothing to him, she would be sanctioned. Every instinct in her rebelled and she fought down an angry feeling of betrayal. Since he was willing to go as far as he had, she thought, he might, for her sake, have gone all the way without making an issue of it.

"I suppose that's about it," he said, finally. "It isn't really what I want . . . but then nothing of what I want is possible anyhow. I've told you—if I could wipe out all that other one, I would. I'd like nothing better than to have this the first time . . ."

"Oh, Mike, really..." She felt unutterably weary. How lightly she and Lucia had talked about it. How blithely they had dismissed the possibility of problems. How little they had known. She felt surrounded by problems, prickled and nettled by them on every side. Marrying a Catholic who was going to be excommunicated because of it held nothing *but* problems. It was beginning to be almost more than she could cope with.

Remorseful, then, because he could not help it any more than she could; the problems were no more of his making than of hers; what he felt was too deeply ingrained in him. She put her hand on his knee. "It doesn't matter. But I think it might be best if we simply went to the judge's chambers. Lucia and Tom can go with us."

He covered her hand. "I hate to do you out of your wedding. Lucia will be disappointed, won't she?"

"I expect she will be . . . but she'll understand. It will simplify matters, really." She leaned her head against the back of the couch and allowed herself a little wistfulness. "It would have been nice. I was married in a justice of the peace's office before."

He was silent a moment. "I didn't know," he said. "Look, darling. Forget what I said. It isn't that important. Go ahead and have the wedding the way you want it . . . you're due that much."

"And you're due what little peace of mind you can get." She roused herself. "No. I've cost you enough in any event. We'll leave your door open for you."

She tried to keep the slight bitterness she felt out of her voice and apparently succeeded, for he smiled at her and reached out to rumple her hair. "I keep telling you—it isn't you at all. It's just the situation."

"But I'm part of it. Let's don't talk about it anymore, Mike. Let's call it settled. Will your people be coming?"

"I think not." He rested his chin on her head and rubbed it.

It irritated her for some reason and she drew away. "It's too hot. Not even your mother, Mike? Have you told them yet?"

He stood and walked to the window, played idly with the cord of the blind. "Not yet." He swung around suddenly. "Mama has a birthday next week. I've been wondering . . . would you like to go up with me? There'll be a big family party, of sorts. Not all of them, of course, but Teresa will be there and Anna plans a big dinner and so forth. I thought I'd tell them then, and you can meet them at the same time."

She felt panicky at the thought of meeting his mother and his sisters. They wouldn't approve—they couldn't, under the circumstances. It would be a trying situation for all of them, next to impossible for her. She would be the siren who had lured him from the fold. They couldn't possibly like her, and they would be weighing and measuring her. It might even spoil his mother's birthday entirely.

All these things ran through her mind and she had the unreasoning wish simply to put it off, to find some excuse for not going. A little desperately she tried to think of a good one, one that would stand up, and realized there really was none. She had to meet them some day. It would do no good postponing it. She couldn't simply ignore them. They were his people and they loved him and they had a right to expect her...She put an end to it, conscious of his waiting. "Of course, darling. I rather wish," she laughed ruefully, "you'd told them first, though. It would be a little easier for me."

"Well, then," he came over and slid his arms about her, "why don't I write them immediately about it, and tell them I'm bringing you up with me."

She leaned against him, thinking how hot they both were, how there was a wave of heat generated between them which made touching almost unbearable. Wherever they touched a small pool of perspiration was immediately created, as on their arms now. As soon as the workmen were finished they must have air conditioners installed. She felt drowsy and lethargic leaning against him and thought she could almost have gone to sleep. She forced herself to become more alert, blinked her eyes and drew away from him. "That would be fine. I wouldn't be sprung on them quite by surprise then."

Letting her go and wiping at his bare arms with a handkerchief, he laughed. "Isn't it funny the things a man doesn't think of? I only thought what a nice surprise you'd be."

She looked at him quickly. He couldn't really believe that, surely. He couldn't be so naive as not to know what he had done was simply to postpone the inevitable pain he must give his mother. He couldn't not know, surely, that he had only procrastinated, hesitated, because of his own reluctance to face the issue with them. His face was quiet and relaxed, entirely calm, and she realized he had done just that.

He had done an excellent job of fooling himself. She could see almost how his mind had worked. When the decision was taken, he had had the impulse immediately to write to them. Finding it difficult, he had found good reason to put it off . . . until there was some definite date to tell them, perhaps . . . when the divorce would be final, when the wedding would be. When that information was in hand, something else just as logical had done equally as well. His mother's birthday was very likely an occasion the family honored annually, and quite simply he had decided it would be the best time to tell them. It had the added virtue of enabling him to tell them in person, and of his being able to present her at the same time. In her presence, probably, they would be restrained. He was not at all conscious of having been devious in avoiding any responsibility. "Well," she said, "being a woman, I know they would rather be warned."

"I expect you're right," he said cheerfully. "I'll get a note off to them tomorrow."

"You'll not forget, will you? It's important to me, Mike."

"Of course I won't forget. Do you think my memory is as untrustworthy as that?"

"A man's memory is notoriously untrustworthy," she retorted, laughing it off, not wanting him to know that it was not his memory she distrusted. "You'd better go now, darling, and let me get back to the kitchen. I wanted to get those designs on the cupboards started this afternoon. You've distracted me enough."

"I wish I could distract you entirely. If I were free I'd suggest . . ."

"Not today," she said, firmly, "no fishing. I'm going to work today."

"All right. I couldn't go anyhow."

The telephone rang and he crossed the room to it, finishing over his shoulder. "I won't be through until late."

She left him at the telephone and went back to the kitchen, surveyed the unfinished cupboards with sudden dislike. She didn't want to paint today, she found. She would botch it, certainly, if she went on under pressure. They wouldn't come out right at all. What she'd better do, she thought, was leave them until tomorrow, take a fresh start early in the morning when it was cooler. Mike was right. She *was* pushing herself too hard. It couldn't matter that much. They still had several weeks before the wedding. She wished now that Mike was free for the rest of the afternoon and they could get out into the country. Summer in this part of the country was most unpleasant. She didn't know when she had felt such heat and it would last, she had been told, well into September.

She heard him coming rapidly through the dining room and turned toward the door. "I have to make a call in the country," he said. "*Couldn't you drop all this and come with me?*"

"I was just wishing you were free. I'm going to let it go until tomorrow. It's simply silly to press so hard at it. Have I time to wash my hands and face?"

It was good to get off the paved streets, away from the reflected heat of buildings, into the open country. Mike drove very fast and the wind blew strongly through the car. It was a hot wind, but at least it was moving air. The sun was glaringly bright, but in the southwest a dark bank of clouds was forming. "Do those clouds mean rain, do you think?" she asked, hopefully.

He gave them the briefest of glances. "Probably. Our summer rains usually come from that direction."

"It would be so nice if it would rain and turn a little cooler. They look very dark." She asked, almost idly, "Do you ever have tornadoes here?"

"Occasionally. Not very often—but there have been a few."

She sat up straighter and looked at the clouds with more respect. "You're very casual about it. I've never seen a tornado. Aren't they rather terrifying?"

"If you had time to think about it. But they're usually too quick. They're on you before you know it and gone by the time the damage is done."

"That," she said laughing, "would probably give me time to die of fright."

"Are you afraid of storms?"

"Well, no—not really, not normally."

"Only of heights and depths," he said, teasingly.

"Yes," she agreed, unashamed.

He patted her knee. "You're very lucky if that's all. Here's where we turn, I think."

He swung the car into a narrow, rough road that wound back toward the hills. It seemed to have been made only for wagons and as they slowly made their way the low-built car often dragged on the high centers of the ruts. "Mike, are you sure you can make it up here?"

"If I can't, I'll have to walk. Unless it gets worse, though, we'll keep on trying."

"Is it an emergency?"

"I don't know. Probably not. A farmer's wife is in labor, prematurely by about ten days they think. It's one of Barton's patients, actually. He's out of town today."

"Why didn't they bring her in to the hospital?"

"I don't know."

They had come to the foot of a long hill and the road dipped to cross a rather wide, shallow creek. "You'd think they'd bridge this creek," she said, as Mike shifted gears to make the crossing.

"It's probably a private road. From the condition of it, I'd say so."

The farmhouse, when they came to it at the top of the hill, was very small, merely two rooms covered with the false brick siding used so much in the country, but it was new and everything about it was neat and clean. There was no clutter of farm implements, and the grass was freshly cut. A rose bush was tied up to a painted scaffolding, and a walkway of creek stones had been laid windingly to the door. The barn was a good one, big and new. She guessed that the farmer and his wife had sacrificed a better home for the time being in the interest of the barn.

When they drew up, a man so young he looked little more than a boy came out of the house hurriedly. He stopped uncertainly when he saw Mike. "I thought you were Dr. Barton," he said, hesitantly.

"Dr. Barton is out of town today," Mike explained. "His nurse called me. I'm Dr. Panelli. Are you the husband?"

"Yes, sir. This is our first one. We've not been married but a year. She's pretty sick, Doctor." The boy's face was wrung with anxiety and his eyes were bright with fear.

"She's probably not as sick as you think," Mike said encouragingly. "You're pretty scared, aren't you?"

"Yes, sir—but she's been sick since yesterday, and she don't get any better."

"Well, we'll see."

They started in the house and then the boy turned. "Won't you get out, ma'am?"

"I think I'd better wait outside," Regina said, "but thank you."

They disappeared into the tiny house and following them with her eyes she thought of what was happening in there. Judging by the age of the boy, the wife would be pitifully young. She would be frightened by the pain and by their lack of experience. She would be lying in the bed they had shared in such joy, and which now had brought her to this solitary pain, in which no matter how much he wished it, the boy could not enter. She wondered if they had wanted the baby, if they had planned for it and looked forward to it. For the girl's sake, she hoped so. It would be her reward for the lonely journey.

The clouds were moving up into the sky, she saw, growing increasingly blacker and obscuring the sun. There was an ominously yellow cast to the light and she watched it curiously. The tops of the trees were beginning to sway in a rising wind and the chickens in the barnyard were skittering before it, their feathers ruffled and turned backward rakishly. The cows, misled by the gathering darkness, were slowly coming up to the barn. She hoped Mike could finish soon and they would get started back to town.

She felt no uneasiness, however, until a bucket was sent flying across the yard, and at the same time a young maple tree was bent almost to the ground under the force of a sudden blast of wind. A piece of tin which had been propped against the side of the barn was caught up suddenly and swirled high into the air, turned over several times and taken on in a high spiral, so slow as to remind her of a ballet movement, entirely over the barn. Why, it's blowing a gale, she thought in astonishment.

Then she watched, almost hypnotically, as the edge of the barn roof, also of tin, gave way and flopped, ripped loose and folded back on itself, until it tore free and sailed into the air. At almost the same moment she felt the car heel over, then settle back. The wind had lifted one side entirely off the ground. The air seemed suddenly to be filled with flying trash, limbs, dust, whirling objects whose identity she could not make out, and in one sudden, unbelievable, second she saw a rooster being blown over the car.

Terror overtook her, a blind, unreasoning terror. It was a tornado. She knew it was a tornado. She wrenched at the car door. She had to get into the house. She had to get to Mike. The car careened again and the door flew open and she fell out, quickly recovered herself and ran, stooping, to the house. Great, cold drops of rain were beginning to fall as she burst in the door, which because of the wind she could not close behind her. She was in the kitchen, and the young man came, hurrying to thrust his big shoulder against the door. He managed to shut it and latch it. "It's a tornado," she gasped, some of her fear subsiding at being inside again.

The boy peered out the window. "I don't think so, miss. It's just a rainstorm. There's a lot of wind, though."

"It's blown your barn roof off—part of it."

"We get some pretty high winds around here." He turned back to the other room, but Mike appeared suddenly in the door. "Regina, I was just going to call you."

Shakily she laughed, wiping the spattering of rain from her face. "I didn't wait. I was too scared. I told you I'd be terrified."

He looked at her blankly. "Terrified of what?"

She waved at the window. "Of the storm. I thought it was a tornado. I was certain it was. I came flying before the car overturned."

He went to the window and looked out. "I was going to have you drive back to the nearest phone and call the ambulance. This girl has to go to the hospital."

The rain was slashing down now, almost drowning out his words with its heavy drumming on the low tin roof just over their heads. The window became a river of water as they looked, and the little house shook under the impact of the wind. She stared at Mike dazedly. No one could drive through this, she thought, no one.

He stood, pinching his mouth, watching the rain, listening to the solid pounding on the roof. Gusts of wind tore at the house and shook it and her fear mounted again. She wondered if it would stand. "You couldn't possibly . . ." Mike said.

"I'll go," the boy said instantly.

Mike was still looking out the window, however. There was nothing to see, she thought, wondering why he should continue to look. The window was blind with rain. He wheeled around to the young man. "That creek at the foot of the hill . . . how quickly does it get up?"

The boy's face showed he had forgotten the creek. Dismay wrote itself across his features. "Pretty fast, sir, in a rain as heavy as this. But I can get across it, somehow."

"You can, I've no doubt, but in thirty minutes, which it will take at a minimum, the ambulance can't."

Miserably the boy looked at the sheeted window. "I've been meaning to throw a bridge across that creek . . . but there's been so many things to do."

"Never mind." Mike made an impatient gesture. "We've got to do what we can, *now*. Regina," he swept around and pointed, "get clean sheets and cover that table, and put a big pan of water on to boil. The dishpan will be best." He went for his bag, leaving her still dully not understanding, and returned before she had recovered to give her a handful of instruments. "Boil these twenty minutes. You come with me," he told the boy.

Slowly the import of what he had said sank in and she looked about to see how the kitchen was ordered. He was going to take the baby, she supposed. The stove was electric. She gave thanks for that. She doubted if she could have managed a wood fire. There was a small tin sink in the corner, with a pump attached. Under it she found a big dishpan. She pumped it almost full of water, laid in the instruments, which looked to her, shudderingly, like instruments of torture. She turned the burner on high and left it to boil.

The house creaked in the wind. In the middle of an operation, she thought wildly, it was likely to be blown out from under them, or the roof taken from over them. Sheets. Where would the girl keep the sheets? In the bedroom, likely.

She tiptoed into the bedroom softly, not thinking how unnecessary it was for her to be quiet in the noise of the storm. She only followed her instinct not to disturb. Mike was beside the girl, a hypodermic needle in his hand. They boy was on the other side of the bed, talking to her. Horrified with one glance, Regina turned away. She looked as if she were dying already, her swollen body making a distorted lump under the thin sheet, her face oily and purplish in its darkness, her hair dragged out over the pillow in limp strands. She was moving her head restlessly, and moaning, not loudly but constantly, and Regina wondered if she could hear anything at all the boy was trying to tell her.

With her back to the bed she searched for sheets. In the bottom drawer of a pink-painted chest she found them. They must have only one change for the bed. The sheets were immaculately clean, however, and smoothly ironed. It occurred to her that the neatness they had observed outside carried over within—that the girl had taken pride in her tiny house. She had painted this chest and an old dresser. The floor was bare except for a small, braided rug, but it was colorful and bright in its newness. The kitchen, too, had been clean and orderly. Pity struck her. They were so young and vulnerable. With such love they had evidently begun their life together, and with such pride made the only home they could afford.

Mike looked around as she made her way back to the kitchen, the sheets draped over her arm. "Are the instruments boiling?"

"They will be soon. I've put them on."

"Good. There isn't much time."

When she had drawn the table under the light and draped it as best she could, trying to think how he would want it, there was nothing to do but stand and watch the instruments boil. They were bubbling now, and she looked at her watch. Twenty minutes, he had said.

A fresh blast of wind hit the house and she felt the floor shake under her feet. Dear Lord, she thought, what a time and place for an emergency. Just let the house hold firm, she prayed, keep it from blowing away with all of us.

The rain was leaking in, she saw, in one corner. Probably the roof had been torn loose there. She wondered if she should put a bucket or pan under it, saw it was already spreading and nothing could catch it. It was already a widening pool on the floor.

She brought her attention back to the instruments. Towels, she thought—he would need towels. He might need another sterile pan or two. He would surely need more water. Her mind left the storm to take care of itself and she hurried about, gathering together the things she could think of. He would need another table. The small one by the stove would do. It was porcelain and he could lay out his instruments on it. She arranged it beside the larger one, thinking as she did so how little the young couple must have known as they ate their last meal here that its next use would be to save the girl's life—if it could be saved.

When she looked at her watch again the time had gone. She stepped to the door. "Mike—they're ready."

"Good. I'll carry her, Bradley."

She went back to prepare a basin of water for him. She had probably forgotten the most essential things, she thought, looking around, but she had done all she knew to do. As she took the basin of water to the sink she noticed that a stream of water was pouring across the floor. She looked but could not find a mop. It was probably on the porch outside. She grabbed up some dish towels that were hanging beside the cupboard and threw them into the water, began scouring them about. "Leave that alone," Mike said, "and come here. I need you."

The girl was on the table, now, the boy holding her hand helplessly. Mike had finished laying out the instruments and was washing up. Passing the table Regina looked at the girl and thought she was not conscious. She looked too waxen and inert. The boy's face was set in despairing lines. She wondered if even Mike could save this girl, so far gone she seemed. Desperately she hoped it was only a layman's ignorance which made it seem so hopeless.

"Bradley is useless," Mike told her in a low voice when she reached him. "You'll have to give the anesthetic." He did not even look up when she drew in her breath in dismay. His voice went on firmly, professionally. "I've given her something and she's already unconscious. I'm going to have to use ether, in the most primitive way."

"Mike, I don't understand . . . what are you going to do?"

215

"I'm going to do a Caesarian, what did you think?"

"I thought you were going to . . . can't you take the baby? Do you have to do a Caesarian?"

"I can't take the baby without killing it. It's too large. That's what's wrong."

"But it would be quicker, wouldn't it? Surely the girl would have a better chance."

"I don't kill babies," he said coldly without looking at her.

From some deep place within her, that remote place which stores up thousands of various and assorted memories, she dredged up one more thing she had heard about Catholics. In a crisis such as this, a child's life was equally as important as the mother's. Where had she heard that? Where had she known it? There had been a newspaper story once—when was it? She couldn't have been more than ten years old—her mother had been condemning. A Catholic doctor had refused to take a child which was slowly killing the mother. It had been a Catholic family, and they had agreed with him—but when the mother died it had become a scandal, and the hospital board had asked for the doctor's resignation. Terrified, she knew that this was another such crisis and that, worse, it was Mike who was involved. "But if it's a matter of saving the girl's life?" she asked, unwilling to believe he would risk it, unable to believe it.

"I *am* trying to save her life. I won't quit trying as long as she breathes, but I won't kill the baby to do it. I have no right. That's God's choice, not mine." He had finished washing, stood with his arms and hands dripping.

"If she dies," she said, slowly, "you will be a murderer. If she dies, Mike, there is nothing for us. I can't . . . we can't . . ." She met his eyes, feeling sick at heart.

"If you feel that way about it, very well. Now," he dismissed the matter, turned about and indicated the girl's head. "Stand there, and do exactly as I tell you. There's going to be blood and there will be ether fumes. But for God's sake, don't faint."

At her place at the girl's head, with the first faint ether fumes coming up into her nostrils, feeling such a mixture of emotions she could not sort them out, she wondered if he had given the boy any choice at all. She wondered if they were Catholics, this boy and girl, and if the boy had agreed to the critical risk, to the harder thing. But they were Barton's patients, she remembered. They would have gone to Mike in the first place had they been Catholics. Surely Mike had no right to impose his convictions on them. The boy must certainly want his wife to come first. Any man would. Bitterly she altered that. Any man but a Catholic would.

His voice recalled her. "More ether."

She dripped it slowly, as he had showed her, looking at the girl's blood-drained face. She was breathing, at any rate, very slowly, very shallowly, but her chest was rising and falling regularly. There was hope as long as that frail breath continued to be drawn in and pushed out.

Mike was working very rapidly, very economically, with no wasted motions, his hands as sure as they were on the wheel of a car, or with a fishing rod—surer, because this was what they had been trained for. She had managed not to look at the incision, but there was no evading the swiftness with which he reached for one instrument after another. He had sent the boy into the bedroom, knowing how cruel it would be for him to watch, she supposed. Just they two were there, trying to bring a miracle to pass. She prayed they could.

She realized suddenly that her feet were wet and looked down. Water was sloshing about her ankles, and still the rain poured. The house shook, but she had long ago forgotten the storm, in the storm of her own jangled and confused emotions. If there was danger outside, it didn't matter. There seemed so terribly much more of it here, on this table.

The ether was making her sick. She gagged and retched. Mike looked at her quickly and she forced herself to control it, swallowing down the lump of nausea.

How long it took, she did not know. She lost all sense of time, all feeling except that of the automation doing what she was told, dripping the ether, stopping it, as Mike bade. It could not, however, have been very long before there was the new life, red, bloody, repulsive, handed unceremoniously to her. She took it, helplessly, looked at it and, oddly, her first thought was, it's a boy. Then she looked around in bewilderment. What did he mean for her to do with it?

The small man-child, inordinately fat for one so newly born, began to squall lustily. Mike looked up, met her eyes and nodded, smilingly. Then he was busy again. Suddenly she felt a queer and strangely protective instinct for the baby. She reached for a towel, wrapped him in it and continued to hold him, cradling him comfortably against her breast. There was an upsurge of joy in her. He was so angry, so resentful of being disturbed in his dark nest, he was speaking out so loudly. She held him and tried, in her ignorance, to hush his cries.

Busy with the mother, doing things very swiftly, Mike did not again look at the child. The young father, however, came to the door, his eyes wondering. "You've got a son," she told him, not at all aware that she had used a time-old cliché. It seemed terribly important to her.

The boy, however, had no eyes for the baby. They were fixed, after a first glance, on the table and the girl. Mike called to him. "Can you help me here. If we work very fast she's got a chance."

They boy went to him in a rush. Regina felt her own knees go weak and she sagged into a kitchen chair, closed her eyes and thought gladly, thank God.

The girl was finally back in her own bed again and the baby attended to. When he had swabbed the infant off Mike handed him back to her. "He's a fine one, isn't he?"

She took the child and somehow felt no awkwardness in handling him. She lifted him up to lay her cheek against his small, plump face. "He's wonderful."

Shyly the boy brought her some clothing from the chest. "I don't now which things you'll need, ma'am."

"Just a diaper and blanket for right now," Mike said.

When she had him warmly wrapped again she could not bear to put him down. He was so warm, so soft, so round and fat. Guided by nothing she recognized she drew up a small rocking chair and sat in it, the baby in her arms, and instinctively began rocking and humming to him. His small fuzzy head rested trustfully against her arm. Lifting and easing it a little she had a shocking thought. That tiny head, so fragile and delicate, would have now been crushed and lifeless if it hadn't been for Mike. If he had done what she thought best, what almost instinctively she had felt he *ought* to do, the child would never have breathed at all, would never have cried, would never have slept, as he now slept so peacefully in her arms. She lifted stricken eyes to Mike and felt the salty wetness blind her. Who could afford to play God?

All night Mike was at the girl's side. He was like a demon in his attention to her, watching her closely, seeing the slightest change in her, ready with what she needed immediately. All during the long hours he fought for her and Regina had the feeling that almost barehanded he brought her through. She helped when he needed her, but there was very little anyone but Mike could do.

At daybreak he turned to her. "Will you drive into town, see if Barton is back—but have his nurse send someone, at any rate. She can't be moved for a few days and she will need care. If you can't reach anyone else, call Miss Hopkins, tell her to send a nurse."

"Of course."

He stepped outside with her. The sky was pearly in the east and the whole wet world lay new and cool and cleanly washed before them. They stood on the steps of the tiny house and breathed it in. "When did it stop storming?" Mike asked. She saw how very tired he was.

"I don't know," she confessed, "I forgot it was storming." Wonderingly she turned to him. She felt as if he had wrought a miracle and as if she had had some small part in it. "Will she live, Mike?"

"I think so. Unless something comes up—the worst of it is over."

"Oh, Mike," she reached her arms about his neck, sobbing, "I'm all mixed up."

"I know. Darling, don't cry. You were wonderful."

She shook her head, burying it in his shoulder. "He wouldn't have lived if it hadn't been for you. But she might have died . . ."

"I know. God has to decide."

Chapter Twenty-One

"Do you think your mother would like that painting of you?"

"I'm sure she would. Why?"

They were laying a rug in the dining room, both of them on their hands and knees trying to smooth it wrinkle-free over the cushioning mat. It was a rug of Regina's, brought over from the small Georgian house to try, a Herez whose brilliant colors had faded mellowly. "Does it have to be that special picture?" Mike asked, tugging at a corner. "I'm rather sentimental about it. I'd hoped you were going to give it to me."

"Why, Mike . . ." she sat back on the floor, looking at him. "I didn't know. Of course you may have it." She confessed, "I'm rather sentimental about it, too, but I didn't want to be selfish and I thought she'd like it because it's you."

"Well, she would, I expect. Perhaps I'm the selfish one. But it seems peculiarly ours, doesn't it?"

She agreed. "Where did you think to hang it?"

"In the library—over the fireplace. I like to look at it and remember that you painted it when you didn't yet know me." Teasingly he lifted an eyebrow at her. "I *think* I can detect a little love in it already."

"Nonsense," she said, "I thought you were a farmer."

"Couldn't you have loved a farmer?"

"If he'd been you, yes. But I certainly had no idea of loving that fisherman when I painted him, I assure you. What," she asked, curious, "is loving about it?"

"Oh, the head—somehow."

"This will do, Mike. We'll never get it entirely smooth. It will have to settle to the cushion. Let's bring in the table, now. The head? Well," she admitted, "that *was* painted lovingly, don't you remember?"

"I was teasing. But I *am* fond of it and I would like to keep it."

"Then keep it, darling. I painted one of the house before we started work on it and made changes. She would probably like it, too."

"She'll like it even better, I expect. It will remind her of when Papa was living and we were all at home here. It was her happiest time, she says."

"It would be, naturally—when you were all children. You know, Mike, I'm very glad we decided to keep that massive table and sideboard of hers. I can just see all of you, when you were small, around the table."

"We were a noisy crew—but it was fun. I remember once Teresa and I got into a bread-throwing fight. Heaved rolls at each other the length of the table." He chuckled, remembering. "Teresa was by far the best shot. She caught me right in the eye."

"Your mother allowed it?"

"Oh, no. She stopped it, and we were both sent upstairs without any more supper. There was chocolate pudding, too, I remember."

"Do you suppose ours will throw rolls at each other?"

"Very likely. And you will send them upstairs without their supper."

"No," she shook her head, "I doubt that. You may—but I think you'll have to be the disciplinarian. I shan't be able to forget long enough . . . Mike, I can still feel how round and soft and fat that baby was the other night. He felt exactly as if he had no bones at all. No, I shan't send them up without their supper. I couldn't, ever."

"You'll see." He was fitting the top on the huge pedestal of the table, screwing the bolts into place while she steadied it for him. "When there are three or four getting into mischief all at once, it won't be too difficult for you to discipline them. You'll forget how soft and round and fat they were and remember only how many hands and feet there are to get into trouble."

"Maybe. How is the girl doing now?"

"She's mending, slowly. Barton has taken over, of course."

She shuddered. It had turned out well this time, but some day, some time, it might not. "Do you have many such cases?"

"No. I watch my obstetrical cases more carefully. I wouldn't have allowed that baby to get so large, and when I expect difficulty I get my patients into the hospital well ahead of time."

"Was Barton slack about this girl?"

"Not particularly. You always run across people who won't cooperate. I expect those youngsters were just ignorant and didn't see Barton until the very last."

"What do you do when they won't cooperate?"

"Tell them to get another doctor. There, it's finished."

They stood off to look at it. The old, round oak table, stripped of its blackened and aging varnish, gleamed goldenly on its massive center pedestal. Not all the finisher's skill had been able to remove the scars made by six youngsters' impatient hands, but Regina only smiled at them lovingly. The tremendous mirrored sideboard was already in its place and she thought how beautiful her silver coffee service was going to look on it. She set the chairs about the table. "Where did you usually sit?"

"There. At Papa's right—so he could thump me on the head."

She gave the chair a little pat, as if the small Mike were still sitting in it. "How did you have the courage, Mike?"

"The courage?"

"The other night—to make a decision."

"There was no decision to make, darling. It's very simple and very plain. 'Thou shalt not kill.'"

She looked at the big hands, tightening one last screw. They had worked with such skill to save both lives. He had gone according to his conviction, in faith that God meant what He said and would take care of the issue, whatever it was. Quickly she pushed out of her mind the sharp edge of the thought that very simply and plainly he was also told, "Thou shalt not commit adultery." That one he chose to ignore. She supposed there was some way of rationalizing . . . it involved no one but him, for instance. It was not life or death for someone else. There was no understanding—there was only accepting.

She backed away and tilted her head, looking at the rug, judiciously. "It will do, don't you think?"

"The rug? I never had any doubt of it."

"I did. I was afraid there was too much gold in it. But there isn't. It's mellowed nicely. Well—the dining room is complete now." She glanced at her watch. "It's four-thirty. I'd better run along home now, get dressed."

He nodded. "I'll pick you up in . . . will an hour rush you?"

"No, that'll be fine."

They intended to leave in time to have dinner before going to his sister's, where they were to spend the night. His mother's birthday was the next day. He followed her to the car, leaned on the door as she fitted the key in the ignition panel. "Rosa will be there," he said, a little diffidently.

She found the slot and inserted the key. "Rosa?" For a moment she did not remember, then it came to her. "Oh, your sister who is a nun." Something in his face told her he had not counted on this, and that it troubled him. "You'd rather she weren't coming, wouldn't you?"

"Well, she will not approve, naturally. I'd rather Mama learned to know you before . . . it doesn't matter, actually. But promise you won't let Rosa throw you off . . . she may be . . ."

"She may be unfriendly?"

"Oh, no, I don't think so . . ."

She laid her hand over his. "Mike, after Father Vincent there isn't much that can be said, is there?"

"No—if you just realize that."

"I do. You might remember, darling—I've made my decision, too." She leaned over to kiss him briefly. "I'll not be shaken."

They were such a loving family, so warmly affectionate and close, so demonstrative. She had been reared under her mother's cool tutelage which, she had no doubt, included love, but which had never included many caresses or much petting and fussing. Her mother had simply been temperamentally incapable of expressing love in such a way. It left her unprepared for the way not only Mike's mother but his sisters flew to him so gladly, kissed him a dozen times, hugged him, patted him and glowed at him so warmly.

Anna lived in a big house in the suburbs, a house so rambling and shabbily comfortable that it reminded her very much of Mike's. As large as it was it seemed bursting its seams when they arrived, teeming with children who flew to climb up Mike's legs, onto his shoulders, to swarm literally all over him. "Hey, now," he said, laughing, struggling with them, "give a guy a chance, will you?"

They were all plump, rosy, shining children, with the dark hair and skin which belonged to him too. He named them off for her benefit. "This is Julius, this is Sophie, this is Tony, this is Maria, and this one," lifting a small cherub high over his head, "is Tina."

Then his mother came flying from the door, a small, brown dumpling of a woman, her arms spread wide, her face shining with joy. "Mikey, Mikey, you've come—you've come."

"Mama!" Mike enveloped her and swung her off her feet. "Mama, you're prettier every day. What do you do to yourself?" He held her off to look and she beamed at him, her heavy, curly hair blowing about her face. "You look younger than Sophie, here."

"Ah, listen to him—listen to that Mikey. Flattery—he always flatters his mama."

"No, I mean it, Mama. You look wonderful. How is the blood pressure, Mama?"

She shook her finger at him. "Never mind the blood pressure, Doctor Mike. The blood pressure can take care of itself today. Today is for the party, not for the blood pressure."

Standing a little to one side, Regina caught the love in the banter, looked on smilingly, content for the moment to be an onlooker. Mike did not allow her to remain one for very long, however. With his free arm he drew her toward him. "Mama, this is your new daughter, Regina."

The mother turned to her, and it was impossible not to see the glow fade a little . . . not much, it was rather a reordering of the face, a collecting of it into the moment, the duty, the requirement. "How can we make you welcome, Regina? How can we tell you that we are so glad you came today?" She reached out her hands, letting go of Mike, and gave them both to Regina. They were small, warm hands, soft and brown. They squeezed Regina's reassuringly. The brown eyes were still moist with love. "Come in, come in. Teresa is here already—and Rosa will be coming tomorrow. Anna has cooked and cooked." She raised her hands helplessly. "All day she has been cooking. She has made the noodles for you, Mikey, the way you like."

Nothing being required of her but a smile, Regina went with them into the house, the children still chattering about them, clinging to them. Anna came hurrying from the kitchen. "Mikey!"

She was a younger duplicate of the mother, small, brown, plump, the same intonation of voice, the same loving welcome. But her acceptance of Regina was freer. She turned to her and gathered her into a capacious embrace. Regina smelled the odor of herbs and spices in her hair, and her hands left small, floury marks on her dark linen dress. Anna released her and stood off to gaze at her. "My, but you're pretty. Mikey, you didn't say she was so pretty. So slim—me?" She tugged at her wide hips and grimaced, "so fat! I eat too much. Julius!" She snatched at the oldest boy, "Leave your Uncle Mike alone. Teresa?" She shouted up the stairs, "Come down, Mike and Regina are here. Come in, come in," she steered them out of the hall into a large family room where a huge table was set. "We've waited supper for you."

Guiltily, Regina looked at Mike. They shouldn't have stopped for dinner on the way, but he hadn't said. He grinned wryly at her. She couldn't eat another bite, she knew, but apparently he was not going to confess they had already had dinner. She would have to try.

It was Teresa's turn next. They all moved so fast, she thought, so swiftly and lightly, and they all talked the same way, all at once, flitting from one subject to another, screaming at each other, shouting happily with excitement, and the children were all about, crawling on laps, scrambling over chair arms and sofas unreproved. It was terribly confusing and at the same time very warm, very Latin and very family-like. There was no need for her to say anything. It was all taken care of by the confusion and excitement. She simply seated herself where she was told, looked on, listened, tried to take it in and make sense of it.

Later, when the noisy, happy evening was over and she was in the bedroom which she was sharing with Teresa, she confessed to her inability to keep everyone sorted out. "Who is Turi?" she asked, "and Francesca?"

Teresa laughed sympathetically. "Turi is our sister Nella's husband. And Francesca is our brother Tony's wife. There are so many of us, aren't there? I expect it's very confusing."

Ruefully she admitted that it was. "I'm afraid I don't even have the brothers and sisters straight yet."

"Oh, in time you'll have us all sorted out. I wouldn't try right now, if I were you." She fitted a cigarette in a long ivory holder, and sitting on the bed, lit it. "Regina, let me say at once that I am all for this marriage—yours and Mike's. Some of the others will not be."

"I know that. I am sorry for it, but . . ."

"But it cannot be helped. I am perhaps not as religious as the others . . . but I want Mike to be happy, and he could never be happy living as a priest."

Startled, Regina looked at her.

She went on. "Oh, I don't mean he would take orders. But it would amount to the same thing, if he didn't marry again. Mike is a family man. He needs a wife more badly than any man I know—a home and children. It would be a waste of his life if he didn't have them. He told me . . . when I was there."

Regina lifted her head. "About us? He couldn't have. We didn't know yet."

"*He* knew. He had made up his mind just then. Of course, he could only hope that you loved him, too."

Swiftly Regina's mind went back through the months. It had not been long after Teresa's visit, she recalled. "Did you help persuade him?"

"Oh, no. He didn't need persuasion. But he did need to talk to some- one about it. I remember that as he drove me to the train I told him he had my blessing and I would stand up for him with the family."

She remember the scene in the care, Mike's happiness, Teresa's touch on his face. It might even have been that moment, she thought. She felt warmly drawn to this sister who understood. "I'm glad—for his sake. It's your mother I mind most about, though."

"Well, Mama will grieve, of course—for a little while. But I think even Mama would want him to be happy."

The light out, in the darkness, Regina tried to be reassured. His mother would want his happiness, naturally. As a mother she could hardly help it. But this way? The way that would take him out of the Church? Would she ever come to think it could lead to happiness? Wouldn't she always believe that in the end it was a sacrifice of happiness? Didn't one's immortal soul weigh the balances too heavily? Wouldn't she forever think that, with grace, he could have been happier alone? She probed and questioned, tossed and turned, and came out always at the same end. The mother would have to be hurt, would have to learn to live with the hurt. It had been Mike's to decide, and he had decided. She denied that immediately. It had also been hers to decide, and she had also decided. It was one of the things to which there was simply no alternative, however much they winced from it.

It was the next morning that the crisis came.

They were in the family room, talking volubly and happily, going about trying to hide the gifts they had brought down, while the mother and Anna set the table for breakfast. Mike came in, yawning. "When is breakfast? I'm famished."

The mother turned to him, beaming. "But Mikey, we are all going to church this morning. A mass will be said for Papa. We will eat when we come home. Rosa will join us there and come home with us, and then," she smiled archly at the entire group, "there may be, just possibly there might be, a few little things for Mama to open, eh?"

Regina saw the shock strike him, saw it go deep and hit home. She saw his mouth quiver and saw him lift his hand to hide it. His eyes, on hers, held despair. He had not counted on this. In pity she watched him. What would he do? He could not go to church with them. He couldn't *not* go, either. Not without breaking his mother's heart. This, they had done between them. Because they had not waited, he could not go to Confession. Because he could not go to confession, he could not, now, take Communion with his mother...enter fully into the mass for his father. She turned away, unable to watch him any longer.

"But, Mama . . ." she heard his voice stumbling, "why didn't you tell me last night? I've . . . I've eaten something already this morning." The lie, so quickly found, did not come well from him, and as if it had been a lash on her shoulders, she winced.

"Mikey, you haven't!" The mother's voice was reproachful, grieving.

From the corner of her eye Regina saw him go to his mother quickly. "Mama, I didn't know..."

"When did you eat, Mikey?"

"Just now . . . I came through the kitchen... there was a sweet roll . . ."

He *had* been in the kitchen, then. He wouldn't have dared mention what he had eaten otherwise.

Regina lifted her eyes from the pattern of the rug which she had been studying and found Teresa looking at her, sorrowfully. Teresa knew he was lying, too, and probably knew the necessity for the lie. She suddenly felt weary of it all . . . of Mike and his lie, of the big, noisy family, of being here among them, an intruder, not wanted, not needed—of all of it and the part she had to play in it. She shouldn't have come. Nothing could ever be right for her with them. She didn't belong here, and Mike shouldn't have tried to include her. It was the worst mistake they had yet made. She squared her shoulders, wondering how she could possibly get through the rest of the day. There was still the nun, the nursing sister, Rosa, and her disapproval to meet.

Teresa broke in then. "Mama, surprises never work out right, remember? It's your own fault for not telling Mike last night."

"I didn't think . . . it's so early. Why should you go nibbling in the kitchen, Mike? You could have waited, couldn't you?"

"But I was hungry, Mama—and there was no good reason."

"There *was* a good reason—the mass for your Papa. Rosa and I planned it."

The entire family broke in, arguing noisily, Anna scolding her mother, also, and then when the mother began to weep, they all tried to console her. "Mama, of course I'll go to church," Mike assured her.

"It isn't the same. I wanted us all to take Communion together."

She might as well have added, Regina thought, one last time.

The day was already so hot she felt headachey, and the noise was so bewildering. Perhaps they were accustomed to such squally settlements among them, but it sounded like nothing so much as a flock of geese cackling and hissing to her. Mama, Teresa, Anna, and Mike, all talking at once, Mama crying, the others alternately scolding and comforting. Even the children were taking part, their high, shrill voices almost unbearably piercing. She would be listening, she thought, to this sort of thing the rest of her life—whenever the family gathered this is the way it would be, and in time even her own children would be part of it.

There was something, she thought grimly, to be said for the kind of emotional restraint she had always known. For one thing it certainly was less noisy, and for another it had more dignity. She put up her hand to her hair, wearily, feeling the heat under her arms and realizing her dress was already sticky from perspiration. Being a Panelli, among Panellis, was going to require a considerable amount of patience.

A degree of peace settled over the family eventually, although Mama continued to look at Mike reproachfully and to wipe her eyes. It had been a bitter disappointment to her and she did not allow it to ease quickly.

They dressed and went to church. Regina sat through the long service quietly, Mike beside her, feeling too numb to care any longer that he must continue to sit there when the rest of the family, even the children who were large enough, filed up to the Communion rail. His mother's eyes were sad when she turned them on him as she left the pew, and Regina saw him smile wanly at her, shaking his head. It was as if she knew, somehow, that it was more with him than having broken fast.

When they came out of the church a black-habited nun came over to join them, embraced her mother and sister, and Regina knew it was Rosa. She was now Sister Mary Marguerite. She looked directly at Regina when she was presented to her, and her eyes, level, cool, and disapproving, rested briefly on her. She spoke as briefly, then turned back to her mother.

There was no joy in the day for Regina, though the mother exclaimed rapturously over the painting of the old house. "It is just the way it always was—when Papa was still living and all the children were little. Just the way it looked. Only there were always some little boys up in those trees, ready to fall out and break an arm. Ah, the times I have

228

scolded them about that." She planted a kiss on Regina's cheek. "It is nice of you to think of Mikey's mother."

Regina felt, however, she would have gladly done without the painting if she could only have been rid of the painter. It was a mixed blessing, that picture. It carried an expensive price tag on it—her son's soul.

When all the gifts had been opened and exclaimed over, the tissues bundled up and thrown away, a semblance of order restored, the big breakfast meal was set. It was so bountiful and rich a meal that it served also as dinner, and the family gathered about it hungrily. She heard, for the first time, Mike's voice in the table grace . . . "Bless us, O Lord, and these, the gifts of Thy bounty . . .," saw all the right hands around the table close the prayer, "in the name of the Father, the Son, and the Holy Ghost," with the soft, swift touches that made the sign of the cross. Awkwardly she waited, aware of how very much outside the circle she was, wanting only to get the meal over with, to get a little more time out of the way until they could decently leave. Dear Lord, she prayed, as earnestly as they, let me not say or do anything amiss. Guide my words and guide my actions now. Let me somehow get through the rest of this day.

It was not accomplished without effort. Soon after the meal she went upstairs to the bathroom, and coming out found herself face to face with Rosa, who, when she would have passed with a murmured apology, put out her hand to stay her. "I must talk with you, Mrs. Browning."

Mrs. Browning—not Regina. "Of course," she said, instantly, feeling the need to brace herself, ready to ward off something. This, she knew, was the rest of what she had been dreading, hoping to avoid.

The nun's black cowl turned, looked about the hall, searching, apparently, for some place to talk, and Regina, seeing it must be met, threw her last refuge away. "We can go to my room. Teresa and I share it, but she is downstairs."

The nun followed her into the room and immediately the door closed behind them. She said, "You must not do this thing to Mike, Mrs. Browning. Nor must you do it to my mother."

Regina stood before her, feeling very much like a prisoner before the bar but unwilling to sit as long as the nun stood. Sparring for time, and despising herself for it, she said, "I don't quite understand you, Sister." What a farce it was, she thought, the use of the ecclesiastical name— sister to Mike, Sister to God.

The nun's voice was calm and judicial, her eyes direct and refusing. "I think you do. I think you know precisely what I mean."

Slowly Regina said, choosing her words carefully, "The problem is entirely Mike's, Sister. I am not a Catholic."

"That is why it must be you who takes the action."

"What action do you mean?"

"Break off with Mike, Mrs. Browning, before you do him irreparable harm . . . before my mother's heart is broken."

"I don't think you have any right to ask that of me. Why don't you go to Mike himself?"

"Because he would not listen, naturally. He is bewitched."

Regina could have laughed at the use of the stilted, meaningless word. She shook her head. "He is so far from being bewitched, Sister, that he took months to think this through. He talked with Father Vincent about it. He is a man, you know, not a child."

"He is a child emotionally—and he is a child of God, spiritually."

"I do not think he is a child emotionally—and I do not see how he can ever cease to be a child of God spiritually. We who are not of your faith can occasionally see some facts so much clearer than you, Sister. I believe God is too loving a God to disown Mike if he marries me, and your Church cannot make me believe otherwise."

"But what you believe cannot change the Church's rule, Mrs. Browning. He will be excommunicated. Do you know what that means?"

Regina bowed her head. "I know exactly what it means. Father Vincent took great pains to tell me."

"You have talked with Father Vincent? And still refuse to give Mike up?"

"I refuse to make any decision alone. If Mike wants to break it off, give me up, let him tell me. I shall, then, of course. But I will *not* play Mike false for a rule of your Church in which I do not believe."

"It is a man's immortal soul you are condemning, Mrs. Browning."

Her patience broke under the sting of the words. "*I* am not condemning anyone's immortal soul, Sister. You are . . . and your Church. It is you who should examine your conscience."

The nun drew back and Regina saw the horror on her face. She had been blasphemous, she supposed, but this was getting to be too much. She rushed on. "I am sorry, truly sorry, if our marriage grieves anyone in Mike's family. I am sorry, moreover, that it cannot be done within his faith. I was willing. But I think human love counts for something, too, and a human life. I cannot live, as you do, for eternity. I cannot put the salvation of my soul before my human welfare. I think they are a part of each other, a fulfillment of each other . . ."

The nun's hand waved her words away. "Please, Mrs. Browning . . . I can't listen to you . . . you mustn't talk so."

Regina felt her legs quivering and thought she must surely sit down before they gave way entirely, but she compelled them to stiffen, to bear her up somehow until this was over. "I must remind you that it was you who asked to talk to me."

"Yes." She looked pleadingly at her. "Doesn't my mother's grief mean anything to you?"

"It means a great deal to me. But I love Mike more than I love your mother. His grief would mean a great deal more to me."

"He would recover . . . God would help him."

"God will help your mother, too, will He not?"

The rosary at the nun's belt jangled as she turned. "My mother will grieve as long as Mike is out of the Church. Her heart will ache and bleed for him and she will pray for him, and she will never know another happy day as long as she lives. She will not be able to think of him except as doomed . . . your heart must be very hard, Mrs. Browning."

Once again she was standing, alone, as she had stood in Father Vincent's study, under a storm of pelting words. Once more they bruised and hurt, and in spite of her resolve, shook her. They would not see, they could not see, and she knew it was hopeless that they ever would. There was one rule, one law—it was not to be broken, ever, under any circumstances. It was irrefutable. It was simple, it was plain, it was final. In the wake of its abandonment remained only sorrow and pain, and condemnation. How could Mike have exposed her to this? she thought, crying silently. How could he not have known what it would be like for her? How could he have deliberately brought her here, to be tried and condemned this way? She raised her head and looked at the nun. "My heart is not hard, Sister. It is very heavy, just now. But the simple truth is that I love your brother. He has convinced me that his happiness lies with me rather than with your faith, and his happiness means more to me than yours, or your mother's, or Father Vincent's, or anyone else's. It means more to me than anything in the world."

"If you mean that," the nun said swiftly, "you will break off with him. If you truly mean that his happiness means more than anything in the world to you, you will surely see that he can never be happy with you. For a time, yes, perhaps—but in the end you will bring him only the bitterest remorse and unhappiness."

Ah, there lay the wound. There lay the doubting, questioning sore spot. The nun had seen it instantly, had pierced, stabbing it open more widely. Regina closed her eyes and swayed tiredly, small circles of pain spotting the eyelids shut over the pupils. "Mike must decide," she said weakly, wanting to cry, wanting this inquisition to end. "It is Mike's right to decide." She could not bear any more of it.

A call came up the stairs. "Regina? Rosa?"

It was blessedly Mike's voice, but she was too tired to answer. She waved to the nun to leave and she collapsed on the bed. The black habit swished by her, without pity or mercy. Irrelevantly she thought that she would forever hate that black garb, now.

The door opened and closed softly. There was the murmur of voices, then the door opened again. "Regina? Darling . . ." He was beside her instantly, his arms warmly about her. "Has Rosa been . . . oh, my darling. I never intended for her to get to you . . ."

She began to weep heartbrokenly, sobbing aloud, her breath catching in her throat. "She was so terrible, Mike . . . so awfully, so terribly cruel. She was worse than Father Vincent . . ."

"I know, I know. You shouldn't have let her. You should have told her . . ." He gathered her close. "It's my fault. I should have kept an eye on her. I expected her to try something like this. It would be what she thought right."

She clung to him. "Only Teresa understands. Your mother hates me for it. Rosa—Anna—none of them want it . . ."

"It doesn't matter. It doesn't matter at all, darling. Don't cry so hard. I shouldn't have brought you here. They should have . . ."

It did no good—the blame and counterblame. It had been done, with whatever hope and in whatever love, and it had failed. There was only left to them now to leave, their defeat ashes about them. "Can we go, Mike? Can't we leave, now?"

"Of course. This minute." He was on his feet at once. "Is your bag ready?"

"Yes. I thought we might be leaving . . . I packed it this morning."

She could not even collect herself enough to go downstairs with him. The weeping was uncontrollable. She heard the clamor and guessed he had told them, something at least, of what had happened. When the door opened again she was still lying on the bed, feeling ill and desperately wondering if she could even make herself go down to the car. Teresa's voice was tender when she spoke. "Mike says Rosa . . . Regina, please try not to mind too much. All her life she has been so certain . . . she had a vocation from the time she was tiny, and she made a burden of it for the entire family. It was a relief when she was old enough to go away. Don't cry, darling. We all love you so much."

Regina could only shake her head.

Teresa sat beside her and held her hand, smoothed her hair. "Mike is getting the car out. I think he has even made Mama afraid, a little. He was wild at Rosa."

"He shouldn't have..."

"Yes, he should. Rosa had no business interfering. Don't blame the rest of us too much, dear, please. Anna thinks as I do. Mama will, in time. Mama loves you, even now. And Rosa you can do without."

The gentle voice, sweetly reassuring, almost pleading, had its calming effect and she could at last check her sobs and sit up to make some effort at pulling herself together. "I am ashamed—but it came so suddenly."

"I know. Here, let me bring you a wet cloth for your eyes. And a comb. You needn't see the others, if you'd rather not. Mike has arranged that."

She applied the cold cloth to her eyes, felt it begin to draw the soreness from them. "Oh, no. I must speak to your mother and Anna."

"Well, if you'd rather. But it's not necessary."

She shook her head, refusing the easier way out.

When Mike came for her, she had repaired the ravages as well as she could and the mirror told her, reassuringly, that she hadn't done too badly. As if she were ill, Mike held her arm down the stairs, stood belligerently beside her for a moment as they confronted the others. Rosa was not among them, and over their heads she could see her, retired to the window, and could see her hands busy with her rosary. Tell your beads, she thought angrily, tell them to the very end and see if they can forgive you for what you've done!

Gravely she told Mike's mother goodbye and was rewarded by being taken in her arms and held consolingly close. Anna was equally as comforting, angrily glancing at Rosa's back as she came to hug her. "Don't mind," she whispered, "don't mind. We love you."

None of it was enough, however. She lay back in the car, her head on the back of the seat, her eyes closed, feeling more exhausted than she ever remembered feeling before in her life. It was so much worse than what Father Vincent had said. This was the family...not the priest, and this went all the way inside to the covering of the heart, piercing even it, and causing it to bleed. Break it off . . . break it off. Peace lay that way.

Break it off, and give back his mother's happiness. Break it off, and let the Panellis fade from her memory. Let them be as if they had never been, nothing to her, no part of her, just a big, noisy Italian family, like the ones who had lived next door in her childhood. Break it off, and sleep again, untorn by conflict and doubt and hurt and black accusing robes of priest and nun. Black—mourning—the mourning of dead love, lost love, lost life.

The sad song sang through her mind as the car wheels hissed on the pavement, rapidly bearing her home, mounting and mounting to a delirium of words and phrases and colors and sounds and denials and circling, endlessly circling, maddeningly circling thoughts. Break it off . . . break it off . . . break it off . . .

Like a dark and bottomless chasm it yawned before her and she felt herself being thrown into it, being torn from Mike and cast into its fearful depths, Rosa and Father Vincent standing at the brink, grinning horribly, screaming at her, refusing her pleas . . . break it off . . . break it off. It was filled with black water and the water closed about her head and she choked and went under, gasping. "You can walk on the water if you try." It was Mike's voice, deep, calm, reassuring.

But this time it did not comfort. This time there was no hope. This time she knew. The waters closed over her as she tried to tell him, screaming the words at him, "You can't! You can't, Mike! You can't walk on the water, no matter how hard you try!"

Chapter Twenty-Two

❧

He was unhappy to see her leave, two days later, and reluctantly he drove her to the airport. "You look so tired and ill," he said gloomily. "Can't all that business up there wait awhile?"

Muddled by weariness, deeply disturbed, still haunted by the nightmare visit to his people, she hadn't the heart to tell him that she longed to get away—that the trip offered a heavenly prospect of peace and rest, that she felt she had to go or break down from the pressures that were so implacably closing in on her. Instead, she told him, "It's better to get it over with now, I think. It would just be hanging over us, darling. Fall is a good time to sell a house, and we do need the furniture.

They were in the airport restaurant, drinking coffee as they waited for her plane to be called. They sat near a wide pane of glass through which she watched the planes. They circled on silver wings, their long bodies looking remarkably like swollen darning needles; they came in to land, appearing suddenly to float lightly and to hover, then touched down gracefully and effortlessly, wheeling eventually up to the long fingers of the ramps. Idly she sipped her coffee, wondered why she had ordered it. She had breakfasted at home and did not really want it. She wondered why passengers always, at train stations and airports, with time on their hands, wandered into the restaurants and ordered coffee. It was time one did not know what to do with, she reflected, an undesirable gift, and it hung heavily and required to be spent. In traveling, she thought, one is for a brief time nothing at all. Left behind is the familiar everyday self. Ahead at one's destination, there is the different person one must become upon arrival. In between one is a sort of cocoon wrapped about a vacuum, held in suspension and belonging nowhere.

She watched a plane arrive. The landing steps were rolled into place and people got off, were met, embraced and taken into the fold of the waiting family, or were not met and then hurried briskly and alone up the ramp and into the enclosure. Their faces, she noticed, all looked purposeful, were intent with purpose—they had some place to go immediately, some one to see at once. She had a purpose, too, but it had become dim and hazy, mixed with her emotions. At the moment her only purpose was to get on the plane, lean back and close her eyes, become nothing, blessedly nothing, for a few hours.

She looked at Mike, who was looking, as she had been, out the window. She studied him with detachment, seeing him as a stranger. She looked at each feature separately, as if only thus could she put him together again into the man she knew. She looked at the tight, gray-salted hair, grown so neatly to his well-formed head. She looked at the wide brow, the straight, beautiful nose, only slightly flared at the nostrils, at the long, firm mouth and the dark, thick mat of his skin. He was a very handsome man, she decided, as if seeing him for the first time. Anyone would concede that—and she knew, better than most, how good a man he was. Perhaps it was, she thought wearily, his very goodness which made it all so difficult. A less good man would be stronger.

In amazement that, even off guard, she should have thought such a thing, she wavered between following it through and dismissing it. Somewhere she had read, she couldn't think now where, that strength required ruthlessness, and that all very good men lacked it—that the very quality of goodness was so permeated by mercy that it was weakened by it. It sounded like Hadrian, she thought impatiently.

In the silence that lay so strangely between them she knew that what she really wanted of him was relief from the burden of her own weakness. She wanted him to take over for her. She wanted, as all women want at some time in their lives, to lean heavily on the rock-like strength of a man. Where did he lack it?

The air conditioner was noisy and its constant humming began to be an echo in her own head, another distraction and discomfort. She felt exhausted and incapable of any effort, either physical or mental. It would have to wait, any more thinking. There would be time at home. She would reorganize her thoughts and her emotions there—alone, away from him and from anything which reminded her of him.

"I think that's your plane that just came in," he said, recalling her to the present.

She gathered up her gloves. "It hasn't been called yet, has it?"

"No. But isn't it Flight 342?"

"Yes."

"We may as well go on out, then."

He paid the check and walked out to the gate with her. They waited in the oppressive heat. Another virtue of this trip, she thought, feeling the stickiness of her clothing, would be the cooler weather. She felt almost as if her brain had turned mushy and soft. Summer was undeniably the most unpleasant season of the year.

The gate was opened. Mike kissed her quickly. They had, after all, been taken by surprise and people were beginning to flow around them through the gate. "Try to rest," he told her. "Don't scurry around too much. Call me tonight."

"I will," she promised to all he said, and left him with relief that his presence could be left behind for a few days. It had somehow got mixed up with her tiredness, her dislike of the heat, her confusion over the many problems—it had become as overpowering and oppressive as any of them, and was one with them.

As the plane wheeled around she looked back. He was still standing at the gate. She knew he could not see her, but she lifted her hand in farewell, with a sudden dismal feeling of loneliness and a sudden unaccountable feeling that she shouldn't be going. It was as if she were telling him goodbye forever, as if she would never see him again. It was as if suddenly she knew there *was* a rock-like strength in him which she was leaving behind and would badly need. She quenched her sadness, told herself not to be silly, and fastened the safety belt. She would rest, as she had promised herself and him; she would get the house on the market; she would do what was necessary with the furnishings; and within a week she would be returning. It was all arranged and ordered.

The house was empty, for she had given ample notice to the people who had been renting it, and it was blessedly cool. For two days she did nothing but sleep, wander through the house, eat occasionally, and sleep again. She did not want to see her attorney, to decide about the furniture, or to do anything. She wanted only to exist in this suspended state of blissful coolness and freedom from care.

She called Mike, as she had promised, the first night, feeling very remote from him. Not even his voice over the wire made him come near. She told him the trip had been pleasant and uneventful, the weather was at least twenty degrees cooler, the house was comfortable and she was going immediately to bed. They agreed there was no need for her to call again until she was ready to come home. He had receded into a kind of cloud-like oblivion for her, and she was willing for him to remain there for the time being. "You still think about a week?" he asked, at the last.

"As far as I can tell," she replied, so sleepy she barely understood him.

"I miss you," he said, softly, "terribly."

Automatically she said she missed him, too, knowing he expected it, but aware that she did not yet, that the feeling of relief had taken possession of her again, and that instead of missing him she was happy to be alone. They said goodnight and she stumbled into the bedroom, fell into bed, and slept without waking for twelve hours.

On the third day, feeling revived, slept out, and refreshed, she went downtown to see her attorney. It was hot, but it was not the kind of soggy, steaming heat they had in Hilton. It was a direct sun heat, a dry, baking heat which once one was inside, or under shade, was not noticeable. There was a brisk freshness to the air, and a clean, sparkling sky.

She walked down the streets taking pleasure in their old familiarity. Here was the department store where she had bought most of her household things; here the dress shop which had clothed her for several years; here the grocery store, the bakery, the post office. Tempted, she even went inside some of them, to see if there had been changes. It was warming to be recognized and spoken to. "You're quite a stranger around here, Mrs. Browning. We've missed you. When are you coming home?"

She said the same thing to them all. "Never, I suspect. I'm here to sell the house." For some reason she did not add that she was being married. It entailed too much discussion, she told herself.

They were all regretful, but they were all quickly optimistic and dismissed her. "Well, a person has to go where he can do the best for himself. Hate to see you sell out, though."

Her lawyer was a middle-aged man who had handled Walter's affairs for him. His name was Sam Stewart. He stood when she entered his office, his round, plump face shining with pleasure. "Regina—I thought you were arriving Wednesday."

"I was—I did." She confessed it, laughing. "I was so tired I've been doing nothing but sleeping. The heat is very bad in Hilton and I was completely exhausted."

He was sympathetic. "It's been pretty hot here, too."

"You have to live in that steamy blanket they have out there to know what heat is really like, Sam."

"I expect you'll get acclimated in time." He drew up a chair for her and seated himself behind his desk again.

"I hope so. Probably after a few summers I won't notice it. You got my letter, of course."

He nodded. "I'm very glad you're going to be married, Regina. You're too young to be wasting your years."

"Yes."

She felt an inability to talk about it with him and hoped he wouldn't ask questions. He was such an old friend of the Browning family he might easily. But he shifted to a discussion of the house. "It shouldn't be hard to sell, Regina. Property values have gone up in that section of town, and it's a very desirable location. I suppose you've noticed the building going on all around you out there."

She nodded. "It was always a pretty place. Walter used to say we'd made a wise choice when we built there."

"You did. Now, do you want to sell it furnished, complete as it is? It would make a considerable difference in the asking price."

"No. I'll dispose of the furniture. Some of it I want to have shipped through—some of it can be sold. I haven't gone over it yet, but I will—within the next several days."

"I see." He studied the blotting pad on his desk, idly tapped a pencil against it, thinking. "Well, then—what figure did you have in mind?"

"I have no idea, Sam."

"What did it cost you to build? I've forgotten."

"About twenty thousand, including the landscaping."

He thought some more and then said, "Well, I believe I'd ask thirty-five thousand, Regina. As I said, property values have gone up out there and I believe you can get it."

"That much?" She was surprised. She had thought only to get back out of it what Walter had put in it, and she had thought she would be lucky to do that.

Dryly the lawyer told her, "People are paying almost unbelievable sums for homes these days. It's a kind of madness—to own a home. That figure may even be a little low. It's a nice house."

"Yes, it is a nice house. Well, then—will you attend to it for me?" She stood. "Give my love to Carrie."

"Oh, but you'll be seeing her. She wants you to come to dinner one night."

"I'm afraid there isn't time, Sam. I must go back in a few days and I'll be so busy. I've had the telephone connected. If there are things I must sign before leaving, you can reach me."

He escorted her to the door. "Do you want the money, when the place is sold, deposited here to your account, or shall I invest it for you?"

She hesitated. She ought, she thought, to have talked this over with Mike, but it hadn't occurred to her. Well, it was, after all, her money. "Deposit it," she said, deciding impulsively. If she needed it, she thought, it would be available.

The attorney looked a little surprised. "It will be rather a large amount to be left lying idle."

She defended her decision. "We shan't leave it idle long. I need to discuss it with my . . . with Mike, though."

"Of course. Is there any way I can help with furniture?"

"You can tell me right now which company to see about having it moved."

"The Central Allied people, I'd think. They're the largest and should be fully equipped. And if I were you I'd send the things you want to sell to the Bulwer Auction people. Or I can handle it for you."

"I wish you would." She held out her hand, pleased at the directness of their talk, at its brevity and succinctness. She felt as if she had managed admirably. "It's been so good to see you again. Of course I expect you to continue to handle my personal affairs, Sam."

He bowed slightly, laughing. "I'll be happy to."

"I'll be in touch with you before I leave, then."

"Fine. And if you have time, Carrie will want to see you."

The house, when she returned, was dim and cool, the light tempered by the shade of the trees about it, its thick gray stone walls a buttress against the heat. She changed into more comfortable clothing and meant to get at once to the chore of selection—choosing, discarding.

The dining room furniture, she thought, must go. She looked at it lovingly, remembering when it had been bought and how carefully. It was fruitwood, pale, amber, beautifully and gracefully designed. It was a pity to sell it. The old and massive oak of Mike's mother's, she remembered now, was heavy, ugly, and bulky beside it. How much lovelier it would be, this long satiny table with its gently curving legs, on the old Herez rug. How much more fitting the brass engraved breakfront would be in the place of the huge, mirrored sideboard. Running her hand over the surface she thought how much lines, the grain of wood, its finish, meant to her. She almost wished she had not agreed to the old oak things.

She left the dining room and wandered into the living room. Here, at least, she might salvage much of what belonged to her. The sofa, especially built for her, long and luxurious, the great, thick-piled Chinese rug, the chairs, the small tables. These she could take with her. She examined each piece carefully. The people had really been very good about them. There was a small scar on one of the tables, a ring, left by a wet glass. It would come off. The rug scarcely showed any further use—but then one could abuse a Chinese rug terribly. She looked through her books. They were in good condition. If they had been handled, they did not show it. This room, she decided, could be shipped almost intact.

She left it behind and went into the large bedroom. Here, as in the small Georgian house in Hilton, her own personality shown through decidedly. This had never been Walter's room. She had done it over after his death. The rug was missing, for she had taken it with her, but the bed, the chests and her dressing table, were an extension of herself. It was not a feminine, fussy room. It was rather the opposite, but it had been put together lovingly, each piece chosen selectively for its effect with the whole. It leaned heavily on its simplicity and color for elegance. She had found the delicate brass headboard of the bed, she remembered, at a country antique shop upstate. The small desk was Italian, its nacre inlay pearly and lustrous. The curved Napoleon couch under the windows had brass fittings that went well with the bed, and she recalled the months of patient searching for the exact faded red for its cushions. Making a home, she had always felt, was too much of an art to be hurried, and she had always taken her time and found exactly what she wanted. She reflected on the odd sensibility in her which required this of her. Beauty was as much a necessity to her as food. She could not live without a setting. Given only one room, she thought, she would have been under the necessity of ordering it and of providing it with grace.

This room, too, could go with her, but not to be possessed by her any longer. No longer would it be an expression of herself. It would be offered to guests. For her there would be the ornate rosewood. Down through the years that great double bed, bought three generations ago by an Italian peasant, in which Mike and Teresa and Anna, and even

Rosa, the nun (strange to think a nun had been conceived and born exactly as other people—they ought somehow to spring full grown into life), had been conceived, would be her place of rest and love. She felt a quick, shuddering revulsion for it. Unwisely, she now thought, and too late, she had allowed her love for Mike to guide her. She had allowed his sentiment to replace her own sure knowledge of herself. She had allowed the wistful hope that his mother would love her and approve of her to weigh too heavily, and she hung the mother's bulky possessions, albatross-like, about her neck. They would hang there the rest of her days.

She left off her task. She would eat lunch, she thought, and then get back to it. Some of this defeat of spirit was undoubtedly because she had breakfasted lightly and needed food.

When she had eaten, however, a friend of the old days came by, pressed her to visit other friends with her, and too easily she allowed herself to be persuaded. She promised herself that in the morning she would get up early and go straight through with the chore until it was finished. She must, if she meant to return to Hilton on Wednesday. The weekend would intervene, as it was, to interrupt her. Guiltily, but grateful for the delay, she went.

It was over the long weekend, as she tried disconsolately to rid herself of a haunted and harried feeling, make herself pack books, dishes, and linens, that the final admission came from her. What lay back of all this reluctance, this lethargic unwillingness, this distaste for breaking up her home to make a new and strange one, was really quite simple. She had better, she thought, face it honestly, come to grips with it once and for all. She changed from jeans into a skirt and blouse, put on sturdy walking shoes and left the packing boxers in the middle of the floor. It would come clearer in the open, not closed in within the gray stone walls.

She took a trail which led through the cool, dense woods back of the house, which she knew as well as she knew the grounds of the house. She knew the exact spot to which she must go—a small rocky waterfall in a fern-ringed glen. It was where, often, she used to go with a difficulty, and where she knew from memory there would be silence and peace.

She stubbornly refused to think as she found her way, putting every thought which strayed into her mind away from her, keeping it stoically quiet, observing only the growth of vines and wild bushes, the rise and fall of the path, the smell of the pines and the feel of the moist, damp air which flowed over the tiny, trickling stream so cooly. She refused, also, to quicken her steps. She let herself linger a little, instead, knowing that the ultimate confrontation awaited her and that she was trying no longer to evade it. Already, having recognized it, she felt a kind of peaceful acceptance and unexpected clarity of vision which allowed her to loiter, enjoying the woods.

Coming at last to the small fall of water, she sat beside it and dipped her hand into it. She had known, actually, she reflected, that this was the inevitable end toward which they had been traveling since her talk with Father Vincent. It had been inherent, really, from the beginning. One less blind, less ignorant, could always have seen it. She had been refusing it, in obstinacy and, she credited herself with the small generosity, in hope. The priest had been right. Mike hadn't the strength, and the inescapable burden must be hers. Just as in the beginning the decision had been in her hands, in the end it must come back to her. It must be her cross to give Mike back his cross. That was the essence, the heart of the whole thing. A line from the Antigone, which the Chorus spoke, came to her: "Nothing that is vast enters into the life of mortals without a curse." Nothing—neither love of human beings, nor the divine love of Heaven. Both had a price and demanded payment.

She thought sadly of the reasoning in the beginning . . . that they were adults, that they had no one to consider but themselves, that they owed no responsibility to anyone else. It was never so. The human ties of his family bound him very tightly, but not, she thought, inescapably. It devolved upon many children to bring pain to their parents—it was the way of life that children should grow away from them, make their own lives in the pattern of their own design and freedom. The human frame being what it was, it was rarely mortal pain that was inflicted. That she could bear—to cause Mike's mother and family grief, to cause Father Vincent sorrow. It was not a happy thing to do, but it was a burden they must find the grace, and could, to bear.

The responsibility which they could not escape, the tie they could not break, was Mike's responsibility to himself, and the bond with his God. To ignore that was to invite the slow death of a soul, the infinitely small but daily disintegration and decay which would work on him like rust on a steel blade and which would in the end corrode and corrupt him until he was spotted beyond use. This, they could not do, and it must surely, she thought, cause even Mike's God a moment of sadness that the love he had made possible must thus be denied.

She hoped, with a moment of hatred in her heart, that He had something to offer in its stead, something beyond the painted plaster smiles of the saints and the murmured incantation of the mass. The moment passed as quickly as it had come, for she knew what He had to offer—the peace of the exile returned, accepted again, within the fold—the Body and the Blood making him whole, taken once more upon his tongue, dissolved into his bloodstream, washing clean of sin, giving him grace.

In the end there was nothing to decide, she thought numbly. It had been decided in the beginning. She had only, now, to write Mike that she was not returning. She had only to pick up her life here, where she had left off. A wrench of pain twisted her as she thought of it and thought of the emptiness which would require to be filled in some impossibly unforeseeable and unknown way.

She looked down at her folded hands and wondered that they should lie so quietly in her lap. They had known all the beauty of his body, had been held, been kissed, received all the warmth of his love, and told the measure of hers. They would never again touch him and she thought they must certainly know their loss of themselves and cry out against it. Curiously she held up her right hand and examined it. There was no tremor of any sort. It was as steady as if she had just determined to sheathe it in a glove. It seemed impossible that flesh could not yearn, physically, for flesh, as mind and heart yearned for it. But her hand felt nothing but the cool aftermath of being dipped in the waterfall.

The glen was growing dark. She rose. A great weariness possessed her and made the walk home seem endless. Her feet dragged and she felt as if she bore on her shoulders a tremendous weight. It would be like this for a long while, she guessed, until she got used to it. It would go away only as the raw wounds of pain and loneliness healed and scar tissue formed. She yearned for that time, knowing it was yet a long way off. All she could expect for hundreds of tomorrows was the weight and the loss.

She did not delay writing him. Not that she was afraid of delaying. She had no fear she would change her mind. She did not write with the intention of getting it irretrievably behind her. She wrote because she had never loved him more and this was all that was left to her. Once more, at this distance, she could communicate with him, and then the door would be closed.

It did not occur to her to call him. As if by instinct she knew she must not do that. It must be written. The written word was so final. It surprised her that the words came to her without a struggle. She must, she reflected, have known for a long time what she must say. She had slowly been preparing for this moment until now; without the effort of choosing phrases and words, she wrote steadily and quickly. There was, after all, only the necessity to say that they could not do this thing, that she was not coming back, and that he must return to the Church. The briefest way of saying it was, in the end, the most merciful.

She signed it, saying truthfully that she loved him dearly, folded it, inserted it in an envelope, addressed the envelope and sealed it, stamped it. Then she felt a weakness in the hand which had held the pen, as if belatedly it protested the use to which it had been put. She went out immediately and slipped the letter into the post box on the corner. The metal was cold under her hand.

She felt so little, she thought. It was as if she were sheathed in an armor of numbness. There was only a physical pain, deep in her chest, which kept her twisting to rid herself of it. She remembered the same pain when she had painted too long, bent in one position for too many hours. There was not yet in her, except in small spasms which came and went quickly, any urgency. There was instead a deep tenderness, a passivity, as of dark, formless waters running tranquilly. That it would be disturbed, she knew, but not yet—and she gave thanks for the absence, for the postponement of pain. It would come later, but mercifully she had not yet to bear it.

Chapter Twenty-Three

The next morning, however, which was Monday, it required the utmost effort of her to think what she should do now. She should see Sam, she supposed, and tell him the house would not be for sale. She should write Lucia. She should get in more food. She should unpack the boxes only half-filled in the rooms. There were a thousand things she should be doing. Instead, she sat, idly, in the living room, her limbs too heavy to move, her mind too dulled to come to any decision.

The sudden removal of purpose from her life left it intolerably arid and bleak. It had been so full—there had been so many plans. She had been so busy. To face this sudden nothingness was like having to face death. The wiping out of life could not be more complete. The pain was beginning, she thought, making herself move about—in this empty house, which would always be empty, for she could not fill it of herself. It was beginning and she twisted her hands as she wandered, distracted, from room to room.

Indecision set in now. The letter was already posted. She could not retrieve it. It was already on its way. It would reach him today—tomorrow at the latest. Uncertainty gripped her. How could she have had the conceit to think it was her right to decide for him? She began to weep, harshly and unrestrainedly, walking about blindly, not knowing where her steps took her. She stumbled over the boxes, not seeing them. Her hip struck the dining table and she leaned against it, wondering at the bruises. She went from room to room, the walls blurred by her tears, the furniture somehow always in her way.

She found herself at length standing at the sink in the kitchen, staring at a glass of water in her hand, not knowing when she had run it, or why. The tears had stopped, but she was still shaken by dry, painful sobs. She drank the water, trying to collect herself. This would not do. She could not give way like this. There was her entire life ahead of her and she must some-how get through this day and all the others to follow. If she only had her car, she thought—she could drive until she was too tired to feel any more. The idea fastened itself upon her until it was the only solution for the moment. There were car rentals—she would have one sent out.

She called, and then dressed quickly. By the time she had changed, the car was at the door, and as if it had been a drug she had been denied she hurried out, drove the attendant back downtown and without think-ing where she should go, took a road that led into the country.

When night overtook her she had no idea where she was. She had paid no attention to where she was going. She dismissed it. It didn't matter. There would be a town some place. She would drive until she reached it, find a tourist court or a hotel and sleep. She could find her directions in the morning and go home. She had driven and driven, stopping only once, for gas. She had not eaten nor wanted to. She was hungry now.

The lights of a town loomed ahead of her and she drove into it, slowly. A tourist court on the right advertised itself with a bright neon sign. There was a restaurant attached. Wearily she drove in and got out. Not until she had registered, the man behind the desk eyeing her dubi-ously, did she think about money. Some instinct had made her bring her bag, however, and when she searched it there was plenty. Relieved, she paid him and went directly to the restaurant. The meal over, she found the room, and without turning on the light, without undressing, fell across the bed. She belonged anywhere on the face of the earth. She had no home.

She slept soundly half the night, then waking and finding the room and the silence intolerable, she got up and went out into the night, started the car and drove back the way she had come. She came across a high-way marker, got out the state highway map which she knew she would find in the package compartment of the car—rented cars always had them—located the highway. At the next town she found herself on the map and was amazed that she was less than a hundred miles from home. She had gone in circles, widening and overlapping, but bringing her in the end not farther from, but nearer to, where she had started. She would never know, she thought, exactly where she had driven all that long, pain-blinded day. But she felt better for it. Some little measure of courage had returned, some instinct of survival.

She slowed the car and went more leisurely, less driven by the need of movement and speed. She let the memories of Mike and the hours in his car with him flood her, unrestrained and welcomed. She counted them over, from the first time—all of them, anxious lest she miss one of them—recalled the circumstances, the conversations, the places, the times. She brought him into the car with her, made him accompany her on this slow drive through the darkness. She remembered so much, and she never wanted to forget. She remembered even the sharp whiteness of the pebbles on the narrow little beach. She remembered the glint of the metal roof from the high ridge above the old mill. She remembered the smell of honeysuckles and rain on the night when she had tried to keep him away. She remembered his hand on the light switch and his lifted eyebrow—"You're pretty silly, aren't you?" She would not forget any of it, she promised herself. Each day she would recall it all, she would keep every memory fresh and vivid and unforgettable. She would not allow any of them to escape her, become a part of the past. She would keep them in the present, alive within her. Beginning now, she thought with determination, with him beside her in the car, on the seat with her, his long legs stretched out, his big shoulders touching hers, she would keep him with her. There was panic lest it prove impossible.

Reason returning with a stale, sour taste, she thought she must be a little mad. Nothing, not even memories, could last forever, nor could be made to. He would become ashes, the fire spent, the passion quenched, the radiance gone, the light become dark. She wept again that she could not keep him.

By loitering, the dawn had broken when she returned the car and went home. She sat outside on the steps of the porch and watched the sun come up. The sky was at first a luminous gray, ragged with clouds, touched only slightly by the pink of the sun. By degrees it shifted and changed, became redder, then whiter and more opalescent until at length the first golden edge of the sun lifted up over the horizon. The birds in the woods all around went wild with joy and the first tufted curls of smoke from the chimneys of the town rose lazily in the still air. There was dew on the grass of the lawn, beaded and sparkling. She felt very quiet within, now. She knew she could go inside and unpack the boxes, set the house to rights, order her possessions. She could begin to pick up her life.

Idly watching a rabbit nibbling in the edge of the grass, she thought she would go to see her parents first. If she liked it, if she found something to do there that would interest her and give her some purpose, she might stay. She could go ahead and sell the house. There was not much point in staying here. There was much to be said for a new beginning in a new place. It was a good plan, she thought.

The rabbit edged nearer, then frightened by something, took off hastily, bounding across the lawn with his ears pointed and his hurrying hope carrying him in great leaps. It was a car coming down the road. She saw it slow, come to a stop, then back and turn into the drive. It was a taxi from town. There was no premonitory warning. She watched it with only idle curiosity, her only clear thought being that the driver had mistaken the place. She stood up, however, waiting. He would have to be told.

Not until the cab swung around the circle and slowed for the stop did she recognize Mike beside the driver, and even then she did not believe it. She had the feeling of needing to rub her eyes, to make them see more clearly, as if he were some apparition she had called up, as she had done the night before when she had beckoned him from her memories. She took one step down, one only, felt her knees trembling and waited. He would vanish. It would be only the cab driver, asking the way farther on. Mike was in Hilton, a thousand miles away. This was not he, in the blue suit, rumpled and hot looking, face troubled and drawn. He was in the big, white house they had made over for themselves, with the rosewood bed and the huge oak dining table and the new yellow and blue kitchen. He was safely there, her letter just read, his own pain just beginning.

He was unaccountably here, though, and real, for he was coming toward her, his tie loose, a bag carried in one hand, his coat thrown over the other arm. It must have been very hot, she thought, on the plane. The cab drew away, and Mike came on, slowly, looking at her. When there was no longer any disbelief in her, when it became necessary to acknowledge his reality, movement came to her, and she cried out, went with the surest steps she had ever taken, and surely the fastest, to him. He dropped the coat and bag and she was in his arms, held so tightly she could not breathe, her ribs crushed, her neck once more, blessedly, tilted to the familiar creen which would make it stiff and aching.

There, inside the iridescent shell of the morning, the dawn still misty and new about them, life began again for her. What had been dead was resurrected, came forth in fresh garments from the tomb and touched her with the promise of hope. His arms were around her—it was a golden moment, blazing with light and radiance and a transfiguring joy. I can do no more, she thought—I cannot withstand him. The snare of love is too intricate, the meshes woven too tightly. There is no escape. Her heart went wild with the fever of joy, the ecstasy of his presence, the rapture of his touch. She laughed and touched and kissed, the unquenched, un-trammeled, exquisite hunger, beautiful, capturing, thickly pouring, encompassing her. It was madness. It was a bursting sun and fluting birdsong. It was the sky lifted up and up to Heaven. They were travelers returned from a far, bleak country, met again by destiny and fate.

At last, in a moment of quietness, some of the wildness dying down, she drew back to look at him but could not bear yet to be apart from him. She snatched him back, betrayed by fear into the convulsive movement, the fear that still he might be only her dream. "It can't be," she murmured against his shirt, "it can't possibly be you . . . I am surely only dreaming."

"You are having a very rumpled and worried dream, then, my darling. What possessed you to write that letter? What went wrong when you got up here alone? You surely didn't think I would accept it?"

With the blaze and the flame still burning, the radiance still shining, she could only lean against him and shake her head. "I don't know—I don't know."

"Can we please go in, dear? Let me have a bath and some coffee. Then shall we talk about it?"

"Oh, darling, I'm so sorry. I completely forgot everything—everything. I was so terribly, terribly glad to see you. But I couldn't believe it . . ." She still felt shaky about it and she held to him tightly as she led him into the house.

In a trembling absent-mindedness she tried to think—showed him the bath, forgot the towels, fled to make coffee and couldn't find the canister. She leaned her forehead against the cupboard door and let the tears, the wonderful solacing tears of relief, flow unhindered. She had done what she could. She had been willing, been resolute, been brave. It wasn't acceptable. Whatever happened now was beyond her strength and beyond her wisdom. He *had* to be the rock, impermeable and immovable, to which she could cling. "Are you hungry?"

He came fresh and cool-looking from the bath into the kitchen. "No. I only want some coffee. The air conditioning on the plane went off and the last two hours were stinking. I felt as if I'd been in a steam bath when we finally arrived."

"It must have been terrible. I was on a plane once when that happened." But she was chattering. She poured his coffee, poured herself a cup and led him to the table in the alcove.

He took his coffee and held the cup in this hands, looked at her over its rim. "Now, you will tell me what this is all about?"

She summoned her courage. "You got the letter, of course."

"Of course. It came yesterday afternoon. I didn't get around to looking at the last mail until after six. In fact, I took it home with me, not expecting a letter from you. I tried until midnight to reach you by telephone . . . then I arranged to fly up on that three o'clock plane this morning. I thought," he said, flatly, "you must have gone away. I meant to find some trace of you and follow."

"Darling . . ." Clinging to his hand she told him how she had spent the night.

"That's all very well," he said, when she had finished, "but what made you decide to write the letter? What brought you to such a decision so suddenly? Was it coming back here? Was it this place? Was it some comparison between me and your husband?"

Aghast that he should think it, she hurried to deny. "Oh, no! No, never that! Mike, I told you. I surely told you what it was. It seemed so very clear all at once—Father Vincent said—and Rosa said . . ."

"What did Father Vincent and Rosa say?"

With a feeling of guilt, a feeling of having betrayed him by holding it back so long, she told him. "Father Vincent said I should go away. I should be the one to break things off between us. He said you hadn't the strength. Rosa said it, too. She said if I truly loved you, I would break it off . . ."

"Why?" The quick question sped like a bullet, straight to her heart.

"Because of . . . the Church. Your not being allowed to take Communion any longer . . . your being condemned..."

"I had already told you that didn't matter.'

"But, Mike, it *does* matter. If we are not married, you can go back . . . you are still in the Church. You can belong again to your family and . . . you can take Communion again..."

He set his cup down and crossed behind her, drew her up into his arms. "Has it never occurred to you that we *are* already married? That for several months I have been fully committed—there has been no return for me? The legal ceremony changes nothing, makes no difference at all." He turned her so he could look at her. "Listen, my darling. Do you know what Confession is? Do you know the words I should have to say . . . the words I should have to mean? Do you know what contrition is? Listen . . . 'My God, I am most heartily sorry for having offended Thee...' How can I ever say those words? They are impossible for me. They have been impossible for me since the night we first went to your room and were together. To repent means to be truly sorry . . . to be contrite means to repent. It's why I've said it doesn't matter, darling—it's too late. Whether you marry me or not, it's still too late, for nothing can change it now. There is no way I can be sorry for loving you. Even if I never saw you again, I could not be sorry. That's what Father Vincent does not understand, and what the Church makes no allowance for. If I were dying, my soul in mortal danger, as it will be, I could not even then be sorry. Nothing you can decide now can alter the simple fact that I cannot turn back."

They had trained him too well. The murmured words were not enough. With him the intention must also be pure. In pity so deep that it bordered on anguish she closed her eyes. *I didn't know. I didn't know.* She could give him back nothing, not the Cross, nor the Body nor the Blood.

They would be married, then, since at last she understood what he meant, since finally she knew how irrevocable had been the step they had taken. Nothing could alter it, now. They would be married, and they would have to learn to take hold of this pain and grasp its thorns. They would have to learn to live with this wound that would forever lie open, a throbbing companion to their love all the days of their life. They must in some way, somehow, find the strength and the courage to color their days with enough of human goodness to bridge the pit which the withdrawal of divine goodness left yawning at their feet.

With prophetic vision she knew that there would be times when he would regret it—not repent, the two were different—for no man was strong enough, no man was rock-like enough, to be forever valiant. Having given up everything, even his God, for love, there would be times when love was not enough, when he yearned to undo it, when the exile would cry for his home country. Those would be the times when she must stretch herself into a dimension so much larger, so much wider and more spacious than she now possessed. She felt diminished by it already. The demands of his spirit must be nourished, and she had no choice but to be his nourishment. *Salve Regina. . . .*

She lifted her arms and encircled his neck.

It was a terrible thing to stand in the place of God to a man.